'Aren't you going to order me to leave?' He lift... question.

'Nay, Varin, I am no... him once, forget her responsibilities and loyalties, forget she was a Saxon, then she would hold that memory of him close to her heart for ever. No one would ever know.

'Do you know what you are saying?' He moved behind her, powerful fingers dropping a featherlight touch to the back of her neck. She jumped violently, emitting a tiny sigh of release at the galvanising sensations pulsing under his touch. Her eyelids fluttered down.

'Aye, I do,' she uttered, with deadly certainty.

'Eadita.' His voice shook as he knelt on the floor behind the tub. His firm lips brushed the elegant line of her exposed shoulders, creamy in the firelight. Her breath snagged.

Varin groaned and the dangerous precipice that she neared loomed closer; a thrilling, quicksilver bolt shot through her veins. He lifted her from the tub, water splashing onto his corded thighs as he swept an arm under her knees to lay her onto the furs strewn over the bed.

He lifted his head momentarily, his leonine hair haloed in the golden light, raw desire sparking in his eyes.

'Do not fear me now, *mon coeur*.'

Meriel Fuller lives in a quiet corner of rural Devon with her husband and two children. Her early career was in advertising, with a bit of creative writing on the side. Now, with a family to look after, writing has become her passion… A keen interest in literature, the arts and history, particularly the early medieval period, makes writing historical novels a pleasure. The Devon countryside, a landscape rich in medieval sites, holds many clues to the past and has made the research a special treat.

Conquest Bride is Meriel Fuller's début novel
in Mills & Boon® Historical Romance™.

CONQUEST BRIDE

Meriel Fuller

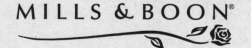

MILLS & BOON®

First published in Great Britain 2005
Harlequin Mills & Boon Limited,
Eton House, 18-24 Paradise Road, Richmond, Surrey TW9 1SR

© Meriel Fuller 2005

ISBN 0 263 84392 0

Set in Times Roman 10½ on 12 pt.
04-1105-87089

Printed and bound in Spain
by Litografia Rosés S.A., Barcelona

Author Note

My story of Varin and Eadita grew from a love of medieval history, a romantic turn of mind and an over-active imagination. I have always been fascinated by the influence of the Norman Conquest on the history of England, the evidence of which can still be seen today in our castles and churches, our landscape and our language.

Conquest Bride is primarily a work of fiction, but I began the story by researching the early medieval period to ensure the background details are convincing and, I hope, correct. However, maintaining accuracy in a period so long ago is often difficult, especially when reference books conflict in their information or provide little material regarding a particular person or event. Although I have used factual evidence and my own knowledge to build up the framework of the book, I have also added a healthy dose of imagination to allow the fictional account of Varin and Eadita to grow and develop into an independent love story set against one of the most turbulent and troubled times in England's history.

Chapter One

West Country, AD 1068

God's blood! Eadita's violet eyes widened in shock. From her precarious position astride a forked branch of a bare oak tree, she watched the group of soldiers approaching on horseback, the sound of the hooves deadened by the sticky mud of the cart track. Sweat sprung to her palms as she gripped the dry, nubbled bark to twist round to her brother, Thurstan, lounging indolently on the next branch.

'How can you sit there like that?' she squeaked, his calm manner unnerving her.

'Have a care, sister,' he warned in a low voice, 'you'll lose your seat swinging round like that.'

'Thurstan, we must move, they'll see us easily. Thurstan, please!' The urgency in her voice betrayed her inner panic. 'They're Normans, they will certainly kill us! They're too small a number to be with Uncle Gronwig's party! There's not a Saxon among them.'

'We're in no more danger than we've ever been in before. They won't even look up.' Thurstan's placid response belied a much deeper hatred of the men who were now advancing on them slowly, a hatred that burned and festered in his breast like a wound. Eadita failed to notice his inner frustration as she studied the outwardly calm lines of his face when he turned toward her, his smooth sable locks ruffled by the harsh winter wind, the lean planes of his face ruddy with cold. *My brother!* Eadita thought proudly, feeling the familiar rush of sibling love.

'If only we had more men with us. I'd fight every single one of them and kill them slowly for what they did to our father, for what they've done to our country.' Thurstan jammed a fist against the bark.

'Now is not the time, Thurstan. Hush now,' Eadita reassured him with gentle tones, trying to hold him back when she feared his headstrong nature would lead him into danger. Not that she could talk! Her father would have had her flayed alive if he could have known what she was up to now!

The plodding hoofbeats were gaining clarity, the deadly 'chinking' sound of the Norman chain-mail hauberks and creaking of leather in the saddle flew to her delicate ears on the strengthening wind. Thurstan had taught her to rely on her hearing, sight often not quick enough in the shady dimness of the woods. Behind the skeletal criss-crossing of bare oak and beech branches, the winter sun started to descend from its high point; even at noon, ice-crystals in the wind settled on her skin like miniature pinpoints of freezing fire. Eadita shivered. She did not want to be here. She wanted to be home, in the Great Hall, or her favourite spot in the kitchens by a roaring fire, surrounded by light and sound and laughter. Instead she sat, some three miles from the manor at Thunorslege, dangling her legs from a tree, passing information to her outlaw brother. And if they weren't extremely careful, they were in imminent danger of being attacked by a group of Norman warriors.

'Thurstan, a plan, now!' she whispered hastily.

'There's not a great number and they're obviously carrying coin and jewels…just look at the size of that cart!' His eyes sparkled, but surely he spoke in jest?

'I truly think you've gone mad, or moonstruck, or both; we are only two this afternoon, we had no plans to—'

'You and your plans, sister. I've always told you, surprise is the best form of attack, but maybe you're right, I don't…' The rising wind drowned his last words. But as she continued to look at him, he smiled and waved. *Upon the stars!* He wanted to strike the Normans! In truth, she had prayed against it, gulping nervously at the size of the men riding out of the trees at the opposite edge of the clearing. She inhaled sharply at the sight of the sweaty warhorses, the bright ribbons flapping on the long spears, the striking reds, blues and golds decorating the oval shields, the dull shine of the hauberks and helmets. Her insides wobbled. Surely Thurstan joked with her, there were at least ten men; yet as she turned to him again, she found he had disappeared. He must be on the ground already, moving into position.

Honed by her brother's steady training over the years, Eadita flexed her muscles and wriggled her legs and toes to get the blood moving after sitting in the tree for over an hour. She set her sights as usual on the leader; a huge man, face shielded by the steel nose piece of the helmet, great arms and legs encased in leather, creased and ridged from use. Her mind flew into panic, then settled. She knew what she had to do.

Baron Varin de Montaigu wrestled to suppress his rising irritation. He'd had no desire to leave his King after the siege at Exeter, but William had insisted, bluntly indicating that this mission was of the utmost importance. His orders had been clear: Lord Varin was to keep a watchful eye on their new Saxon ally, Earl Gronwig, while using his country estate of Thunorslege as a base for the weary battalion of Norman soldiers.

A mission, indeed. Varin threw a cursory glance at the covered ox-cart that lumbered in their wake. It had taken an age to hoist Earl Gronwig in and now he lounged inside, his corpulent body bundled in furs and woollen blankets against the cold. Restless by nature, used to the headlong pace of route marches and intense battle training, Varin balked at their slow, plodding pace. But King William was convinced that Gronwig, despite being a personal adviser to Leofric, the Bishop of Exeter, was not as loyal to the new Norman regime as he pretended. Alongside the Bishop, Earl Gronwig was one of the most high-ranking and powerful Saxons in the West Country; he had access to the hearts and minds of all the lords, earls and thegns in the area. Both Leofric and Gronwig had been instrumental in breaking the eighteen-day siege on the city of Exeter. As part of the agreement negotiated, the Earl had promised to help William gain a foothold in this part of Devonshire, and in return, William had promised him protection.

William had asked Varin, his close friend and finest knight, to stick close to the Earl's side. Gronwig's reluctance to house the Norman battalion at Thunorslege had been palpable; the air thick with tension when William had made the suggestion. Varin would have preferred his battalion to reside near the King, at Bishop Leofric's palace in Exeter, but there had been no room. Thunorslege had been the only option. Reluctantly, Varin had agreed to the timely march to the country; a tense and edgy journey through unfriendly forests and treacherous stinking marshes that threatened to pull their exhausted warhorses down into their miry depths.

Pulling the leather reins sharply to halt his high-spirited steed in the middle of the clearing, his hard thighs clad in fine mesh chain-mail gripping the animal's flanks to steady its gait, Varin addressed his portly charge in French.

'Whither now, my lord?' Most of the Anglo-Saxon nobility spoke his language and Gronwig answered him easily from his comfortable seat.

'Take the right fork, my lord. 'Tis not far now.' A white hand fluttered feebly from within the curtained interior to bid his escort forward. Mud caked the large wooden cartwheels, a sad reflection on the state of the roads in this part of the country. *Why couldn't he ride a horse, like the rest of us!* Varin thought. The ox-cart had severely slowed their progress from the city. He could barely see the track at all, the dense growth of the wood making it difficult to pinpoint the direction with accuracy. Hauling abruptly on the reins, he wheeled the horse around to the right, then threw an arm high to beckon his entourage to follow.

Eeeeeeyarrrgh! A bloodcurdling scream rent the air, then another and another. An entire body weight dropped on Varin's back, clamping knees like a limpet tight around his shoulders and pinning his arms to his sides. Icicles of fear slid through his veins as cold steel pressed against the throbbing pulse at his throat, through the neck hole of the chain-mail. *Sacré bleu!* Under attack from rabid outlaws, having survived the whole siege fighting alongside his King at Exeter. He would not die at the hands of these villainous churls! Raising a gloved hand, he grabbed the arm that held the knife to his throat, but the grip on his shoulders did not lessen and the knife pressed slightly deeper.

'I will spill thy blood, Norman pig,' the voice hissed in his ear. 'We will have your gold…and your life as well if you don't keep still!' So the outlaw spoke French—an interesting quirk of fate. And the weight on his back was not quite so heavy after all.

'I've no time for this, peasant!' Varin spat out, rearing his whole body up and around, sheer muscled force wrestling the attacker from his back, disarming him in the process and slamming him to the muddy ground from the considerable height of his horse. The churl landed with an almighty thump, howling in despair and pain. Swiftly, Varin dismounted, pulling the short sword from his belt as he prepared to finish off the lowly serf. Granted, he'd had enough of the killing and the fighting, but this was just one more annoyance that stood between him, a hot meal and a warm bed, luxuries that he'd not taken the pleasure of for many months.

His attacker was only a lad; sprawled in the burnished mass of fallen leaves he seemed very small, a woollen hat pulled low over his face, a short cloak swirling on the ground behind him. His tunic and *braies* were a dull green colour— no doubt a deliberate choice to blend in with the surrounding vegetation. The boy seemed dazed, an unfocused look in his huge violet eyes, eyes that sparkled out from his mud-spattered impish face. *Violet* eyes! Varin shook himself. He had never been that way inclined and the women that followed the Norman camp were always obliging if the need arose. Varin lifted his sword.

'Stay your hand, *mon ami.*' A warning hand rested on his arm, preventing Varin from making the fatal downward thrust. By his side stood Geraint de Taillebois, his friend and fighting comrade. A lord in his own right, he'd elected to become Varin's steward during the Conquest and had remained a calm and steady companion throughout their days in this heathen country.

'Remember our important Anglo-Saxon charge, Varin,' Geraint continued. 'These are his woods; he may want to decide the fate of this outlaw himself.'

'Granted.' Sheathing his sword reluctantly, Varin turned to the ox-cart where the Earl, as if on cue, pulled back the richly embroidered curtains to view the spectacle. The cart lurched sideways as Gronwig leaned out.

'Good work, Baron,' he praised, a sinister smile playing

across his florid features. 'I'm glad you didn't kill him. I shall have fun torturing him for information about the many attacks in these forests. We must hunt down those responsible. Take the lad prisoner.'

Eadita cursed the ground the Normans walked on. How on earth had she got herself into this mess? Where was Thurstan? He'd managed to disappear quickly enough, *if he had jumped from the trees at all!* Had she misinterpreted his gesture? Tears prickled at her eyelids as she lay, almost bent double over the neck of that *monster*'s huge destrier, a large hand placed firmly in the small of her back. As if she could escape—the situation was laughable if she hadn't been so frightened. Her whole body ached from the sheer force of that brute's attack; all the air had been punched from her lungs and bruises swelled on her arms where he had grabbed and thrown her. He had tossed her on to the horse as if she'd been a sack of grain, but thankfully the dizziness in her head was beginning to subside. Wet oozy mud had seeped into her woollen garments from the forest floor, now making the damp cloth itch against her tender skin. The strong scent of the horse stung her nostrils as her face bumped against the flank of the animal.

She'd recognised her uncle's voice from the wagon immediately, despite being muffled by a hulking barbarian whose intent had been quite obviously to slay her. Her life had been saved by the presence of the very person who hated her; the person under whose guardianship she lived. This group, much smaller than she'd been expecting, were obviously escorting her uncle back to his estate at Thunorslege, where Eadita lived with her mother and the rest of her uncle's family and entourage. An estate that had once been her father's, where he had ruled as the Saxon lord, before that bloody battle at Hastings where he had fought and died bravely alongside his Lord and King, Harold.

Now the Normans had conquered Exeter, helped by her scheming uncle who'd been instrumental in achieving a somewhat tense resolution to the long siege. The Normans had suffered more by attempting to take the city, but eventually the people, urged on by the powerful and persuasive Earl Gronwig, had surrendered, having first extracted favourable promises from the new King, William the First. Her uncle would no doubt be crowing about his efforts at the meal tonight; it seemed like he was the best of friends with these French barbarians now.

Her heart sped faster as the hooves finally clattered over the cobbles that marked the entrance to her home. Her father had had the foresight to build his fortified manor and guard walls in stone; a much longer-lasting building material than the wood that was more commonly used. She heard the thump of the massive wooden gate studded with iron bolts as it closed behind her. Home again, but not quite in the way she was anticipating—the lady of the manor could not be revealed before her people as an outlaw! She prayed that the daubs of mud on her face and her large hat would so obscure most of her features that she would not be recognisable.

'What shall we do with the baggage, my liege?' The harsh tones of the warrior assailed her ears, his big body leaning over her as he dismounted. The horse skittered and slipped on the cobbles as if glad to be free of the controlling force on his back and she began to fall forwards, her stomach and legs slithering on the horse's flank. Her hands flew out instinctively to break her fall as the greasy cobbles loomed. A mighty hand grabbed a handful of cloth at her back and stopped her whole body weight in mid-air as she was dragged unceremoniously back and on to her feet on the Norman's side of the horse. Laughter broke out around her, but she dared not raise her eyes.

'Not so fast, peasant! You're as slippery as an eel. I hope

you've got a secure stronghold, my lord,' he said. *He was laughing!*

Gronwig's daughter, Sybilla, appeared in the arch of doorway, her rounded features stretched in a taut, half-welcoming smile. She wrapped her arms about her chest to ward off the bitter air.

'Father,' she squealed, remaining firmly at the top of the stone steps as she ran a fastidious eye over the mud and animal manure coating the cobbles below, 'we weren't expecting you until later.'

'Greetings, daughter.' Gronwig pulled himself awkwardly from the cart, leaning heavily on his waiting steward as he hesitated distastefully at the state of the ground. 'You!' He jabbed a finger at a servant about to take the reins of a horse. 'You, clean this mess up—what sort of way is this to greet our guests?' His colourless, red-rimmed eyes fixed coldly on his daughter, shivering in her blue woollen gunna. 'Where is Eadita?'

'Who knows, Father?' Sybilla shook her head. 'Probably mixing her potions, or muttering to her vegetables… I *did* tell her you were coming…'

'This is intolerable,' the Earl hissed, as he picked his way through the mire to join his daughter. 'What do I give that maid and her mother board and lodging for, if—?' He stopped himself suddenly, remembering their visitors. ' She will be punished.'

'The evening's feasting is in full preparation,' Sybilla added hastily. Eadita, head bowed under the soldier's grip, suppressed a snort. As usual, Sybilla, who had seen far more than Eadita's one-and-twenty winters, had failed to do anything. It had been Eadita, with the help of her steward, Godric, and her servants, who had overseen the slaughter of the pigs, the plucking of the geese and chickens: meat that was now roasting over the fires. Root vegetables from the cold winter soil had been unearthed and washed, fruits taken out of storage, and flour milled to make loaves to feed the men expected to arrive with the Earl. Silently, Eadita resolved to hold back the best cuts of meat until the Saxon battalion arrived; their reserves were low and she had no intention of wasting good food on these perfidious Normans!

'Come and meet my daughter, Baron.' Gronwig held out his hand to gesture Varin towards the steps, towards the simpering figure of Sybilla. 'The servants will see to your men's needs and settle them in the hall and the guest bowers.' He indicated the circular huts dotted around the perimeter walls with a sweep of his hand. 'And so will my niece, lady Eadita, when we can find her.' He laughed hollowly. 'I must apologise for her absence. She would, as lady of the manor, naturally perform this duty. It grieves me that she is apt to be a little…er…absent-minded at times. Unfortunately my own wife, Sybilla's mother, died some years ago.'

'Please don't trouble yourself,' Varin replied, his manners impeccable. 'But I have no wish to drag this varmint near your kin. Methinks we should deal with him first.' Varin shook the prisoner roughly in his grasp, to be rewarded with an indignant squeak.

'Of course, I was forgetting.' Gronwig sighed. 'Let me deal with him later…I am tired. Let the guards take him below.' Eadita smiled secretly at her uncle's words. She would be able to slip the guards before she reached the dungeon, an intolerable earthen pit beneath the manor. She sensed an approaching freedom from her Norman captor, a captor who still retained a firm grip on her shoulders, the fine chain-mail of his gloves biting into her delicate bones.

'Pray let me take the prisoner to the dungeon myself; I've a care to see he's locked up tight.' Eadita's heart sank.

'As you wish. Not willing to be surprised again, eh?' The Earl smirked. 'A servant will show you the way.'

'Move and you die.' Varin threw a direct order at the peasant's bent head. Passing his gloves to Geraint, he raised his hands to remove his restraining steel helmet, before pushing back the flexible chain-mail hood of his hauberk to his shoulders.

A gasp of amazement spilled out from the bustling crowd of knights, serfs and peasants, previously busy around the courtyard, now pausing to stand and stare at the beautiful man before them. If Varin had been an overpoweringly impressive figure, riding through the gates on horseback clad in glistening chain-mail, face menacingly shadowed by the confines of his helmet, he now emerged as a god from the trappings of war, running his hands through tawny locks that dropped to his shoulders. The eddying chatter swirled around him, rising and falling in hushed tones of awe. Caution deserted Eadita as she lifted her head warily to peep at the man. She quickly dropped her eyes, aghast at the vision she had seen. How could one so cruel be blessed with such good looks? Was it not true that most Normans were supposed to be ugly pigs with their hair shaved halfway up their heads? She stole another look. Sun-bleached, dark blond locks fell vigorously to his collar, framing a visage tanned and ruddy from a lifetime spent outdoors. Finely etched dark eyebrows sprung above eyes washed in pale jade, incandescent with gold flecks and fringed with jet lashes; a piercing look raked the crowd hungrily as if looking for new prey. High cheekbones served only to emphasise the determined squareness of his jaw, which framed wide lips curving sensuously, the arched narrowness of his top lip accentuating the erotic fullness of the bottom. His high-bridged nose ran arrow straight and arrogant as he lifted his head as if to scent the air.

Eadita's toes itched to run, her skin tingling, oppressed by the very closeness of this man. *Look at him basking in the very attentions of the crowd. The very pomposity of the man!*

'Better bar your door tonight, Varin,' Gronwig simpered,

'otherwise the maids of the manor will be after your honour.'
Sybilla preened visibly, smoothing soft hands down the sumptuous wool of her gunna, as if to emphasise the delights beneath. The soldier grinned, the generosity of his smile causing
tiny lines around his eyes to crinkle with humour. Eadita
dropped her eyes hastily, her heart tripping in panic. Upon the
stars, someone help me out from here! Silently she prayed for
salvation. Her captor handed his spear, helmet and shield to
a younger member of his party, keeping his jewelled short
sword hanging at his leather belt.

'Let's go.' Varin grabbed her upper arm, propelling her
swiftly in the direction of the servant who stood patiently at
a side door of the manor. *God in Heaven! What was she to
do?* Appealing to the guards and servants securely in the pay
of her uncle would reveal her disguise and put her brother at
risk; she couldn't trust them. Fear prickled in her fingertips
as her toes bobbed over the cobbles, dragged in the warrior's
wake, the very speed of her legs preventing logical thought.
Bedevilled, cursed man! How could she shake him off?

Fortune smiled on her. A shout hailed Varin just before he
raised a sturdy hand to push against the oaken planks of the
door on the east side of the hall. Cursing under his breath,
Varin shoved Eadita into the strong grip of his companion,
Geraint.

'You take him…other matters need my attention.' He
strode away. Geraint, still tall, but of slighter build than Varin,
gripped a handful of wool at the shoulder of her tunic to drive
her forward once more. She relaxed slightly. Now she had a
chance while they followed the stone corridor, lit at intervals
with tallow and rush torches slung into metal hoops driven
into the wall to ward off the gloom. Advantage lay on her side
in her detailed knowledge of her home; she could gain her
freedom if she were quick.

Although Geraint's hold on her right shoulder remained

tight, her left arm swung free. They approached a large tapestry behind which was a small opening. As the entrance to the dungeon loomed at the end of the flagstone passage, Eadita realised she must make her move now or never. She reached for the neck of the next burning torch, thrusting it round briskly to brandish it in her enemy's face. He loosened his grasp for a second as the flames shoved towards him. In an instant, the burning brand dropped hissing to the floor before him, the tapestry moved slightly and his captive vanished! Astonished, Geraint stood rigid for a mere second, before tearing down the intricate wall-hanging and shouting the alarm back to the Baron and his men in the courtyard. He dropped his head to squeeze through the constrictive doorway. Barely noting the narrow dark stairway, Geraint bounded up the steps two at a time, fearing his reprimand from Varin before it was delivered. Gaining the top, a glance both ways informed him that his ex-prisoner was nowhere to be seen.

'Quick, quick, fill the tub.' Eadita burst in on Agatha, her maidservant, continuing to shout commands while ripping off her filthy masculine garments. 'Make haste, the Normans are after me.' She ran to the ante-room, plunging her hands into a basin of freezing water to scrub her face free of caked mud, drying her skin on a rough linen square till it pinkened attractively. Agatha followed her.

'But the water's cold, my lady!'

''Tis no matter, we must merely give the illusion!' Eadita rushed back into the main chamber. 'We must clear these dirty clothes as well, they must not be found!'

The sound of doors being shoved open along the corridor came steadily closer, shouts and running feet could be heard outside. Eadita unpinned the tight braids, letting them drop like dark ropes about her, before fumbling with the leather thongs that held each braid intact. Her heart pounded as she ran her shaking fingers through each braid to fully unleash the bundle of silky chestnut locks. Slipping a linen chemise over her naked body so it would look as if she were about to take a bath, she cast a keen glance over her chamber to see if any item might give away her double identity.

The door slammed back violently on its iron hinges, thudding against the wall. Eadita turned her head slowly, regally even, refusing to be daunted by the imposing sight filling the doorframe. Upon the stars! Why did it have to be him?

The chamber walls shrank inward at Varin de Montaigu's magnificent presence and, although her feet moved not, her body seemed to lean towards him as if of its own accord. Despite having set aside his trappings of war, the shield, his spear and his helmet, he still wore the silvery chain-mail that clung to his frame like a second skin, emphasising the sheer muscled power of his shoulders and legs. Beneath her thin shift, Eadita's legs trembled involuntarily. Varin seemed unable to speak, his generous mouth set in a taut line as the dangerous glitter of his emerald eyes greedily drank in the gentle vision of femininity before him.

Agatha spoke first, breaking the tense tableau.

'Sire, please, I beg of you! You must leave at once! You should not be in my lady's chamber.' The servant moved towards him, wringing her hands nervously. ''Tis unseemly, my lord, pray take your leave!' The warrior moved not, his eyes fixed on Eadita, Agatha's words rolling off him like oil on water.

'The heathen did not understand you, Agatha,' Eadita explained in Saxon dialect, her tone faintly mocking, ' and once he realises he'll gain no sense from us, he'll leave.'

'My lady Eadita, I presume,' Varin addressed her in French, his angry mood evaporating as his gaze slipped languidly over her flimsy chemise. ''Tis an honour to meet you.'

'Pity I cannot say the same,' Eadita replied in the complicated Saxon burr. Agatha tittered unsteadily. Her mistress, by her scanty attire, had obviously hoped to shame any man entering this room into leaving immediately, but chivalry seemed to have deserted this knight. Eadita clenched her hands into small fists. How dare he not leave, his incisive eyes raking her body instead? Impudent man!

Varin took a step closer, and Eadita lifted her hands instinctively as if to ward him away. ' I do not understand your language, sire. You heard my maid. Now, go, away with you!' She shooed him away with ringless fingers. He couldn't fail to understand the gesture.

Varin laughed out loud, a wide grin lightening his face at the sight of this intriguingly beautiful woman. How this little chit ordered him out of the chamber as if he were a mere fly; her very arrogance was astounding. Either her bravery knew no bounds or she was immensely stupid. Lesser men had died for challenging a Norman lord in such a fashion and she was just a maid! In these times it paid to be prudent and her behaviour was anything but that.

Despite her frigid demeanour, his keen eyes noted her agitation at his continued presence. The transparency of her linen shift did little to hide the sharp rise and fall of her chest, the gauzy material tightening at each breath over the sweet curve of her full breasts and dusky nipples. After three months of hard fighting, desperate living conditions and unnecessary bloodshed, the vision of beauty before him was pure heaven, and his groin tightened involuntarily. If he cared to remember his knight's training at all, the code of chivalry meant that he should have left at once, but the day had been long and arduous: he had yet to reap some reward from it. Her haughty bearing goaded him to spark some reaction from her, despite her bloodthirsty look.

'I need to search your quarters, my lady,' he stated. 'An outlaw has escaped and is possibly dangerous.' The order was issued with all the superiority of one used to having his demands met, as he leant idly against the doorframe. Despite his relaxed stance, Eadita sensed the coiled tension in his body, a wolf about to pounce.

She started to shiver; piercing draughts sneaked through the oiled hides covering the window embrasures. The hem of the white chemise skirted her toes and the sleeves reached to her elbows, but through the loose and gauzy weave of the cloth her naked vulnerability was all too apparent. His frankly assessing gaze told her so. Hurriedly, she grabbed a fox-fur pelt from the bed to wrap around herself.

'Please don't cover yourself on my account, your attire has left little to the imagination.' His provoking words belittled her belated attempt at modesty. Embarrassed, she yanked the pelt around her figure, her wan face whipping around to accost him, amethyst eyes scorched with loathing.

'Just get out,' she hissed in his language, 'get out, you're not wanted here. There's nobody in my chamber and well you know it. Scuttle back to your beloved Conqueror in the city and make haste back to France. Leave…now, this minute.' She turned her back on him with, she hoped, a convincing sob, Agatha placing a comforting hand around her shoulders.

'Accomplished French for one who had little knowledge a few moments ago… I congratulate you, *mademoiselle*.' Varin's feet remained firmly in place; he sensed a mystery and these two women were plotting, he was certain. Whatever it was, lady Eadita was effecting it rather delightfully. The fur around her body served only to enhance the delicacy of her diminutive frame, yet he had caught only a shadowed glimpse of that elfin stature through the gossamer fabric. Warmth amassed heavily in his loins, a feral heat gathering steadily.

Amazed at his reaction to her, he wrenched his mind back to the more statuesque proportions of the faceless whores with whom he occasionally dallied. Women who were far more equal bed partners than this…this slender elfling with her smooth, chestnut locks, the sinuous tendrils curling softly around a fragile-boned face before snaking down to skim her delectable rounded bottom. With her face turned, he was denied the sight of her amazing eyes, eyes a deep, deep blue, the colour of the sky just before dawn, almost purple. Only her title and relationship to the Earl protected her. No knight of honour would dream of bedding a member of the nobility, unless they were prepared to risk the consequences. If he touched her, he would be called to account and forced to marry, no doubt by the Conqueror himself and he had no intention, ever, of being saddled with a wife.

Pure sexual frustration seized his body. Trying to stifle the unwanted desire, he drove an iron fist into the doorjamb to power his body into the room, causing both women to start nervously. Eadita turned to regard him with contempt, eyes awash with fake tears. Varin had planted his great legs in the middle of her sheepskin rug, unmindful of his muddy boots, his massive presence filling the room. The scent of leather and male sweat tantalised her nostrils as he spoke.

'Don't insult me with your feminine wiles, my lady. I'm wise to the devious ways of women. All women.' He laughed disparagingly. 'We come to Thunorslege in peace, in a land that is now at peace, as an escort to your Saxon uncle, to be greeted with hostility and curses.' The harsh cadence of his language rippled with intent, his eyes lively and insistent. ' I would watch your step, my lady,' he cautioned. 'Now, by your leave, may I search the chamber?'

Chapter Two

With a venomous stare, Eadita dropped her head in a tight nod, admitting defeat…for the moment. In the dimness of her chambers lit against the afternoon gloom with tallow candles, the man appeared as a giant, the flames picking up the gold strands of his hair and turning them to burnished amber. The gammelled metal of his hauberk gleamed over the broad expanse of his chest and dropped to mid-thigh, where it met woollen *braies* heavily cross-gartered with leather straps from knee to ankle. The heavy soles of his leather boots guaranteed them weatherproof; eyeing them, Eadita envied the skills of the French cobblers—her thin slippers were no match for the manor's cold stone floors.

'Seen enough, my lady?' The warrior couldn't fail to notice her scrutiny.

'Just get on with it,' Eadita snapped, sitting down on the bed.

Varin moved easily over the wooden floor, despite the obvious weight of his chain-mail. Jaded by months of pitiless fighting, he absorbed the rich details of home life with pleasure. Colourful quilts and fur pelts piled high on the oak-framed bed, spread across a soft mattress of sweet-smelling branches covered with linen sacking. How different from the many nights sleeping on hard, lumpy ground with only his cloak for cover! The bright tapestries covering the dull stone of the walls were fine in their application and choice of colour, if a little threadbare in places.

A derisive snort from the bed stilled his hand as he riffled through the garments in the carved elm coffer.

'You wish to say something, my lady?' Varin raised an eyebrow as he continued at his task.

'You're hardly likely to find the culprit in there.' Eadita didn't attempt to edit the scathing tone from her voice as she perched stiffly on the bed.

'The lad is only small, about your size. He could easily squeeze in here.' A guilty flush invaded her pale cheeks; he wondered at it as he stepped into the ante-room. An enticing array of earthenware pots and jars greeted him, arranged neatly on the wide shelves that covered every wall. Curious as to their contents, he reached lean fingers towards a squat jar. The cork stopper yielded easily, revealing a thick, white cream with a strong perfume. The smell hit him immediately; the scent of rose petals on a hot summer's day. His mother's scent. Suddenly he wanted to shove the pot away, dash it to the floor and watch it break to smithereens, but memory crowded in too fast for him to act, too fast for him to crush his thoughts.

Felice had spent hours rubbing the rose-scented cream into the cold, detached beauty of her face, anxious to preserve her looks for a string of rich lovers. As a young lad, Varin and his brothers had watched in disbelief as she fed his adoring father a steady diet of lies and half-truths, but the gentle Sigurd would have loved her anyway, no matter what she did. What a fool his father had been!

'Twas Sigurd who had brought him up, he and his two younger brothers, Drogo and Ansger. Sigurd, with his wide, all-embracing hugs and his patient understanding as he showed them how to string a bow, to shoe a horse and to do the household chores that Felice somehow neglected to do. As young children, they had fallen over themselves in their efforts to try to please her, desperate to raise a smile from this hard, bitter woman, not understanding when she rewarded their childish efforts with stinging slaps and railing curses. He remembered her banging down cold, sloppy porridge for them to eat and Ansger, the youngest, flinching at the noise, curling in on himself with his thumb in his mouth and refusing to eat. She had beaten him for that. As the eldest, Varin had become quiet and watchful, looking out for his siblings, comforting them in their distress, making sure they were clean and dressed until they were old enough to do it for themselves. As they grew, Drogo and Ansger curbed their natural exuberance, creeping around her nagging, resentful presence until the day she walked out.

Her departure should have been a relief, but Sigurd sank into a decline so deep that Varin worried that he would never recover. It was as if Felice had cut his father's heart out with a knife and had taken it with her, she and her rich merchant lover. Varin could not understand why his father had loved Felice so unconditionally, a woman who constantly belittled him, a woman who broke his heart.

He jammed the stopper back into the generous neck of the jar. He wanted to erase all memory of that hateful woman, that sly, vindictive bitch who had made his father's life a living hell. His father had been a fool to love her, and he, Varin, had no intention of being snared in the same emotional trap. The solution was easy; he had vowed never to love a woman, never to become involved at such an intense level that escape without having one's heart ripped out became impossible. Better never to love at all. His fingers shook as he returned the jar to the shelf.

'What are you doing?' The question rapped at his back.

His eyes moved along the serried ranks of jars slowly, as he used the time to bring his thoughts under control. 'I'm just doing my job, my lady,' he managed to say, reaching up for another jar.

'Please don't touch them! All the jars are sealed against the air!' Eadita moved swiftly around to place a restraining hand on his arm. He stared down at her shining hair, each strand picking up a glimmer of candlelight as it tumbled around her. His breath caught. Something about her seemed familiar, but what was it? Her hair, her eyes, her scent?

'A might possessive, my lady.' He shook her off.

'There's no one here!' She bridled at his nearness, intensely aware of his impressive magnitude in the smaller chamber.

'What do you do with all this?' He ignored her irritation, instead indicating the drying bunches of herbs, the jars of creams and liquids with a sweep of his hand.

''Tis none of your business, soldier.'

Before she could prevent him, he pulled open a linen bag stuffed with dried twigs to discover a smell so acrid it made his eyes water.

'Serves you right. I told you not to touch them.' She chided him as if he were a child, yet he towered over her. Removing the bag from his hands, she hung it carefully from its hook below the shelf. For some unknown reason, he wanted to trace the gentle curve of her upper lip with his fingertip.

'Are you a healer?' He dragged himself back to reality. 'Several of my soldiers could do with your help.'

'I don't help my enemies!' She turned to go, but he caught her upper arm in a rough, punishing grip, all soft thoughts of her driven from his mind. What a little bitch! She might look like an angel, but inside that diminutive frame beat the heart of a viper. Just like every other woman that he knew...

'I've warned you already to watch that tongue of yours,

mam'selle.' She glanced pointedly at his hand manacled around her arm. He dropped it immediately, disgusted at his behaviour. Surprised by her own uncustomary rudeness, Eadita glanced in panic at the bowl of water on a chest behind Varin, a dirt-encrusted cloth floating in the muddy water.

'Come on, there's nothing to see here, 'tis just a few potions that I dabble with.' She tried to lighten her tone.

'Don't hustle me, *mam'selle.* I'll take as long as I need.' He dropped down gracefully to dip his fingers in the wooden bathtub. 'Isn't it customary to heat the water in this country?' He chuckled, the bleak memory of his childhood draining away. She felt the warmth of him suffuse her slender body as he raised himself from the floor, a feral heat branding her from toe to crown. The piercing intensity of his dragon-green eyes made her shift uncomfortably.

'You made it go cold,' she accused childishly. 'It was perfectly warm before you barged in.' His silence unnerved her. 'I owe you no explanation.' Her voice trembled guiltily as his eyes bore into hers, trying to garner some reaction from their iridescent depths. Blood seeped into her limpid skin, but she refused to drop her eyes under his intense exploration. Did he guess? Did he guess that she was the one, the peasant who had leapt on his back screaming a blood-curdling war cry? Now, as he stood before her, she marvelled at her own courage from the very size of him…or was it just the folly of her mind? *Be careful,* an inner voice warned.

'Do you torment all women like this, or is it just me?' Eadita flounced back into the bedchamber, her spine ramrod straight, drawing him from the ante-chamber before he discovered the grimy dregs of her double life. Agatha scuttled from the partition door, and began folding already-folded clothes. Two large hands descended on Eadita's shoulders. A husky whisper at her ear made her jump. 'I treat all women in the same way.' She shuddered, closing her eyes against the chaotic invasion of her senses.

'As you have found no one, maybe you should be about your business.' Eadita struggled to hold on to her self-control. 'My uncle will not be pleased that an outlaw is at large.'

'Oh, I'm confident he'll be found.' He bent towards her again, his masculine scent enveloping her as he growled in her ear, 'And closing your eyes won't make me go away. I'm real, not just some bad dream.' Chuckling, he strode briskly towards the door. 'I'll take my leave, *mam'selle*. It's been a pleasure.' Varin flashed a quick grin and was gone.

Insufferable man! With trembling fingers, Eadita rearranged the perfectly aligned jars in her anteroom. How dare he shove his way in here and ask—nay, demand to search her room! Consumed with indignation, she scarcely noticed the hesitant knock that heralded the belated pail of hot water, nor Agatha helping her frozen limbs into the steaming tub.

'Don't you ever do that to me again, mistress. That was too close for me.' Agatha sucked in her cheeks at the vivid bruises mottling Eadita's slender back. 'What in God's name happened out there?'

'Nothing that I haven't been through before!' Eadita set her mouth in a mutinous line. She'd be damned if she allowed that man to make her feel vulnerable!

'You've never been caught before! You must have been out of your wits to attack a Norman escort!'

Eadita groaned suddenly, the truth of Agatha's words impacting on her conscience. 'Don't remind me, Agatha. I made a mistake out there, I must have misunderstood Thurstan's gesture.'

'I thank the Lord that knight didn't recognise you. Despite what you think, that man is no fool.' A pair of jade-green eyes pushed intrusively into Eadita's mind.

'All men are fools, Agatha,' she snapped, derisively, shaking her head to drive the image away. 'You just have to find their weak spot. And they all have a weak spot…even Lord Varin of Montaigu.' She uttered his name with a sneer.

'I wouldn't be so sure, my lady. They say he's a knight trained to the highest order and a close personal friend of the new King. If he finds out what you are up to—'

'But he's not going to, Agatha,' Eadita interrupted confidently. She rose from the water, rivulets sluicing over her flat stomach and lean thighs, before Agatha threw a towel around her. Once dry, Eadita reached for a dollop of her favourite lavender cream to smooth it generously over her body, imparting a delicate perfume to her damp skin.

'He's not like the men you're used to,' Agatha muttered.

Eadita lifted her arms wordlessly as her servant dropped a dark blue wool undertunic over her chemise, appreciating the luxurious warmth of a garment she had spun, dyed and woven herself. Next, a heather-coloured gunna was slipped over her head, gold silk tablet embroidery decorating the hem and V-shaped neckline. The wide cuffs, also embellished with fine gold thread, dropped to a point near her ankles, revealing the tight sleeves in the blue of the undertunic beneath. She frowned at the frayed edges. In her father's day, the ladies of the manor had been able to purchase fine cloth from abroad to make up their gowns, now there was scarce enough coin to buy the thread to sew them together.

'Agatha, apart from my father and brother, all men are the same. They take control physically, rule with their bullying strength and bluster. That Norman is no different. Nay, I lie, he is worse! Not only is he a man, but he is also my enemy.'

'Forgive me, my lady. But 'tis rare to see you lose your good humour before anyone….except…with him. You must be careful, for that will be your weakness. He may provoke you enough to speak the truth.'

'Never. I would never jeopardise Thurstan's life in such a way.'

'Since the day that you were born, you have been in a position of power, the daughter of a Saxon thegn. How could people not do your bidding?'

'What are you trying to say, Agatha?' A knot of foreboding gathered in Eadita's stomach.

'That you cannot control everything, my lady, or everyone. Especially him.' Agatha paused to draw up the leather laces on either side of the overdress to tighten the garment to Eadita's curves. She looped a heavy gold belt studded with amethyst below her lady's waist, the squares of metal linked together to sit easily on the slenderness of her hips.

'Since your father's death and your mother's self-imposed mourning, you have managed the estate with a firm but fair hand…you have done well, mistress, especially with your uncle holding the purse strings.' Eadita sat on a low stool, her initial bravado ebbing. Agatha brushed her hair, catching back the soft chestnut tresses into a loose plait that fell like a thick rope down her back.

'But…?' Eadita prompted, wincing as Agatha secured an exquisite gold headrail with jewelled pins to her head, anchoring a gossamer silk veil in place.

'Mayhap you should curb your activities with Thurstan for a while…'

'Nay, he needs my help. That means keeping my eyes and ears open here and taking food and medicines to the forest when I can. Think of all the poor people that will starve to death if Thurstan doesn't help them. 'Tis because of the Normans and their taxes that we have to do this! If I stop now, it means those barbarians have won!'

Agatha pursed her lips into a thin, disapproving line. 'Don't you mean "that barbarian"? He is, after all, the only Norman you have met, so far.'

'What! Him? He isn't fit to look at the sole of my shoe. I'll not stop helping Thurstan…especially not for him!' Eadita fiddled with the amethyst beads at her neck, dismayed at the worry in Agatha's face. She had no wish to upset her loyal servant. Placing a hand upon her servant's gnarled one, she tried to appease her. 'Fear not. I will stay out of his way. You can be sure I will avoid his odious presence like the very devil. Besides, he will not concern himself with the daily management of the estate. I will be free to come and go as before. He is as like to stay next to Gronwig, as he is supposed to be his protector.' A prickle of doubt needled her. 'Yet...?'

'Yet...?'

'From what you say about his status, it seems he is an unlikely person for the job. Why wouldn't the King send some lower-ranking soldier to protect my uncle?' Her maid shrugged her shoulders, intent on arranging Eadita's veil to her satisfaction.

'Mayhap he will take charge of the battalion due to arrive later this eve?' Agatha suggested.

'The Saxon battalion?' Eadita queried.

'The Norman battalion, my lady.' Agatha's hands covered her mouth as she viewed Eadita's shocked face. 'Oh, my lady. I thought you knew! You talked to the messenger yourself.'

'But...but...?' Eadita remembered the wiry young man galloping headlong into the courtyard some days earlier, stumbling out his message while still gasping for breath from his breakneck ride. *Prepare the guest bowers and victuals for two score knights and ten,* the order from her uncle had been. Eadita laced her fingers to a tight knot. She had used up valuable stores in order to welcome the battalion with a tolerable feast; now she cursed her mistake. She had used up food that could feed the village and manor for a month.

'I thought the battalion was Saxon,' she mumbled dully. A shudder ran through her. 'They mean to overthrow us, Agatha. And my uncle is too stupid to see it. Now they hold Exeter, the King needs to use Thunorslege as a base to suppress the rest of the West Country.'

'Nay, mistress. Your thoughts run away too fast. The Normans come in peace.'

'The Normans never come in peace. Agatha, these men have my father's blood on their swords!' Rising abruptly from the stool, she rounded on her servant, arms crossed defensively. 'They have raped and pillaged and burned their way through the country, do you think they'll change their ways for us? They attempt to lull us falsely.'

Agatha shook her head. 'I think you are mistaken, my lady. Have faith in the foreigners.'

'Nay, I do not trust them. I must speak with Gronwig directly.'

As she ran along the dark passageway to her uncle's chambers, the sensation of her once-ordered life crumbling around her strengthened. She had known the feeling once before, on being told of the death of her father and brother. Numb with grief, watching her mother descend into a stupor of mourning, Eadita had stood by helplessly as her father's brother, Gronwig, commandeered Thunorslege for his own and assumed the position of *eolderman* for the area. Despite being a close adviser and attendant to the Bishop of Exeter, he had relished the additional power that the country estate gave him, the ability to control the justice and the taxes for the area, as well as a responsibility for the local *fyrd,* the troops for the military. Yet, in reality, Gronwig spent little time at Thunorslege, preferring the luxury of Bishop Leofric's palace in Exeter, leaving Eadita and her steward to run the estate with minimal interference. Only her mother and Agatha knew of her brother's survival at the Battle of Hastings and how he had returned as an outlaw to the forests of Thunorslege. Eadita's help was vital to her brother's success, for by passing him information on wealthy travellers and merchants passing through the vicinity, he was able to take their gold with ease and pass it on to those most in need of it.

Her uncle sat resplendent in his purple velvet robes, quaffing a pewter tankard of mead. He placed it carefully on a side table after his mean-faced servant, Hacon, opened the door at Eadita's knock. A fire burned brightly in the hearth; his chambers benefited from being above the Great Hall, thus sharing the great chimney that rose from below. Gronwig's small eyes gleamed disagreeably at her.

'About time, niece.'

'I'm sorry, Uncle…I had no idea you wanted to see me.' Eadita's voice remained unapologetic.

'I expect you, as lady of this manor, in place of your sad lackwit of a mother…' he emphasised each word heavily '…to be on the steps to greet me and my guests. You had the messages, pray tell?'

'My apologies…the kitchens had my full attention.'

'Not my problem, niece.' His thin lips, almost hidden in the fleshy folds of his white face, worked in agitated motion, every so often flecks of spittle emerging as he talked, his temper growing at the cool, unperturbed manner of his kin. Whilst everyone around him cowered under his bullying behaviour, his niece refused to be intimidated. He hated her for that. She reminded him so much of her father, his elder brother, Edwin—good, kind, clever Edwin whom everyone had adored. Well, he hadn't been so clever to get himself killed, had he? Gronwig cackled, running his eye over Eadita as she stood unflinching before him, seemingly detached from his anger. She would never leave this place, trapped by her mother's fragile mental state, and that was to his advantage. He would bring her down eventually.

'I expect you to be on the steps to greet me and my honoured guests,' he repeated. 'Today you failed in that duty and you will be punished. You will serve at the meal tonight.'

'You can't hurt me with your petty humiliations, Uncle,' she replied simply. 'It will be a huge relief not to sit at the same table as your visitors, listening to their lies, wondering when they plot to kill us in our beds. I do not consider them to be honoured guests. They murdered my father and brother…they do not deserve my attention.'

Gronwig hissed a foul expletive at her disdainful outspokenness. 'You go too far, Eadita!' Glancing nervously at the shadows behind him, his pudgy digits reached out to grab her hand, crushing her wrist in a cruel grip. 'Remember, I am your guardian and you are mine to control. I can do what I want with you. Do not challenge my authority.' Eadita's expression remained openly mocking, despite the kernel of fear scratching at her innards. She would not give him the satisfaction of pulling away. His blotched face leered close to her own. 'You, niece, need to learn some respect!'

'Respect!' Her eyes flashed angrily at him. 'You do not deserve my respect, Uncle! You dishonour my family's name by bringing the Normans here, by helping to hand Exeter over to the King…how could you do it?'

'Watch your words, niece.' Gronwig licked his lips, eyes rolling back skittishly. 'You speak with a traitorous tongue.' Dropping her hand, he took a deep slug of mead, the tankard wobbling in his hand. Rubbing her wrist stealthily, Eadita wondered at his odd behaviour. The fire had obviously not been burning for long, for the chamber still held a cloying chill, yet shining beads of sweat studded Gronwig's brow.

'How many of these men are we expecting? I've already encountered one…and he had the manners of a very dog.' Her uncle recoiled at her brusque dismissal. It was almost if he were frightened…but…of what?

'A battalion follows us. William wants to quell the Saxon uprisings in this part of the country. Thunorslege is the ideal place to base his soldiers.'

Tension clenched at the base of her neck and unconsciously she put up a hand to rub at the stiffness. This couldn't be happening! She had to reach Thurstan, to talk with him, to warn him! His life was in jeopardy.

'Can't you send them back? Tell William that we'll deal with the uprisings ourselves.' Anything to keep those Normans away from her brother!

The Earl threw her a wry smile. 'William trusts no Saxon, not even me. Why do you think he's sent de Montaigu to lead his men? The man is known for his fighting prowess and incisive leadership.' Eadita remembered the hiss of Varin's sword as she lay at his mercy on the forest floor. She didn't doubt that he would have killed her if his steward had not prevented him.

'We will rue this day, Uncle. Do you really want the Normans to conquer what little we have left of Saxon Britain?' She laughed harshly at the sickly, bemused expression on her uncle's face. 'Aye, of course you do...now you're in the pocket of the King, you'll do anything to please. No wonder he's furnished you with such a highly qualified bodyguard.'

'You meddle in matters that do not concern you, should not concern a maid. You've no right to question me in such a manner. 'Tis obvious you have been too long without a firm hand to control you—would that I had found you a husband sooner!' He sniggered towards the thin figure of Hacon at his elbow. 'No matter, no doubt we'll find some burly lord to tup you soon!' She flushed at his crude words, the alabaster purity of her skin stained with a haze of colour.

'You stray from the subject, Uncle. My being married, God forbid, has nothing to do with this. I'm afeard for Thunorslege and the people I have grown up with. What are the Normans about?'

'I have already told you, if you attended my words.' Gronwig smirked. 'I expect our Norman guests to be treated in the proper manner, do you understand?'

Eadita stared at her uncle, hating him. 'We do not have

enough food to feed a whole battalion for months on end. I will need more coin to buy in extra supplies.'

'I give you all the coin I can spare. Most of it goes in taxes to King William. You know I support his new regime fully.'

'While your villagers starve,' Eadita informed him bitterly. 'How can you entertain these Norman infidels while your own people grow sick and die from hunger? My father made sure that none of his villagers suffered, even in the lean years.'

'Your blessed father! How sick I am of hearing about Saint Edwin's good name!'

'He was thrice the man you are. You leave us here to work and scrape and starve, still expecting us to give you an income to support your life of entertaining and luxury in Exeter! You're a disgrace to the Saxon name!'

'And you, my girl, are looking at a spell in the dungeon if you don't hold your tongue!'

'Do you think I care? All I care about is Thunorslege and the well-being of our people.'

'It might not be yours to care about for much longer…'tis a tiresome estate run by an extremely tiresome niece.' His well-padded fingers traced the delicate carving on the arm of his chair. A horrible thought captured her.

'Do you intend to hand the estate over?' Her pulse began to race as she awaited his answer.

'Not yet.'

'Not yet? How can you say such things?'

'I can say what I like, 'tis not for you to put words in my mouth.' The Earl was pleased to have found a subject with which to needle her.

'You can't…you mustn't do this, you cannot give away what my father took so long to build up!' She fought to keep the pleading tone from her voice as a vague sense of unreality wreathed around her.

'Then you'd better start doing what I tell you to do!

Thunorslege is mine to keep and mine to give away. You would do well to remember that!'

'This is intolerable!' she hissed. 'I cannot let you betray my father's name like this! I will kill you first!' A log spat noisily in the grate, sending a crackle of sparks on to the wooden planking.

'Then you will have me to deal with.'

Chapter Three

Eadita's blood ran cold. The husky words slipped quietly towards her from the dimmest corner of the room. Varin emerged from the shadows.

'Oh.' Eadita swallowed hastily, trying to rid her throat of a sudden dryness. Her limbs turned to liquid at the looming figure, taking a hesitant step backwards.

'Oh indeed, mistress.' Varin folded his leather-clad arms across his burly chest. His green eyes glittered in the candlelight. So he had been here all along! No wonder her uncle had appeared so apprehensive.

'Forgive me, Lord Varin, I tried to stop her…' Her uncle gestured ineffectually, his robe sleeves flapping.

'Pray do not apologise. Short of killing her, I doubt anyone could have stopped her mouth.' Eadita rocked back on her heels at the alarming coolness of his tone. 'Besides, I heard nothing that the maid has not told me before. It appears she has quite definite views on our presence here.'

'She *has* offended you…!'

''Tis nothing.' Varin dismissed with a wave of his hand, digesting the finer details of Eadita's attire. Hidden in the shadows, he had stared in amazement as Eadita entered.

Dressed in her evening finery, she was simply stunning. Her violet-coloured gunna, laced tightly to her sweet contours, emphasised the bewitching svelteness of her body, a slenderness surprising in a woman who barely reached his shoulder. Now, he clenched his fists against the sudden desire to hold her body against him, to feel her soft curves beneath him. A silky veil spilled around the pale oval of her face, lending her skin an ethereal sheen that dug at the pit of his belly. Shaking his head slightly, he chuckled. It would not do to be entranced by this one—the woman was a hellcat! Why, even now, aware that he had heard her every damning word, she viewed him with contempt.

'How dare you lurk in the shadows? Why did you not show yourself?' Eadita challenged him, her arms flung towards him. The open accusation in her glance made him want to laugh. Did the maid have no fear? As she stood some four feet away from him, brimming with scantily shrouded fury, she reminded him of the Viking valkyries of old folk myths, eager to throttle him at the merest encouragement.

'The conversation was more interesting without my involvement,' he responded drily, his profile lean and intense in the firelight. ''Tis fortunate the King didn't hear your words. He wouldn't want to think his men weren't welcome at Thunorslege.' Eadita bridled at the edge of threat.

'I cannot pretend. You heard my words.' She shrugged her shoulders, the soft wool 'V' at her neck dipping enticingly towards the shadow between her breasts. A muscle jumped in Varin's high cheekbone.

'Eadita!' Gronwig recoiled at her rudeness. 'Maybe you need some time in your chamber.'

'Nay, at least the maid is honest.' Varin waved her behaviour away. 'There will be time enough for reprimand.'

Eadita's stomach turned over. 'I will take my leave,' she pronounced hurriedly, aware of the implicit warning in Varin's words. 'I am needed in the kitchens.' The hem of her gown swished over the straw-strewn floor as she turned to go.

'Not so fast, my lady. I have need of your services.' Despite the swiftness of her step, Varin now stood before her, a vast tower of masculinity, blocking her exit. She stared purposely at the blond hairs emerging from the slashed neck of his shirt, furious that he should use his physicality to bar her way, refusing to savour the musky aroma that arose from the bare skin at his neck.

'Ah, yes.' The Earl rushed his words in his eagerness to appear willing. 'Lord Varin has several men carrying wounds from Exeter…attend to them now, Eadita. You have the skills. Maybe you can make amends for that brazen tongue of yours.'

'Over my dead body,' she muttered, but only Varin heard her.

'It will be, if you don't get a move on.'

Her heart thudded. 'I will help them after the feasting,' she relented fractionally. As a committed healer, she would never willingly let another human suffer, despite her previous words to this warrior.

'Nay, my lady, you will help them now.' Varin's eyes narrowed dangerously, a frightening adversary to her wilful behaviour. His fingers itched to shake her for her mulishness, as he watched her rapid pulse beat at the silken hollow of her neck.

Gronwig watched the interplay between the couple with close interest.

Suddenly, Eadita felt very, very tired. The rough manhandling she had received in the forest began to take its toll; the bruises and scrapes peppering her skin began to ache uncontrollably. Varin sensed her acquiescence a moment before her shoulders slumped. With any other woman, he would have chided himself harshly for his overpowering behaviour. But with a spoiled vixen such as this? Despite her fragile demeanour, he had no doubt that she was a force to be reckoned with.

'I will get my things,' she said, sweeping her veil lightly around her shoulders.

Varin nodded grimly.

* * *

Eadita drew on a thick fur mantle to brave the freezing air. The sun had set, bringing the peasants in from the fields and outhouses. All around the estate, fires were lit and chores attended to before supper took place in the Great Hall. Despite her animosity towards the Normans, Eadita hoped that Gytha the cook was coping with the preparations for the influx of visitors.

She stepped reluctantly along the ash-strewn path towards the guest bowers, Agatha in her wake. Between her outstretched arms she carried a rush basket filled to the brim with unguents and bandages that slowed her pace. A feeling of dread engulfed as she approached the guest bower. Fear was a sentiment she had never before associated with men, having grown up in the close company of her brother and his friends, yet now, now, she couldn't be certain what was happening. Varin de Montaigu was certainly a formidable figure, despite his boorish manners, but as a man, he should pose her no problems. So why did her stomach churn uncontrollably? Why did her pulse pick up speed as she neared the lighted entrance of the thatched timber hut?

'Prepare yourself,' Varin warned Geraint as he caught the flash of golden headrail in the doorway. 'The termagant has arrived.' Grinning, he allowed his steward to remove his heavy chain-mail to place the hauberk and leggings in a glistening pile at the end of the oak-framed bed. Viewing the lady Eadita's scowling face across the hut, noisy with his busy soldiers, he murmured, 'Mayhap, I should be wise to keep that on.' He gestured towards his armour.

'But she looks delightful,' Geraint commented quizzically as he divested Varin of his padded gambeson. Eyeing the wooden tub steaming with hot water, Varin's lean, tanned fingers unbuckled his belt as he stepped out of his woollen *braies*.

'You deal with her. You know who needs attention.' Varin sank up to his neck in the baking liquid, an involuntary sigh fleeing his lips as the taut sinews in his arms and back stretched and relaxed. Resting his tousled locks against the rim, he allowed the exhaustion of the past few weeks to seep from his limbs.

Bolted to the threshold, Eadita threw a disdainful eye around the hut's interior. Knights in various states of dress and undress bent to their various tasks. Some sat cross-legged on the beds, polishing their swords and spears. Others oiled their chain-mail hauberks to stop them seizing up with rust. Some simply sat and stared at the wall, fatigue clouding their features.

Of Varin, thank the Heavens, there was no sign. Unless…

Time squeezed to a pinprick, then magnified. Eadita swayed, blood rushing to her head, the contents of her basket threatening to topple. Behind the thickly woven hanging, she caught the flare of naked flesh, flesh spangled with water as it sluiced from firm, honed limbs. Rising from the water, Varin had his back to her, the rugged cord of his spine indenting gracefully to muscular buttocks. The glimmering braziers delineated the brawny contours of his thighs, the coating of fine blond hairs darkened wetly. Breath punched from her lungs as the pale linen towel caressed the muscles rippling across his broad back, before he slung the material low about his hips, tucking it at the front. He murmured something to his steward, his lean, aquiline profile half-turned towards her.

She gasped for air, clawing hurriedly for some sense of normality, some sense of reason. Her senses unravelled like looping skeins of silk tumbling to the floor in a chaotic jumble. Raggedly, she hauled her traitorous gaze away, a crimson wave sweeping her face and neck. Perspiration dampened her underarms, a sinful lethargy invading her legs. What was this sickness that consumed her? She had seen naked men before, so why was this hateful man so different?

'My lady. 'Tis an honour to meet you.' A dark-haired man stood before her, blocking her view. 'I am Geraint de Taillebois, steward to Lord Varin.' He bowed gracefully. Eadita expelled a long, shuddering breath. This was the man who had stayed Lord Varin's hand, who had quite possibly saved her life! Similar in height to Varin, and as dark as he was fair, Geraint smiled at her. 'Thank you for helping our men.'

She nodded, grudgingly, unable to trust her voice.

'Young William is the most badly wounded.' Geraint's kindly, open face encouraged her to focus on her purpose as he lead her to a soldier lying on a pallet. Dried blood encrusted a large patch around his shoulder, fresh blood continuing to seep. Aware that Agatha had already organised a pot of near-boiling water to be carried from the kitchens and suspended over the central fire, Eadita removed her cloak and smoothed her damp palms over the heavy cotton apron she had donned to protect her finer garments.

'I will be as careful as I can.' Eadita smiled at the wariness in the man's eyes, trying to reassure him. Dipping a cloth into the bowl of water that Agatha placed by her side, Eadita's fingers soaked and teased the stiff linen away from the wound.

'It will need stitching. Have you drunk some mead?' The man nodded, his scared eyes focusing on the bone needle and gut thread she now held between her fingers. 'You must drink some more. It will dull the pain.' Geraint lifted the tankard to the man's lips, encouraging him to drink deep. Agatha moved closed with a candle, so Eadita had a good light by which to sew.

Eadita lost all sense of time as she moved diligently from one man to another, wrapping poultices around septic wounds, issuing herbal tinctures and sound advice. She forgot the daunting presence of Lord Varin behind the curtain, forgot her own aches and pains and forgot the reasons why these men were at Thunorslege at all, treating them with the equal deference deserved by the sick.

Drawing a dark green tunic over his linen shirt, Varin observed Eadita's steady hands with interest as she tended to his soldiers' wounds. 'Twas obvious the woman had great skill, for her relaxed repose suggested a knowledge in healing that belied her tender years. The lady was a puzzle. The rebellious, spoiled chit he had encountered earlier had been replaced by a maid whose calm, assured manner drew looks of respect from his men. With her voluminous aprons disguising her slender figure and worn, wooden clogs on her feet, the lady of the manor looked more like a peasant. Cursing softly as he pulled up his supple leather *braies* over the smarting wound on his thigh, he strapped on his sword belt. For all he knew, given the amount of noxious liquid she poured into his soldiers, she could be poisoning them all.

'My lady, we're not quite finished…' Geraint drew her attention as he helped her from the kneeling position. Accepting his arm gratefully, Eadita looked puzzled. Surely she had attended all those that needed help?

''Tis no matter, Geraint,' Varin pushed the curtain aside and moved towards them. 'Let it be.' Realising the identity of the last casualty, Eadita thanked the stars that he spurned her help. Treating him would be a nightmare!

'But, my lord…' Geraint turned towards him '…the cut seemed red raw around the edges. Maybe the lady has a poultice or—'

'The lady can look if she wishes.' Varin grinned suddenly at Eadita's dismayed expression. It amused him to goad the insolent chit. The words hung in the air between them. His wet hair was raked back, emphasising the unyielding lines of his closely shaven face, the slash of high cheekbones arrowing down to the tense angularity of his jaw. With the stubborn line of his chin, the effect would have been harsh but for his generous bottom lip, which lent him an intriguing sensuality.

He was testing her, she thought. His eyebrows, arching up

at the outer corners, gave him a searching look, challenging her to take him on. The fresh, invigorating tang of his clean skin played with her senses. Damn him!

''Tis no matter. I have tainted my hands already with foreign blood.' Geraint's eyes narrowed at her rudeness as she gestured around the room. She regretted her enthusiasm as Varin shucked his *braies,* sitting down on a nearby pallet. Despite a linen loin cloth covering his lap, she stared in panic at the long, deep cut that stretched lividly from groin to halfway down his thigh. The edges were dull red and puckered; the cut, although not bleeding, gaped ominously. The wound festered.

'When will you men learn to take care of yourselves?' she snapped, trying to cover her confusion at the near nakedness of the man. 'You should have cleaned it properly.'

'Careful, my lady. It almost sounds as if you care.' As she stood before him, a handspan from his outstretched knees, her unusual elfin beauty became even more apparent. *Diable!* He still held the memory of her flowing glossy hair in her chamber, hidden now by a floating diaphanous veil of the finest silk. He yearned to pluck the formal headrail from her locks, to run his fingers through the silken loops, yet knew he should know better.

'It needs stitching.' She wished desperately that it wasn't the truth. The cut looked septic; if she left it now, the poison from it could spread to the rest of his body. As much as she hated this man, she couldn't allow her personal feelings to interfere.

'Then stitch it,' he growled. Sweet Jesu! It was difficult enough keeping himself under control with her standing right next to him! How in the Lord's name would he cope while her slim fingers stitched his skin! He would definitely need the services of a woman tonight!

Eadita nodded, kneeling down before him, her skirts belling out over the rushes. Sloshing hot water over the wound to clean it, she took the threaded needle from Agatha, biting her lip as her short, pink nails grazed Varin's thigh with a but-terfly touch. Luckily, the sharp prick wrenched his mind from sensual thoughts. She hadn't bothered to ply him with mead, no doubt to make the pain worse to bear! His mind cleared of conscious thought as he tried to remain detached from the woman's proximity.

'Varin! Geraint!'

Eadita started nervously at the strident masculine shout, driving the needle into the hair-roughened skin far harder than she intended. Varin sucked in his breath swiftly, snaking brutal fingers about her wrist to drag the needle out.

'Take heed, mistress!' he whispered. 'Concentrate on the task in hand!'

'I will, if you let me go!' Her eyes stung with angry tears. It had been an honest mistake.

'Ah, Varin. Up to your old tricks, I see.' A tall, lean warrior had entered the hut, throwing his helmet down on an empty pallet. His obsidian eyes assessed the scene disparagingly.

'Count Raoul.' Varin acknowledged his fellow Norman with a nod, his lips clenched.

Why hadn't she started at the top of the wound? As the tight, neat stitches worked towards the crux of his groin, Ea-dita feared her knuckles would brush the intimidating swell of his loincloth. Pausing, she closed her eyes momentarily.

'Looks like the maid's got her hands full!' Raoul chuckled, a lewd grin splitting his gaunt face.

'Leave it, Raoul!' Varin grated. 'I'll be with you shortly.'

'I…' Eadita faltered, lifting her eyes to his, her hands still frozen. His dragon eyes swooped on hers, at once fierce and commanding.

'Finish it!'

The oppressive heat from the fire pushed into her skin, as she took three quick stitches to close the wound and sat back abruptly on her heels. Though she missed touching his manhood by a hair's breadth, the heat from her fingers flared over him. He fought hard for control.

'The battalion?' Varin questioned Raoul. His voice held a shred of unsteadiness.

'Aye, they are here. Settling into the other huts. Some may have to sleep in the hall,' Raoul replied, his interested gaze dwelling on the servant girl at Varin's feet. He suspected a tolerable figure hid under that tent of a gown; she might be just be the maid to warm his bed tonight. Raoul licked his lips 'I thought I'd borrow your tub.' Eadita scrambled to gather her things together, rising to her feet. A heavy hand on her shoulder pressed her down.

'You, girl! You wash my back!'

Eadita viewed Count Raoul coldly. 'Agatha stays with me.'

'I didn't mean that old crone, you silly wench, I meant you! Come here!' Looping a hand under her shoulder, he pulled her roughly upwards.

'Get your filthy Norman hands off me!' she hissed, trying to push him away.

'If you value your life, Raoul, I would remove your hands now.' Varin stood at her side. 'This is the lady Eadita, Gronwig's niece.'

'A Saxon,' Raoul replied scathingly. His hand still gripped her underarm.

'Let her be.' Varin locked eyes with his compatriot, unflinching at the intense hatred in Raoul's eyes. The Count dropped his hold.

'Forgive me, my lady.' Raoul bowed his head. 'Would you do me the honour of sitting beside me at the meal tonight? I am at pains to correct this grave error of judgement.' Eadita regarded him indifferently. The silence stretched and lengthened. Raoul's ingratiating smile dropped away. 'I can see I have offended you deeply. How can I make up for my lack of manners?'

'You cannot, sire. As I have made perfectly clear to Lord Varin, I find it difficult to tolerate your presence at Thunorslege, let alone sit at table with you!' Eadita stalked to deftly scoop up her cloak, flinging it vehemently around her shoulders. 'Make haste, Agatha!' She moved towards the door, her back a rigid line of disapproval.

Raoul's eyes blackened angrily, his face changing rapidly to a sinister mask.

'I will have her, insolent wench!' he muttered, low enough for the women not to hear as they pushed through the oiled skins covering the doorway. 'A lady should know her place, especially a Saxon lady.'

Chapter Four

Eadita stepped down lightly into the bustling kitchens. All around her, servants scuttled and scurried, making ready for the feasting that eve. Hogs roasted over open fires, the dripping fat crackling and spitting in the flames while smooth rounds of kneaded dough burst forth their yeasty smell as they rose imperceptibly in the ambient warmth, soon to be pushed into the bread ovens at the sides of the fires. She wanted to shout to them all to stop; not to waste their precious energy on their unwelcome guests. But the damage had already been done, the food already prepared and the only thing that she could do was make certain that only half of it reached the table. The other half she could hold back for those whose need was greater.

Despite her chagrin, she inhaled deeply, the familiar scents and sounds filling her nose and ears: it was as if she had suddenly washed up to safety upon a shore, after struggling in the deep waters of an unforgiving sea. The kitchen hubbub formed a safe haven for her careening senses; here, she knew what to do, what to say, how to act. Here, she would be able to muster her defences. Those men, and one in particular, had thrown her off course. Count Raoul's lascivious behaviour had made her skin crawl, but she had handled worse than him. But her reaction to Lord Varin bothered her; by tending him, she had exposed a rich seam of vulnerability that she had no idea she possessed.

'My lady, thank the Lord that you are here!' Gytha the cook rushed her wide girth forward, wiping grease-slicked hands over the ample spread of her apron. 'Godric tells me there'll be over two score at the feasting.'

'Aye, and none of them our friends, more's the pity,' muttered Eadita. She glanced over to the corner of the kitchen where her steward berated a kitchen boy. A figure of trustworthy reliability, Eadita had learned all her skills of management from Godric. He had nourished her from a grief-stricken maid, distraught at the death of her father, to the efficient and capable mistress of the household that she was today.

'Godric's just checked the stores, some of the vegetables have gone rotten…the damp has seeped in.' A ragged note of panic crept into the cook's voice as she busied herself scrubbing the kitchen table, pitted and scratched from years of use.

Eadita leaned on the table, her palms flat down on the rough wood, and faced her cook. 'I wish we had nothing to give them, Gytha. I wish our stores were empty so they would move on, stay anywhere but here.'

Gytha frowned. Her mistress prided herself on her well-stocked storerooms, full of preserved meat, jams and jellies to carry the manor and its inhabitants through the scarcity of the cold months. Lady Eadita made sure that all of the surplus produce from the summer and autumn harvests was carefully preserved; nothing went to waste. In truth, circumstances had been a lot harder since Gronwig had become lord; Gytha knew the meagre amount of coin her mistress received as a household budget and her uncle continually demanded provisions to be sent to the palace in Exeter, leaving little for them.

A pair of serving girls came back from the great hall, their eyes round and excited.

'They say he's killed over a thousand men in battle,' Eadita overheard one of them say, as she leant over a bubbling pot to taste the sauce.

'I can believe it,' said the other. 'The size of him!' The younger maid clapped a hand over her mouth.

'Makes you wonder, doesn't it?' the older servant replied saucily, jabbing her friend with an elbow. 'I wonder if he's the same size all over?' They dissolved into ribald laughter, as they began to load the large serving platters with hot food.

'Cease your prattling!' Eadita whirled around to the pair, her stomach churning. Held aloft in mid-air, the wooden spoon dropped spots of sauce over the flagstones. An unwanted memory of hard, corded thigh lurched into her mind, tearing forcibly at her roughly pieced control. The serving girls stared in amazement; it was rare to see their mistress in a temper. She almost never reprimanded those who worked for her, having earned their loyalty with clear directions and unending patience.

'Is there ought amiss, my lady?' The softly spoken Godric appeared at her side.

'Nay…*nay,*' she emphasised the negative determinedly, placing the spoon back in the pot. 'These Normans have disrupted me, 'tis naught. I resent giving them all this food.' Food that she could take to Thurstan and his men, when she had the chance.

'I know 'tis difficult for you, my lady. Our memories are still so fresh.' She nodded. 'But do not fear as to our supplies,' Godric continued, 'we can always send them out to hunt for fresh meat.'

'Aye, they need to earn their keep. In fact, I will tell them now.' Lifting a platter of succulent trout, still steaming, she turned for the door.

'My lady…?' Godric looked puzzled. 'What are you doing?'

'My uncle bid me serve tonight, Godric.'

Her steward looked at her aghast, his mouth twisted in sadness. The people of Thunorslege had suffered under Gronwig's rule, but none more than Lady Eadita. 'Forgive me, mistress, but that man treats you, a noble-born lady, like a servant. Your father, God rest his soul, would have been appalled.'

'But my father is not here,' Eadita replied, her voice tinged with sorrow. 'And we must survive to the best of our abilities under my uncle's lordship. Remember, 'tis only whilst he's here. Soon he'll tire of the country and return to Exeter, you'll see.' A false hope tinged her voice.

'But he treats you like a slave, like the lowest peasant.'

'I would rather be a slave than sit next to those Normans.'

The chattering level in the great hall was directly proportionate to the amount of mead being served. By the smell of honey in the air, Eadita guessed the amber liquid had been flowing for some time. Skating her eyes over the ranks of freemen and servants clustered noisily along the trestle tables, her gaze flew to the high dais where the brightly dressed nobility sat.

Sybilla perched alongside Varin, her yellow silk gunna standing out gaudily against the more sombre hues of the men. Her face turned up to Varin's with such an expression of pure idolatry that Eadita had to bite her lip from cursing out loud. Stupid chit! Her cousin made no secret of the fact that she was unmarried…and available.

With half an ear to Sybilla's constant chatter, Varin's cat-like scrutiny stalked Eadita's fluid path towards them. She carried no excess weight, as if honed by the wind, moving with such effortless grace, such suppleness, that he suspected an inner muscular strength. It mystified him; most ladies he

knew spent their days at looms and spinning wheels with little opportunity for exercise.

'Ah, niece, glad to see that you are following my orders…for the nonce.' Gronwig, seated between Varin and
Raoul, slurped noisily, fixing his small, pale eyes on the platter she held aloft as she approached the top table. 'I'll have
one of those.' He stabbed his jewelled short sword, diamonds
flashing in the hilt, into the largest trout, adding it to the
mound of pork and chicken crustade on his plate. 'Lord
Varin?'

Varin declined the fish, his emerald eyes sparkling wolfishly
at Eadita, the memory of her cool fingers on his thigh igniting
vividly. He would challenge any full-blooded male to remain
resistant to that maid's nimble fingers on their skin. He drew a
deep breath. Divested of her all-encompassing apron that she
had worn in the guest hut, her amazing figure was once more
revealed. The purple gunna fitted her soft curves exquisitely, the
bodice clinging to her full high breasts, the fabric indenting at
her slim waist before flaring out over her hips. His fingers itched
to run themselves along her alluring flanks, to pluck deftly at
her leather side lacings, to…! He gripped the stem of his goblet stonily, hardly aware of Sybilla's talon-like grip on his forearm. By the rood! He must keep himself under control; his duty
was to his King, to keep his wits amongst these treacherous
Saxons and not to tarry on this noble lady! Hadn't he learnt anything from his past? Why had he spent so many years in the thick
of battle, trying to stamp out his own memories? Now, more
than ever, he needed to behave according to his chivalric code,
especially when it came to dealing with Eadita of Thunorslege.

'I'll have some of that!' Raoul demanded sullenly, a scowl
twisting his thin, bony features. He stabbed down at the fish
aggressively, deliberately, causing Eadita to nearly drop her
load. Winding crushing fingers around her wrist to stop the
fish falling on to the table, he bared his yellow teeth at her.

'Good to see you know your place now, mistress.' His grip tightened. Behind him a large candle guttered in its metal cup, sending out a wreath of acrid smoke.

'I know my place, but do you know yours?' Eadita lifted her chin.

Raoul hissed angrily, dropping his hand at her insult, stabbing his knife into the wood of the table.

'You must take no notice of that one,' the Earl reassured Raoul benignly, as Eadita moved off to serve the rest of the table. 'Her mother has turned completely mad since the death of my brother Edwin, her husband. I have always suspected that his death has affected the maid in the same way.'

'She needs to learn some manners,' growled Raoul, staring after her bitterly.

'You would do well to honour our hosts, Count,' Varin cut in with a reprimand, ignoring Gronwig's attempts to pacify Raoul. 'William would not want any antagonism.'

'Oh, and you'd know all about that, wouldn't you?' Raoul replied sarcastically. 'You and William are such good friends.' He stuffed a chicken leg into his mouth, oily juices spilling down his chin. 'The King now honours friendship above nobility, is that the truth?'

'He needed someone he could trust to send to Thunorslege,' explained Varin patiently, a warning thread to his tone. On the other side of Sybilla, Geraint shifted uneasily. A burst of raucous laughter rose up from the trestles at some jest or other.

'One would have thought he would send a more noble compatriot, one more high-born perhaps.' Raoul's hostile tone was unmistakable.

'This is old ground, Raoul. I have earned my place in the knighthood, just as you have.'

'You can do as much earning as you like. Some things you must be born into.' Raoul, with his noble-born lineage, had never quite forgiven Duke William, his liege lord, for taking in Sigurd the armourer's three sons and training them up to be his household knights. That Varin had earned the title of Baron, as well as a castle and lands in Normandy, was of particular insult.

'The subject is closed, *mon ami.* Pay courtesy to our hosts by talking of other things.'

Raoul noticed the Earl's interested glance in their conversation and slumped back in his seat, lips pursed in a cruel line.

'I do hope you like your quarters.' Sybilla seized the pause in conversation to turn Varin's attention back to her.

'Aye, my lady,' he responded politely, ''tis a great deal different from our wretched tent in the marshes.' The many bitter nights spent under frozen canvas, awaiting the end of the siege in Exeter, had become an ordeal for him and his men; many had suffered with the coughing disease, a few had died. He had to be thankful for the Earl's sensitive negotiations with their own more volatile Conqueror so that the eventual ceding of Exeter to the Crown had been achieved quickly, but still with too much bloodshed.

'You poor thing,' Sybilla simpered, 'camping out for weeks on end. You must be desperately in need of some company.' She leaned forward on to the table, allowing her ample bosom to swell the confines of her bodice. Varin looked down his aquiline nose at her. He was used to the loose morals of the camp followers, women who sold their sex to willing knights thirsty for a night of bedding, wishing to lose the vile thought of battle in warm, soft flesh. It surprised him to find the same behaviour in the daughter of a Earl. 'We'll do our best to make you comfortable,' Sybilla continued, pushing back her veil coquettishly, 'but you only have to ask if you need anything more. Anything.'

'Lady Eadita has been kind enough to tend to my soldiers.'

The sexual transparency of Sybilla's conversation began to irritate Varin.

'Aye, I know, but she has not the skills in…other areas.' Sybilla licked her lips, tucking a wayward strand of greasy blonde hair behind her ear.

'Really?' Varin replied blandly, taking a mouthful of curd cheese pie. Geraint smiled discreetly. His lord was not known for complicated relationships; idle dalliance with camp whores involved no parlance and no commitment. A lady was far too risky a proposition.

'Oh, aye.' Sybilla warmed to her subject, her jealous hatred of her cousin fuelling her words. 'Eadita has no idea how to treat a man properly—why, the poor maid wouldn't know where to start.'

'Aye, that's true enough,' the Earl interjected, waving his tankard as if to make a point. 'She's scared off every potential suitor that either her father, or I, has brought before her.'

'No doubt with that caustic tongue of hers,' Varin chuckled, almost pitying the love-lorn swains who dared declare an interest.

'I must find her a husband soon,' Gronwig continued. 'As you saw from this afternoon, Lord Varin, her behaviour becomes more unmanageable by the day.' He belched noisily.

'Who'd have her, Father?' Sybilla crowed with laughter. 'She's far too whimsical.'

Sybilla's words snagged Varin's curiosity. He told himself it was merely because William had told him to be alert to anything unusual. Lady Eadita was certainly unusual, different from any woman he had ever met.

'In what way?' Varin asked quietly.

'Well, let me see. She likes to walk, for example. No lady walks for any great distance, but Eadita does…for pleasure. The peasants say they've even seen her running…can you imagine? And she dabbles in all sorts of potions and powders made up from her herb garden. Some folk are afraid of her healing powers…they cross themselves when they pass her on the farmstead—'

'But she has far more obvious pleasures,' Raoul interrupted, his gaze scrolling over Eadita's petite figure with avaricious eyes as she emerged once more from the kitchens. 'And if she's not spoken for…'

''Tis not our purpose here to find you a wife, Count Raoul.' Varin's rapier glance quelled his compatriot. 'You would do well to remember our duties at Thunorslege.'

Eadita has lost count of the number of times she had trodden the cold flagstones between kitchen and hall along with the other serving maids. Her feet ached and hunger growled like a physical pain in the pit of her belly. The tantalising aroma of the food teased her nostrils cruelly, although she had managed to grab a few morsels, in between her duties. Her aim was to get the evening over with so that she could find Thurstan and his men, discover what had gone wrong earlier in the day and to warn him of the worrying influx of Norman soldiers.

Every time she entered the Hall, the merry crowds appeared drunker, Sybilla's headrail became more askew and her uncle slumped further into his high-backed chair. Choking smoke combined with the heavy smell of mead thickened the air to blur her vision and slow her progress as she lugged the platter of roasted chicken. Nearly tripping over one of the many dogs that roamed the hall looking for left-overs, a strange light-headedness swept over her. Her foot found the step to take her to the top table but she stilled abruptly as the dizziness surged over her, threatening to swallow her up. Grimly, she fought to hold the plate level, her footsteps halting as she fought the jumble in her mind.

'Here, let me take that from you. You've done enough.'

Strong, cool fingers touched her own as the heavy weight was lifted from her wrists and forearms.

'I'm perfectly able,' she snapped, immediately hostile at Lord Varin's interfering presence. Raising startled eyes to his, she held fast to his gaze, a gaze like warm, melted honey that poured over her face and body, seeping into her very soul. Shards of heat flamed through her blood, appallingly, her nipples stiffened in response. *She must be ill!*

'Let me alone, *please.*' She had been hoping to slip away unnoticed once her uncle had been in his cups, and now Lord Varin had scuppered her plans! Hoisting the platter to one massive leather-clad forearm, Varin encircled her other arm to sweep her up the steps. She had no choice but to keep alongside him or be dragged like a sack of potatoes.

'Methinks the maid has done enough.' His tone, though melodious, held the steel of authority. Gronwig barely focused on his niece through his alcoholic haze.

'Aye, let her sup,' he grunted, 'if she can find anything.' Eadita's retort that she'd rather sup with the animals was cut short by Varin pressing her down on to the bench beside him, squeezing her in between himself and Sybilla, who looked suitably outraged. Wordlessly, he filled her a tankard and selected some choice cuts and pies for her to eat, pushing them before her.

'Eat,' he commanded.

She bent her head quickly to the trencher to avoid looking into the jade depths of his eyes. 'It seems I have little choice in the matter,' she muttered disconsolately, taking a sip of mead.

'Would you rather still be lugging the food? 'Tis an ungainly sport for a lady.' A rich vein of steel hardened his words as he looked down at her, making her acutely aware of their close proximity on the bench.

'Not one I am unused to. 'Tis none of your affair.'

His thighs pressed sturdily against her own. As the definition of his leg muscles imprinted on her delicate skin, she tried to hitch her hip away from him.

'Do you mind?' She regarded him peevishly. 'Your sword is pressing into me.' Sybilla hooted with ribald laughter and even Varin smiled at her confused innocence. *Now what had she said?*

'My apologies.' He reached down between them to unfasten his belt and discard the sword. As he fiddled with the buckle, his fingers brushed along her waist. The butterfly sensation shot carnal desire, innocent and newborn, stampeding along her veins. A perception of rushing faster than herself, of spiralling upwards, of nearly bursting, flooded over her, all-consuming. With trembling fingers, she unwittingly lifted the cup of mead with her bruised hand, the legacy of Gronwig's previous cruel grip, to watch it slip from her weakened wrist and soak the contents of her trencher. Dismay shadowed her tired face as the runnels of sticky liquid poured in rivulets amongst the thinly sliced chicken, the chunk of pigeon pie, the curd tart. Tears pushed behind her gritty eyelids.

'Careful!' squeaked Sybilla peevishly. 'You could have spoiled my dress.' She began to search for an invisible stain. Eadita stared hollowly over the crowd below, laughing, joking, chatting, and wished she were somewhere else.

'No harm done.' Varin righted the errant tankard and swapped Eadita's flooded plate for his own. So the virago had a chink in her armour after all, he mused, sensing the lady's weariness. 'What ails your hand?' he asked kindly, lifting the offending member from where she had tried to hide it in the folds of her gunna.

'A small bruise, 'tis but a trifle.' She couldn't bear his touch…or his kindness! His eyes narrowed as his lean, tanned fingers traced the obvious circular bruises around her fragile wrist, taut muscles working under his high cheekbones as he remembered Gronwig pulling the maid towards him. *Sacré bleu!* The grip must have been excruciating to leave such a mark, yet the maid had given no indication of pain.

The nourishing food began to revive Eadita, her quick wits returning with every mouthful. Reluctant as she was to sup with these men, it presented her with an excellent opportunity to glean their plans. The more information she could gain as to the Normans' movements, the more information she could give to Thurstan…and keep him and his men safe. Biting daintily into a pork pie, she turned to Varin.

'So tell me of your plans for the morrow,' she asked pleasantly. His rugged eyebrows slashed upwards in question, the corners of his eyes crinkling with humour.

'You wish to talk to me now? I thought that we did not merit conversation.'

'You caught me indisposed, my lord. No lady likes to be discovered at her toilette.'

'Especially one who is quite so dirty.' So he had noticed the bowl of muddy water!

'My hands were muddy from the garden.'

He knew she was lying. Even he, a soldier, knew that hardly any plants grew in the winter months. He let it pass.

'Why do you want to know of our plans?' he asked, equally pleasantly, watching her touch the fine pastry crumbs that lingered on her lips with the pink tip of her tongue.

''Tis mainly a matter of food,' she replied patiently. 'You have swelled our numbers somewhat. How long do you intend to stay?' She fixed him with her lustrous eyes, each one a pool of deep purple liquid, a fathomless lake that he would happily drown in.

'As long as it takes, mistress.'

'What sort of ridiculous answer is that?' she snapped, all attempt at an agreeable approach flown away. Really, he was the most obtuse kind of man!

'Aha!' He lifted an admonishing finger and had the utter

temerity to wag it at her. 'I knew you were acting out of character; it quite put me off my food!' Pushing his platter away from him, he scanned the high revelry in the hall that almost drowned out their quiet conversation. 'I will put my men through their paces in the morning. We will have the use of the fair field during our stay.' She nodded. The large expanse of grass at the back of the manor was often used for tournaments and travelling fairs.

'And in the afternoon?' she prompted.

'And in the afternoon—' his eyes sparkled '—we will go hunting.'

'Oh, good. You will need to bring back some fresh meat for our stores. Our supplies will dwindle rapidly otherwise.' She bit into an egg custard tart.

'Not that kind of hunting, my lady.' Something in his velvet tone made her wary, suspicious. She raised fine eyebrows.

'We will hunt outlaws.'

The piece of tart lodged in her throat as she sucked in her surprise. She started to choke, eyes watering madly. Varin slapped her in friendly fashion on the back until the food dislodged and she was able to swallow it.

'Do you think you'll catch any?' A hoarse undertone invaded her voice.

'Do you think we will not?' His eyes bore into hers.

'I've no idea,' she hedged. 'I know not what lies in the forests of Thunorslege.'

''Tis my job to find out.'

'I don't hold out much hope…you've lost one already.'

'Aye, Geraint was unlucky,' Varin commented, 'for the lad obviously knew all the secret ways of this manor.' Eadita squirmed uncomfortably in her seat, a niggling tremor of fear fluttering in her stomach. 'I must ask you to keep your ears and eyes open, my lady, for that outlaw may still be among us.'

'I doubt it,' Gronwig chipped in, slurring his words. 'He's

probably long gone.' He heaved his bulk from the chair, swaying unsteadily, Hacon supporting his elbow. 'I am to my chamber; I bid you goodnight.' He shuffled off, weaving slowly from side to side as Hacon guided him around the trestle tables.

Once out of earshot from the great hall, Gronwig grabbed Hacon's arm. His face twisted into a mask of pure evil. 'Get a message to Thurstan, and quickly. I don't care how much danger he and his men are in…he promised me he would finish Lord Varin on the way to Thunorslege. I cannot be certain why the outlaw bungled the job, but, unfortunately, Lord Varin is still very much alive, with his wits about him. 'Twill not be long before he discovers what we are up to. Tell Thurstan that I want the man dead.'

Chapter Five

'Mother, fare thee well?' Eadita rushed forward to clasp Lady Beatrice's hands, while curling her frozen toes back and forth in her thin leather slippers to warm them.

'Come and sit by the fire, child, you look chilled to the marrow.' Her mother drew her towards the stone-circled fire pit, the smoke wreathing up like dirty lace to the hole in the apex of the roof. Beatrice pushed a steaming cup of mead into her daughter's stiff fingers.

Eadita had only herself to blame for this utter coldness. Through the early morning mists, the ringing shouts of combat from the fair field had deterred her from treading her normal path, for it would have taken her directly past the commanding figure of Varin as he steered his soldiers through the finer points of sword-play. Her spirit quailed at any more encounters with his overbearing personality and she decided to take a longer, more circuitous route around the melee of cottages, huts and outhouses clustered around the manor house.

'I *am* frozen, Mother. I will sit, thank you.' Sitting on a low stool, she turned her knees towards the glowing flames. 'You look well rested.' She admired her mother's clear skin and bright blue eyes.

'Daughter, I have never fared better. Unlike you, I heard about your escapade.' Her slim fingers began to wind a ball of wool.

Eadita sighed. 'I am not the one you should be worried for, Mother. 'Tis Thurstan we must concern ourselves with…'

'They will never find him. He's too well hidden.'

'Lord Varin is not stupid. He might easily find a way to navigate the forest.'

'What was that name?' Beatrice leaned forward slightly, her fingers stilling on the brightly coloured yarn.

'His name is Baron Varin de Montaigu and he's an arrogant, rude—' She stopped suddenly at the look on her mother's face.

'De Montaigu.' Beatrice appeared wistful, the name stirring old memories.

'Yes, Mother. That's what I said. Is ought amiss?'

'Nay, daughter, 'tis nothing.' Beatrice decided now was not the time to explain. 'But you, I fear, are in a quandary?'

Eadita shrugged her shoulders. 'I just want them to leave.'

'They may not…'tis not unusual for a Norman lord to take over the running of a Saxon manor. Look what they've done with the rest of the country.'

'Mother! Do not speak of such a thing!' But Eadita nibbled her lip as she remembered Gronwig's threats to hand the estate over to the King.

'Then let us see what the future holds for us.' Beatrice's parchment hands reached down to open the well-worn leather pouch that dangled by a cord from her waist.

'I have no need of the rune stones, Mother, I do not want to know the future.'

'They may steer you in the right direction, my love, or provide the answer to a tricky question.' Her mother spread the angular stones fashioned from bone on to the table before her. 'Why not choose your stones and find out?' Eadita's hand hovered over the stones, stones that had once been her father's, each showing a strange carved symbol. She picked three stones out absent-mindedly, her whirling thoughts on other matters.

'I hope those barbarians haven't disturbed you.'

'Nay, daughter; 'tis good to hear my language spoken properly.' Her mother swept the remainder of the rune stones back into the bag.

'Mother, how can you say such a thing! These men are Norman warriors, descended from the Vikings; they are not the *true* French, not like you.'

'Maybe, maybe not.' Her mother shrugged her shoulders, elusively.

Eadita exhaled, annoyed by her mother's evasiveness. Since her husband's death, Beatrice preferred to live a more simple life in a small hut next to the guest quarters. Decorated with colourful wool hangings, the timbered hut held a small loom and embroidery frame by the window, testament to her mother's industry during daylight hours, and a bed-frame.

'They are the fighting elite, Mother.' Eadita tried again. 'No match for our humble West Saxons… I fear we will be slaughtered in our beds.'

'They appear to have come in peace…as protection for Gronwig.'

'I don't trust the heathens. They are a whole different breed, despicable manners, unchilvarous behaviour, standing higher than our doorframes. I live in hope that a few skulls will be cracked on entry.'

'Place the stones on the table,' her mother ordered, not listening. One of the rune stones slipped from Eadita's fingers to the earthen floor. She bent to pick it up, drawing away suddenly as if scorched. The rune with no symbol faced her from the floor, the blank rune: a bad omen. Eadita shuddered.

'It bears no significance, daughter. Calm yourself. Take

another six stones from the bag.' The stones clicked beneath her mother's fingers as she set out the familiar pattern, three lines of three stones. As the stark, black symbols mapped out her past, present and future, Beatrice started to speak.

'*Daeg* is a confusing stone, but I suggest it represents a change of position, a change that will be long and difficult.'

'Is it me who will change?' Eadita decided to humour her mother's fanciful ways.

'Not just you, you can see *Beorc* here, symbolising growth, and *Tir*, indicating a warrior, a conquest. Someone will change with you. With *Pertra* nearby, you must also be wary of deceivers and intriguers…'

'Hah! That I know already with all these Normans around me!' she scoffed. Her mother's eyes told her to remain silent.

'Someone very close to you will betray you…'

'Mother, cease, I do not want to hear any more.' Eadita clapped her hands dramatically over her ears. 'I'll start to fear what's around every next corner.' She rose in agitation. 'Now, I must change my clothes and find Thurstan. He needs to know what's happening.'

'Tread warily, my daughter.'

'I bid you farewell, Mother.'

As she left her mother's bower, Eadita wished she had put on her fur cloak instead of the woollen one she wore now. The biting needles of the east wind cut through the heavy-gauge fabric; although she had on her gown, underdress and linen chemise, she still felt chilled. She staggered back suddenly as a large warhorse snorted beside her, rolling his eyes malevolently, baring big yellow teeth.

'Have a care, sire. Your horse might do someone an injury. Pray do not ride your animal in the grounds, 'tis safer that way.' Her tone was dismissive as she raised heather-coloured eyes to confront the rider, her heart sinking as she recognised the weak chin of Count Raoul behind the steel helmet.

'Good morrow, Count. I trust you slept well?' She remained courteous but reserved.

'Very comfortable, my lady. And warm too. Everything a man could wish for. Well, almost.' His smile drew back just a little too far back over his teeth…very like his horse, Eadita thought.

'You must excuse me. I have duties to attend to…'

'Forgive me, *mademoiselle,* but you seem to have too many duties for a lady. In France our ladies spend a good deal of each day sitting and chatting.'

'Fortune smiles on them,' Eadita commented wryly, thinking exactly the opposite. To not use her body physically seemed like a sin. The infinite joy she gained from walking and running in the forest far outweighed the risks she took.

Count Raoul dismounted to stand rather too close to her, the faint rotting smell of his breath wafting over her. 'I would have words with you, *mademoiselle.*' The urge to run became overpowering, but she held her ground, rapidly assessing her situation. The Count had neatly boxed her in, his horse on one side pawing the ground with menacing regularity, and himself on the other in the lee of a storehouse.

'You and I would deal well together, *mam'selle,* if only you would unbend a little.' He clasped her forearm heavily.

'I am not in the market for a husband. Good day to you, sire.' She made to move, but his grip tightened nastily.

'I'm not talking wedlock, my dark-haired angel. Only a little bedsport now and again.'

'How…dare you proposition me in such a way?' Her voice dripped disgust. 'You…a Norman. I made it quite clear last night that I want nothing to do with any of you. I can barely tolerate your presence here.' Her mocking look died as she watched the anger flare up in Raoul's face.

'You...insufferable little prig. Look down your nose at us, would you? I'll soon show you who's master around here.' He took a tighter hold of the fabric on her sleeve, bunching it savagely as he jabbed into the soft flesh beneath it and started to drag her off behind one of the huts. Instinctively, a scream began to rise in her throat, before she snuffed it. She knew what to do; Thurstan had shown her enough times. This bully needed to be taught a lesson and to hell with the consequences.

Swinging her captured arm down in a chopping motion, she released his hold smartly, before aiming her knee viciously at his groin. Raoul howled, bending over in wincing pain. Quickly, she rolled her lithe body through the mud under the horse's belly, her skirts flying out around her. Springing up, she slipped quickly around the corner of another circular hut. Recovering slightly, his face registering shock, puzzlement and fury, Raoul clumsily pushed his horse away in a mild attempt to pursue.

Varin, showing a young knight how to position a sword correctly, had spotted a flash of purple on the periphery of his vision. Turning his head, he groaned at the sight of Eadita's petite form, her gown startlingly vivid against the mud-coloured hut, dwarfed by the thuggish Raoul. Would that man never give up?

His heart lurched as the huge destrier skittered beside the couple. A stallion bred for its aggressive qualities should never be around people unused to them. He sensed the horse's unease, its hooves pawing at the rutted mud, tail swishing as it towered over the diminutive Saxon lady. Phantome did not have a reputation for docile behaviour.

Varin began to cover the field in long, rapid strides, seeking to halt any mishap that might occur, then stopped, astounded. Did his eyes play him false? Lady Eadita had performed an almost unbelievable manoeuvre, folding her body to fit neatly under the belly of Phantome, before pitching forward through the tussocky earth to flick smartly upwards on her feet again. Never pausing, nor looking around, she vanished around the side of the hut.

Raoul, a thunderstruck expression on his face, pushed Phantome aside venomously, striding purposefully towards Varin.

'Did you see that? Did you see it? The little bitch is out to get me.'

'I thought it was the other way round.' Varin replied drily.

'Nay, she is teasing me. She knows full well what the end result will be.'

'I wouldn't be too certain of that, Raoul. The lady is fairly opinionated on her likes and dislikes.'

'She will learn.'

'Raoul, leave her alone.' A mild exasperation peppered Varin's tone. He gestured towards the untethered horse. 'Take Phantome and tie him up in the stables. He's too dangerous to be out.' Raoul's eyes blazed, but he registered the steely command and knew he was beaten…for now.

The elegant drape of Varin's long cloak swung around his leather boots as he walked back to the mock fighting in the field, resolving to speak to the lady about her risky behaviour. He knew Phantome's unstable nature—it was lucky that she hadn't been crushed to death. He imagined the lady's haughty response to his reprimand, the imperceptible raising of her head as she sought to defy him, her expression inscrutable. He smiled softly. Where had she learned to carry her body like that? She moved with an underlying grace, a lissom flexibility that reminded him of the acrobats in the travelling fairs who amused their audience with backflips and somersaults.

'Lord Varin!' Eadita interrupted his idle thoughts; her tone held authority and complaint. She must have retraced her steps to have words with him. He looked up at the grey skies, clouds starting to build, idly watching a flock of geese honking their way east, mentally preparing himself.

'My lord! I demand speech with you!' She placed a hand on the worn leather cuff strapped around his forearm. His cloak swirled in the freshening wind, reaching out to whip around her ankles, enveloping the brilliant hues of her hooded cloak. Varin looked down imperiously at the delicate bones clutching his arm, trying to forget her fingers on another part of his body.

'You…demand?' Her audacity seemed overwhelming in a woman; no other lady would dream of hustling for his attention in the fashion of this elfin chit. It astounded him that she saw nothing wrong in the way she addressed him.

'Aye, my lord…I have cause for complaint.' She followed the movements of his men on the field as they plied their swords overarm to attack an imaginary enemy and frowned, suddenly distracted. 'Twas a snippet of useful information she could carry to Thurstan.

'Why do they use their swords in such a way?'

'So they can thrust down over the enemy's shield and thus break the shield wall. Why are you so interested?'

''Tis of no real interest.' *He didn't believe that.* She was watching his men intently. Whisking her vivacious face back to his, her limpid eyes scrolling over his implacable features, she folded her arms high on her chest.

'My lord, I have resolved to tolerate the presence of the Norman battalion at Thunorslege…'

'How gracious of you,' murmured Varin, knowing she had little choice in the matter.

'…but Count Raoul is becoming offensive. He has just propositioned me in the most vile manner. He is quite…libidinous.'

'Libidinous?' Varin strove to keep a straight face at the prudish formality of her words. His eyes, the colour of unfurling leaves in spring, sought her own, but she refused to look up at him, maintaining a steady gaze towards the thrust and parry of the cavalry in front of her.

'Yes, libidinous behaviour. 'Tis unseemly…I have certainly no wish to have any involvement with a Norman, any man for that matter—' She stopped abruptly, embarrassed by the sudden flood of words. What on earth was she saying?

His lips twitched. 'You don't wish to be involved with *any* man? You do surprise me, *mademoiselle*. I thought Saxon folk carried the reputation for being extremely libidinous in their behaviour. In France we hear tales of good men and women stripping naked before huge bonfires before tumbling in the undergrowth with their chosen partner.'

'Those ceremonies are for the peasants; not everyone joins in,' she replied, defensively. 'The year is long and difficult, at least the feast days allow them to enjoy themselves.'

'Ah, you admit they enjoy themselves. Then all is not lost, *mam'selle*. You admit there must be some enjoyment when a man and a woman tumble together.' She glanced up at his unsmiling visage. Was he teasing her?

'I…um…' Desperately, she searched for the correct words. How could she tell him that she had no idea what happened when a man and a woman were together? That, at one and twenty winters, she had scarce kissed a man, let alone lain with one. Varin noted her discomfort, the hesitant nibbling of her full underlip, causing blood to redden its perfect rosebud beauty, set in the magical oval of luminous skin. He started to feel a building discomfort of his own, shifting his weight uneasily.

'Just tell the Count to leave me alone! I had to endure his odious presence yestereve and just now by the storehouses.'

'I know, I was watching.' He lifted a gloved hand to brush the congealing mud atop her veil. 'That was quite a performance you gave…where did you learn to do that?'

'Why didn't you stop him?' Her eyes flew wide as she avoided a direct answer.

'You were merely in conversation, my lady. I couldn't hear

the words spoken. Obviously he offended you greatly, your reaction was most extreme.'

''Twas all I could do in the circumstances.' A gleaming brunette strand escaped from her veil, the curling end catching the breeze to clasp lovingly about his arm. His breath snagged, the heavy fullness in his loins gathering heat as she stepped back hastily to sever the contact.

'Indeed, you might not have thanked me if I had rushed over. I may have been breaking up a budding romance. Count Raoul is not a bad prospect for a husband; his lands are vast in Normandy. You could do worse.'

'You must be insane,' she spoke sharply. 'I've no intention of yoking myself to a husband.'

At least we agree on something, thought Varin. Marriage is for fools only. One kiss from me would mean nothing to her and, by the rood, he was sorely tempted; he just needed a taste of those sweet lips to dampen his interest. Warning bells clanged in his head as he slid his gloved hands around Eadita's enticing curves under the butter-soft wool, marvelling at the narrowness of her back. Excitement bubbled through his veins, blood pumping heavily. In one swift move he lifted her to him so that her slippered feet dangled above his boots and bent his leonine head to claim her lips for his own.

She bit him.

She had bitten him! The impudent little chit! Rage boiled up to replace the desire that had ravaged his body only moments ago; a red flush streaked along his cheekbones. He threw her away, causing her to stumble a little. Watching the anger play across his face, she quavered as his eyes hardened to green ice.

'I suppose I deserved that,' he ground out, wiping the back of his glove against his smarting lip.

'You did.' Eadita, head perched proudly on her elegant shoulders, stood resolutely before him. 'Your manners are inexcusable, but I can't say I'm surprised. Who could expect more from the savages who slaughtered my countrymen? I shall be speaking to my uncle about how long we must endure your insufferable presence—I do hope that it will not be overlong!' She whipped away from him.

Varin told himself he welcomed her scornful rejection, but, oddly, her disgraceful behaviour and quick wit had begun to needle his carefully built defences, sneaking between the gaps to catch him unawares. His lack of control around her surprised him; hadn't his father's experience taught him anything? Eadita's beauty drew him like a moth to a flame, but he had no intention of being burned. Staring moodily after her retreating figure, her white veil flapping madly in the stiff breeze, Varin prayed for restraint.

Chapter Six

'Why not try the red against the purple? Eadita suggested, her nimble fingers unravelling a dark red skein from the colourful bundle in the wicker basket at her side. Perched on a small stool, she smiled at the woman sitting at the wide treadle loom, offering up the bright yarn. Touching her fingers briefly to her face, Eadita was aware that her skin still carried the flush from her encounter with Lord Varin. Damn that man!

'I agree. I hadn't thought of those colours together,' the older lady replied, biting her lip in concentration as she threaded the wool into her work. The faint morning sun trickling into the windows of the women's solar touched the rich colours in a haze of gold. Rolling her tense shoulders under the sun's warmth on her back, Eadita looked around at the ladies who worked on their various forms of needlework. Some did vital repairs on the household linens, others worked industriously at the looms, weaving the yarn to cloth. Two ladies sat spinning in the corner, their skilled hands feeding the bulky sheep's wool into the wheels to produce a fine weaving yarn. Eadita had prided herself in continuing a tradition of her father's: to provide each villager and servant of the estate with a new set of clothes every year. Pulling at a piece of wool between her fingers, she realised that, this year, she might not be able to give them anything.

Resting her eyes on the ladies working on the bare patches of some of the huge tapestries, Eadita shook her head slightly, amazed that so much could change in the two years since her father's death. She stood up abruptly, the yarn falling to the floor. Now was not the time to wallow in her constrained circumstances! She just had to make sure that all the women had enough work to keep them busy, then she would slip away to the forest, and to Thurstan. Her eyes alighted on a bundle of shirts, unusual in their design.

'Whose are these?' she demanded, picking the top shirt up between disdainful fingers.

'Oh, 'tis a pile of shirts and chemises from the Norman soldiers. They are ripped beyond belief.' One of the ladies stepped forward with an explanation. Eadita stared at the mess of torn linen, lips compressed, rage beginning to simmer within her. The pure insolence of those men! First they wanted her to tend their wounds and now they expected, above board and lodging, for her women to fix their clothes!

'It will not take us long,' Alfreda, one of her most experienced seamstresses, answered Eadita's frowning face.

'It will take you no time at all,' Eadita retorted, whipping the basket from the floor to hoist it beneath one arm, 'if I take it back from whence it came!'

'Oh, my lady,' Alfreda gasped, a shadow of worry flitting across her features, 'maybe 'tis best to just do the work? I wouldn't want to offend them.'

'I shouldn't worry about that,' Eadita replied recklessly. 'We have enough work of our own. Hopefully the less we do for them, the sooner they will go!' She whirled about, hem flying, and stepped straight into Varin, standing quietly in the doorway.

'You again!' she breathed. 'Why aren't you on the fair

field?' Was he following her? Did he suspect something? Her eyes flew guiltily to the obvious red mark on his bottom lip.

'My job is finished there.' He grinned slowly, his dark-green eyes bright with humour. 'I see your behaviour towards your guests has not improved.'

'As has yours?' She widened her eyes to reprove him for the attempted kiss. 'Excuse me, please.' Behind her, the high bubbling chatter dwindled to nothing. The clicking of the looms had stopped. Her face heated under his direct gaze as she remembered the brief press of his lips upon her own before she had… She had to get away! She made to step past him, but his huge frame filled the doorway. His eyes flicked over her neat headrail, her chestnut hair braided into two fat plaits hanging either side of her face. A pulse beat rapidly under the fragile skin at her throat.

'Where are you going?' he growled softly.

'Is it any business of yours?' Her heart lurched at the possession in his voice.

'It is where my soldiers' clothes are concerned.' He picked up the top garment, ripped and dirty, and met her eyes in mild rebuke. 'Forgive me if I don't congratulate you on your sewing skills.'

'We haven't mended them,' she replied slowly, trying to keep her temper under control. 'Surely that much is perfectly obvious!' The weight of the heavy basket began to drag uncomfortably on her upper arms. 'My ladies are hard pressed as it is to keep apace with the household requirements.'

'Your continued hostility is beginning to irritate me,' he lowered his voice silkily. The outer corners of his well-defined lips twitched slightly. She could have sworn he was trying not to laugh.

'I am trying,' she retorted, 'but you're making it very difficult.'

'Then I suggest you try harder, *mam'selle*. Maybe I should

make you mend every one of those garments with your own fair hands,' he suggested. 'That might put an end to your spoiled, irascible manner.'

'Just you try!' she flung back, watching his golden head tip back a little at her challenge.

'I've made you tend to my men against your will, my lady,' he pointed out calmly. 'Do you really believe that I couldn't make you do this?' The chamber behind Eadita held its breath. Scanning the full, powerful length of the man before her, Eadita acknowledged in panic that she was out of her depth. The magnetic pull of his eyes taunted her, as she refused to answer.

'You couldn't make me kiss you!' she blazed, realising only after the words were out what a stupid thing she had said.

'I wish we were somewhere more private so I could prove you wrong, my lady.' The rough seductive edge of his voice sent a mercurial tremor of excitement vaulting through her body. He stood too close to her! She shifted uneasily, trying to move the basket from where it rested on her hip to the front of her where it could form a more effective barrier between them. Her fingers slipped on the smooth wicker and the basket lurched downwards. She jumped as his large, warm fingers curled over hers, relieving her of the cumbersome weight to set it on the floor.

'I didn't come here to argue about mending.' He straightened up. 'I want you for something else.'

She folded her arms defensively over her chest, trying to ignore the erotic quality of his husky tones. Why did everything he said seem to have a double meaning? Without realising, she shook her head slightly, trying to distance herself from the bewitching, captivating effect this man, this Norman, had on her!

'Your uncle suggested that you might be able to show me around the estate. He assures me that you know everything there is to know about managing Thunorslege.'

'Oh, he did, did he?' Gronwig would have delighted in handing Lord Varin over to her; he knew it would rile his niece to have to show the enemy around. She pushed her bottom lip out.

'Don't pout, my lady. It doesn't become you.' She glared at him, willing herself not to react to the brilliant flare of his eyes.

'What possible interest could you have in a Saxon estate?'

'Let's just say I'm mildly curious,' he explained, shrugging his massive shoulders. 'Gronwig doesn't need me by his side constantly.' She had to get rid of him somehow. Reaching Thurstan was her priority now, finding him before the Normans did.

'I thought you were supposed to be hunting outlaws?'

'Not until this afternoon. My soldiers need to rest after Exeter. I have time enough this morn.'

'It will take longer than that.' Her mind hitched on to a different tack. Maybe, by showing him all of Thunorslege, down to the last detail, she could prevent him and his men going out at all today.

'We plan to be here for some time, my lady. I thought I had made that clear. Whatever we don't cover this morning, we can do on another day.'

She gripped her fingers together in disappointment.

'Has Thunorslege always been in your family?' Varin asked conversationally as they stepped out of the main door into the sunlight.

'Aye,' Eadita replied. Of independent spirit, she was unused to a man walking at her side, escorting her. Trickles of apprehension streaked through her slender frame as the tall warrior matched her steps considerately. What is he trying to find out by coming with me? she wondered, eyeing him surreptitiously as she pulled her voluminous hood over her shining hair. His cloak swung in one long fall from his broad shoulders to sweep a few inches from the ground. Lined in fox fur, the dark colouring of the fur indicated its expense.

Eadita marched on grimly towards the outer palisade of the manor. She supposed she ought to try and be civil to him. Glaring at the sun's elevated position, she realised that a good portion of the morning had elapsed. Thankfully, this meant her time with Varin would be curtailed because of the mid-day feasting.

''Twould make this easier if you volunteered slightly more information, my lady.' Varin viewed her truculent profile in amusement. Her volatile manner made her easy to tease, easy to keep their relationship on neutral ground. He followed her down the wide steps and through the high stone walls that formed the inner defence to the manor. Over to his right lay the village of Thunorslege, a small church nestling in its midst, a river glistening in the distance.

''Tis pretty, this estate of yours,' he remarked.

'I think so,' she replied. ''Twould be a great shame if it were to fall into Norman hands.'

'Your bluntness is astounding.' He grinned. 'Unusual for a woman, but then…you are an unusual woman.' She flushed under the teasing nature of his words. 'I must assure you, 'tis not our intention to take over Thunorslege—Gronwig is now a confirmed ally to the King.'

Eadita shrugged her shoulders. 'I suppose I have to believe you, since my uncle appears to trust you.'

'But you do not trust your uncle,' he observed equably. Eadita clamped her lips shut, not about to confirm or deny his intuition. 'Twas no business of his! She trod along the stony path that bounded the perimeter, lifting her skirts away from the mire. Varin regarded her trailing hem thoughtfully.

'Would you prefer to show me around on horseback, my lady? 'Twould keep your clothes from becoming dirty.'

She rounded on him, her tones sarcastic. 'You have much to learn, Norman. We Saxons only ride when there's hunting or hawking to be done.'

'How could I forget?' he murmured, as they set off again. 'Twas the Norman cavalry at Hastings that had overwhelmed the Saxon foot soldiers and ultimately won the battle. If the Saxons had been on horseback, the ending of the battle might have been entirely different.

Reaching the north side of the boundary, Eadita stopped to sweep her hand over the view. 'These are our lands,' she said, unable to keep the small touch of pride from her voice. A myriad of patchwork fields, hedged and bounded on all sides by drainage ditches, lay below them.

''Tis a sizeable amount.' He looked on with interest. 'What do you farm?'

'Wheat for the flour. Oats for the animal fodder and our porridge. Peas and beans in summer.'

'And the livestock?' Varin was impressed by her knowledge.

'Cows and pigs, of course. We keep chickens up near the kitchens. And our fyrdsmen hunt whenever they can, especially in winter when stocks are low.'

'But I suspect they are never allowed to become that low,' he suggested, 'considering the amount of coin your uncle has available to him.'

She frowned. 'Nay, you are mistaken. We work hard to preserve our crops for the winter. There is precious little going spare.'

He reached for the material of her sleeve, rubbing it between two fingers. 'You dress in expensive cloth.'

She stared for a moment at his hard, muscled hand, callused from many years of controlling warhorses. 'Most of my garments are the legacy of a generous father. Nowadays, we make our own cloth,' she spoke lightly, reluctant to alert Varin to the poverty at Thunorslege. 'You saw how busy my women were this very morn.' He dropped her sleeve, one eyebrow quirking in suspicion.

'But you can buy extra stores at the market?' he probed once more.

'Nay, we do not have enough coin.' His constant, searching questions worried her. What was he trying to discover? 'All the taxes that are collected and any income from the estate go directly to Gronwig. 'Tis he who gives it all to the new King. Or had you forgotten that?' He watched her shifting uneasily from one foot to the other, sensing a mystery. Something was not quite as it should be at Thunorslege. Something he couldn't quite put his finger on…

''Tis a lot to manage.' He whistled admirably, changing the subject. He glanced down. The tightly wrapped sleeves of her underdress emphasised her lissom arms, the fragility of her wrists. 'Especially for a young maid. Why do you stay, my lady? Surely marriage to some rich, love-struck swain is preferable to this hard existence?'

'Godric, my steward, manages much of the daily business. ''Tis not so difficult.' How could she even begin to explain what Thunorslege meant to her, to her mother? It was her home.

'Your uncle treats you badly, like a servant.' She caught the note of kindness in his voice, and gripped the edges of her cloak, drawing the cloth around her. She didn't want this Norman to feel sorry for her!

'Gronwig treats everyone badly.' She shrugged her shoulders, staring blankly ahead.

'And what about your mother?'

'She is a virtual recluse…because of my father's death,' she explained limply. 'To her, the estate still belongs to Edwin, my father. She would never leave Thunorslege.' And I would never leave her here, alone. Gronwig would destroy her, Eadita thought. 'You will not see her; she blames you all for his death.'

'King Edward promised the English crown to William. I cannot change the past,' he reminded her.

'Harold of Wessex should not have died. The crown was his.'

'Then we must agree to differ, my lady.' A corner of his finely drawn mouth lifted. Her heart thudded at the curving sensuality of his bottom lip. 'Do you hate me because I am Norman, or because I am attracted to you?' His words hit her like a thunderbolt. Her chest bumped awkwardly. Why did he say such odd things? It threw her off balance, like a child's spinning top about to wobble over.

'What utter foolishness,' she chided, sternly. 'I just hate you, hate you for what you've done, for what you stand for, that's all.' Was he attracted to her?

'That's *all!*' The corners of his eyes crinkled with humour. 'It seems for every minute in your company I must pay the price one hundredfold for being a Norman. Lesser men would have run for cover by now.'

But you are not a lesser man, she thought, guilty at the way her mind worked. He stood but a foot away from her, surrounding her, engulfing her with his large, domineering body. He made her feel like a woman; he forced her to acknowledge feelings that she had no idea she possessed.

He tipped his head to one side, observing her. 'When two people desire each other, my lady, it doesn't matter from whence they came.' Now why had he said that? He had no intention of becoming involved with this maid, but surely it didn't hurt to flirt a little? It amused him to watch her innocent reaction to his goading, he told himself, 'twas a light diversion from the long months of battle.

'Oh, do not tease me so,' she admonished, unbending slightly. But she refused to relax her proud, defiant stance totally, knowing it was her only defence before him. God forbid that she started to enjoy his company.

Varin flexed his leg, an unconscious gesture.

'Your leg?' she questioned, staring intently at his thick, muscled thigh banded in supple leather before twisting her eyes away, embarrassed. 'Is it healing properly?'

'Would you like to look?'

'Nay.' She shook her head, too quickly. 'I trust your judgement when it comes to your own flesh.'

'It begins to itch.'

''Tis a good sign. It means…' She trailed off.

'That the stitches need to come out,' he finished triumphantly. She quavered under the dynamic brilliance of his eyes.

'One of your soldiers can do it.' She had no intention of being in such intimate proximity to this man again, especially after he had tried to kiss her!

'My soldiers' hands are more used to wielding a cumbersome sword than a delicate blade.' He laughed. Eadita turned her back to him, starting to walk briskly back to the manor. He followed her. 'Why do you run away so, *mam'selle?* You put the stitches in…surely you are not shy about taking them out?'

'Nay, of course not, but now I know you better, I may find my hand is not so steady,' she threw back over her shoulder, relieved to be away from his intimidating nearness.

'And I might lose more than just a leg.'

'Which can only be a good thing,' she responded maliciously. 'I am not going to do it. Just make sure they burn the knife point and wash their hands before they start.'

Varin winced.

Thurstan pursed his lips to make the familiar bird call. He listened intently. It came again. Once, twice, thrice. His sister waited for him! Moving silently over the sodden vegetation, his leather-shod feet sinking into a mess of decomposing leaves and bracken, he pushed noiselessly through spindly branches and tugging brambles. He paused on the edge of the clearing. The small figure sat solemnly waiting on a large, flat stone, her head bowed as if in prayer. Dressed in sombre colours of brown and green, her angelic visage marred by streaks of mud, a pang of guilt made him question the validity of his cause.

With the Normans at Thunorslege, Gronwig was nervous. That much was apparent by the message Thurstan had received from Hacon the previous night. Eadita had scuppered Thurstan's plans to kill Lord Varin by jumping from the tree too early. She had no idea he was in league with Gronwig, believing that the gold they robbed went to the poor and needy, not directly to their uncle to build a Saxon army! But Gronwig had promised to return Thunorslege to him once the Normans had been overthrown, and the dream of holding his family home again was too much of a prize to resist. Ever since he had returned from the Battle of Hastings with his father's blood splashed over the Thunorslege markings on his tunic, he had vowed to avenge his father's death. What better way than this, for his dream was the same as Gronwig's. He prayed that Eadita would understand once it was all over.

'Thanks be to the Lord that you are safe,' he whispered, moving to touch his sister's shoulder. She jumped slightly, then rose to clasp her brother in a bear hug.

'Thurstan, what in God's name happened yesterday? What was amiss?'

'You jumped...I didn't.' Thurstan clasped her shoulders. 'You mistook my signal, Eadita. I was only funning, I had no intention of attacking.' The lie burned his lips.

'Thurstan, that was not the time to play the fool,' she admonished severely, 'I could have been killed by that oaf.' A pair of green eyes stirred her memory. 'Thurstan, I came to warn you. The Normans plan to search for outlaws this afternoon. I only managed to slip away because they are all eating.'

'They will never penetrate the greenwood,' Thurstan replied confidently. 'A man can walk for days and days and not reach the other side. With no identifying landmarks, 'tis difficult to know one's place.'

'Even so, Lord Varin is no lackwit. You must lie low, do naught without thinking carefully. Please, for my sake.' Her beautiful amethyst eyes implored him.

'Nay, sister, 'tis you who should take care. You took a chance coming to visit today.'

'I had to know what had happened to you. Besides, you have need of provisions.' Thurstan noted the two heavy net bags stuffed full of muslin-wrapped packages. His mouth watered. His men would be glad to see her as the hunting had been poor of late.

'Did you bring the lungwort for Kenelm's cough? I fear it has worsened today.'

'Aye, brother.' She patted the pouch at her waist. ''Tis the cold, damp air. Come, I would see him.' Thurstan drew a long woollen scarf from the thick leather belt girding his overtunic and tied it securely around his sister's eyes. By not knowing the way to their camp, it kept her safe.

'Do you think we'll find anybody?' Geraint asked.

Stones bounced out from beneath the horses' hooves as the Norman battalion rode down the deeply rutted embankment from the gatehouse.

''Tis enough to gain our bearings,' Varin replied. 'The forests are vast, it'll take several days to cover them.'

''Tis a shame Gronwig could not supply a guide—' Raoul laughed harshly '—'twould make our job a good deal easier.'

'Aye, it would have.' Varin had not been surprised by the Earl's reticence to help them. It merely confirmed William's suspicions about the man.

'Do you really trust Gronwig?' Raoul's eyes narrowed as he drew his horse alongside Varin's. 'Five days since he held Exeter in siege against our King.'

Nay, I do not trust him and neither does William, Varin thought. But with Raoul's headstrong nature he was not about to commit that information. Only Geraint and he knew of William's uncertainty regarding his most recent ally.

'There are enough of us to hold Thunorslege if he decides to challenge us,' Varin answered mildly, pulling on the reins to prevent his horse from stumbling too fast down the hill. Raoul frowned, aware that Varin suppressed the true details. 'Twas always the same, he thought resentfully, kicking his spurs viciously into his horse's flanks. Why in God's name did the King trust this low-born dullard over him, a high-ranking noble? The Villeneuves were an old French family, descended from Charles the Simple, while the de Montaigues… Vikings, the lot of them.

'To the village?' Raoul swept a gloved hand towards the number of cottages and huts down by the river, disguising his jealousy with the action.

'Nay, the forests are more likely to yield our outlaws. Take your men and start combing the west side.' Varin despatched the Count and his men with practised ease, while he and Geraint elected to take the middle path into the dark woods. The horses plodded quietly, but soon the undergrowth made headway difficult. They tethered the animals, deciding to walk.

'Have you noticed anything strange?' In the depths of the trees, Geraint knew it was safe to talk about their true purpose.

'The King was right. Gronwig is certainly up to something. But I suspect he is gaining help from an unusual quarter.'

'What do you mean?'

'Lady Eadita has exhibited some unusual behaviour…'

Geraint's laughter rumbled in his chest as he hacked at a mess of brambles. 'Isn't that just towards you, my lord?'

'Nay, she doesn't like me, that much is clear. But there are other things.'

'Such as…?'

'The muddy water in her chamber, for example, that she tried so hard to prevent me seeing; her interest in the sword-play on the field—when have you ever known a woman to be interested in something like that?' Geraint shook his head. 'And that move away from Raoul, so quick, so practised…oh, I know not, Geraint, but there's something about her that I cannot unravel. Seeing her that first night, I could have sworn I had met her before…' Varin thrashed at a tangle of nettles in exasperation.

'Wishful thinking?'

Varin grimaced, his expression implying the opposite.

'She seems to have the measure of you,' Geraint continued his teasing vein.

'Her mind is quick, I'll give her that. But her behaviour!' Varin fingered his bruised bottom lip. ' That scrawny under-sized chit is unbearable! Nothing would make me happier than to see her topple from her impossibly high perch.'

Geraint smiled to himself. His lord was used to women falling at his feet, but the lady Eadita seemed immune to his handsome good looks.

The two men trudged till the sun was nearing the horizon, working hard against the hostile vegetation to clear a way forward. Occasionally they found a track, worn into the ground by the deer or wild boar that roamed the forest and it made their headway easier. Keeping the sun in the west made them confident of their route homewards.

'Methinks we should turn back, my lord. The eve draws near and we have no direction without daylight.' Geraint drew a hand across his brow, removing his hat.

Varin drew a finger across his lips, silencing him immediately. Both men dropped soundlessly to their haunches, years of training kicking in instinctively. Varin strained his ears against the yawning hush of forest to catch the tiny crackle once more, trying to gauge the direction. He heard the stream running, a continuous burbling to his right, and then another sound, an uneven splashing against the more regular rhythm.

Creeping forward, Varin raised his tawny head into the wind as if scenting his prey. Geraint's sinewy hand inched over his stomach to grasp the hilt of his sword. Through the thicket of brambles, a circle of brilliant green grass had caught their attention; a clearing banded by a small stream. And at the stream, a prone figure lying forward on the grass leaning over the bubbling water to drink steadily…

On leaving Thurstan, Eadita had hurled herself into a fast sprint. She loved the feeling of her feet sprinkling over the ground, dodging the trees and brambles, ducking this way and that. Unhampered by the heavy gowns, the freedom became uplifting as she jumped over fallen branches, ever sure of her direction. She had run many furlongs before throwing herself flat on the ground in a clearing to assuage her thirst. As she leaned her head over the dank edge of the dancing water, her hat fell in and she caught it with one hand to scoop up a crownful of the sweet nectar. Sitting up in one easy movement, she gulped deep, letting the cool liquid trickle down her mud-streaked face and neck, closing her eyes briefly as she lay back again to rest on the moist, spongy grass. The freshening evening air took the heat out of her skin as the shadows started to close around her.

A twig snapped. Sweat cast a pearly sheen on her brow as she lifted her head, alert now. There, in the dimness of the trees beyond the clearing, stood the tall, formidable hulk of Lord Varin and, behind him, the rugged form of Geraint. Clapping her hat on her head, water spewing over her face, she sprung to her feet and ran, jumping clear over the stream to plunge into the undergrowth.

'Halt, in the name of King William!' Varin's fierce shout

fell on deaf ears as he started pursuit, muscles bunching in his powerfully built physique. Throwing off his thick fur-lined cloak in order to gain speed, he leapt over the brook to pursue the lad who had taken off like a young gazelle. Varin could run fast, but he had already lost sight of his quarry.

Eadita forced her muscles to work faster, harder, blood pumping through her veins. He was behind her, and gaining; the solidity of his relentless strides covering twice the ground that she could. Her lungs couldn't take in the air quickly enough; dread rose as strength ebbed from her body. Her previous long run had been exhausting. Yet nimbleness and the gathering night both championed her and, as she nipped in and out of the gnarled trunks, she gained the vital seconds to change her plan. Her mind racing with adrenaline, she grabbed a low bough to swing herself up into a spreading oak, almost losing her hat in the process. Her toes caught on to an obliging foothold and she hefted her body weight into the branches. Praying that the half-light would conceal her, she climbed quickly, scrabbling for available foot and handholds to lie low along a branch, like a cat.

She was only just in time. A moment later, Varin appeared beneath her…and stopped. Her heart almost stopped too, her limbs frozen to the bark. He lifted his head; she pushed her face into the tree to hide, ripples of exhaustion and fear snaking through her. Fortune had deserted her.

'Come down now, boy. You cannot escape me,' he ordered, his voice echoing authoritatively among the branches. She didn't budge. He started to climb the tree towards her, deftly placing his feet in the forks, drawing ever nearer to her pathetic hiding place. A sob rose shakily in her throat. *He must not discover her true identity!* As he climbed steadily, staggeringly agile for such a big man, she sat upright on the branch. As he drew level, she shimmied to the end of the bough, which still took her weight, but would not support his.

The forest floor looked very far away, at least twenty feet or more, but as she viewed the forbidding lines of his face, jumping to the ground seemed like the only option.

'Don't even think about it,' he cautioned fiercely, surveying her from the main trunk. 'I want you alive.'

No words came forth, for she still had a chance. If she spoke now, he might recognise her as Lady Eadita and all would be undone. Varin watched in amazement as the boy placed his hands next to his ankles around the branch and swung underneath to jump to the next one down, balancing perfectly. He did it again, and again, until he had almost reached the ground. Varin slid down the main trunk haphazardly, the rough bark tearing at his clothes and just as the boy gained the lowest branch, he launched himself forward, crashing his weight and the boy's downward.

The brambles tore at her face, stinging her skin cruelly as she lay face down on the damp soil once more. Air had squeezed from her lungs with the force of the impact and her chest hurt as she struggled for air. Tears pricked under her eyelids. Everything she had fought for now hung in the balance as the great hulking oaf lay on top of her. Oh, Thurstan, she thought, forgive me.

'Geraint!' His voice yelled deep in her ear. 'Over here, I have the lad.' His weight shifted momentarily as he flipped her on to her back, a heavy knee in the middle of her ribs. Keeping her eyes clamped shut, she wondered if she could feign death.

'Open your eyes, boy. I know you're pretending.' The knee pressed further into her torso. The linen strips she used to strap her breasts down bundled uselessly around her waist but she prayed he wouldn't notice. Varin repeated the order again, this time in garbled Anglo-Saxon; at the unbelievable pronunciation, she nearly opened her mouth to reprimand him.

'Boy, give up. You will not escape me. Where are the others?'

'Mayhap a little water will loosen his tongue?' Geraint suggested, having caught up with the pair. With her eyes closed, she missed the smile between the men. Varin grabbed the leather belt slung below her waist and hauled Eadita up by it. Her legs buckled beneath her.

'So that's the way you want to play it, eh, lad? Don't play me for a fool.' Varin chuckled and hoisted his reluctant prisoner on to the wide expanse of his shoulders and they marched back to the stream. The deep pool where she had drunk only moments ago was now to be her destiny. Varin threw her in.

She suppressed a rising scream of panic as the freezing water closed over her head, then a mighty hand grabbed her neck to pull her to the surface. Through the rivulets of stream water gushing over her face, blocking her eyes, her ears, her mouth, she barely registered the giant torturer before her, his blond hair tousled and a mocking grin on his face.

'Where are the others? You do not run alone,' he rapped out, ducking her once more to bring her up again, coughing and spluttering. 'Speak French. I know you can. *"I will spill thy blood, Norman pig"*, I think the words were.'

'Never!' she spat out in a guttural croak as the water poured from her, spewing from her saturated clothes. Varin held her in a tight grasp of overtunic at her throat as he plunged her under once more.

'My lord, remember we must keep the lad alive!' Geraint cautioned as Varin pulled the outlaw choking and gasping for breath out of the water by the scruff of his neck, before shoving him in again.

'This wretch will not escape me again.' Varin's firm foothold on the flat stones beneath the water meant he could torture his quarry indefinitely. Geraint, watching from the bank, frowned as he noticed a peculiar aspect of their victim.

'My lord—' Geraint tried to gain Varin's attention '—my lord, 'tis but a maid.' Varin paused momentarily to stare astounded at his friend, holding his victim under slightly longer than intended, then plucked her out briskly to deposit her pale and lifeless on the bank.

'Your eyes are sharp, Geraint.' His eyes gleamed appreciatively over the rounded curves starkly delineated by the wet cloth as the limp form lay on the ground at his leather boots. He noted the chestnut plaits braided closely to the head, the curling jet-black lashes over alabaster-pale skin, the dainty tip-tilted nose and the sensual pink curves of the lips. He shook his head in puzzlement, then amazement. She had no need to open the jewelled beauty of her eyes to confirm her identity.

'No doubt she's a maid, Geraint.' Varin smiled, a rakish, lopsided grin brightening his face. 'And not just any maid.'

Chapter Seven

Stunned, both men stood for a moment as they considered the full implications of their catch. Against the criss-crossed fretwork of the oak branches, stark against the dusky twilight, their powerfully built frames hulked over the girl. Her slender figure twisted awkwardly, supine on the springy grass where Varin had dragged her, her soaking garments clinging to her svelte curves. In the hurrying darkness, a ghostly pallor infused her face, her lips turning greyish-blue with cold. The tight wet braids hugged her skull, making her wraith-like vulnerability even more apparent. Varin cursed profusely, eyes igniting with guilty vexation.

'The maid has truly lost her wits! How does she think she can pit against us?' A myriad of emotions crossed Varin's face, anger stirring his blood at her utter foolishness, at the merry dance she had led them, yet he couldn't forget the impressive speed with which she had looped and turned like a young deer through the trees, almost outrunning him.

'Geraint,' he intoned slowly, 'do you realise who this is? This is the lady Eadita and our outlaw, the person who gave you the slip on the first night.'

'And the person you nearly ran through with your sword,'

Geraint replied. 'I can scarce believe it. She's either very stupid or very brave, but right now I think she needs our help. Her breath draws shallow. Methinks the water has taken its toll.' Concern creased his brow as he hunkered down beside her and placed two fingers at her neck. 'Her heart beats sluggish.'

'Do not concern yourself, Geraint.' Varin observed Eadita disdainfully. 'This maid is not to be trusted. No doubt she's listening to our very words, trying to plan her next move. She's played us both for fools, but this time, she's played once too often.' Varin continued to stand above her, great legs astride her daintily shod feet, massive arms crossed over his gambeson. 'I suggest we take her back to let her uncle deal with her. Maybe that will spur her into action!' He laughed hollowly.

'Sire, her breathing weakens.'

Jolted from his lazy observation of her beautiful curves, Varin marked the rapid change in her skin colour, from chalk white to a deathly grey. Dropping fluidly to his knees, he straightened her on to her back, ripping open the neck and chest of her overtunic and chemise to watch her chest. No breath swelled her delicate bosom. Adroitly tipping her head back, he closed her nostrils gently with two lean fingers and bent his leonine head, sealing firm lips to hers to fill her lungs with the breath of life. His keen eyes watched along her breastbone to see her chest rise, turning his ear to her mouth to listen for the expulsion of air.

'Come on, Eadita, breathe,' he demanded, exhaling into her again. The frail structure of her ribcage suddenly heaved with great effort as Eadita greedily sucked in the cool forest air, coughing, spluttering. Anticipating her actions, Varin turned her smartly on her side as choking racked her frame, holding her head as she spewed water on the verdant turf.

'She lives, my lord. Her breathing is sound.' Geraint's voice appeared far away. Varin sat back on his heels, hard, his toes grinding into the turf through the tough leather of his boots. An uncommon fear chased his blood, a feeling of intense culpability at nearly killing someone, someone who did not deserve to die. Despite the constant antagonism of this maid, he had no wish for her to lose her life. He shuddered.

'Dieu merci.' The raggedness in his voice disturbed him. Thank God.

In the still evening air, the crows had gathered en masse above the tense tableau, circling and wheeling to gather in a black bunch on the tree-tops, to break and circle again at the slightest disturbance. Eadita emerged from the swirling mists to hear their harsh cawing, an unsettling memory of firm lips upon her own teasing her mind. A familiar smell, a spicy scent mingled with leather and horse, tantalised her senses, before unwelcome, strident tones assailed her ears.

'My lady, wake up.' A large hand shook her shoulder. 'We have tarried too long playing the nursemaid. Wake up.' *God have mercy! Varin!* Blue-veined lids quivered open, as she lifted a shaking hand to her forehead, rawness scraping along the inside of her throat.

'Water…please,' she rasped. The unnatural croaking of her voice surprised her. Her braids pulled her scalp, hurting her skull. She was unable to prevent a low moan falling from her lips.

'Haven't you had enough water?' Varin mocked unevenly, angered at his own uncommon concern for the maid. Had she no idea how much trouble she was in? 'What on earth possessed you to behave like this?'

'Sire, have a care.' Geraint drew a small drinking horn from the embroidered pouch at his waist to fill it from the stream. Returning to Eadita, he knelt by her side, lifting her head carefully to let her sip.

'I'm sorry,' she gasped out, struggling to sit. Geraint pushed her prone as a stultifying weakness invaded her limbs.

'Nay, my lady, rest awhile. Do not tax yourself overmuch,' Geraint coaxed sympathetically. He turned to glare at Varin. 'Go easy, sire. You have just brought her back from the dead.'

'I did little. She would have come back on her own,' Varin snapped, playing down his own involvement. 'Why do you hover like a nursemaid? She can rise now, surely.' His own guilt ate away at him; he masked it with his frustration. The shivering Eadita served only to remind him of his near folly as he watched the chills ripple through her willowy figure.

'Come, we all need warmth and shelter,' he announced imperiously. 'I am not about to lose you to sickness after saving your hide.'

'Saving my hide!' she spluttered. ''Twas you who tried to drown me!' With eyes still sore from the constant barrage of stream water, she squinted up at him, a towering menace of barely suppressed anger. How on earth was she going to explain her presence in the forest? It had been a stupid mistake to run from him. 'Twas a sure admission of guilt.

'I would not have let you drown,' he announced, imperiously. ''Tis merely an excellent method of extracting answers.'

'Aye, probably in men twice my size!'

''Tis no defence, my lady, especially as you seem quite able of attacking men twice your size! You must be insane!'

So he knew. He had already realised it was she who had ambushed him that first night. She covered her face with her hands, unwilling to let him see her disappointment.

'Aye, *mam'selle,* you're right to feel ashamed. I've no idea what you're involved in, but I aim to discover it, one way or another.' The words thudded around her ears, berating her. Varin looked up at the sky, then at Geraint. ''Tis too dark to return to Thunorslege without losing our way. Think you to remember the direction to those caves we passed?'

'Aye, my lord.'

'Now, can you walk?'

Varin watched, arms folded, as Eadita struggled to rise in her wet, heavy clothes, swaying precariously. How could he have been so blind to her deceitfulness? The fragile beauty of this maid had hoodwinked him successfully, and no mistake. Had he even begun to think she was different from any other woman? Nay, she was as cunning as a vixen. Just like his mother.

As she sank to the floor, exhausted by her efforts, he cursed under his breath, realising he would have to help her. He grabbed her with a strong hand to support her back and another beneath the crook of her knees to swing her slight frame into his chest. She protested vaguely, pushing weak fingers against him.

'You have caused me more than enough trouble already, my lady,' he rumbled against her head. 'Be still.'

A rocky outcrop jutting out from a high overgrown bank heralded the caves. Eadita, recognising their location, sighed in relief. It would be an easy task to find her way back to Thurstan once full night had arrived. Now Varin knew her identity, she must disappear completely and become a true outlaw herself. It was the only way to keep her brother safe to continue his mission. Life would be more difficult, with no support coming from the manor, yet they would surely find a way.

Pressed tightly against her captor's chest, she acknowledged Varin's superior strength as he carried her easily through the undergrowth. Sneaking a look at his rigid face, she knew herself to be the source of his irritation and welcomed this barrier between them. His anger cocooned her in a wide blanket of protection, the prospect of managing him becoming easier. An irate Varin was far easier to deal with than a Varin who treated her as if he cared. If he looked at her with those passionate eyes, eyes glowing with the promise of undiscovered sexual waters, as he had on the fair field, as he had when she showed him round the estate, then the bonds of her self-control loosened with ease. She feared that more than anything.

Dumping her unceremoniously on her feet in the dank confines of the cave entrance, Varin stood back, hands on hips, regarding her proud, erect stance. His *braies,* wet from the stream, clung to his thighs, emphasising the bunched muscle underneath. Energy began to return in swift degrees to her young, fit body as she glared back at him, an open challenge in her huge, violet eyes.

'Off with your clothes, *mam'selle,*' he ordered brusquely. 'You'll catch an ague if you remain so.' Turning away from her, he began to pick up small pieces of wood to start a fire. She remained perfectly still.

'Do it.' He didn't even bother to look at her as he repeated the command.

'I will not.'

'If you refuse to help yourself, then I must help you.' Varin drew two flints from the leather bag at his waist, striking them to produce a spark. As the flame curled around the damp leaves, starting to burn smokily, he carefully laid twiggy sticks crossways until a scant flame sprang to life from the vegetation.

'Aren't you afraid of outlaws? They might attack once they see the flames,' Eadita taunted.

'I have a feeling that, with you by my side, we'll be safe. Now, will you remove your garments?' Hearing the determined set of his voice, Eadita realised he had effectively cornered her.

'I would have your cloak,' she ordered brightly, raising her pale chin in opposition.

''Tis done.'

He undid the jewelled neckpin at his throat to sweep the rich cloth from his broad back. Eadita maintained a stony silence as he wrapped the voluminous folds around her, refusing to delight in the delicious body heat that emanated from his garment. He moved away to tend to the spluttering wood, hissing and spitting as it threatened to go out. Wriggling against the fastenings, Eadita discarded her shoes and woollen *braies,* glad to remove the itchy wet fabric from her sensitive skin. She struggled with her overtunic and undershirt to eventually wrest them over her head without allowing the cloak to slip. Keeping her wet chemise next to her skin, she all but threw the garments at him.

''Tis done.'

'All of them.' Varin poked a stick into the flames.

'My chemise stays on.'

'Your chemise is soaking wet and it needs to dry. My cloak is thick enough to give you warmth and coverage.' He noted her lack of industry and started to rise. 'Do you need some help?'

'Nay, never,' she responded hurriedly. With a sharp laugh, he crouched down again. Eadita pulled the sticky shift from her body, colour rising in her cheeks as she produced the brilliant white linen hanging limply from her fingers.

'Hang them over the branches near the fire so they dry,' Varin directed. Eadita was painfully aware that the only fastening on the cloak was her own hand at the neck. If she lifted her other hand to hang the garments, her naked body would be revealed. Besides, the warrior's litany of orders began to grate on her jangled nerves.

'That I cannot do.'

Varin glared at her, mercilessly searching her graceful features. Purple shadows under her brilliant eyes evidenced her recent ordeal, yet the testiness of her behaviour served only to bedevil him. Men of far greater stature than she had quailed visibly in his presence, yet this feisty witch showed no fear of him or her current predicament. Did she not realise that her future lay in his hands?

'Well?' she questioned boldly. He swore he could hear her

foot tapping. He sighed, preparing to give in. Eadita heeded the barely discernible movement in his lean stature and scented a possible victory.

'Let me.' The ever-gallant Geraint stepped into the halo of light cast by the fire and swept up the bundle of clothes, plucking the virginal linen from Eadita's fingers. Varin snorted, denigrating his friend's behaviour.

'Be careful, Geraint,' he mocked, 'you'll be dressing the lady's hair next.'

'My thanks, Geraint,' Eadita said, softly. 'You have better manners than your lord.' Geraint nodded furtively, dropping his head as a dark blush suffused his broad cheeks. He strode to the mouth of the cave, where the fire now burned brightly, to string the wet clothes on the low bushes framing the entrance.

'I will try to find the horses,' Geraint said, as he finished his task.

'Good idea,' Varin agreed. He patted the dry earth beside him. 'Come and sit by the fire, my lady. There's no need to stand on ceremony.'

'And there's no need to mock me,' she answered, pulling the cloak around her as she sank down gratefully before the leaping flames. 'Remember who I am.' She made a great show of arranging the cloak's folds around herself, so not an inch of flesh was exposed. Even so, her naked skin beneath the wool puckered with goosebumps.

'And who is that, *mam'selle?*' he questioned dryly. 'Are you a lady of the manor, a Saxon maid of high-born family who appears to lack for nothing, or are you a common outlaw, intent on hiding your identity to commit some dreadful crime?'

''Tis none of your business,' she retorted smartly.

'Oh, but it is my business,' he returned, a dangerous eddy in his voice. 'You became my business the moment I met you.' Her heart plummeted, as if a solid rock had hit her square in the chest. Her captor sat with his massive back supported by the curving rock of the cave entrance, his elbows resting comfortably on his upraised knees. He twisted a twig idly between his fingers. 'Why do you do it?'

'My head hurts,' she complained, refusing to answer him. Varin muttered something unintelligible.

'Unbraid your hair,' he suggested. 'The drying water pulls your plaits too tight.'

'It takes two hands to undo them,' she explained. Two hands that she needed to keep the cloak wrapped securely about her.

'Sweet Jesu!' He levered his body away from the cave entrance before she realised what he was about to do.

She shuffled backwards. 'Nay, it doesn't matter, the pain will ease once they are fully dry. Do not trouble yourself.'

'I cannot have your headache distracting you from answering my questions, my lady.'

'But you cannot, 'tis unseemly!' She began to panic as he moved closer. Varin laughed out loud, the fine creases around his green eyes turning up in chorus to his generous mouth.

'I do know that unmarried Saxon women should not reveal their tresses in public for fear of being branded a whore, but, *mam'selle*—you sit before me wearing my cloak with nothing underneath. Surely that is worse?' She nodded, eyeing him warily. Varin watched her dilemma with detached amusement.

'Let me do it.' He scooted over to kneel behind her, deftly undoing the leather laces securing the braids. Eadita laughed to hide her nervousness, acutely aware of the cool tips of his fingers moving sweetly against the stretched skin of her scalp.

'Hah! You taunt your steward for playing the lady's maid, yet now you perform the role yourself!' She sighed blissfully as the long chestnut coils slipped from their bindings to spread over the luxury of the warrior's cloak. A drift of lavender pervaded the air; she caught the scent of her other life on the wind and prayed for her salvation.

Varin prayed for his own salvation as he watched each gleaming section loop and tumble to her hips like long skeins of slippery silk. His fingers twitched with a need to plunge into that mass, to bundle it to his face, to drape it over his skin. Aware that he had not answered her jibe, Eadita turned her head, sucking in her breath sharply at his sensual contemplation. Ripping her own gaze away, she dropped her head forward to let her hair fall like a curtain around her face, hugging her knees.

'Why don't you just let me go? I am of no use to you. I am a bored, idle lady who occasionally likes to adventure out. That is all.'

'And you expect me to believe that,' he grunted, sardonically. 'Let's list the misdemeanours that this *bored lady* has managed to achieve. By the rood, you make it sound as if you were doing needlework in the forest!' He moved back to sit against the wall of the cave.

'You have no right to keep me prisoner like this,' she mumbled into her hair.

'I have every right, Eadita,' he returned, evenly. 'Firstly, you try and slit my throat in a manoeuvre worthy of a high-ranking soldier, then you escape my steward by thrusting a burning brand in his face—'

'Not my fault he wasn't concentrating,' she interrupted.

'Then you escape Raoul by rolling with extraordinary dexterity through the mud and take off like a scalded hare when I discover you in the forest.' He raised his eyebrows. 'Hardly nothing.'

Eadita stared glumly into the flames.

'Does your uncle know what you are up to?'

She glanced up, startled. 'If he did, then I wouldn't be sitting here. He takes the greatest pleasure in curbing my freedom.'

'It seems that you've had a little too much freedom,' Varin reasoned.

'Are you going to tell him?' Eadita reached up within the cloak to rub the back of her neck.

'Only out of courtesy. 'Tis not his matter to deal with, for your misdemeanours fall under Norman law now. You're in serious trouble, my lady, a traitor to William and all that rule under him, unless you aid us in catching the other outlaws who run with you.'

'That is impossible.'

'Then I am duty-bound to reveal your treachery.' His clipped vowels echoed around the cave, with ominous foreboding.

'I work alone, Lord Varin,' she lied. 'After the Conquest I couldn't bear to see the suffering of my people, poor and starving under the crippling new taxes. I sought to find gold to keep those families alive.'

'You expect me to believe that!'

'Who was there when you were attacked? Just me. No one else.'

In one swift movement, Varin leaned over, clamping her face between two large hands, pulling her towards him. 'You're a foolhardy maid, make no mistake. I will discover the truth, Eadita.' He grinned wolfishly, his lips inches from her own. 'You would do well to start trusting me, before life becomes more difficult.' He threw her back on to the earth, before springing up to stand.

'You can threaten me all you like, Lord Varin, but I will not speak. How can you ask me to trust you, you above all people, a Frenchman, a murderer! I'd rather die!'

'I do hope it won't come to that,' Varin replied smoothly. *Dieu!* He wanted to wring her neck and help her at the same time. Surely full-on warfare was easier than dealing with this maid? Noting the miserable slump of her shoulders, and the noble effort she made in attempting to stop shivering, Varin decided to take pity on her, for the moment. 'We need to sleep, *mam'selle.* Let us move into the cave.'

'I prefer to sleep by the fire,' she argued, unwilling to spend time near him. Once he was asleep, she hoped to be able to make her escape.

'Nay, my lady,' he replied in low, burnished tones. 'You stay by my side, lest you hatch any more plans to slip my grasp.' He held out his hand to help her up. Eadita swallowed. His brawny form, outlined by the crackling flames, threatened to overwhelm her. Better not to goad him further, she decided, and go with him meekly for the moment.

Holding herself rigidly away from the powerful length of Varin stretched out beside her, Eadita tried in vain to stay awake. It should not have been a difficult task; the ground held many stones that poked into her left side; her stomach growled alarmingly from lack of food and her bare feet seemed to become uncovered by the cloak with alarming regularity, however much she tried to scoop them beneath the thick fabric. Yet the events of the day gradually overcame her and her eyelids drooped as she succumbed to a deep slumber.

In what seemed like only a few moments later, she awoke, shivering jerkily. A congealing numbness invaded her body, all limbs turned to ice. The fire had died out at the mouth of the cave. Silvery moonlight washed the grey rocks around in a luminous, eerie light.

'My lady?' A voice questioned sleepily at her ear, warm breath washing over her lobe. 'What ails thee?'

'I'm…so-o-oo…cold,' she stuttered back. Immediately, the warm bulk of Varin pressed into her back, tucking her delicate frame into his big body as a muscular forearm snaked firmly around her waist, pressing her hips into the natural hollow of his lap. He had unlaced his padded gambeson and he now wrapped the heavy leather flap over her side for extra warmth.

'My…?' Eadita started to protest.

'If you value your life, do not protest,' he whispered back, cutting her short. 'You must warm up and this is the quickest and easiest way to do it. Do not fight it, go back to sleep.'

Screaming in silent outrage, Eadita acknowledged the futility of attempting to pull away, yet this close proximity made the focus of her world tip crazily, listing heavily against the maelstrom of emotion inundating her senses. Never before had she lain so close to a man! A kernel of desire budded deep in her chest, a warm spiralling whirlpool that threatened to grow and engulf her. Desperately she clamoured to remember Varin as her enemy, the man who might have slain her own father on the battlefield. Her few hours of sleep had sharpened her senses.

'Sir! You are too bold! I will not have this. You cannot lie with me like this!' She bucked her neat *derrière* into his groin, attempting to gain leverage to pull away from his warmth.

'Don't try that again,' Varin warned, growling in her ear. 'You may gain more than you bargained for!' Eadita coloured hotly at the aroused edge of his voice, squeezing her eyes tight shut. She hadn't failed to notice the prominent bulge that had nudged her backside and vowed to remain impassive, at the very limit of Varin's hold. With the thick padded leather of the gambeson around her, this was no easy feat.

Varin was indeed fighting his own battle, attempting to douse the fierce flames of desire that urged him to bed the maid, and cursed his own tiredness the previous night for not venting his passion on a willing manor wench. Without a woman for some weeks, the sheer proximity of this elfin chit made his senses tingle with anticipation.

He sighed with relief as he finally noticed her deep, even breathing, heralding sleep. Listening to the night sounds of the forest, he caught the low whinny of a horse as Geraint led their animals into the clearing, securing the bridles over a low branch.

'As the moon came up, I knew my direction,' Geraint answered Varin's questioning eyes. 'We have almost come full circle in our pursuit of the lady; the horses were not far. How fares the maid?' Varin looked down at the petite figure bundled against his own, as he propped his head carefully on an upraised hand to talk to his companion.

'She sleeps deeply, now that she's warm.'

'She must be exhausted. I'm amazed at the strength in that little body.' Geraint grinned suddenly, noting the possessive curve of Varin's arm. 'You look very comfortable.'

'Comfortable is not the word,' Varin grimaced. ''Tis pure torture.'

Geraint smirked. 'What are you going to do with her? The circumstances are not that simple.'

'William's suspicions about Earl Gronwig may well be tied up with this maid's activities. But I can't be certain. Her surprise at my question about her involvement with Gronwig seemed genuine. There appears to be little love lost between them; you've seen the way he treats her.' Geraint nodded, throwing a few more sticks on to the fire. 'But she's a clever piece,' Varin continued, keeping his voice low, 'and their antagonism could merely be a ruse to throw us off their scent.'

'Has she told you aught?'

'Only a bundle of lies. I will gain the information somehow.' Varin's white teeth gleamed in the moonlight. He swiftly countered his friend's look. 'Nay, *mon ami*...not in the way you think. With her innocence, 'twould be the easiest way, I grant you. Her beauty tempts me, but she's a noblewoman. Think of the consequences, my friend.'

Geraint grinned. 'Aye, William would not be pleased. Will you tell the Earl?'

'Nay. If they are working together then 'twill alert him to our conjecture. I would rather bide my time, use our eyes and ears to find out what goes on at Thunorslege.' At his side, Eadita shifted restlessly. 'We'll take her back just before dawn, 'twill be easy to access her chambers unseen.'

'Why not now? We can see our way in the moonlight.'

'She needs her sleep.'

Geraint was surprised at his lord's accommodating manner. He unbuckled a blanket roll for himself and another for Varin from the back of the horses and, flinging one over the couple, he tucked himself up warmly to snooze for the remainder of the night.

One small kiss; 'twas no great thing! As her sweet bottom nudged Varin's groin once more, driving him nearly to the brink of bursting, his thumb instinctively brushed against the fullness of breast above his hand that gripped her waist. A nipple peaked, pushing under the fabric. Although asleep, a vague moan whispered from Eadita's parted lips. Desire jolted through his blood, firing pinpoints of yearning along his limbs. His lips tingled. Her drowsy body turned towards him like a flower to the sun, the dark cloak falling open at her bosom. The shadowed swell of her breast caught his breath; his stomach churned with an incessant craving. The ache in his groin jeopardised his usual controlled finesse, threatening to explode with the bungling incompetence of a young novice. Despite dredging for constraint, Varin lowered his lean visage to Eadita's graceful features.

Eadita dreamed. A beautiful, delicious dream. Devoured by strange, buffeting fires, her insides swirled. A man kissed her, firm lips pressing inexorably against her own, urging, urging…!

Confounded, her eyes shot open in full comprehension as masculine lips roamed her own. Toiling against the burning weakness suffusing her flesh, she opened her mouth to speak and his tongue drove in to flick against her own, battling her to submission, forcing her to meld with him. Her mind railed against him as her tongue twined with his, an exquisite invasion of her mouth. He withdrew, planting feather-like kisses on her lust-roughened lips, to plunge in once more. Eadita shuddered, stifling a cry at the intensity of the sensation. A honeyed pain gripped her at the juncture of her thighs, a clutching, searing convulsion that drove through her like a bolt of lightning. Logic deserted her, as her arms crept around the massive shoulders to bring him closer, closer to her. Varin chuckled throatily, threading his fingers through the shimmering mass of hair to draw her even nearer, moving a thick, iron-hewn thigh over her own to push his knee gently between her legs. An owl screeched suddenly, shockingly close.

The sound galvanised her. Panting heavily, she ripped her face away, clamping her mouth shut, pushing at him with both palms flat on the broad expanse of his chest. Her feeble attempts at escape made no impact on him and in desperation she grabbed a handful of hair, tugging viciously.

'*Merde!* That hurts!' Varin raised himself on forearms planted either side of her, staring at her quizzically, high colour in his prominent cheekbones.

'Get…off…me!' Eadita ground out. 'Get off me…now!' She shoved, but he was already drawing away in one easy movement to his feet. Eadita sat up abruptly, drawing the cloak primly about her. Her head spun as she glared at his feet.

'How dare you…how dare you?' she spat. Varin raked an unsteady hand through his hair. In truth, he wasn't sure how it had happened. His complacent words to Geraint mocked him now: 'Her beauty tempts me, but she's a noblewoman.' A Saxon lady, an argumentative chit just half his size who sought to outwit him at every turn. How could he have lost control like that?

'Have no fear, *mam'selle.* 'Twas only a kiss.'

Only a kiss! Her jumbled brain tried to make sense of his words and the blinding, exhilarating effect he ignited within her body. What on earth was the matter with her? A trickle of fear pooled in her chest as she stared up at him, willing herself to remain detached as she eyed the leonine set of his head, the arrow-straight bridge of his nose, the sensual lips curved into a mocking smile…

'You were…you were going to…' she stuttered.

He laughed with cruel disdain. 'Nay, my lady. You fool yourself. Think I would lie with one such as you? I prefer my women with more meat on them.' The harsh barbs bit into Eadita, as he sought to bury the intriguing memory of her. He began to gather the damp clothes from the bushes around, bending down to shake Geraint's shoulder. The warrior sprang instantly awake.

''Tis time to return.' His face set in a hard mask as he directed his words towards Eadita. 'Dress yourself and ride with Geraint. We'll get you back before sun-up.' The clipped commands railed around her bowed head. So there was to be no chance of escape from this horrible man, she thought. If only Thurstan was near, for he and his men would overpower the two Normans easily. Maybe if they stayed in the forest a little longer…?

'We will certainly lose our way. Why not wait until dawn?' Eadita stalled, resolutely unmoving in her warm cocoon of Varin's cloak.

'We have light enough…' Varin indicated the gleaming moon '…and despite the fact that you seem to possess an intimate knowledge of these woods, I wouldn't trust you to take us back. No doubt you'd lead us on some never-ending trail to thwart us once again. Now dress, *mam'selle.*' He thrust the garments into her arms, before striding off towards the horses.

Her heart sank. Varin spoke the truth. With the moonlight to navigate by, there was no reason not to return to Thunorslege. Turning her back on the two men, she dressed briskly in the shadows.

'What do you plan to do with me?' she questioned, walking towards Varin. His hands stilled on the stirrup he was adjusting.

'What do you think I should do?' His answering question tipped her off balance. She patted the horse's neck to cover her confusion, her mind sifting for the right answer.

'I think you should forget this ever happened.'

'Aye, you'd like that, wouldn't you? As if anyone would believe such a feeble-looking girl runs wild and savage through the woods.' He touched the tip of his finger to her ear lobe and she flinched as the erotic pulse sliced through her limbs. His finger moved along the evocative line of her jaw, before he gripped the curve of her chin in his hand. 'You, *mam'selle,* are now under my jurisdiction. You will do as I say, obey no one else. You will not leave Thunorslege again, except in my company, or with my permission.' His green eyes glittered a warning at her.

'And if I don't?'

'Then I will tell your uncle and hand you over to the King.' Eadita tried to curb her rapid breathing, panic rising within her chest. Which was worse? Subjecting herself to this devil, or being punished by Gronwig and the King?

Varin eyed her sternly. ''Tis a good offer, my lady, lenient in the circumstances. Your unrestrained code of conduct is hardly the correct behaviour for a lady.'

'You pompous oaf!' she flashed back. 'And you think your behaviour is worthy of a knight? Making love to me in the forest against my will, making me strip my clothes, unbind my hair…what sort of chivalry is that?'

His fingertips tightened on her chin. 'You seem to forget, *mam'selle,* that you are at my mercy, under my control. You would do well to guard that flaying tongue of yours, lest it brings you more attention than you expect. You will do my bidding.'

'I haven't agreed yet,' she returned, haughtily.

Tension rippled across the lean planes of his face. 'You will, my lady. I will guard your secret, but you have to give me something in return. All I ask for is your co-operation.' There must be a way out of this, she thought wildly. But her mind was too scrambled and confused by tiredness to deduce any obvious solution.

'Then we had best return to Thunorslege before sun-up,' she replied, 'otherwise prying eyes might link the two of us, and Gronwig will have us married before tomorrow.'

'God forbid.' Varin dropped his grip, grimacing. 'I couldn't imagine anything worse.'

Chapter Eight

An uneasy silence blanketed the trio of riders as the horses picked their way slowly through the moon-washed trees. Slowly, as the new day approached, the vague shadows took on more definition as the night turned to soft greys. Ahead, Varin rode with customary arrogance, a casual grace defining him as an experienced horseman. In truth, he still seethed in frustration at the indomitable spirit of the maid—commendable in a man, her very stubbornness would very likely put her in danger if she didn't start to place some confidence in him.

Eadita occasionally glimpsed his formidable profile as the Norman warrior rode up ahead and shuddered, welcoming the broad chest of Geraint against her back. Secretly, she had been relieved when Varin suggested she ride with the uncomplicated and easygoing Geraint. 'Twas uncertain how her body and mind would have coped with the brooding nearness of Varin. He seemed to possess an unerring capacity to set her in a muddle; her thoughts became disordered in his presence, her body traitorous. She believed him when he promised not to reveal her exploits, but 'twas obvious he would not leave the issue. She had to think of a way of guarding her brother's secret and keeping him safe without Lord Varin suspecting anything. The days ahead loomed with a sense of foreboding.

They reached the manor just before dawn. Eadita's eyes ached with fatigue, purple rings emphasising the hollows beneath her eyes. The solid wooden gates were firmly closed and to raise the guard would be to expose Eadita to prying eyes and gossip. Varin turned to her, lips tight, skin taut over his prominent cheekbones.

'Is there another entrance? We need to get you in unseen,' he rapped.

'Nay, this is the only one. It makes the manor more impenetrable.'

'I can see that, my lady. But it doesn't help us.' His snarl shocked her.

'No one would question it, my lord, if you brought her in as your woman,' Geraint chipped in, smoothly.

'In case you have not noticed, Geraint, she is hardly dressed as a woman,' Varin hissed, gesturing the sorry state of Eadita. Dirt streaked her delicate features, her boyish clothes were torn and damp. Varin grimaced at the gaping rent visible at her neckline; a poignant reminder of how close to death she had come. He sucked his breath in, sharply, cursing her ability to affect him so. Against the hulking form of Geraint, she appeared small and fragile; her hair, unbound, flowed over her shoulders, the tresses curling in glorious abandon. By giving her no regard throughout the journey, her utter beauty brought him up…hard. Despite her attire, she was definitely a *woman*. Acutely conscious of his intense regard, suddenly aware of her neglected state, Eadita started to braid her hair, raking fruitlessly at the matted locks.

'I need a bath,' she mumbled, distractedly. Varin raised his eyebrows.

'How like a woman to think of a bath at a time like this,'

he replied, scathingly, leaning forward in his saddle to address her slowly. 'I must remind you, *mam'selle,* 'twas you who pointed out the dire consequences of us being discovered together.' Her violet eyes flicked up to his. He laughed, but there was no humour in the sound. 'Aye,' he muttered, 'I thought that would gain your attention. Now, think, *mam'selle.* Use that quick-witted brain of yours to devise a way to gain entry to the manor house unseen. Marriage to a virago such as you is something I would not, could not, tolerate.'

'Oh, my lord, do you really think I would let it come to that?' she replied slowly to give her brain time to think. She knew how to get into the manor, but it would mean showing these Normans her access in and out of Thunorslege. Could she afford to let this secret slip? As the east sky began to lighten, she knew her time was limited.

Kicking aside his stirrups as his horse skittered restlessly, Varin bounded down, grabbing Geraint's bridle to look up at her.

'Pray tell me, *mam'selle!* How do you propose to get yourself into the manor without being seen?' His eyes held scorn. Loathe to divulge any more information, Eadita finally acknowledged that she needed their help to gain entry.

'Lead me round to the north walls,' she commanded. *She'd be damned if she had to walk!*

'And then?' Varin prodded.

'And then I'll tell you what I'm going to do next.' Varin swore softly under his breath at her continued thwarting of him. He noted smoke starting to rise from some of the cottages in the village as the pink wash of sunrise started to stain the horizon. Behind Eadita, Geraint dismounted and the two men led their horses and their charge around the grassy slope that edged the fortified manor walls. The verdant grass changed to small rocks and gravel as they reached the back wall, Eadita telling them where to stop. The two men looked curiously at her as she jumped agilely down from the destrier, flicking off Varin's cloak and bundling it into his hands.

'I have no need of this,' she stated confidently. Both men watched open mouthed as she placed one small foot on a thin ledge of stone jutting slightly out from the wall on a level with her waist. She reached up an arm to stretch for a handhold on a similar stone above her head.

'I bid you *adieu!*' She smiled and pulled her lithe figure smartly up the wall. Varin started first.

'Not so fast, my lady.' He placed large hands about her waist to drag her back against the bulk of him. 'What do you think you are doing?'

'Only something I do on a fairly regular basis. 'Tis easy when you know how. I only have to get to that narrow window.' She pointed to a shadowed opening about the height of three men above the ground and smiled sweetly at her captors. Varin groaned.

''Twill be the very devil keeping an eye on you,' he admitted, grudgingly, still annoyed with her.

'Granted,' she smirked. ' Can I go now?'

'Aye, we can catch you if you fall.' Somehow, Varin knew by the dimple in her rosy cheek that that would not happen. Correct in his assumption, the two warriors watched amazed as she swung herself speedily up the wall, pulling her lissom body through the gap in the stonework.

Beatrice pulled at the wispy sheep fleece to feed it skilfully into her spinning wheel. The yarn had been dyed a pale grey-green, but its colour wrapping around the spindle was deeper than she originally had expected, and she smiled in concentration as her foot pressed rhythmically on the treadle. The regular clacking sound lulled her as she worked, pulling the hanks of fleece into manageable yarn. Eadita would give this wool to her ladies, who would weave it into fabric for clothes.

Immersed in her work, her ebony hair caught back in a thick plait under a green silk headrail, Beatrice looked far younger than her thirty-nine winters, despite the utter grief at losing her beloved husband, Edwin…. Her fingers stilled on the fluffy yarn.

The years peeled back.

Judhael of Totnes stood in the doorway, blocking out the morning light.

With a cry of delight, she rose in pleasure, lacing her arms around the stout man's neck. 'Judhael! What in God's name are you doing here?'

'It gives me much happiness to see you as well, Beatrice,' he rumbled, a wide smile splitting his grizzled features as he squeezed her in a tight, bear-like embrace. 'I wanted to see you before I sit in the Shire Court this afternoon.'

'Of course!' Comprehension dawned on Beatrice. Naturally all the lords and thegns from the several manors in Devonshire would attend the Shire Court held once a month at Thunorslege. The Earl would demand their presence to deal with the more problematic matters of judgement.

Pushing away momentarily, she reached up a dainty hand to touch a shell-pink fingertip to the grey hairs at his temple. Despite standing only a handspan above her, his burly physique dominated her sylph-like frame.

'Age becomes you, Judhael,' she commented, clasping his hand firmly to lead him inside the hut.

'Careful, my lady. I am but a few winters older than you.' Seating her friend by the fire in the centre, she searched his kindly features. Apart from the grey hairs, they had scarcely changed since the day he had helped her escape her native France, bringing her on one of his merchant ships to the bustling trading centre of Totnes, to his castle.

Love might have blossomed between them, if a certain Saxon, Edwin of Thunorslege, had not been staying with Judhael. As the romance developed between his good Saxon friend, Edwin, and the girl he had rescued from an arranged marriage to an elderly Count of Brittany, Judhael had tried hard to hide his sorrow.

Now, he appraised her thoughtful look. 'Tell me all your news, Beatrice.'

'You mean the arrival of these Norman French.'

'Aye, be careful of those fierce barbarians—nothing but a heathen race.' Judhael sought to distinguish himself from the blond-haired giants from Normandy, descended from the Viking king Rollo. Beatrice picked up the iron poker to stir the dying embers of the fire, watching it spring to life again.

'You forget, Judhael,' she whispered. He clapped a hand to his forehead in consternation.

'Beatrice, forgive me. I forget your lineage.'

'Do not speak of it. I became a Saxon on my marriage to Edwin.'

'But King William could come to Thunorslege!'

'Aye, but 'tis not likely that he would recognise me.'

Judhael nibbled his nail dubiously. To him she appeared exactly as she had then, stood on the prow of his ship, some twenty-two years earlier. He had yearned for her then, as he ached for her now. Not even his good wife, who had died of an ague after bearing him three sons, could turn his thoughts away from this magnificent woman. A place in his heart had always been reserved for her.

'What about Lord Varin de Montaigu? Didn't you know his family?'

'Only when the boys were little. When Felice upped and left them motherless and William took them all in to raise them as knights. What a terrible time for those boys.'

'And for Sigurd too.'

'Aye, he took it bad. I don't think he ever recovered from her betrayal.'

'So Lord Varin might well recognise you.'

''Tis doubtful. He was just a young lad when I knew him.'

'Hmm. I'm not so sure.' Judhael lowered himself on to a wooden stool and stretched his fingers out to the fire. ' Maybe you should tell Eadita the truth, before she hears it from another.'

Beatrice turned away, wrapping defensive arms around her body. She ached to confide in her friend, to tell him how proud she was of her two children fighting for their Saxon heritage, helping those who needed it most in these hard times. She wanted to tell him that her son lived, that he had not fallen beside his father on the battle ground. But she knew Judhael would encourage her to halt their unfettered behaviour. Both could be tried as outlaws!

'I cannot,' she responded simply. 'By not speaking of it sooner, I would surely lose her trust now. I cannot risk losing my daughter.' Judhael drew his lips together in a grim line.

'I suspect Eadita is stronger than you think. You may be surprised by her reaction.' Beatrice was already shaking her head.

'Nay, she loathes the Normans; she will never forgive them for taking her father away, for their aggressive invasion of England.'

'Aye, I must admit that the wild stories one hears of their outlandish, brutal behaviour is enough to set one's teeth on edge. But should all Normans be described in such a fashion? I certainly couldn't describe you as being a typical Norman…'

'I understand what you are trying to do, Judhael, and I thank you for it. Maybe circumstances will force me to speak…' She hoped they wouldn't.

'How have the Normans behaved since they have been here? Have they subjected anyone to their outlandish behaviour?' Judhael warmed to his theme.

'Nay, their behaviour seems above criticism. They claim to form a bodyguard for Gronwig, as well as hunting down any Saxon uprising against the King. They already comb the woods for outlaws.' *My own daughter among them!* Her voice shook. 'Oh, God, but that you had not brought me to this country, Judhael. Then I would never have met Edwin, to have to endure his loss after all that time together…! And then to be in this tangle now…' A light film of tears sparkled brilliantly in her eyes, threatening to spill at any moment.

'Hush, Beatrice, hush now.' Standing, Judhael pulled her up into his comforting arms. She caught the smell of the road upon him, of horses and of woodsmoke. Like a soothing balm, the warm masculine fragrance calmed her jangled reason. 'Would you have rather married that old dry stick of a count, and have never known true love? Isn't it better to have had eighteen years of happiness as opposed to a life of discontent?' His leathery thumb smoothed the wet tears seeping down her cheeks, wise eyes scanning her sadness with disquiet.

'Aye, your words have truth, I must be thankful for the years I have had with Edwin and now must move forward. But to tell Eadita who I really am? I don't think I am ready…' She trailed off limply.

'But you must, Beatrice. For her to hear the truth from another quarter would be unbearable.'

The Earl pushed back the oiled cloth at the window embrasure and stared moodily down at the Norman soldiers training in the morning mist. 'You have missed your chance with Lord Varin. Too bad your lad bungled the attempt.' He swivelled on his heel, turning his lumpy silhouette towards Thurstan.

'The lad jumped too soon. There will be another opportunity.'

'Nay, Lord Varin plans to attend the Shire Court this afternoon. He wants to know everything, no doubt to see whether we follow the new-fangled Norman law.' Wiping his clammy brow with a pudgy hand, he fixed his nephew with a malevolent stare. 'Nay, you must make haste to the Bishop's Palace in Exeter.'

'You mean…?' Thurstan hesitated, his blood beginning to pound.

'I mean,' Gronwig enunciated slowly, as if talking to a dim-witted child, 'that you must kill the King. No blunders this time. I have no care as to how you do it, but in God's name, Thurstan, it has to be soon, tonight if you can. William has sent Lord Varin here to investigate us, I'm certain of it. If we wish England to wear a Saxon crown once more, then this is the only way.'

Thurstan walked over to the oak chest and poured himself a tankard of mead, his hand unsteady as he carried it to his lips.

'You never said it would come to this.'

'I had no thought that it would. 'Twas unfortunate that William claimed Exeter. I tried everything in my power to stop him.'

'I'm not sure.'

Sensing Thurstan's wavering retreat, the Earl lumbered over to him to stand toe to toe, searching his nephew's face for a chink of weakness.

'You are ideally placed.' Gronwig jabbed a finger in the middle of Thurstan's leather jerkin. 'Everyone believes you to be dead. You will be able to slip in and out, like a ghost.'

Thurstan shrank back further. The malice in Gronwig's eyes shocked him.

'Remember what happened, Thurstan. Remember the shouts and cries of the battle, the screams for help of your fellow Saxons, your father's dying words as the blood bubbled on his last breath, God rest his soul. Can you remember?'

Thurstan's head swam; he clenched his fists, trying to forget, to squeeze out the memories branded on his brain. His uncle's words leaked into him, burrowed into crevices to unearth the shouts of horror, the French horses stampeding over his friends, the frenzied bloodbath of two years ago.

'You must kill King William,' Gronwig repeated, his pasty jowls an inch from Thurstan's lean features.

A craziness whipped around him, frustrated rage plucked his innards. A crushing headache rose ominously from the base of his skull. His teetering mind began to resonate with bitter acrimony, making him groggy and confused. Since his father's death he had found it increasingly difficult to control his fluctuating moods. A tide of rancorous despair seized him on most days, except when Eadita appeared, steady and nurturing, ready to set him on an even keel once more. He craved her unstinting love, her unbending loyalty, but he needed her admiration as well. Surely she would embrace this honourable act; she hated the Normans as much as he did. Thunorslege would belong to them once more. Aye, she would approve.

'I'll do it.'

The lid of the oak coffer banged down. Heart racing at the jarring sound, Eadita jerked awake, her mind confused. Where was she? Under her fingers, she touched the softness of her own perfumed sheets, heard the familiar rustling of Agatha moving around her chamber.

'Agatha?'

'Oh, my lady, forgive me, I didn't mean to wake you.'

'God in Heaven, Agatha, what time of day is it?' Throwing back the furs, Eadita swung her shapely limbs to the side of the bed, pushing back the ropes of hair from her eyes.

''Tis not long after the noon bell, my lady. You have time enough to prepare for the Shire Court.' Agatha held out a heather-coloured underdress.

'Shire Court be damned!' Springing nimbly from the bed, Eadita rushed to the coffer, flinging open the lid, digging into the neatly folded clothes within. Even with the little sleep she had had, her mind shot through with clear, logical thought.

'My lady, whatever is the matter?'

'I must leave Thunorslege, Agatha. We must leave, Mother

and I. Lord Varin caught me in the forest last night.' Her servant paled, fluttering hands rising to cover her mouth.

'Thurstan…?'

'Is safe, do not fear. I told Varin nothing. But he will torment me until he finds out the truth.' She blushed faintly as she recalled the imprint of his thighs upon her own. Dear God!

'But where will you go?'

'Anywhere away from him.' Her questing fingers stilled as they found the leather bag and she began to stuff garments into it. Stopping suddenly, she pushed the bag towards Agatha.

'Here, you finish this. I need to dress.' Luckily, Eadita had managed to bathe when she had returned earlier that morning. Flinging the underdress over her chemise, she topped it with a thicker gown of dark green, banding her waist with a girdle of gold and amethyst. In the light of day, she could not risk being seen dressed as a boy; no one must think that anything was amiss.

'Do you think lady Beatrice will go with you?' Agatha began to braid her hair.

'She will be reluctant; Thunorslege holds many memories for her. But 'tis imperative that I persuade her. Now Lord Varin knows my secret, I have become the greatest risk to my brother.' I don't trust myself with Varin, she thought, shocked at her own revelation. The very fact that she had turned to him last night, albeit in her sleep, sent her into a turmoil of confusion. Her body, unprepared and unused to such a powerful onslaught of sensation, had betrayed her…betrayed her with the wrong man.

Giving Agatha a hug, she smiled at her worried face. ' Do not fret, Agatha. It will not be for long.' She pointed at the overstuffed bag. 'Throw that down when I'm on the ground, I cannot go through the hall at this hour. He's bound to be there.'

Sticking her head through the window, Eadita glanced

around hurriedly. No one was about. Throwing her leg over the sill, hampered somewhat by her long skirts, she sought the familiar hand- and footholds to bring her to the ground, jumping the last few feet in a swirl of fabric. Raising her eyes back to the window, she waved at Agatha to throw the bag down.

'Going somewhere, my lady?'

The bag crashed down beside her, missing her by inches.

Chapter Nine

Varin unsnagged her veil from the abrasive stone behind her, his fingers impatient.

'Well?' he snapped, dropping the material distastefully.

'Nay, I…' She grappled to hold back despair.

'Do not lie to me, mistress,' he growled, allowing her no time to forge an answer. 'Unless I'm very much mistaken, you are about to run away.' Wrenching open the leather toggles, he turned the bag violently upside down, pouring out the jumble of serviceable gowns, underdresses and chemises on to the stony ground. Within their folds, the jewelled hilt of a knife glinted. Picking it up, Varin revolved the blade between knowledgeable hands, his face inscrutable.

'You have defied me.'

Eadita's heart lurched, then plummeted. She stared dumbly at the incriminating pile of colourful silk, linen and cotton. Two big hands clasped her shoulders, the warmth permeating her skin beneath the soft wool.

'Look at me, Eadita. Look at me.' She angled her head derisively, her neck heavy with guilt. Unwilling to let him see her wretchedness, her stormy eyes linked boldly with his. His emerald gaze scalded her, searing her face and neck. 'Did you believe me not, when I vowed to watch your every move? Did you think I would not notice?' A ridged thumb placed in the middle of her lips prevented her from speaking. Varin shook his head, the blond strands of hair fanning out in the hazy afternoon light. 'Nay, do not speak. I want no more of your lies. I only want the truth, Eadita, the truth.' His words yanked at her.

'I cannot,' she whispered. The craving to brush the tip of her tongue against the pitted surface of his thumb bubbled up, but he drew it away, leaving a lingering imprint.

'Cannot or will not?'

She placed her hands in the middle of his chest, wanting to push him away, wanting to pull him closer. He glanced down scathingly at the innocent fingers spread over the supple leather of his jerkin. Nay, not innocent! The coquettish smiles and pretty lies of his mother wrenched at his gut; this maid had all of the guile and deceit of Felice.

He pulled roughly at her wrists, flinging her hands to her sides. 'Be careful, mistress,' he snarled. 'I am wise to your devious ways.'

'Who are you to do this to me?' Her voice muted to hushed sibilance, nervous energy sapping from her. Whenever he was near, her body seemed possessed, refusing to follow the commands of her brain, becoming chaotic, confused. With her mind she hated him, yet her body sought to defy her with every meeting. She swayed. Varin stepped back from her, folding his arms high on his chest, a mocking grin on his face.

'Do not think to trick me with these womanly wiles. Remember, I have witnessed enough of your bad behaviour to know that you will do anything you can to gain your own way.'

'Not everything,' she replied in a trice.

He raised his eyebrows in a questing arch. 'If I made that judgement on your conduct last night, then I beg to differ.'

Eadita flushed, locking her knees rigidly as they threatened to buckle.

'Do not speak of it.'

'Why? Because you don't like to hear the truth? *Exactement!* You don't like the truth at all, do you, *mam'selle?* Because you don't like to remember how you lay next to me, closer than a hair's breadth, warm and pliant in my arms?'

'No!' she shouted. 'No!'

'Because you liked it?' His pitiless regard burrowed into her very soul.

'You…bastard!' She turned her face away, swinging her veil down so it covered her features.

'Aye, that's right, *mam'selle*. Shun reality; loathe me if you must, but you will not escape me.' He cursed inwardly, viewing the delicate oval of her wan face, knowing he was being unfair. But he wanted to goad some reaction out of her, to needle her to full confession. Fighting a compulsion to loop her in his arms and comfort her, he picked up the bag instead and began to steer her back towards the main entrance.

'Lord Varin. Eadita.' Sybilla hovered by the doorway, her pasty face greeting them suspiciously as she saw the bag in Varin's hands. 'Gronwig is looking for you both, the Shire Court has already started.' She eyed the tall warrior greedily. 'Lord Varin, you go on. I beg a word with my cousin.'

Varin threw a quelling look at Eadita. 'Remember my words, my lady.'

'Have no fear, my lord, I am not going anywhere,' Eadita ventured tremulously, her shoulders slumped in defeat. A prickle of guilt stung Varin as he swung away down the passageway, confident that she had no intention of fleeing. Her slender figure seemed barely able to hold itself upright, drained of energy.

'I spy a mystery,' announced Sybilla, planting her bulk across the passageway. She tapped her nose conspiratorially.

'Where were you at the feasting yestereve? Father became most agitated as to your whereabouts.'

'I had urgent business to attend to in the village.' The excuse sounded lame, even to Eadita's ears. The intense stare of Sybilla's eyes fixing on her own brilliant orbs started a kernel of a headache.

'Oh, I'm sure you did,' spat Sybilla, her mouth twisting insultingly. 'And I can guess who you had urgent business with, you filthy little harlot. And with him again just now, unless my eyes play me false. You couldn't wait to see what he was made of, could you?' Sparks of jealously emanated from her snake-like eyes. 'Tongues are a-wagging, Eadita. I won't let you get away with this.'

Eadita laughed bitterly. 'How addled can you be, Sybilla? Lord Varin's hands are stained with Saxon blood. I hate him and everything he stands for. Now, let me pass.'

Temporarily deflated, Sybilla tried again. 'Father will not be happy that you're rutting with the enemy,' she continued crudely, drawing pleasure from the immediate pink stain that washed Eadita's cheeks. 'He sees your virginity as a great prize; 'tis a pity you've given it away with your sluttish behaviour. He'll be furious when he finds out.' She cackled triumphantly. In the sombre light of the corridor, her countenance adopted a sadistic gleam; she enjoyed humiliating her cousin. 'Now hear me, cousin, and hear me well,' Sybilla continued. 'Lord Varin is mine. He's wealthy and has vast lands and castles in Normandy. I want that and I want him and a little chit like you is not going to stand in my way.'

'You can have him with my blessing,' Eadita replied coolly.

'Just keep your filthy paws from him. I've seen the way he looks at you.'

'You're mistaken, Sybilla. Lord Varin can't stand the sight of me and I intend to keep it that way.'

* * *

Eadita paused at the entrance to the Great Hall, her knees shaking. She didn't dare try and make her escape now, feeling Varin's scrutiny upon her before anyone else noticed her appearance. She noted where he sat and vowed to place herself as far away as possible as his burning look followed her across the room.

The trestle tables had been pushed back against the stone walls and replaced by wooden benches set in a horseshoe formation before the high dais where her uncle and the various high-ranking nobles sat, including Varin. Peasants, serfs and freemen crowded on to these seats, more people standing behind. A case had obviously just finished; Hacon, serving as court bailiff, rolled up a manuscript ceremoniously, as Gronwig dismissed the plaintiff. People rose to congratulate the man, slapping him on the back, offering words of encouragement.

'Ah, Eadita, at last. You are showing an exasperating ability for tardiness.' Gronwig spotted her trying to step around the thronging mass. The crowd parted respectfully as she made her way to the top table. 'Perhaps you would be kind enough to serve us with some mead,' her uncle added, sarcastically.

Eadita nodded, hefting the earthenware pitcher of honeyed liquid from a side table. Walking behind the motley collection of high-ranking lords and *eoldermen* gathered from around the county, she leaned over in between them to fill their goblets. Most of the men had known her father; now they greeted her with wary, protective smiles, which she dutifully returned. As she brushed against them, Varin's blond head intruded on the fringes of her vision, tormenting her from the end of the table. Heart sinking, she wished her task could be performed with less bodily contact.

'How now, my pretty!'

She floundered awkwardly as a large arm came around her waist, nearly tipping her backwards. The jug keeled crazily, but she just managed to save it from spilling the contents over her assailant, setting it firmly on the table with a thump.

'Watch it, you fool,' she rounded hotly, then smiled in relief as she recognised Judhael's comfortable features.

'Only an old fool! Have mercy, my lady,' he chortled, still clasping an arm about her. She bent down to kiss him on his lined forehead.

'Oh, Judhael, I am so pleased to see you.' A tiny frown marred her smooth brow. 'Have you seen my mother?'

'Aye, and spent a pleasant morning in her company. We always find much to talk about.'

'She is fond of you,' Eadita acknowledged, winding the trailing leather lace from her belt around her fingers, backwards and forwards. Judhael's gnarled fingers curved over her hands.

'What is the matter, Eadita? Is it the Normans?'

'Judhael, I need your help.' She dropped her tone a couple of notches, although the surrounding commotion effectively masked her conversation. Her heart raced. She had to escape Varin's clutches. In a flash, she knew he would prise the truth from her; her own weakness around him would betray her shamefully. In the end, he would win, and for Thurstan's sake she did not want to be around when that happened.

'Oh?' Judhael's brows lifted.

'We need to leave Thunorslege, Mother and I. The situation becomes intolerable. Lord Varin marks my every move…'

'But why does he watch you? Beatrice says he is bodyguard to Gronwig.'

'I know not. But he frightens me…' She paused. Nay, he did not frighten her. He had insulted her, infuriated her, outwitted her and pushed her to the very limits of her reason, but he did not frighten her. He…excited her. Shame rose like bile in her gut; she studied the floor miserably.

'Has he hurt you?' Judhael demanded, half-rising in his seat.

'Nay, nothing like that.' Her eyes met his wise orbs as she patted his arm in reassurance. 'I think Mother and I would be safer elsewhere, just till they have moved on.' And once I have my mother settled, I can live with Thurstan in the forest, she thought. 'Maybe we could stay with you, in Totnes?'

'You're going nowhere, Eadita.' Gronwig, turning from his conversation with Baldwin of Athelton, snared the final words of her plea. 'I need you here to deal with our…guests. And right now, by chattering incessantly, you fail in your duty. I need some mead…now, before I die of thirst.' He thumped the tankard on the table, his irritated eye on the pitcher.

'Don't worry, Eadita. I plan to stay for a few days at Thunorslege. We will have plenty of time to talk,' Judhael murmured as she began to serve once more. She threw him a bleak smile. Her heart began to pound as she neared Varin, the thick locks of his unruly hair taunting her as he talked to Geraint. Her stomach twisted crazily. Astounded that the nearness of his presence should cause such enhanced sensitivity, she almost buckled in her effort to discipline her catapulting logic. Their last exchange had been bitter; think on that, she challenged, rather than on the set of his wide shoulders clad in the finest buckskin, on the flaxen strands brushing the neckline of his jerkin. Her urging fingers begged to touch the downy hairs nuzzling at his nape… No more! Clamping down sternly on her untrammelled instincts, she gritted her teeth to lean between Geraint and Varin. With God's grace he would ignore her.

Varin caught her delicate perfume long before she slopped the mead into his goblet. As she leaned forward, her gunna gaped to release another heady waft from the warmth between her breasts and his thoughts wrenched abruptly to the bittersweet recollection of a luscious body pressed close to his own. Why did the little vixen have to smell so wonderful, like the summer fields of lavender in Provence?

He strove to recall the treachery of the woman, the sheer perfidy of her nature, the open dismay on her face when he caught her sneaking from her chamber window earlier. He scowled as the branding curve of her bosom touched his shoulder, an inevitable contact given the crowded conditions. His tapered fingers snaked out to grab her wrist savagely. Anger was the only way to fight his desire for her.

'Let go of me, you brute!' she whispered. His punishing fingers dug unmercifully into her wrist, pulling it under the table, tipping her closer, nearer, to the length of him.

'What business do you have with Judhael?'

'None of yours!' she hissed, enraged at his behaviour. 'Let go of my hand!'

'Not until you tell me.' His tone held the steel of command.

'Judhael is an old family friend.' She regaled him with a fiery look. 'There, are you satisfied?'

'Never,' he whispered. Cheeks flaming, her amethyst-washed eyes met his as she pulled futilely against his unsparing grip. Panic welled in the pit of her stomach as she fought hard to halt the senseless careening of her hurtling blood. The abrasive tips of his fingers seared into her flesh, sending pinpricks of desire leaping along her veins. Through the acrid smell of the woodsmoke she acknowledged his musky scent, an invigorating combination of tanned hide and her own thyme soap. *God have mercy on my soul*, she thought.

He laughed, unexpectedly, fracturing the hostility between them. Her limbs melted into a hopeless puddle. His calming fragrance lulled her into a strange torpor; she had to shout for help…drag herself away…smash the pitcher over his head. *Smash the pitcher over his head!* Her fingers curled determinedly around the earthenware handle, lifting it to her shoulder height to bring it around.

'How could I have forgotten your bloodthirsty nature, my lady?' Varin's left hand whipped around to anchor the makeshift weapon and her other wrist to the oaken planks. 'After all, 'tis only two nights since you tried to murder me; I should have anticipated the next attack.'

'I wasn't going to murder you. I just wanted you to hand over the...' she dropped her voice to a whisper '...gold.'

'Only that time you met your match.' His eyes glittered dangerously. On a level with his shoulder, she shied away from meeting his gaze, acutely aware of his body heat through her gown.

'The *only* time,' she rallied, arrogantly. From the corner of her eye, she saw the next plaintiff led in. 'My lord, I must sit before my uncle notices. Please let me be.' His grip relaxed.

'Aye,' he agreed. 'We draw too many interested glances.' She made to pull away, but he swept an arm around her hips, swaying her back to him. 'But remember, mistress, we are far from finished.'

Thronged on all sides by the amassed peasants stood a young woman, uncovered brown hair straggling down to her waist, a ragged hem encrusted with mud. Her painful thinness served only to highlight the late stage of her pregnancy. Great hollows were carved out beneath her dull eyes, emphasising her exhaustion. She looked on the verge of passing out...and no oath-helpers, no one to cite her innocence. My God, thought Eadita, the woman wouldn't survive, whatever her crime might be.

'Fetch this woman a chair, Hacon, and quickly,' Eadita ordered, rising from her seat. With her knowledge of midwifery, she judged the woman's labour to be imminent. The peasants muttered uneasily, the worrying chatter rising and falling in waves of disapproval. Hacon turned to Gronwig, seeking his assent.

'As usual, niece, you are too soft. Let's hear her crimes before we give her a seat.' Gronwig smirked, the blue silk of his tunic drawing tight over his chest as he slumped back in his seat.

'She needs to sit, Gronwig—' Varin's imposing tones supported Eadita's request '—otherwise she will be unable to speak her crimes.' Judhael, and the other *eolderman* murmured their agreement. Curling his bottom lip petulantly, Gronwig nodded grudgingly at Hacon, tapping his pale fingertips on the table. The woman lowered her bulk gratefully on to the stool, a glimmer of a smile tracing her lips as she glanced at Varin. A pang of envy whipped through Eadita and she quashed it brutally before it had time to flourish. Hacon cleared his throat theatrically.

'The villagers of Thunorslege bring this case, my lords. This woman, named Margaret, came to the village seeking shelter and a place to birth her child.'

'Our villagers always help people in need. Why not her?' Gronwig questioned against a growing, dissatisfied chatter. The sun, peeping through the upper window embrasure, sent a bright shaft down on to the woman's head. The collective grumbling grew louder, the crowd shuffling restively as a few of the peasants crossed themselves.

'She has the mark of the Devil.' Hacon deepened his voice melodramatically. The jumbled words of the crowd became more distinct.

'Out, out, out with her!'

Margaret faced the jury of thegns, lords and *eoldermen* impassively; indeed, she appeared too tired to fight.

'Silence!' roared the Earl. 'Someone speak for the villagers.' Heads turned; a large man stood up, clutching his woollen cap nervously between agitated hands.

'What is this mark?' Gronwig asked.

'Her foot, my lord. She has the Devil's foot,' he stuttered.

'Show me!' Gronwig ordered the woman. 'Show me your foot!' Lifting the tattered skirts, the woman stuck both feet out in front of her, a touch of defiance on her face. One bare foot, besmirched with mud, was dainty and high-arched. The other,

wrapped in filthy, stained cloth-bindings, took on the ungainly proportions of a clubfoot. Eadita sucked in her breath.
It was common practice amongst the peasants to smother
babies with this affliction at birth, because of its associations
with evil.

Hacon seized the momentary pause to continue. 'The villagers don't want her or the newborn babe in the village; she
will bring bad luck, turn our water sour, affect the crops…'

'I say cast her out, to whelp in the forest,' Gronwig announced. 'We cannot risk the bad luck in the village, especially at this hard time of year.'

Eadita rose, annoyed with Gronwig's callous dismissal. 'I
don't agree. Just because the woman carries a supposed mark
of the Devil,' she spoke above the rising chorus of disapproval, 'does not mean we should cast her aside. The woman
needs help in labour, like any other, with childbirth. She would
very likely die in the forest.'

'No one will touch her, my lady, no one wants to put their
hands on her, or the child,' someone shouted from the crowd,
'we'll all be touched by the Devil.' The Earl smiled slowly,
turning his bulk towards his niece. His eyes narrowed beadily.

'Unless, of course, you would touch her, Eadita? Would
you help her as you do with the other women in the village?'

'Aye, I am not afraid. I will help her.' Her voice rang out
true and clear, echoing through the hall.

'Nay, my lady. Do not do it!' A woman stood up in the
crowd, shaking her head violently. 'Other women will not
want your hands on them after you have touched one such as
her. Don't risk our own babies!'

Eadita bit her bottom lip, searching the familiar faces for
an answer. She had assisted the village midwives at many
birthings, her knowledge of medicinal herbs complementing
their care of the labouring women. Eadita knew her potions
could bring on a late baby, or ease the excruciating pain in

delivering a breech, but due to her status, she had never held a new-born head in her hands. But she had seen enough to know what to do. Old Mother Taynor's words held a warning, and the truth: the villagers were so entrenched in superstition that they would not let her aid them if she touched this stranger and her babe. And she would surely touch her as no one else was prepared to help. She doubted she could even persuade Agatha. Could she really turn her back on her village, the village where she had grown up, to help one woman, a stranger? The mark of the Devil meant nothing to her for all she saw was a woman in need, a woman who needed help.

'I will help her.' The measured tones came as a shock. It was Varin who spoke. Several mouths dropped open, before a hostile uproar broke out in the gathered crowd.

'Are you insane, Norman?' the Earl shouted, appalled, turning his wobbling frog-like complexion on the warrior, who reclined with feline grace against the back of his chair. Eadita's head whipped round, eyes stark with astonishment at his relaxed attitude.

'What is the problem, my lord Earl? I have no fear of the Devil…and your niece needs some help. I am prepared to give it.' Varin cast his hands forward, shrugging his shoulders in typical Gallic style. 'I do not see the difficulty.' Eadita sat down shakily, bewildered that this man, a Norman knight, was prepared to help with a birthing. The bringing of a child into the world was women's work, yet he had offered to assist when none of her Saxon womenfolk could bring themselves to touch the woman. The Earl echoed her astonishment.

'The problem, my friend,' the Earl snarled slowly as if talked to a slow-witted peasant, 'is that you are a *man*. The Church does not allow men within the birthing chamber. It is an unclean act; why defile yourself so?' A fleck of spittle sprang from his lips to land on the table before him; Eadita watched it disintegrating as Varin's words reverberated in her mind. *I will not let you out of my sight. We are far from finished.*

''Tis not viewed that way in France. Childbirth is seen as a cause for celebration.'

'Well, Lord Varin, who am I to dissuade you from such a demeaning task? I only request that you purify yourself with holy water in the church afterwards. What say you, niece?'

''Tis not the best idea…' Her questioning gaze swept over the upturned faces. Margaret's hollow eyes pleaded with her. 'Are the villagers in agreement?' Old Mother Taynor stood up, thrusting a crooked finger at her.

'Just make sure you never touch the girl.'

'Then 'tis decided,' proclaimed the Earl. 'She can live without the walls until her time comes; food can be dropped and she can easily find shelter.' Gronwig flicked an invisible crumb from his rolling stomach. 'Take her away.'

There was no time to be furious at Varin's interference. A noisy scuffle had broken out near the main doorway, but the crush of people made it difficult to see the cause. The crowd surged then and broke apart, clearing a path for the imposing chain-mail clad figure of Raoul.

'Count Raoul, we have missed your presence.' Gronwig raised his arm in greeting. 'Do come and join us, we are having a most entertaining afternoon.' He glanced archly at Varin, before rising slightly in his seat to see what baggage Raoul dragged haphazardly behind him. Kicking and screaming, fighting like a wild cat, was a boy of about ten years old. Annoyed by the slowness of his advance towards the high table, Raoul picked the boy up to deposit him on his feet in front of the Shire Court.

'I, too, have been having a most entertaining afternoon hunting outlaws,' Raoul said. 'You will be well pleased with me, my lord.' Raoul shifted his eyes stealthily toward Eadita. 'I have your attacker. This boy was in the forest the night you travelled to Thunorslege and jumped your party to kill for gold. He has been handed over to me by reliable witnesses so we can punish him according to the King's Law.'

Under the table, Eadita's legs started to shake violently; sweat sprung to her palms in disbelief. Climbing anger quelled her fear at the sight of the wretched, struggling child, deathly afraid of the fate that awaited him. Mud daubed his thin face, his eyes gleaming round and terrified towards the imposing rank of lords and thegns facing him from the high table. She rose, almost knocking her chair backwards in haste.

'You must be mistaken, Raoul. How could a lad such as this attack such a heavily defended party? Just look at the size of him compared to them!' She pointed at Varin, who frowned slightly. Was that a warning he held in his eyes?

'My lady,' Raoul addressed her in patronising tones, 'forgive the assumption, but what possible knowledge could you have of such matters? I have the information on good authority. He must be punished.'

'On who's authority?' Eadita sounded shrill, even to her own ears. 'How much money did you have to pay them?' *Why wouldn't Varin speak? He alone could save the boy!*

'My lady, forgive me, but I resent that outspoken accusation,' Raoul replied smoothly, noting with glee Gronwig's obvious annoyance at his niece's continual interruptions. 'Methinks you would rather see the boy attempt to murder us again, than bring him to trial. Is that right?' Raoul's eye roved the length of her well-fitting gown, tracing the lines of material that clung to her figure.

'No, of course not,' she replied, scornfully. 'I merely want to see fair justice.'

'And so you shall, niece, if you cease your accusatory interruptions.' Gronwig fixed her with his pale stare. 'You are beginning to irritate me, niece. Now sit down before you say something you regret.'

'Well, my lord Earl, is it the lad or no?' Raoul grew impatient, sensing a loss of direction with his main intention. He relied on the fact that one peasant lad would look very much like another. The Earl stared heavily at the thin, wiry ragamuffin, who stood more silently now, occasionally wiping his nose with his free arm. Gronwig stroked his chin, considering the lad. Eadita fidgeted, her eyes cast down into her lap as she realised what she must do if the boy was found guilty. The scrawny urchin had no oath-helpers to speak in his defence. Frantically her eyes reached along the table, searching Varin's impassive profile for some clue that he would save the boy. *Save the boy!* she willed him under her breath, but his mouth didn't open.

'Hmm!' the Earl finally said. 'I find it hard to decide about the lad; I gave him no regard after his capture…what say you, Lord Varin…Geraint?' He turned to the Norman lords. Now, Eadita prayed silently, now he would speak. A scavenging fear rifled through her bones; she gripped her hands together as the knuckles whitened.

'I agree, 'tis difficult to say…' Varin's calm, melodious tone did nothing to convince her terrified heart. Surprised, he stopped mid-sentence as Eadita sprung in panic from her chair, shaking her head violently. She would not let this poor boy take the blame for her own crimes.

'Stop! Stop this madness; the lad is innocent…please, please listen to me…' Her eyes roved the room wildly as she summoned the courage to speak the words of confession.

Chapter Ten

'Lady Eadita is ill.' The words came close to her left ear. 'I would get her some air.' In a trice thick arms grabbed her around the waist, turning her speedily from the crowd to push her face into a broad chest.

'Varin!' she uttered angrily, but the rich fabric of his overshirt muffled her speech. He swooped an arm deftly under her knees, crooking them so she lost her balance, and hoisted her light weight casually into his arms. Before she had time to struggle, before she could clear the quickening dryness in her throat to scream, Varin had marched out into the passageway with her, through the astounded kitchens, and outside to the back wall, depositing her heartlessly on the mossy bank.

'It would not be a good idea to confess.' Varin raked her face with his lean, hungry look.

''Twas my only option since you were obviously not going to save him,' she jibed at him.

'You hardly gave me much time to even speak of his innocence…' he countered, folding his arms high over his chest.

'What do you mean?' She fought to control the trembling in her voice.

'Do you really hold me in such low regard that you think I would allow an innocent boy to suffer unnecessarily?' He arched one eyebrow as he deciphered her contemptuous look. 'Aye, I can see that you do.' He placed a sturdy hand at her elbow. 'Well, hear this, my lady. I would not have.'

'Then why did you hold your silence?' Her voice sounded shrill in the still air.

'Sometimes it pays to bide one's time.'

'And let that poor boy suffer at your expense; 'tis why I leapt in to save the boy.' She tugged at his arm, anxious to be away from the intimacy of the situation. 'Come, we must hasten back inside so you can tell everyone.' A blast of wind whipped her skirts around, the freezing air clearing her head keenly after the musty, fuggy interior of the hall.

'Not so fast, little one. I will save the boy…on one condition.' She turned leaden eyes upon him.

'I beg your pardon?' The haughtiness of her tone belied her fear.

'Tell me what you were doing in the forest. I can help you if you learn to trust me.' She frowned at the tenderness in his eyes, so different from his earlier disdain. *Remember Thurstan,* she reminded herself.

'And…what?' she demanded suspiciously.

'And I will say the boy is innocent.'

Eadita gasped, grabbing the bunched muscles of his upper arms in shock. He regarded her dispassionately.

'You…you bastard!' she breathed. 'I knew it! You speak against your word already! And you ask me to trust you! Hah!' She jabbed a finger between the lacing on his chest. 'You would lower yourself to blackmail a confession out of me! You would make a young boy undergo a trial by ordeal where his hands are deliberately burned to test his guilt! Oh, no, no, Varin, it will never happen, because I will certainly confess! I would give my life for that innocent boy!' At every word she poked his chest, hard. A muscle jumped in his cheek, pinkened and raw in the wind.

'And who else would you give your life for, Eadita?' he said softly. 'Are you protecting someone, is that it?' She regarded him blankly until he held his palms up toward her in gesture of defeat.

'*Mon Dieu!* You would try the patience of a saint!' He ran exasperated hands through his golden locks, several gleaming strands falling over his forehead. Suddenly he laughed, the smile transforming his face.

'It seems I have underestimated you, my lady!' He had the grace to appear abashed. 'But you must give me some praise for trying to garner the truth.'

She shook her head. 'Nay, I do not praise a blackmailer. You stoop too low.'

'You judge me too harshly, *mam'selle.*' He laid a hand theatrically over his heart. 'How else am I to prise out your secrets?'

'I have no secrets. My actions in the forest were entirely innocent. Can't you accept that?'

'No, I cannot. I have seen too many curious things to believe you are acting within the law. My first duty is to my King, whom I must protect above everything. Believe me, my lady, when I say that far lesser crimes have attracted greater punishments.'

'Then punish me,' she dared him, impulsively. 'You caught me fair and square, why not throw me in the dungeon, torture me? I will say nothing. Why not hand me over to the King's guard right now?'

'I am the King's guard.' His concerned look bothered her. 'You are in my care until I decide what to do with you. The less people know about your double life, the better. 'Tis safer for you.' His voice held a protective edge.

'I'm in no danger.'

'Don't be so certain.'

He glanced down at her sylvan features, the deep violet of her cat-like eyes regarding him intently. As the wind carried her gossamer veil across her face, she lifted her arm impatiently to push it back. Distracted, he traced the spellbinding curve of her underarm down towards the upraised swell of her breast. As his eye travelled downwards, he yearned to pluck the leather laces from her svelte waist, to drag the gunna from her smooth, pliant limbs. *God have mercy on him!*

'Varin?' she prompted, bringing her arm down suddenly. A hectic flush roved her cheeks under his steady regard. They stood a mere handspan apart, his arm planted heavily against the wall to box her in. Desire burst through his loins like igniting flame, the scent of lavender from her skin flirting with his senses. Desperately he tried to wrest himself away from the magnetic pull of her body as he swayed from the impact of his passion. The hankering to bed this woman, to bury himself so wholly in her body, to encircle himself night after night within her smooth, velvet limbs so that his imprint would remain for eternity, gripped his body in a fist of steel.

'Oh, no, you don't, *petite!*' He grabbed her shoulder as, disconcerted by his intense gaze, she made to duck under his arm. Frantically, Eadita looked about for someone who might help her.

'You can't make me stay here!' Balling her fists in frustration, she aimed a sharp kick at his shins. His white teeth flashed with amusement.

'Can't I?' he goaded. 'Although I admire your amazing agility and speed, I doubt you could win when pitted against me.' Eadita doubted it too, but only because she had lost the element of surprise. The top of her head scarcely reached his shoulder; his big body loomed over her, a body honed and muscled from years of training. Despite his lazy stance, she was all too aware of the power in his frame.

'Let me go, you big brute!' She opened her mouth to

scream. In a whirlwind movement, Varin had lifted her up and pinned against the wall with his body, chest to breast, thigh to thigh, as firm cool lips claimed her own to silence her outrage. Her feet flailed a good foot-length above the ground as she sought to stand, but to no avail.

As her mind bellowed in sheer fury at the violation, her innocent body suffered a gamut of sensations. The taut harpstring of control threatened to break as she strained in fury to resist the relentless onslaught of his mouth slashing rudely across her petal-like lips. At first he explored the contours of her mouth with tantalising gentleness, then opened like a hot flower across her lips, pressing insistently with the rough tip of his tongue to gain access to her mouth. An enervating pull sucked powerfully at her, coiling with deceit in the pit of her stomach. The bunched muscles of his hefty thighs rode heavily on her own, his chest crushed against her painfully constricted nipples, sending waves of hungry need arcing through her blood. *Resist! You must resist!* To obey her self-instruction was complicated by a soporific sluggishness engulfing her limbs. She wanted to relent, to cast control aside and surrender to the welter of awareness that swarmed her body.

As his tongue probed incessantly along the tightly clamped line of her lip, she opened her mouth to shout, 'No!', at the same time attempting to shove him away. She realised her grave error as he pierced the defence of her mouth with ease, pushing a questing hand under her veil to thread tanned fingers urgently through her silken hair. By pulling her head back slightly, he gained greater access to plunder her mouth more efficiently. Against her will, her body cleaved towards his, trying to achieve a greater closeness. Varin groaned: a deep guttural yearning. Her heart raced, her breath coming in short gasps, hands stealing from his chest to clasp tightly, possessively around his neck. Her legs itched to swing from the wall, to straddle his pelvis; to draw herself nearer…

'Ahem! I say…ahem!' The coughing and throat-clearing seemed part of a dream. Her mind cleared, she wrenched her lips from Varin's to cast a dazed look at the avuncular figure of Judhael.

'God in Heaven!' she breathed. 'Judhael!'

Varin let go of her slowly, reluctantly even, sliding her down his body so she was patently aware of every contour before her slippered toes brushed the ground. He stood back then, a brooding promise in his eyes. Flustered, embarrassed, Eadita smoothed her palms down her gunna, trembling a little. It was all Judhael could do not to laugh—the pair of them looked so guilty: Varin trying to conceal his annoyance at being interrupted, Eadita fluttering like a trapped bird.

'Well,' said Judhael sheepishly. 'I came to see how the maid was faring, but I can see now she is in capable hands.' He nodded briefly at Varin.

'Nothing of the sort. He dragged me out here, against my will,' Eadita jibed critically. Anger had replaced the earlier passion; she was vexed at this horrible man for engendering such new feelings in her; such delicious uncontrollable feelings that taunted her every time she looked at him.

'And why would he do that, my dear?' Judhael asked kindly. 'You seemed to be getting on quite well.'

'Oh…er…well, I was feeling a little faint at the time.' Eadita realised that she couldn't tell Judhael the real reason why she had been dragged out here. She turned to Varin, a silent plea in her eyes. He nodded, understanding.

'Come,' he said, spinning her along with his lengthy strides. ' I must declare the boy's innocence.' They followed Judhael into the manor house.

'I cannot bear this; I cannot bear the pain!' The woman groaned out as she gripped the sides of the makeshift pallet, knuckles whitening as she tried to fight the constricting agony of a contraction. 'How much longer do I have to suffer?' Lying awkwardly on her back, Margaret's eyes rolled up to the ceiling, unfocused on the serried branches ranked over the wide cross-beams.

'Tell me what I have to do.' The bright curiosity in Varin's eyes found Eadita in the damp shadowy confines of the tumbledown hut.

'You don't have to do this, Varin; to lower yourself like this.' Dropping her bag to the earthen floor, she knelt down to unpack her herbs and tisanes. 'The menfolk think it strange that you should help at all.' Her gunna pooled around her, highlighting the narrowness of her waist.

'As I explained, 'tis not the way in my country. Childbirth does not frighten us men away.' Varin unbuckled his sword, flinging the jewelled hilt into the corner. He began to roll up his tunic sleeves, slowly, deliberately revealing massive forearms corded with muscle. The fine downy hairs riffled in the breeze that blew into the temporary shelter. Outside, grey clouds amassed heavily. 'If I hadn't stepped forward yesterday, this maid might well have died.'

'But why do you care? The maid is Saxon, none of your concern.' Eadita turned her bright eyes towards him, conscious of his power and strength within the confined space.

'We are all one people now, Eadita, and the maid needed help.'

'I would have helped her on my own.' Eadita ducked her head.

'And be forever shunned by your kinsmen? Never be able to attend on the women in your village? It would have been a high price to pay, Eadita.'

He spoke the truth, but she was reluctant to admit it. She needed his help. Margaret groaned again, head lolling back on to the heavily-embroidered linen pillow. Yestereve, after the Shire Court, Eadita had persuaded Agatha to help her carry some spare linens and furs across the rutted fields to the run-down hut in order to make Margaret more comfortable for the night. Varin had ordered one of his soldiers to accompany them, no doubt to prevent any escape attempt. When she and Varin had returned early that morning, Margaret was obviously exhausted, yet her labour had only just begun. Her distended bump, covered in dirty rags, seemed huge against her frail stature.

'She needs us. Both of us. Put aside your hatred of me for the nonce—we must work together.' Varin's eyes, hard as ice chips, flicked over the pale, sweating girl, one thin arm thrown over her eyes.

I don't hate you. The words sprang unbidden, but remained unspoken. His generosity of nature in offering to help had confused her. Flustered, Eadita tossed her veil back imperiously, hooking back the trailing sleeves of her overdress, cursing the impracticality of her garments. In normal circumstances, she would have worn just her underdress, with its fitted sleeves, but Varin's presence prevented her. She hadn't expected Margaret to be in labour so soon, but when Varin had escorted her over the fields to check on the maid, they had found her in a state of painful shock, surrounded by a pool of liquid. Her waters had broken.

'Tell me what to do,' Varin asked, his voice calm and steady.

Eadita ran her eye over the girl, assessing her condition. 'She must walk around, Varin; it will encourage the babe to move down. Could you help her?' Eadita's voice was unsteady as she looked for a suitable place to build a fire. Varin nodded, his strong arms lifting Margaret as if she were a child, supporting her as another contraction gripped her womb. Margaret howled in agony, her screams reverberating around the timber hut.

'This cannot be right!' Varin looked over to Eadita, concern etching his features. Eadita smiled tightly. 'Nay, 'tis right. Welcome to the world of women, Lord Varin.' He grimaced, but encouraged Margaret to shuffle forward on her water-swollen feet. The maid's head buried into Varin's chest, her groans muffled as her arms clenched on to his elbows. Watching the new smoke curl from the fire, adding sticks to feed the tiny flame, Eadita's hands stilled. She had forgotten how painful these early contractions could be.

'I want to sit; I want to lie down.' Margaret pulled against Varin's unyielding body.

'I will give her something; the babe will be long in coming and I fear for her strength.' Eadita drew a pestle and mortar from her bag and began to pound the bundle of dried leaves with a slug of water from a leather flagon.

'How long?' Varin questioned, as he lowered Margaret on to her side.

'Pray that it is not above two days.'

'I had no idea.' Varin raked his fingers through his tawny hair, hunkering down beside Margaret to draw the woollen blanket over her. Eadita stared, fascinated. She had not thought the barbarian to be capable of such kindness. He caught her look.

'Believe it or not, mistress, we want the same thing here, despite having spent most of my life on the battlefield. Here, let me give her that.' He reached for the bowl of green liquid mush, wrinkling his nose as he helped Margaret to sip. The maid's eyes fluttered shut, her scrawny frame beginning to relax as the rigidity peeled from her body. Her breathing slowed; she lapsed into a shallow doze. Eadita sighed in relief.

'Now, we wait.' Her amethyst eyes brushed over him, before turning to her fire, smouldering dismally in the rain-soaked air. Varin chuckled at her obvious dismay.

'Your knowledge of childbirth is to be congratulated, *mam'selle,* but your skills in fire-making are sorely lacking.' She pursed her lips as he kicked aside the soggy, charred twigs, using his dagger to cut a neat bowl shape in the earth. 'You picked a good place, though,' he continued. 'The wind blows away from us; it will not smoke too much.'

'If you say so.' Eadita shrugged her shoulders, turning away. He eyed her slim back.

'This is not the time for your spoiled ways, mistress. We have a difficult job ahead.' She knew her behaviour seemed churlish, but his kind manner had thrown her off balance. Who would have thought a warrior capable of such tenderness?

'I'm sorry.' She confronted him, met his piercing green gaze full on. ''Tis difficult for me to forget your true purpose at Thunorslege, to forget whom you are, what you represent.' Folding her arms across her body, she searched the taut angles of his face.

'And…?' he prodded, lacing the sticks crosswise.

'And…?' she questioned, confused.

'And 'tis difficult to forget what has occurred between us.' The words tumbled out before he could stop himself, damn it! After the intensity of their last kiss, he had vowed to keep a level head around her, yet some unknown bewitchment constantly lured him, like a dim-witted moth to a flame. He should know better than to tangle with a high-born lady! Irritated with himself, Varin drew his flints to set a spark to the newly laid fire, the smoke curling merrily. The silence elongated, punctuated by spots of rain sporadically hitting the flames.

Eadita traced his broad back as he squatted on his haunches in the bare dirt. How could she answer him? With the truth? Her mouth still carried the burning imprint of his lips; her body tingled with the memory of his insistent thighs. She had enjoyed every sweet minute of his last kiss, a kiss that crushed her hard-won defences, a kiss that forced her to crave the sensation of his large body cleaving into her own, a kiss that would surely send her to hell.

'Forget my words,' he growled bitterly, rising abruptly to loom over her. 'You're a beautiful woman, Eadita, but nothing more! I am attracted to you…physically, like every other man at Thunorslege.'

'I can't help it if you can't control yourself!' she lashed at him, hurt by the vehemence of his insult, the rapid change in his manner. 'But don't take it out on me!'

His dragon eyes meshed callously with hers. '*Faites attention, petite!* You are fast becoming the most likely person I would take *it* out on!' She held her breath, toes curled in fearful excitement, but he swung away from her, the rigid line of his shoulders tense with fury. 'Underneath, you're like all the rest of them.' He made her sound like a whore.

Eadita gasped, astounded that his verbal rebuff should hurt quite so much and bit her lip, sliding her gaze from his dominating figure to Margaret to cover her humiliation. Surely his rejection was the very thing she wanted? Surely she wanted him to spurn her, ignore her very existence?

'Why are you being like this?' she probed softly, her voice catching. ''Twas you who said we should lay our personal feelings aside today.'

He caught the tint of sadness in her tone and cursed, frustration rippling from him. He sensed a trap closing in on him, no doubt the same lure with which his mother had reeled his father in to a lifetime of misery. He could not, would not, let it happen! Wheeling away, he stared out over the flat pasture of Thunorslege, hedges and ditches pattening away in the distance, breathing deeply to rein in his anger.

'Aye, you're right. You don't deserve my insults. Forgive me.'

She smiled at him, the incredible purple depths of her eyes absolving him, thanking him, understanding the effort it had cost him to apologise.

His breath hitched. He didn't want her forgiveness; their mutual animosity made it easier to keep the distance between them. Could he believe for the slightest moment that she wasn't like all the others? Her duplicity enraged him, her spirit and determination enthralled and annoyed him simultaneously, yet underneath lay a gentle kindness that he was reluctant to acknowledge. He would tie himself to no woman after what that lying whore had done to his father! For his own sanity, he wanted to believe Eadita was like all the rest, but at this very moment, he was not so sure.

'I do believe that is the first time you've apologised.' Her calm words, lightly teasing, broke the stretching tension as she lifted the pot to boil over the fire.

'Remember it well, mistress, for it will most likely be the last.' He laughed, a sharp husky sound, his enticing eyes lacing with her own, mirroring her mood. They were on steady ground once more. On the bed, Margaret whimpered as another contraction took hold, yet she slept on.

'The effects of the tisane may not last that long,' Eadita warned, her mind adjusting swiftly to the task in hand. She sat down on a heap of straw, drawing her cloak around her to ward off the chill and took a piece of embroidery from her bag.

'Go, if you wish, my lord. Send me a lad so I can summon you if things start happening.'

'I will stay.'

'Oh, for goodness' sake. I am hardly likely to flee when this maid needs me!'

'Even so, *mam'selle,* I will stay.'

'Why don't you just turn me over for King William to deal with?'

'Because I prefer to deal with you myself. William trusts me to do the right thing.'

'You seem remarkably close.'

'Aye, we're good friends. He trained me up as a knight from the age of eight. Geraint as well.'

'Something that Raoul seems displeased about.'

Varin frowned. 'Raoul resents the fact that my father was a lowly armourer, a Viking descended from King Rollo of Denmark, not a high-born French noble like his own father. Normally, you are born into knighthood.' His gold-fringed eyes clouded over.

'And you?' she prompted.

'Sigurd, my father, saved William's life from an assassin. William never forgot and promised to train myself and my two brothers under his banner when he became Duke of Normandy.'

'How did your mother feel about that?'

A tiny silence descended in the hut, broken only by the crackling of the firewood shooting glimmering sparks into the gloomy air and the occasional stifled moans of Margaret in the shadows. Varin threw another stick onto the fire, resting his elbows on his knees, his expression bleak.

'I have no idea.' His voice was so cold a lump of ice lodged in Eadita's stomach. Her embroidery needle drove into the tip of her finger, and she sucked it to stop the blood spotting her work.

'Is she dead?' Eadita asked tentatively, wondering at his distant look.

'She is to me.'

A rasping scream drew them both to their feet in a moment.

Chapter Eleven

An eerie silence filled the hut as Eadita lifted the small life-less bundle into her arms; it had been a long struggle to haul the baby out. Eadita's hair hung in damp wisps around her tight-lipped expression, her veil and headdress long since discarded. She had broken her promise not to touch Margaret, but she cared not. Tasting the salty perspiration on her top lip, she laid the baby boy on a linen rag, starting to wipe away the blood and murk from its tiny limbs.

Varin, stripped to his shirt, lifted a blanket over Margaret who shivered with the exhaustion of her labour. His concerned regard questioned Eadita. She shook her head sadly, kneeling to wash her hands in the pail; the child had been dead long before he had entered this world.

'My baby?' Margaret stuttered timidly as she laid a weary arm across her eyes. Varin spoke to her in hushed tones. A low keening wail trickled from her mouth, a tragic sound of loss filling the ramshackle walls. Eadita closed her eyes, biting her lip in consternation. No stranger to death in childbirth, this loss was particularly hard to bear. Most villagers had family and friends to comfort them when tragedy struck; Margaret had nobody. How cruel Fortune was, to allow this woman her hopes and dreams in all those heavy months of waiting, only to have nothing at the end of it. She swaddled the child, her mind parched with sadness.

'Can I hold him?' Margaret asked in a shaking voice. Eadita frowned.

'It can do no harm.' Varin left Margaret's side to wipe his own hands. 'Let her spend some precious moments with her baby.' Drawing solace from his calm, assessing tones, she picked the baby up to place him carefully in Margaret's arms. Turning her head quickly to avoid witnessing the devastating scene of mother and child together, she struggled to hold back the tears.

'The child must be christened and buried,' she announced tonelessly, her face a white mask. 'I would fetch the priest.'

Varin blocked her path.

'Eadita.' His big arms came around her as he folded her into his sturdy chest. She breathed in the familiar smell of leather and woodsmoke, his scent lapping around her like a soothing balm, blunting her sadness. Without his woollen tunic, the heat of his skin pressed through the gauzy linen of his shirt, warming her cheek as she rested against his chest. Her limbs became weak; the need to sink into his body teased her senses. Conscious of her own vulnerability, she pushed futilely against the enticing embrace.

'Nay, do not fight me now, *petite*. Just let me hold you.' His breath tickled the top of her head, stirring shining strands. Beneath her ear, his heart bumped steadily, a reassuring affirmation of life. Tears clustered around her eyes; she couldn't bear for him to see her like this, but her emotion would not be stopped. She wept openly, big, choking sobs, her fingers clutching the stuff of his shirt, working their way into the folds to cling as if on to life itself.

'Why does God let this happen? Why does it have to happen?' she gasped, flinging her tear-streaked gaze up at him.

'God's ways are a mystery to us, Eadita. We have to accept his decision.' The words mumbled up from his chest as he stroked her hair. Over the sweet perfume of her lustrous hair, he watched Geraint approach, holding aloft a wicker basket of food in greeting.

''Tis so hard.' She stood back abruptly in the circle of his arms, wiping away tears with unsteady palms, taking a juddering breath. She jumped as Geraint appeared, his ruddy face anxious.

'How fares the maid?' He gestured towards the bed, setting down the basket of victuals.

Varin shook his head. 'She lost the child.' Geraint's mouth set in a grim line.

'I must fetch the priest; he must christen the child so that he is accepted into God's house,' Eadita announced. Making decisions allowed her to stop thinking about what had occurred. Her practical nature often took over when grief was near. ' Geraint, would you stay with Margaret until I return?'

'Until *we* return,' Varin corrected her. 'It will not be easy to persuade the priest, given the child's mother. Why not let it go?'

'I think 'twould mean much to Margaret to have the babe christened, knowing that his soul would rise to Heaven. I would try for her.'

Varin nodded. 'Then I will accompany you.'

Back over the fields the pair trudged, Varin's large frame dwarfing Eadita's slight stature as they walked to the stone church nestled amongst the wooden houses and huts that formed the village of Thunorslege. Her father, Edwin, had insisted that all his manor follow the path of Christianity and had even installed a priest, Aelfric, to preside over the church and its services for the many feast days and festivals.

They walked along the field boundary, an easy path of flat

earth untouched by plough, bounded on one side by a drainage ditch that stopped the meadow waterlogging and a high stockproof bank topped by prickly hawthorn. Today, her mind disorientated with the traumatic events of the morning, all the evidence of her father's hard work slipped by, unnoticed.

Varin increased his step to walk beside her as the path widened, glancing at Eadita's solemn face, flushed now from the exertion and the cold. Despite the emptiness of her expression, so unemotional after her initial outpouring of grief, he knew she was in despair. Her fists bunched at the sides of her cloak; her mouth set in a determined line as she scanned the horizon ahead. She had firmly brushed his hand away when he offered his arm to help her over the rutted fields, the earth softening in the continuous drizzle. Aching to comfort her, wanting to kiss away the pain and sorrow that etched her delicate bone structure, he knew he should relish her indifference, knowing that his iron-clad self-mastery, imposed at his mother's desertion, lay in serious jeopardy. By witnessing Eadita's unselfish act in helping Margaret, by witnessing every deft movement of her experienced hands and every softly spoken command, he had begun to question his harsh initial judgement of the maid: that she was a wilful, spoiled bitch. With a jolt, he suspected he couldn't be further from the truth.

The rhythmic ringing of metal on metal from the blacksmith's forge concentrated Eadita's mind on the cluster of houses and huts before her. Her innards echoed noisily; seeing the stream of peasants spill out to the fields reminded her that it was not long after the noon repast. The walk tired her, the rain soaked through the thin leather of her slippers and dribbled down the neck of her gunna, lending her garments an unforeseen heaviness that dragged at her feet. The faster she tried to walk, the further away the church spire appeared. A stultifying weakness invaded her limbs; the sustained effort of attempting to keep level with Varin's commanding strides began to erode her strength, and she stumbled. She didn't even come close to the ground. Varin's mighty arm hooked her up, his sensual radiance scalding her back, before she wrenched away to face him.

'Thank you,' she murmured, her eyes studying the darkened hem of her gunna made sopping wet by the long grass.

''Twas my pleasure,' he commented drily, studying the pearl-like lustre of her skin, the well-defined bow of her lips a dusky rose against its brightness. Her lashes fell spikily over cat-like eyes as she heaved her ethereal violet gaze to his. Varin's heart pounded, the beat bumping faster, heavier, against the muscled inner walls of his chest. His emerald gaze riveted her to the spot, once again awe-struck by her beauty, an angel in this godfor-saken country. A need burned in his loins and seized his vitals, a need to lay her down in the spongy vegetation and make slow, sweet love to her. A rigorous tremble yanked through his body as he fought to curb the powerful attraction.

'Will you let me go!' Eadita demanded imperiously, breaking his mood. He lifted both hands sardonically and waggled his fingers in front of her face.

'*Mam'selle,* I hold you not!' Flushing, she realised it was true. It had only been his dragon-green scrutiny that held her in thrall. 'Well, make haste then,' she snapped, realising her mistake, 'the priest will not wait for ever.'

'Such a temper, *mam'selle,* in one so little,' he chided gently. 'But 'tis understandable in the circumstances.'

'I don't need your sympathy. I have witnessed scenes such as that before.' The slight pressure of his fingertips on her arm prevented her moving.

'Listen to me, Eadita, you don't have to be so brave all the time. Not many women would have done what you did today, especially one so high-born. You helped Margaret when no one else would.'

'Aye, that may be so,' she acknowledged, 'but Margaret is no better off than if she had whelped on her own. She has no child to show for all her labouring.' Eadita hung her head sadly, tears threatening once again. Varin released her hand, moving to cup her beautiful elfin face, her skin feather-like under his large thumbs. Eadita registered the flare of desire in his eyes as his face moved closer.

'You've no strength left in you, maid.' The green flare of his eyes searched her face. Did his amused expression mock her, knowing that she had expected a kiss? That she would welcome it? 'You haven't eaten all day,' he persisted, 'and if we continue plodding in this manner, you'll be in no state to meet with the priest, let alone argue your case.'

Her stomach lurched at his kindness. Why did he seem to care so much for her? As much as she wanted to resist, a small part of her welcomed his nurturing concern, his protection. Pulling the edges of her cloak together, she viewed him warily.

Varin's widening smile crinkled the corners of his eyes. 'Don't look so suspicious, maid. 'Tis my own stomach that is hungry too!' He stopped her returning his words with a flat palm, inches from her face. 'Nay, do not answer. We must eat, not talk. You can thank me later for having the presence of mind to snaffle this from Geraint.' The wicker basket dangled from his lean fingers, as he nodded in the direction of a barn a few steps off their path.

Eadita almost squealed in delight as Varin's decisive fingers pulled off the muslin wrappings to reveal floury rounds of bread, pork pies and slices of cooked meat, her stomach growling in anticipation. She ate with gusto, her neat hands breaking the crusty bread to offer a piece to Varin, before taking a bite herself. The dusty scent of hay permeated the two-storey barn, evoking the endless, balmy days of summer. A few bales remained on the top floor where they sat, wisps of hay swirling around in the draught from the uncovered window. Varin, his thick shoulders braced against the wall, stretched the muscled length of his leg out before him, crooking the other leg so he could rest his forearm. The flexed planes of his face sat in shadow as Eadita sat cross-legged opposite him upon the billowing softness of her cloak, the skirts of her gunna spread demurely as she selected one delicious morsel after another.

'Careful, mistress. Do not make yourself sick.' Varin's amused eyes glinted like emeralds through half-shuttered lashes.

''Tis unlikely,' she informed him between mouthfuls, 'I have always had a healthy appetite.'

'No doubt due to all that exercise in the forest,' he remarked drily, taking a bite of crumbly cheese.

'I like to run, to walk, to feel the wind in my hair,' she defended herself. 'I hate feeling trapped, day in, day out, by the stone walls of the manor.'

'And for that I do not chastise you, mistress. But 'tis unusual in a woman.'

'I had a brother; we grew up with the forest around us; 'tis a part of my life.' Did she tell him too much?

'Had?'

'Had,' she fabricated bitterly, guiltily. Thoughts of Thurstan reminded her of all the reasons why she should not be sitting alone with Varin, sharing a meal with him. She brushed away the speckles of loose flour that had fallen from the bread on to the napped lavender-coloured wool of her gown. 'Let us talk of other things. I am sad enough today.'

Varin prowled her exquisite features, solemn with memory. She would not confide in him, refusing to drop her guard. It annoyed him, but at the same time, he admired her determination. They ate without speaking for a few moments, the silence comfortable between them.

'Do you think Geraint will be able to cheer Margaret?' Eadita spoke suddenly.

'Aye, Geraint will know what words to choose. He is used to women.'

'As you are.' The words spilled before she could stop her tongue.

One dark eyebrow quirked upwards. 'Is that what you think, *mam'selle?* That I endlessly court the company of women? That I spend my days rampaging through a raft of whores?' His words pierced her with their crudeness, unsettling the easiness between them. 'Why does it not surprise me that you hold me in such high esteem?'

She flushed, cornered. 'Nay, 'tis not what I mean. You deliberately misunderstand me.' His accusations stung her. 'You handled Margaret well today. I just didn't expect it.'

'You didn't expect a battle-hardened, sexually experienced, full-blooded male to help. Is that what you mean? Is your understanding of men really so limited?' Yes! She wanted to scream at him, yes!

'For God's sake, Varin, I am trying to thank you.'

'I know.'

His leather jerkin creaked a little as he leaned across the middle of the half-eaten food. She didn't draw back. The lean angles of his face loomed close to her own, his flinty eyes holding her within their emerald spell, pillaging her mind of all sanity.

A butterfly kiss. A kiss of understanding. A kiss of friendship. That was all it was supposed to be as his lips claimed the pliable nectar of her own. Blissful awareness seeped through Eadita, enervating her exhausted limbs. The heated brand of his lips flirted insistently with the fragile edges of her mouth, beguiling, searching…for what? For some clue that she was different from all the rest? He lifted his head abruptly, feasting on the polish of her skin, the jewelled brightness of her eyes, the rapid breath from parted lips. He groaned, the enchantment of her lips too strong to resist. His capable hands curved around her neck, fingers snaking into the damp tendrils of hair, anchoring her head to his own. Suddenly on their knees, facing each other, she gasped as a controlling hand at her waist sealed her to him. His tongue drove into her slightly parted mouth.

Reason tried to tell her that the pain of the last few hours had destroyed her defence mechanisms, that Varin took advantage of that fact, but she would be lying. Instead she swallowed greedily at the vital energy pouring into her as the kiss inflamed the flickering, life-enhancing passion that danced along her veins. She hated him. She wanted him.

Weakened with desire, she fell back against a cushioned dome of hay. His wide bulk followed her down, sprawling heavily across her. She relished the feel of him, the possessive set of his shoulders enclosing her in a wild, passion-filled cocoon. Lean fingers at her throat yanked at the lacings, sweeping the bodice from her shoulders. A nub of lust scrolled stealthily within her, innocent in its tardiness. His well-defined lips tracked the length of her collarbone, plundered the hollow of her throat. She threw her head back, allowing him greater access, savouring the intensity of the moment as the wet strands of his hair cooled her fevered skin.

His hands, running over her as if he had no sight, marvelled at the lean lines of her petite, honed body. She shuddered as a big palm neared her breast, then rounded it, a blistering graze through layers of clothing. His fingers shook as he tore down the bodice of her gown, the tattered threads trailing uselessly in the still air, as the pale globes of her full, high breasts were revealed.

'Mon Dieu!' he whispered, his breath scorching her breastbone, his eyes dilated to obscure their brilliant green. Her body arched upwards as his lips claimed one rosy-tipped nipple.

Eadita moaned. The sound whispered out from her barely parted lips, swollen from his kisses. Desire gripped him anew, an incandescent fireball. He had to have her, to possess her, to consume this woman who tortured his every waking moment, tempted him at every turn, a seductive will o'the wisp. Then he would be rid of this incessant craving, this perpetual hankering that forced him to forget his loyalties, to forget his duty. Self-control fled. Grabbing the hem of her gown that bunched around her knees, he pushed it higher, running his hand along the flimsy length of stocking until his fingers met her warm, silken thigh.

Eyes closed, Eadita began to thrash her head from side to side, uselessly searching for something she did not know the answer to. The knowledge of their identity had long since fled. She was a woman. He was a man. Blood pounded through her veins, her pale skin flushed with passion. The well of desire had spread and widened, bursting now into a swirling whirlpool of need, a maelstrom of craving that scampered along the fringes of her consciousness.

'What do you do to me?' she gasped, as his fingers inched towards the centre of her womanhood.

'You're about to find out, maid,' Varin growled, his voice heavy with unfulfilled lust. He lifted his body to loosen his *braies*.

The church bell tolled in the distance, sonorous, a warning.

Maid. *Maid.* Her frenzied mind clutched at his drifting words, a rope of safety dangling before her. She was a maid, a virgin, about to offer her body to a man she hardly knew, a man who, not three days ago, she had despised. Now she stretched raggedly beneath his muscular weight, breasts bare, legs spread wide beneath his burgeoning manhood. Grim reality insinuated itself, thrusting its unwelcome presence into the logic of her brain.

'Nay, nay, Varin. 'Tis not to be!' Her voice, tremulous at

first, yelled at him in panic. Her clasping hands now thudded on his back, trying to break the spell. 'Nay, Varin. Do not do this! Remember who I am, who you are! 'Tis not to be!'

Her words stilled the urgency of his actions, sloshing over him like cold water. He collapsed on to her, taut with passion, drawing on the very limits of self-discipline. She squirmed uselessly under him, trying to wiggle away from his intoxicating weight. He pushed her shoulders roughly to the floor, stilling her upper body movements, lifting his chest away from her bared breasts.

'Do…not…move!' he breathed, teeth clenched, 'unless you wish this to continue!' Beads of sweat appeared on his brow. Her limbs quieted, wrung out with desire, her emotions punched and tattered.

He cursed angrily, mangled frustration gripping him as reality engulfed him. Her words rang true. He forced himself to breathe deeply, to bridle the coursing tide of blood that pulsed at breakneck speed around his body, before raising his tawny head. Still conscious of the breadth of him against her body, she stared aghast at the brilliant anger in his eyes, the rigid set of his mouth.

''Tis fortunate that you stopped me when you did, my lady. For by now you would be maid no more.' He rolled away from her, adjusting his trousers, his expression empty. Sitting up shakily, she followed his stilted movements with dismay, still wanting him, missing his big body covering hers. If only circumstances were different, she thought. If only I hadn't a brother who I must protect at all costs, if only he weren't a Norman. If only.

'I am sorry,' she mumbled, eyes downcast. 'I…I changed my mind.'

'Never, ever, do that to me again!' His disapproving tones iced her spirit. 'For next time I will not be able to stop.'

'There will be no next time,' she vowed numbly.

He came beside her in a moment, dropping to his knees before her as she tried to hold together the ragged remains of her bodice. He gripped her chin with forceful fingers, wanting to strangle her.

'Unfortunately for us, mistress, our bodies crave what our minds do not.' She flushed guiltily. He tracked the colour seeping into her skin and nodded. 'Aye, mistress, you know it, as I do. We are not finished.'

Chapter Twelve

Gronwig peered gloomily at the horse's rump rolling in front of him; steam rising from the gleaming hindquarters in the weak sunlight. All day, the hunting party had been pelted with driving rain; now, as they returned to Thunorslege, the weather began to improve. At least he had been spared Lord Varin's watchful presence, although Count Raoul rode with him and the rest of the nobles from the Shire Court who had elected to take advantage of Gronwig's hospitality. Hopefully, he'd be relieved of the Normans soon enough, if Thurstan had accomplished his mission in Exeter. If he had successfully murdered the King, then the French would almost certainly pull back to London and the West Country would be his once more.

'Father, Father, wait for me!' Sybilla's thin whining hailed his ears on the breeze. His lips curled sardonically, remembering his amusement at the rare sight of his daughter in the early morn, dressed in practical clothes and ready to join the hunt. All day she had clung to her poor, unfortunate mare, slipping and sliding as she fought to retain her precarious seat in the side-saddle.

Pleased to take a rest, the Earl reined in his stallion and prepared to wait for his daughter. He frowned as he cast an irritated glance over the wobbling ox cart that carried their scant pickings; only two deer and a wild boar. Every so often the wheels of the cart bounced over a log or dipped into a rut, threatening to disgorge its bloody contents on to the path. Judhael and his men rode some distance away, laughing and joking after the exhilarating thrill of the chase.

''Tis a pity Lady Eadita did not join us today.'

The Earl turned his pallid features towards the arrogant set of Raoul's head. He hadn't realised the knight had reined in beside him.

'The chit never learned to ride, more fool she.'

''Tis surprising. She seems so accomplished in other matters.' An unmistakable slur threaded his words.

'Sybilla is the horsewoman in the family.'

Raoul could scarcely contain his sneer as he watched the ungainly advancement of the Earl's daughter. 'Twas not an attractive sight.

'Maybe lady Eadita will join us afterwards?' Raoul suggested.

The Earl shook his head. 'Nay, the chit has too much work to do.'

''Tis a pity to see such a beautiful noblewoman working as a peasant.'

'What do you know of it? Remember, you are a guest in my house.'

'A guest on the King's orders.' Raoul's words held a threatening timbre.

'You are my bodyguard. William and I struck a deal. He agreed to send a battalion to Thunorslege for my own protection.'

'Aye, and we fulfil that duty. It doesn't stop me looking around at what's on offer.'

'What do you mean?'

'I want your niece for my wife, my lord.' Raoul yanked viciously on the reins to stop the nervous dancing of his horse, his bloodshot eyes narrowed obsessively.

'Why on earth would you want her?' Gronwig returned lightly. *What was wrong with his own daughter?* 'The girl is a hellion, like her father, completely wild and uncontrollable. Now take my Sybilla, now she—'

'I like my women wild.' Raoul curtailed his words. 'There are ways and means of breaking a woman's spirit. The fun comes from doing just that.'

Gronwig smiled slowly, comprehension dawning. 'I know exactly what you mean, Count. But you might have to impress me more than you did yesterday in order to win her hand.'

Raoul flushed slightly. 'That boy was guilty and Varin knew it. He will do anything to contradict me.'

'And why is that?' the Earl asked smoothly.

'Because I contest Lord Varin's right to be a baron. William took him and his base-born brothers under his wing when their whore of a mother deserted them.' Resentment edged his words.

'So, there is dissension in the Norman ranks.' The Earl eyed the Count, sensing his weakness. 'How can you persuade me to give you my niece's hand?'

'I have money,' Raoul offered, 'and my father has lands in Normandy that will eventually be mine. Naturally, I would be happy to take on Thunorslege; it would provide an excellent dowry for your niece. Our King is eager for Anglo-French marriages to strengthen his realm.'

'I'm sure he is.' The Earl smiled, his thin lips stretching over the yellow pegs of his teeth. Very soon the King would be an insignificant memory, if his plans unrolled with no complications. He just had to wait. Idly he wondered how loyal Raoul was to William; it might be interesting to offer him Eadita in return for his…help.

'Good afternoon, Count.' Sybilla finally pulled up, gasping, her face blotched unhealthily with exertion. Raoul scowled, forgetting his manners. He would have to pursue his suit at another time.

'My lady…' he nodded, pinning a facile smile upon his features '…you are enjoying the hunt?'

'Well, not exactly enjoying…' Sybilla started to moan, before she remembered her audience. Initially disappointed that Lord Varin had not joined them, she had quickly decided that Raoul was handsome enough to fritter away the time with.

'You go on, Father,' she hinted boldly. 'We are slower than you.' Raoul concealed his irritation at being forced to accompany the maid; to refuse to ride with her would be the height of rudeness. The plump angles of Sybilla's face beamed in delight at her orchestration. She turned coyly towards Raoul, allowing her cloak to fall away to reveal the tight-fitting lines of her gunna. Raoul pressed his horse into a slow walk, low branches rasping along the leather at his shoulders.

'What were you talking to Father about?' questioned Sybilla, intent on engaging him in conversation.

Raoul looked at her coldly. 'About marrying your cousin.'

Sybilla's face suffused with colour, deathly white followed by a fiery red. Her fingers twisted aggressively in the reins as she strove to repress her rising temper.

'What…! Are you insane? That girl is fit for nothing!'

'I can think of plenty of things she is fit for!'

Sybilla couldn't fail to notice the insinuation. The urge to scream and shout in childish outrage gripped her like a seizure. Why did Eadita always gain the attention? None of the Normans, nor any of the Saxon thegns, paid her any regard whatsoever, yet she was just as attractive as her scrawny cousin.

'Well, if that's what you're after, then why didn't you just say?' Quelling her ill humour with a sultry look in his direction, she cast her lashes downwards in mock subjugation. She wasn't about to let another man drop through her fingers.

Raoul absorbed her obvious behaviour with faint surprise, aware that the noisy bulk of the hunting party had moved on much further ahead of them. An Earl's daughter, no less, he chuckled to himself, offering herself up for a bit of fun. His eyes raked the padded curves of her face, the yellow locks snaking from underneath her veil, then travelled the length of her body. She was not Eadita.

'Another time, perhaps.' His mouth twisted derisively, as he kicked his heels into the horse's flanks. The blatant snub flooded through her like physical pain; it was if he had slapped her. Oh, cousin, Sybilla vowed silently as she wrenched her mount towards the manor, I will make you pay for this.

Aelfric the priest burped extensively in the confines of the vestry, a coarse appreciation of the excellent noon fare he had recently gorged in the main hall. The food had definitely been one of the more positive aspects of taking up residence at Thunorslege. Pushing through the dusty vestry curtain, he glanced at the kneeling figure and bowed head of Lady Beatrice, lost in prayer. He had almost forgotten her silent existence, her mouth working endlessly in silent prayer, as he resumed his task of changing the old candle stubs for new ones.

Aye, Thunorslege had been a fine place for him to settle. Here, he could dabble in a little underhand debauchery with the girls in the village without attracting too much attention to the infringement of his ordination. In truth, young Ailith had been quite delectable last night. Such firm, delicious limbs! He could hardly believe his luck!

The sensual pathway of his thoughts halted as the aged wooden door at the end of the aisle creaked open and a couple entered. Lady Beatrice appeared not to notice, elbows resting motionless, hands clasped against her forehead.

Aelfric's heart jumped excitedly as he recognised Lady Eadita, the perfect oval of her face shining luminously in the half-light, then plummeted as Lord Varin ducked his sun-streaked head to avoid knocking it on the stone lintel. In the shadows, his impressive musculature appeared like the devil, a devil with an angel at his side. Only his bright flaxen strands, contrasting strongly with the chestnut locks of Eadita, allevi-ated the hellish suspicion. With deliberate slowness, Aelfric bent over to place the handful of candles back into the rush-woven basket at his feet. Rising again, he ran his sweating palms down the front of his greasy, food-stained cassock be-fore turning to his visitors.

'I bid you good day, Lord Varin, Lady Eadita.' He nodded to each in turn. 'How may I be of assistance?'

Eadita began to explain the events of the morning. In the tense walk from the hay barn, Varin had agreed to remain si-lent when they met the priest. For the moment, he kept that promise, resting one hip idly against the end of a pew, his long legs reaching out to cross at the ankles. As Aelfric listened, head cocked to one side and a sly smile touching his lips, he watched only the fiendish cast of Varin's face. A *frisson* of fear chilled his body.

'Whose babe did you say it was?' Aelfric hadn't heard the last of Eadita's words.

''Tis Margaret, the stranger from the Shire Court yesterday.'

Aelfric crossed himself fervently and took a step back, nearly tripping over the hem of his cassock. 'She is marked.' The ominous timbre in his voice boded ill as he started to shake his head.

'She has a club foot, Aelfric,' Eadita explained wearily. 'She is no more akin to the Devil than you or I.' The priest's eyes bulged at her blasphemous statement.

'My lady, you seek to link us with…that women! I can do nothing, save pray for both your souls.' His vehement glance encompassed Varin. 'You have put yourselves at great risk be-fore the eyes of God.'

'But…but…you must help her!' Eadita's fingers sought the end of the pew, trying to draw strength from the whorls of intricate carving she touched. ''Twill be the only good that comes from her labouring.'

Aelfric snorted. 'I will not do it.' He couldn't resist running a sneering, lascivious look down the length of Eadita's body.

'Enough!' roared Varin, drawing his short sword; an insidious rasp of steel hissing through its leather sheath. The sound echoed hollowly around the stony confines of the church. Hoisting the dumpy figure of Aelfric up in a grasp of fabric, Varin pointed the tip of his weapon inches away from the thick vein beating in the priest's neck.

'You *will* do this,' Varin commanded. Aelfric's feet thrashed above the wooden floorboards, kicking the dust into whorls that puffed like ash against his dark hemline. One hand reached out to try and secure the edge of a wooden pew to lever himself away from his captor, but he did not succeed.

'Lady Eadita, help me!' Aelfric floundered, his tone beseeching. 'Can't you see that it goes against everything the Church teaches us? What would your uncle say?' He gulped noisily as the sword tip pressed a little deeper.

'The Earl does not need to know.' Varin gave a half-smile. 'And you believe that baptising this child goes against the teachings of the Church?'

'Aye, that's what I said.'

'And how does the Church view your activities in the village?' Aelfric's mouth dropped open. Eadita looked at Varin in surprise.

'I…er…what are you implying?' Aelfric stalled.

'That you engage in sexual congress with a number of women in the village on a regular basis,' Varin stated in clear, sonorous tones. A wild puce colour suffused Aelfric's pasty skin.

'I…I…' he spluttered.

'Now, I'm sure you value your position here, and would

not wish the Earl to know about this behaviour…so…?' Varin let the question hang.

Aelfric slumped in defeat. 'I will do it.' He dropped his head. 'But not here, I will perform the baptism down by the river.'

'And the burial?' prompted Eadita.

'Aye, that as well. But Earl Gronwig must not hear of it.' He didn't bother to await their reply, but turned towards the vestry. 'I will fetch my cloak.'

As the curtain flapped behind him, Eadita jabbed an accusing finger at Varin.

'You promised not to intervene! There was no need for violence!'

'That was not violence, *mam'selle,*' Varin countered angrily, unwilling to forget the priest's lewd perusal of Eadita. ''Twas merely gentle persuasion. Do you think he would have agreed otherwise?'

'I know Aelfric well enough. Words would have worked eventually.'

Varin folded his arms high on his chest, his eyes impassive, mesmerised by the fervent pulse at her neck. 'What would you have me do, Eadita? Stand by and watch him insult you with his eyes and speech? Would you have it so?'

Her heart jolted, her body still carrying the flush of their intimacy. 'I'm surprised you care after—'

'After what you did? After what *we* did? With hindsight, 'twas a blessing that we stopped, my lady, but I cannot say that I didn't wish it. 'Tis naught to be sorry about.' His eyes glowed possessively. 'I will not stand by and let that priest treat you with such—' His gaze skimmed the top of Eadita's head, a movement in the shadows arresting his speech. Beatrice stood at the church door, one hand on the heavy iron latch, one hand pulling her veil hurriedly across her features.

'Damn! I had no idea that someone else was here!' he muttered, frowning, before raising his voice to acknowledge the woman. 'Forgive me, *madame,* I was unaware of your presence. I am sorry you had to witness that scene.' Distracted by his tone, Eadita turned to follow his glance, smiling in relief as she recognised her mother.

'What are you doing here?' She skipped along the aisle to hug Beatrice, lifting solace from her comforting scent.

'Same as I do every day, daughter. Praying for Edwin…and for Thurstan.' She had dropped her voice to a whisper, one hand fumbling with the cumbersome door latch. 'Let me leave, Eadita. I am in no mood to meet your companion.'

'Let me help you with this door, my lady.' Varin materialised beside them. Beatrice clutched at Eadita, pulling her closer as if using her as a screen from the imposing warrior.

'Varin, step back. You frighten my mother!' Eadita ordered, wrapping a reassuring arm about her mother's shoulders. Varin ignored her, a distant memory stirring as he regarded Beatrice's lowered profile. 'Varin, my mother has been in mourning for some time. She is unused to public scrutiny.' Eadita raised her voice a notch, annoyed by his lack of action.

Varin took a step back. 'Forgive me, *madame.* But I think we have met before? Your face seems familiar.'

'I have my daughter's likeness, 'tis true, my lord.' Beatrice kept her eyes downcast.

'Aye, 'tis true, but your voice is different. You are French, are you not?'

'I speak French, as all the nobles do in England.'

'Nay, *madame,* you mistake me. 'Tis the clarity of your accent. You were born in France?'

He examined her reaction closely, scrutinising her features that were so like Eadita's. Of the same height, their heads together, the two women could almost pass for sisters. A violent trembling had seized the fingers that held the veil close to her face. Now, he was almost certain they had met before, in another time, another place.

'Varin, leave my mother alone,' Eadita chastised him. 'She *was* born in France, but she's not a barbarian like you…' Her words faltered.

'I am sure I have met you before,' Varin repeated sternly.

'I would have remembered one such as you,' Beatrice whispered. ''Tis not possible.' Eadita frowned. Was it her imagination or did her mother's voice hold a thread of fear?

'No?' Varin drew his brows together. He shrugged his shoulders as if discarding the thought. 'No matter. It will come to me.'

Thudding hoofbeats approaching at great speed outside the church made the three twist in unison. Responding to the loud shouts, Varin reached for the door first, wrenching open the rain-swollen planks. Hubert de Bonneville, King William's squire, faced him, breathing rapidly. Behind him, his horse, foam-flecked from the exertion of the ride, pawed the ground irritably.

'My Lord Varin…' he began, then eyed the two women, unwilling to elaborate. ''Tis the King.'

'Stay there.' Varin's order was curt. Eadita and Beatrice, following his broad shoulders out into the tepid afternoon sunlight, stopped suddenly, blinking after the dimness of the church. Varin drew the young boy out of earshot.

Eadita faced her mother, confused. 'What happened back there, Mother? Why were you so defensive with Lord Varin? You were acting as if you have something to hide.' Beatrice shifted uneasily.

'You know I am unused to strangers. He is particularly imposing.' Beatrice placed a tentative hand on her daughter's arm, eager to change the subject. 'I haven't had a chance to say how sorry I am that you lost Margaret's babe today.'

'I'm sorry too, Mother.'

'Let me take Aelfric to Margaret, daughter. I'll make sure he carries out your wishes. Let me help you.'

'Are you sure?'

'I have spent too long in isolation. Seeing Judhael again has made me realise that my life must continue alongside my grief. I'm just sorry you had to deal with Margaret's labouring on your own.'

'Not quite on my own.' Tight-lipped, Eadita allowed her gaze to roam reluctantly over Varin, towering head and shoulders above the squire, firing off questions in rapid French. If only she had been alone with Margaret, she thought, acutely conscious of the savaged remains of her bodice beneath her cloak, a shameful reminder of her wanton behaviour.

'What do you mean, Eadita?'

'Oh, 'tis naught. Only that he provokes me as much as he seems to vex you.' She turned to her mother with bold curiosity, but Beatrice refused to be drawn on the subject. Behind them on the threshold of the church, Aelfric cleared his throat noisily, pointedly riffling the parchment sheets of his Bible. He stopped fidgeting as Varin came striding back, his face thunderous.

'Something to please your ears, ladies.' His clipped tones rained down on the pair of them whilst he strapped his sword belt more tightly to his flat stomach. 'King William is ill. I must fetch Geraint and go to him directly.'

'My mother is to take the priest to Margaret,' Eadita offered, amazed at the anguish she saw in Varin's face. 'She can send Geraint back here.'

'Nay, there is no time. I have sent de Bonneville. Would that he had come to me sooner!' He ran an agitated hand through his blond locks, giving them a rumpled look. Already, the stable lad was leading a pair of saddled horses down the cobbled track from the manor to the village, scattering peasants as they shied away from the high-stepping hooves.

Varin turned to Beatrice. 'Thank you for helping with Margaret. Lady Eadita has had enough heartache for one day.' Eadita looked up sharply, trying to read his strained expression. What had he meant by that?

Placing two hands on his horse's neck, Varin leaped into the saddle from a standing position, evidence of the latent power in his big body, scissoring his legs to snare a foot in each stirrup. Under snug *braies,* his muscles bunched tightly to weld his body to the horse.

'No chain-mail?' she remarked lightly, trying to conceal her admiration at the formidable sight of him on horseback.

'As I keep saying, *mam'selle,* no time.' He hit her with the words. 'I can only pray that we don't run into any outlaws.' He threw her a hard look as Geraint sprinted around the side of the church, jumping on to his destrier, pulling hard on the reins as it bucked under his weight.

'*On y va?*' he questioned Varin. *Are we going?*

'One moment, Geraint.' Varin leaned down low in the saddle, reaching out to drag Eadita woodenly towards him. 'Keep yourself out of trouble, my lady, until my return. And I will return. I have soldiers posted around the perimeter of this estate, with instructions to apprehend you on sight. If I find you in the dungeon when I come back, your life will not be worth living.' His pitiless grip was uncompromising.

'I don't doubt it,' she returned with equal force, refusing to quail at his callous treatment of her. A roiling uncertainty wound around her chest, a strange feeling of bereavement that made her feel unbalanced. He examined her contemplative expression, her huge eyes paling to lavender in the bright sun, and grinned suddenly, harshly.

'Don't miss me too much, *chérie.*'

Chapter Thirteen

Several hours later, in the depths of the forest, Eadita chuckled, throwing another stick on to the fire. 'You would not believe it, Thurstan! Those dim-witted soldiers were looking for a lady, not a young boy dressed in rags. 'Twas easy to slip through their guard.' Her confident smile belied a deeper sense of guilt, guilt that she had gone against Varin's express command. But he need not discover her recent deception, for with any luck he would be miles away by now!

'You did well.' Thurstan stared at his beautiful sister, the elfin angles of her face mysteriously shadowed in the firelight. A tantalising drift of lavender wafted from her direction generating a keen sense of belonging within him: it was also his mother's scent. He longed to return to Thunorslege; he needed to go back home and be master of his family's lands once more.

'I would not have managed it with Lord Varin there. Or Lord Geraint for that matter,' she continued. 'But they were called away suddenly this afternoon. The King is very ill.'

Thurstan scowled into the heart of the glowing embers, his heart pounding. He still trembled from the magnitude of the endeavour he had undertaken yestereve. From Eadita's words, it seemed he was likely to succeed in his mission. The King would die. And it was all his doing. The sweat of his journey from Exeter still permeated his skin; if his sister had been just a few hours earlier he would not have been in the camp. He wanted to confide in her, but whispers of Lord Varin constantly at her side made him question her loyalty.

'Is aught amiss?' Eadita touched her brother's arm, aware of his unease.

'You have oft been seen with the Norman,' Thurstan stated, picking at the cross-lacings on his boot. Startled, Eadita caught the faintly accusing tone.

'Through no choice of mine. Who's been tattling?' Her voice rose a couple of notches, outraged that her brother should doubt her. Hunching her knees to her chest, she clasped her arms around her calves, linking her fingers tightly. Thurstan's keen eyes noticed the wary gesture, his lip curling scornfully. The darkness of the forest, once her friend, now seemed to alienate and push her away. She shivered.

'Wulfstan saw you returning to Thunorslege with Lord Varin and the other knight—the morning after you met with me in the forest. What in God's name am I supposed to think?'

'I haven't had the chance to tell you. They captured me as I returned from you. It became too dark for them to see their way, so we camped out, to return in the light of morning.'

'I see.' Thurstan replied tersely. 'But you know the way in the dark, sister.'

'Aye, but do you think I was going to let them know? By staying out all night, you might have been able to rescue me.'

'Granted.' He nodded. 'How on earth did they manage to catch you? You can outrun any man, even me.'

'Varin was faster,' she responded dully, aware of her brother's growing displeasure. His blue eyes mirrored her own, narrowing sceptically.

'Two errors in as many days, Eadita. Come on, sister, you can do better than this.'

'That's not fair, Thurstan,' she retorted. 'Varin was faster. No one could have foreseen that.'

'Aye, though for a big man he must be surprisingly fleet of foot.'

'Don't you believe me?' Eadita gasped. 'Do you think I just stood there and let him walk up to me? Don't you think I tried to escape? Good God, Thurstan, what has happened to make you mistrust me so?'

'I can't understand why he hasn't handed you over as a traitor. What possible incentive does he have in protecting you?'

Silence hung between them, thick with suspicion.

Why does Varin protect me so? thought Eadita. Does he think to gain the truth by watching my every move, vexing me beyond belief, driving me to distraction…by kissing me, making love to me?

'Had you but slit his throat when you held him on that first eve…' Thurstan murmured, drawing his knife to twist it this way and that in his palm. The blade glimmered evilly in the moonlight. 'You had the chance.'

'Aye, but I would not have killed him. All you want is the money, not needless bloodshed. Remember, we are not like the Normans.' Her eyes grew wide at her brother's ugly expression. Catching her astonishment, his face relaxed.

''Tis no matter anyway. He'll be finished by Saxon hand soon enough, if I have my way.' A chilling spiral twisted in her belly, a trickle of suspicion that something was seriously amiss with her sibling.

'What do you mean, Thurstan?' Her question sounded leaden in the still evening air.

'I will hold Thunorslege again!' Her brother seemed consumed by an unnatural greed; a hunger to claw back what he believed was rightfully his.

''Tis not possible. Everyone thinks you're dead; if you suddenly reappear you'll surely be arrested for your actions.

Even if you evade capture, you cannot hope to wrest the estate from such a powerful force; they are some fifty men strong, with reinforcements at Exeter.'

'The Normans are nothing without their leaders, dear sister.' How he ached to tell her of the plans that he and Gronwig had devised. Longed to tell her that the coin they purloined from travellers went straight into buying support to eventually overthrow the French, instead of going to help the poor as she thought it did. He hated keeping the truth from her, but her guarded behaviour made him uneasy. For the first time in his life he felt unable to trust his own sister.

'There's one thing I want you to do for me' he announced, bending his knees to sit in cross-legged fashion beside her.

'Name it.' Anything to mend this widening rift between them!

'I want you to destroy Lord Varin.' Eadita winced as the hate-filled syllables banged sonorously in her ears.

'W-what?' she stammered. A sparkling pair of dragon-green eyes impinged on her brain.

'You heard me, sister. I want you to kill him. Without implicating yourself, naturally.'

'By the rood, Thurstan!' Eadita grabbed his forearm, shaking it and forcing him to meet her eyes. 'You surely have gone mad! I will not listen to this nonsense!' He jerked away from her hold, eyes intense and brooding, seemingly consumed by a passion that would not release him, that shook him in its jaws like a dog.

'Eadita, just think on it! You are ideally placed within the manor, you have access to his sleeping quarters, to the food he eats. You know of the plants and herbs that would kill a man. No one would ever suspect you. No one knows of your double nature.'

'Except for him,' she announced calmly, though her mind reeled with the full implications of Thurstan's words.

'Exactly. The man knows far too much. And he is an accomplished leader, ready to take over from King William should anything happen to him.' She shook her head in response; Thurstan drew his brows together in consternation.

'Eadita, you must remember whose side you're on. From the information I've received, it would be easy to believe that you've forsaken the Saxon cause to secure a Norman husband…and a wealthy one at that.'

''Tis utter foolishness! Thurstan, stop this! Do not doubt me!'

'If what I say is ridiculous, Eadita, then you will have no qualms about killing the man!'

'This is pure blackmail, brother. It proves nothing about my loyalty as to whether I choose to kill a man or no. The simple fact is that it is morally wrong to do so; it goes against everything the Church teaches us—surely you can see this?'

'Methinks you betray your heritage,' Thurstan declared. She stared into the deep pools of his eyes and wondered where her brother had gone. His fingers curled about her hand to turn it palm upwards, tracing the lines tenderly.

'Look at the strength and determination in your hand. We share the same fate, the same destiny. We are two halves of the whole, we think alike, yet now I feel you draw away from me. Who or what has created this space between us? I like it not.'

Varin. Varin has created it, she thought. But she would never speak the words aloud. 'You imagine it, Thurstan. I would never kill a man in cold blood.'

'Eadita…' his tone became pleading '…you must kill him. I cannot bear to see our Saxon heritage disappear before our eyes.' And with all the Norman leaders dead, the remaining French will be easy to overthrow, he thought.

'I will not.' She pursed her lips in stubbornness, then jumped as Thurstan, enraged, stabbed the ground with the point of his dagger, causing an ugly gash in the soft brown earth. He strode off into the inky gloom. Eadita's eye followed his shoulders shaking with frustration, and sighed.

* * *

Agatha looked on in horror as Sybilla riffled through the oak chest of clothes, spindly fingers digging viciously into the colourful pile of velvet and wool. As she grabbed chaotically, her face contorted into a mask of gleeful vindictiveness. With no mind to the often delicate fabrics, she pulled voraciously, tugging at various garments and flinging the rest in a disordered mess to the planked floor.

'Aha! Now this one is definitely mine! So she thinks to steal from me, does she?' Sybilla wrested a bright green gunna from the jumble of material to try it against her figure. 'What thinks you, Agatha? It looks better on me than her, doesn't it?'

Agatha bent to sort out the clothes on the floor, her face stretched thin with tiredness and worry. The candles by the bed had burned more than halfway down, indicating that the hour was late. Where was her mistress?

'Why not decide what you want to wear upon the morn, my lady Sybilla? The night is near fully grown and I'm sure Eadita will gladly show you all her clothes on the morrow.' Momentarily distracted from her venomous task by the servant's voice, Sybilla turned her pale, watery eyes upon the diminutive figure standing beside the bed.

'Are you telling me what to do?' Sybilla's mouth curled into a tight, little smile, at once threatening and condemning.

'Oh, nay, my lady, 'Agatha rushed the words out to reassure her, hands fluttering up to her lined face. 'Pray, continue. Indeed, there is a lovely red gunna with green tablet embroidery, which certainly would suit my lady. Do you wish me to find it for you?'

'Nay, I'm having more fun doing it myself,' Sybilla replied, nastily. The gradual pile of rippling colour grew carelessly in the middle of the bedchamber and she relished the mess she had made. Since Raoul's rejection of her in the forest, resentment had begun to grow like a slow ulcer, threatening to burst its poison at any moment. 'Where is my cousin, anyway? I've had no sight of her all day.'

'I believe she visited her mother.' The lie crept easily from Agatha's lips.

'That old crone. Father can't stand her.' Agatha chose not to comment, more worried that Eadita would return at any moment.

'Why not take that whole chest to your own chamber, my lady? Then you might look through Eadita's clothes at your leisure. I can summon a couple of servants to lift it for you.' The eagerness behind her words carried too much strength. Sybilla glanced at her sharply.

'Why do you want to be rid of me?' Sybilla's eyes constricted warily. 'It's something to do with Eadita isn't it?'

A thumping at the door interrupted their conversation, making both their heads turn in that direction. 'Go and see who that is, Agatha,' Sybilla ordered, watching the servant open the door, nod her head, then go out in the passageway to mumble something to the unseen visitor.

A sound at the window embrasure startled Sybilla and she leapt around in astonishment as the leather curtain over the gap started to shake and bulge inward. Her mouth rounded in an astounded 'O' as a human form bulked the curtain out from behind and a shapely leg emerged from beneath the hem, toes seeking a foothold on the floor. A raft of cold air drenched the chamber as the material was flung aside and a mud-spattered, owl-eyed urchin jumped into the room.

'God save us! Help us! We are being invaded. Help!' Sybilla screamed out loud, failing to recognise her own cousin, face caked in mud and a large hat pulled over her brow. Agatha came running back into the room at the noise, leaving a confused servant clutching a wooden pail of steaming water in the corridor.

'Saints alive!' Agatha thought quickly and seized Eadita by

the shoulder to physically haul her across the room. ' I'll take this varmint down to the guards. He's little more than a boy.'

'Hold one moment!' Sybilla, recovering from her initial shock, spotted the gleaming chestnut plait that had escaped from underneath the boy's hat. 'Let me see that boy!' Her fingers flicked at the leather brim and she gasped in astonishment.

'Eadita! 'Tis you.'

'Aye, that's right.' Eadita chose her words carefully, trying to read Sybilla's mood. Her cousin's sly intelligence, coupled with a brimming jealousy, could not be underestimated.

'What had you been up to, Eadita? Obviously not visiting your mother…' her snake-like eyes flashed a heated look towards Agatha '…but what? And in such outlandish garments?!' Sybilla flicked the fraying cuff on Eadita's tunic, her brow furrowed in concentration.

''Tis none of your concern, Sybilla,' Eadita replied evenly.

'Ah, now that's where you're wrong, cousin. I've been watching for an opportunity like this, a chance to show my father the kind of woman you really are, and now you've landed in my lap, like a bird in a snare. You've been with a man, haven't you? Meeting in secret, you, an unmarried maid, trading your virginity like a common whore!'

'You're mistaken, Sybilla. I lie with no man.' Eadita shifted uneasily, aware that by allowing Sybilla to spring to her own conclusions, a dangerous situation had arisen.

'I don't believe you. 'Tis obvious what you are trying to hide. Why else would you go to so much trouble to conceal it? You're a slut, cousin, and this time my father will know it!' Eadita flinched at her cousin's vulgarity, her hate-filled words digging into her with the sharpness of a cat's claws. Sybilla grabbed her shoulder. 'Come on! I can't wait to hear what he'd going to say. Let's hope he punishes you well.' She clutched at Eadita's shoulder. 'Guards!' she shouted, 'Fetch the guards, Agatha, or I'll have you thrown in irons.'

'There is no need for this.' Eadita announced patiently. 'I will go with you willingly. It will take no more than a few words to sort this out. Just let me change into something more suitable to attend on him.'

'Oh, no. He might not believe me if you turn up all pretty and clean. He needs to see you like this. Come on.' Eadita threw a despairing glance at Agatha, but her servant just shook her head miserably. Both of them had run out of ideas.

Despite the lateness of the hour, a few people still lingered in the Great Hall. As Eadita hesitated on the threshold, Sybilla's ferocious grip on her shoulder pinched deep to steer her towards the high table. The acerbic nature of the smoke from the charcoal braziers, combining with the sweeter smell of woodsmoke from the fire, smacked sharply at the delicate hairs in her nose. Her eyes watered as she peered through the haze, discerning Gronwig slumped in his customary seat, listening lethargically to some item of gossip that the black-garbed Hacon, perched at his shoulder, was feeding him.

Raoul, seated on Gronwig's other side, was engaged in a game of tabula with another knight. Their hands flew quickly over the board, white bone pieces moving under Raoul's thick fingers, followed by the darker pieces as the Count's opponent took the lead. Other groups of men huddled around the hall, some playing tabula, others playing the easier game of nine men's morris. Mead flowed in abundance, and occasionally a roar of laughter would break open a huddled group as flushing, befuddled faces guffawed up at the ceiling before returning to the board games.

Other men had given up for the night, wrapping themselves in their furs to snore the darkness away. At least here, both French and English seemed happy in each other's presence, Eadita mused idly. If only Thurstan could see this now, the severe shaven heads of the Normans forming a strange contrast to the flowing Saxon locks.

Smiling faintly at some titbit of information Hacon had just spoken of, Gronwig chose this moment to glance around the room. His mouth dropped slackly as he witnessed the peculiar sight of his daughter, Agatha, and another common outlaw being brought before him.

'Daughter!' He greeted her benignly with an outstretched arm. 'I thought you had retired to your bedchamber. Have you been catching outlaws instead?' A guffaw of polite laughter rippled along the top table, the attention of the other guests momentarily snapped up. Eadita pulled herself straight and caught the eye of Count Raoul watching her intently.

'Nay, not an outlaw, Uncle. 'Tis I, your niece,' Eadita's melodious tones spoke clearly into the Hall, as she tugged off the hat and smiled at the stunned faces around her. Sybilla's expression turned from smug expectation to instant displeasure that Eadita had trumped her at the revelation of the prize. Gronwig's parchment skin surged with a chalky white, patches of red mottling his skin in anger.

'What is the meaning of this, Eadita?'

'She's been sleeping with a man, Father. I caught her sneaking into her chamber, dressed in this ridiculous garb.' Eager not to be upstaged once more, Sybilla jumped in before Eadita could cobble together a reasonable explanation for her bizarre outfit. Gronwig's fist slammed into the oak planking, causing the pewter mugs to jump and spill some of their contents. The mead spread onto the wood, soaking it with a dark stain, like blood.

'Who is it? Who have you been with?' Gronwig heaved out of his chair to lean accusingly towards her. Eadita shrugged her shoulders, exuding an aura of confidence that, in truth, had long since deserted her.

'No one, Uncle. 'Tis only Sybilla who believes otherwise.'

'And do you think I would believe you, you…you harlot, over my own daughter?' His spitting sibilance made her shudder slightly. 'Why would you dress in such a fashion unless you were trying to hide something?' His fleshy lips, wet with spittle, gleamed in the candlelight, his eyes accusing with an abnormal hatred. 'You want to remain hidden, to sneak around giving away your virginity…you *wanton!* What godforsaken star were you born under, to act like this? Your maidenhood is *mine,* do you hear me; it is mine, as your guardian, to give to your future husband. You have no right.'

Gronwig was consumed by an unnatural fury: his words, weighed heavy with the right of possession, caused a few bemused stares. Immune to these perplexed looks, he continued to rant. 'Now you are worthless, lower than the filth that is fetched up from the cess pit. You are the bane of my life, niece, and you will be punished.'

'I tell you, Uncle, Sybilla makes something of nothing.'

'What I see before me is not nothing. You are bent on defying me, niece, and this time you have gone too far. 'Tis time I found you a husband.'

Riveted by the spectacularly enticing sight of the maid dressed as a boy, Count Raoul leaned forward, resisting the compulsion to rub his hands in glee. He was enjoying her obvious discomfort and noted the small cracks beginning to appear in her icy composure. Soon it would be time to make his move.

'I do not intend to marry,' Eadita replied haughtily.

'Your intentions do not come in to it, dear niece. It's time someone took you in hand, tried to curb your wilfulness. But to merely hand you over to someone is far too easy; I must think of a more exacting punishment, something to really make you suffer.' Brows drawn together, Gronwig thought in the murky silence that closed around Eadita like an oppressive blanket. She bit on her lip angrily, realising the whole situation was spiralling out of control. She had given her uncle the ideal excuse to exact his warped revenge upon her and seethed at her own stupidity for allowing Sybilla to catch her.

'The trouble is, you are no longer a virgin; we cannot gain a high bride price for you. I ought to sell you to the highest bidder instead,' her uncle mused. His eyes widened, slapping his palm on the table as if struck by the brilliant idea. 'I ought to sell you to the highest bidder,' he repeated with a chortle. 'Aye, that is what I'll do, I'll sell you to the highest bidder. Some men aren't too fussy and you're pretty enough…once you're wearing the proper attire.'

'I would take her off your hand, my lord. Remember our conversation.' Raoul leaned forward ardently, feasting his eyes on the girl before him. 'She causes you no end of trouble, but it wouldn't bother me, damaged goods or no.'

'It's very gracious of you, Raoul, but I like my own idea in preference. Let us stand her on a podium, with knights and men from all around devouring her with their eyes, clamouring for her with gold pieces.' Raoul scowled in annoyance, slumping back in his seat. 'To give her straight to you would be too easy for her; there's no punishment involved. She needs to suffer for her actions, and I know that humiliation is the best way. Is that not so, niece?' Eadita clamped her lips together, jostled by the excited fidgeting of Sybilla beside her.

'Oh, what fun, Eadita!' her cousin chortled. 'To be sold to the highest bidder, like a lowborn slave. Which is more than you deserve, I warrant.'

Eadita's balance momentarily deserted her; she rocked on her heels as the fug of the Hall threatened to close in on her. She couldn't let this happen to her; she was far stronger than this. Raking the length of the top table with a disparaging look, she fought against the stifling atmosphere to challenge her uncle with a cold eye.

'Are you my father's brother to do such a terrible thing to his daughter? How can I ever call you "Uncle" again, as it implies a relationship between us that I no longer wish to acknowledge? You would sell me, your own niece, like a common slave with no goods to her name. You have judged me wrong, Uncle, for I would prefer to do that and leave this godforsaken hole, than to live under the same roof with a man who professes to be my guardian, yet protects me not; a man who has sworn to live under the moral code of Christianity, yet flaunts his position every day; a man who is selfish, greedy and conniving. You had no love for my father, nothing but jealousy and rage. You are a man who will surely go to hell itself.'

The condemning words thudded into the screeching silence like weighty stones, each striking fear into the collected gathering. The Hall held its breath as the people watched the Earl leave his chair unsteadily, and walk down from the dais to face his niece on the level. His very calmness denoted a fury that threatened to spill over at any moment, madness dancing in his eyes; a queer light, demonic in its instability. He dragged one podgy finger down his niece's cheek, before lifting a broad hand to slap her across the face, hard.

Chapter Fourteen

'He looks no better,' Geraint muttered. 'In truth, I fear he worsens faster. The fever has a hold as I have never seen before.' He dropped a wet cloth into the wooden pail at the side of the pallet bed and wrung it out before placing it again on the forehead of his King. The runnels of water dripped down his forearms, soaking the sleeves of his overtunic, but Geraint appeared not to notice.

'Damn it to hell!' Varin cursed, standing at the end of the bed. 'Where's that dim-witted monk gone now? I thought he said he could cure him!'

'He's gone to fetch the Abbot. I have a feeling he's run out of ideas…and methinks he's also scared of your threatening behaviour, Varin.'

'This man is now their King, Geraint. 'Tis their duty to save him. He cannot die now, not after everything he has achieved.'

'I agree with you, but ranting at the monks will not make his recovery faster.' Geraint pulled the downy sheepskin coverlet higher around the neck of William. The man in the bed lay very still, his dry lips chapped and bleeding, open a crack to allow a faint crackle of breath to wheeze in and out. His chest heaved mightily, exuding a tremendous effort to allow the next intake of breath: the smell of death hung in the air like damp, mouldy linen.

'This cell is not fit for a pauper, let alone a King!' Varin blasted, pacing the meagre length of the chamber in two short strides, cursing his own ignorance in the art of healing. Frustration consumed him; he had left William's side for less than a week and already his King was in danger. Curse the day that William had sent him away to Thunorslege! From now on he would not leave his side.

'I doubt he much cares for his surroundings, Varin. He merely struggles to achieve his next breath.'

'As long as it's not his final one,' Varin muttered, grimly. He closed his eyes momentarily, searching for his next move. He was reluctant to send out messengers to the other barons to form a close-knit guard around the King; that would be tantamount to admitting William would die. 'Where is that confounded Abbot?' he slammed.

As if on cue, the door swung back tentatively to admit a wild-eyed monk, preceding the more portly figure of the Abbot stepping over the threshold. Both were dressed in long wool smocks, heads shaved to indicate no indulgence in frivolity of any kind. They were men of learning, seeking to educate the masses, and had no truck with excitation of the spirit. Their drab appearance seemed to incense Varin further, although he struggled to speak calmly.

'He worsens, Abbot. Can you do anything more for him?'

Advancing into the cell, the Abbot shook his head. 'I fear the fever has too powerful a hold; 'tis up to the strength of the King himself to fight it now.'

Varin towered over the Abbot, but the smaller man stood his ground, though the monk by his side quailed visibly at Varin's shining presence. Suddenly Varin caught a faint, barely recognisable smell. Lavender! The pliable body of Eadita pressed up against his own! He shook his head to dispel the memory—why did she intrude on his thoughts now?

'Have you no gardens here, no plants that you can use?' Now why had he asked that?

'Aye, we have gardens, and some plants for medicinal purposes, but I can think of nothing more that can help this man... Yes, what is it, Brother Geoffrey?' He listened attentively to the man at his side. 'Ah, yes, now I think of it, there is one more thing you could try. I know a woman immensely gifted in the art of healing with plants. She dries the leaves to keep a steady supply through the winter and with her vast knowledge she may know of something that we do not.'

'Why didn't you tell me this before?' Varin grabbed the Abbot by the shoulders. 'Who is this woman?' He had a feeling that he knew the answer before the Abbot opened his mouth.

'Why, 'tis Lady Eadita of Thunorslege.'

The day dawned sunless, the morning wrapped in a drifting, scattered mist. From early morn, Eadita had stood by her window, a window now barred with fresh oak to prevent any escape, and had watched the village below stir to life. While the women lit the fires and kneaded the flat bread to break their fast, the men polished their knives and daggers in front of the newly curling woodsmoke, braiding their long Saxon locks with colourful ribbons anxious to look their best for the bride-sale. Eadita clenched her lips together and shivered in the thin linen shift that Gronwig had ordered her to wear. Already in the distance, she saw the bright banners fluttering wildly, marking the arrival of the first of the interested guests.

God in Heaven! Her infernal tongue had landed her in trouble before, but to openly malign her uncle in front of everyone had pushed him over the edge. She touched the sore patch on her left cheek. Marriage. The one thing she had battled against for most of her young life; the one thing she had argued consistently about with her father, until he finally agreed that her wilful personality was not worth inflicting on some poor nobleman. Gronwig had engineered the perfect degradation and with the help of his daughter; she was well and truly trapped. Even Agatha, moving softly about the chamber behind her, was silent, dry of her normally endless chatter and advice.

Where was Varin? She'd been glad to see him go yesterday, but the events of last night had drained her strength. Pushing vexed fingers against the wooden ledge, Eadita twisted back forcefully into the chamber, unwilling to acknowledge the path along which her mind tentatively stepped. She missed him. She needed his strength. Closing her eyes, Eadita imagined him standing beside her and caught the mingling scent of leather and woodsmoke, of pure masculinity. Appalled, her lashes flicked upwards. Why think of him? Varin would no doubt laugh uproariously at her predicament, relieved that she had finally gained her come-uppance. In times of trouble, in time of self-doubt, Thurstan had always been there, her ally, her confidant, her friend. Since when had the Norman Lord replaced her own brother in her thoughts? Berating herself harshly, she strode to the ante-room to splash her hot face with icy water. There must be some way out of this.

Poised on the edge of the heaving, eddying mass of people, a guard at each elbow, Eadita was not so sure. To her right, servants hoisted pigs on to spits, the mouthwatering smell of roasting meat contrasting sharply with the woodsmoke. Dogs lingered, scenting their next meal, trotting expectantly to circle the fires, before being chased away by screaming knots of children. Above their shrieks and cries, the gossiping and chuckling of the assembled crowd, travelling musicians could be heard practising the odd melody on harp, drum and lyre.

Eadita gave a wry smile. Gronwig had not missed the opportunity to make some coin from the occasion. Looking at the number of merchants who had set up their gaudy tents on the outer boundary, she was surprised that word had circulated so fast. Gritting her teeth, she set towards the makeshift platform where Gronwig and his entourage waited like vultures. The crowd, smartly dressed Saxon thegns and ragged peasants alike, fell silent as they parted like the biblical sea to let her step amidst them, a pale wraith of celestial beauty.

'Look, my lord, the harlot approaches.' Hacon nudged his master's shoulder.

'Good, she has kept us waiting with this rabble long enough.' The Earl adjusted his bejewelled finery.

'I don't understand why you continue with this parody,' Raoul grumbled loudly. 'I will have the maid anyway. Why not let me hand over the amount you want now?'

'You fail to understand, Raoul. The maid must be brought to her knees. This lowering of her status before her people is the only way to do it.'

'I know of many ways to bring her to her knees,' Raoul hinted darkly.

'Aye, Count, I am aware of your habits in the bedchamber…' the Earl laughed hollowly '…but they would not be for public consumption. There will be time enough if you mean to have her. Hold back your bid to let the maid suffer for a while. Let me have my fun.'

'Well, what are we waiting for?' Eadita demanded, as she mounted the steps to the platform. 'Let's commence with this farce, Uncle!' Her silken veil, secured with pearl-headed pins, drew attention to her calm, confident expression. As she raked her haughty gaze over the leering, upturned faces, every inch of flesh hummed with the demeaning parade, yet she would not show any weakness. Gronwig's face flushed angrily at her overbearing manner, then waved a ring-laden finger at Hacon. At his gesture, a cheer arose in the front semi-circle of the gathering, a cheer that gathered strength as it rippled through the crowd to its edges. Hacon cleared his throat dramatically, his black robes whipping like rags in the slight breeze.

'Here stands Eadita of Thunorslege, a woman who has brought shame on herself and her family name—'

'Speak up!' someone shouted from the back and the crowd tittered. Hacon adjusted the parchment held between his claw-like fingers and continued in the same dry monotone.

'She has defiled herself with another man, has given away her virginity before her uncle could decide on a suitable husband for her…'

'Shame on you, maid!' a hoarse cry emerged from the mass. Eadita's resolve quavered slightly at the unfairness of the situation; her eyes began to water in the cold, but she would not wipe the moisture away for fear of showing timidity.

'Continue!' her uncle rapped at Hacon.

'Yet she is a comely piece, beautiful as an angel—'

'Hear, hear!'

'If you can forget her insubordination.' The breeze whipped the stark linen against Eadita's womanly curves. Her nipples, hardened by the icy air, stood out against the clinging material, and the shadow of her womanhood was clearly visible. Gronwig's irritation increased at his niece's composure. By the devil! It would take a strong man to keep her in line. He traced the rigid, arrow-straight line of her back from the elegant curve of her neck, barely visible under her veil, to the backs of her leather shoes and willed her to crumble before the crowd, to plead with him, beg forgiveness from him. But she would not. He knew she would not.

'Ten gold pieces!' A young knight started the bidding. The Earl snorted.

'That is a pitiful amount, Guy of Widsham. Go back from whence you came—you haven't gold enough to afford the likes of her!'

'Ten gold pieces and a pig!' the blacksmith ventured, drawing a shout of laughter from the crowd. The Earl drew a linen square across his brow. How these country peasants tried his patience; Eadita's complacent smile merely goaded him further.

An unearthly hush cloaked the gatehouse as Varin, low in the saddle, thundered through on the greasy cobbles. He had ridden like the devil himself from Exeter, and now his horse foamed and snorted with the exertion of the breakneck ride. His fur cloak and leather *braies* spattered with mud, Varin drew the reins up short, causing his horse to buck and fidget against the harsh treatment, as he whirled the animal around in a tight circle, seeking a servant, a guard, anyone, to send for Eadita. He needed her.

Wisps of straw blew about the deserted stables as he led his destrier, calmer now, into the stalls. The animal needed to be rubbed down after the hard ride, but no servant or stable hand came forth. Snatching a bundle of clean straw from the floor, Varin removed the leather saddle and harness to perform the task himself. A growing uneasiness made him naturally cautious as he walked out from the stable, until he caught the roaring of the crowd.

Rounding the inner wall with quick, assured strides, his eyes immediately honed in on Eadita, standing high above a sea of people. He noted the dignified bearing of her sylph-like figure, the supercilious tilt of her chin, hands clasped defensively before her. A quivering fear streaked through him, memories transporting him to the forest when she had lain, scarcely breathing, after he had nearly drowned her. She looked so tiny, her dainty figure indecently shielded in a gauzy shift, her angelic features schooled with confidence as the crowd feasted their eyes on her figure, heckling and boorish. Crude words and gestures reached his eyes and ears as a savage blood-red rage filled his vitals, firing his mighty pace through the gathering as he shoved people this way and that, scattering them like fallen leaves, ignorant of the blasphemous protestations he left in his wake. His eyes never left Eadita; the compelling need to extract her from this evil mess pulled at his conscience, a rope of feeling that tugged at him more powerfully and more uncomfortably than anything he'd ever endured before. He liked it not, yet it drove him on.

'Ten gold pieces and a horse!'

'You obviously have no idea of the sheer beauty of my niece!' Infuriated, Gronwig propelled himself from the chair to stand beside Eadita. 'Why, just feast your eyes on this pretty figure!' In a single, violent movement, Gronwig grasped the neckline of the shift and tore savagely downwards with all the power he could muster. Horrified, Eadita sensed the material tightening on her shoulders, cutting into her skin, before the fabric ripped sickeningly to reveal her pale curves. As the crowd fell into a jolting silence, her fluttering hands sought desperately to piece the tattered fabric over her nakedness, a shameful roaring in her ears. Her lashes shuttered downwards to block her uncle's leering features. She wanted to die on the spot.

'*Sacré bleu!* You go too far!' A familiar, but ferocious voice swooped over her as an enormous fur cloak enveloped her shaking, trembling body. A rich masculine scent arose from the garment, at once steadying her agitation. *Varin!* Instinctively, she rubbed her cold cheek against the supple pelt, breathing in his nurturing smell, her tense diaphragm relaxing.

'What the hell is going on?' Tense with fury, Varin spat the words out.

''Tis how we deal with disobedience, my lord.' Raising his pale eyes, Gronwig threw him a sly smile. 'Sybilla caught Eadita sneaking into her chamber, dressed as a boy. She refuses to tell us where or who she was with.'

'So you thought you'd strip her naked in front of her own people? *Diable!*'

He faced the Earl with brutal scrutiny and took a menacing step forward. Gronwig, frightened, stumbled back into the arms of Hacon, who, unprepared for the weight of his master, skittered back into a nearby chair. The sight of the Earl sitting on his servant's knee spread a raft of giggling and tittering amongst the crowd, easing the tension. Varin towered over the pair as they fumbled to extricate themselves.

''Tis obvious she's been with a man,' the Earl insisted, pushing the scrawny frame of Hacon on to the bare boards, brushing fastidiously at his cloak.

Varin dropped a reproving glare on Eadita's white, drained face, the purple infinity of her eyes seeming to absorb his very soul. She lifted her chin defiantly, wondering at what punishment Varin would mete out. Suddenly the prospect of a weak, rich husband seemed infinitely preferable to this devil radiating fury beside her.

'Why?'

'I beg your pardon?' Gronwig frowned at Varin's question.

'Why do you think she's been with a man?' Varin's eyes remained fixed on Eadita. She flinched at the alarming ferocity of his gaze, a burning flush suffusing her cheeks.

'Hah!' Gronwig indicated with a belittling gesture. 'Just look at her—the shame is painted on her cheeks!' Eadita studied the floorboards, annoyed that Varin stirred her so easily. Gronwig continued. 'That's why she scrambled into her chamber in the dead of night—guilt!'

'Scrambled into her chamber, my lord?' Varin questioned drily. The Earl's eyes popped slightly as he realised the idiocy of his words. 'You say she climbed into her chamber... from the window embrasure?'

'I...er...' The Earl faltered, throwing a glance at Sybilla. His daughter nodded wildly.

'It's the truth, Lord Varin. She scooted through the window like…like a spirit.'

'Then she must have wings.' Varin gestured with a long, leather-clad arm to the back wall of the manor, raising his voice so that the spectators would catch his words. 'The chamber windows are at least thrice my height from the ground; the wall is flat stone.' He laughed. 'I doubt very much that I could climb it, let alone this feeble maiden here. Methinks you might be seeing things, *mam'selle.*' He bore Sybilla with a pointed look, and she cringed. Someone cackled loudly near the platform and a low doubtful mumbling began to hum amongst the spectators. Gronwig started to look sceptical.

'I know what I saw!' spat Sybilla, rising from her chair.

'Well, at this moment, it matters not.' Varin faced her. 'I don't give a damn what the lady Eadita has or hasn't done. I just need her to come with me now.' Varin had grabbed her upper arm to propel her away.

'Lord Varin—' Gronwig rose from his chair '—I bid you to stop!' His squeaking voice rose a notch, irritated that his niece should be absolved so easily. Varin turned, his tall, commanding figure sweeping Eadita around with him. 'You cannot just march in here and drag Eadita away! Why, I have hundreds of potential husbands gathered here!' His arm swept over the crowd. Varin threw him an icy look.

'There will be time enough to find her a husband…later. I agree she needs one. But right now, I need her skills to help with the King. Our King.'

The Earl's eyes blinked rapidly. 'I…er…but…but, the girl's a whore, Lord Varin. She must be punished.'

'Oh, I assure you, my lord, she will be punished.' Varin slanted a mindful look in her direction. Her stomach looped. 'But I wouldn't want to jeopardise the life of King William because we tarried to find lady Eadita a *husband.* Would you?'

Gronwig slumped back in his chair, shaking his head.

'I smell a rat,' Raoul's guttural tones attacked Varin, his eyes narrowing with suspicion. 'She was with you the other night, wasn't she? She says nothing in order to protect you and you protect her. I'm right, am I not?'

Varin laughed openly, appraising Eadita with a scathing look. 'Do you really think I'd be interested in the likes of her? A termagant half my size with a tongue like sandpaper!' He rolled his eyes, as Eadita bit her lip. 'Nay, Raoul, our King is ill and the monks assure me that, surprisingly, Lady Eadita has the skills and knowledge which may help him. Which is why I need to escort her to the monastery. Now.'

Raoul stood in Varin's path, toes inches from his. 'You don't fool me, peasant. Just remember to keep your hands from her. That one is mine.' He placed a possessive hand on Eadita's shoulder, eyes seeking approval from the Earl. Varin swatted his hand away comfortably, pulling Eadita further into his lean flank as he turned once more to Gronwig.

'I would watch your step, Earl Gronwig. My men will keep an eye on proceedings here until I return. The King will hear of your behaviour.' Varin began to descend the steps, his arm around Eadita's shoulders.

'Aye,' Gronwig muttered tauntingly to Varin's retreating back, 'if he is still able.'

Chapter Fifteen

'You didn't need to do that,' Eadita puffed out, as Varin dragged her at a headlong pace towards the manor.

'Nay, I didn't,' Varin snapped. 'You don't deserve my help when you seek to disobey me at every turn.' He stopped abruptly, allowing her slight weight to run into his large frame. 'I should have left you at the mercy of those animals.'

'Why didn't you?' she mocked, nerves jangling. Thank the Lord that he hadn't!

'Because unluckily for me, my dear lady, I need your help.'

'Well, I didn't need yours,' she muttered, stung by his arrogance. 'I can look after myself. You needn't have bothered.'

One eyebrow slashed upward. 'I'll have that back then, if I needn't have bothered.' Varin whipped the cloak from around her shoulders, tutting theatrically at the muddy hem where she had trailed it along the ground. She flushed in embarrassment as he raked her boldly delineated curves beneath the fragile torn linen. 'How much was he planning to get for you?'

'Stop it!' She pulled at the sides of the shift over her spilling breasts. 'How can you defend me up there, yet lower yourself to the rest of them down here?'

'Because you're asking for it with your wilful ingratitude. I didn't see anyone else stepping in to help you.'

Her slight figure slumped as the fight drained out of her. He was right. No one else had stepped in to help her, Saxon countrymen who she had grown up with, families who she tended to in their sickness, children who she had helped bring into the world. They had stood and laughed and jeered at her. She sank to her knees in the soft ground, her skin burning with shame, wanting to curl up and sleep. How could Varin, a man who had arrived in Thunorslege as her enemy, have saved her from this nightmarish ordeal, an ordeal imposed by her own kith and kin? Sometimes it seemed that he was the only person in the world who cared for her. Covering her face with her hands, she shook her head from side to side, her loose hair swinging down to cover her face.

'Eadita, what's the matter?' Concerned, Varin crouched down at her side, touching her gently on the shoulder. But he knew the answer. He had seen the way she had held herself before the crowd, her proud, defiant stance refusing to be bowed, refusing to acknowledge the utter degradation of her circumstances. All her inner strength had been mustered to maintain that dignified bearing; now she was clearly exhausted, spent.

'That was horrible. Horrible.' Tears streamed from between her fingers, dripping down over her wrists

'Don't, Eadita. Don't let him see you beaten.' Hooking one hand under her arm, aware of her body trembling with reaction, he raised her easily to her feet, swinging his cloak back around her shoulders.

'Why did you disobey me, Eadita?' he asked softly. 'Why did you leave Thunorslege when I told you not to?'

She hung her head, ashamed that she had defied him. Ashamed that he should see her brought so low. Ashamed of her own people who had refused to help.

'If you hadn't left Thunorslege, then you wouldn't have been caught.'

'I know,' she replied miserably, looking down at her shaking hands, before flinging tear-washed eyes up to him. 'If it hadn't been for you, I would be sold for marriage by now.' Her voice shuddered. 'Thank you, Varin. Thank you for helping me.'

'De rien,' he replied simply. It was nothing. Securing his cloak with a jewelled brooch at her neck, he cast a harried look at the position of the sun in the sky. ' We have wasted too much time already,' he muttered, almost to himself.

'What do you mean?' Eadita asked, the tears drying on her face as she began to recover her composure.

Varin began to walk again, pulling Eadita in his wake. 'What I mean, dear lady, is that you owe me. Thrice I have saved your skin, now 'tis time to repay.'

'What would you have me do?'

Varin stopped, surprised. 'What, no protest, my lady? No objections, no complaint? I should spring to your mercy more often.'

'I said I would help, Varin. Don't make too much of it.' Preceding him through the outside door of the manor, Eadita realised that she wanted to help him. As he had helped her. Was it possible that her hatred of the Normans had blinkered her to the true qualities of this man?

Varin stared down at her neat head, relieved that the regal carriage of her bearing had returned. Now, more than ever, he needed her support.

'King William is gravely ill.'

At his words, she turned towards him, balanced on the first step, her eyes on a level with his chin, noticing the reddish-blond bristle about his jaw. Dark shadows hung beneath the green flare of his eyes, tired lines creeping from their corners, the tightness of concern around his mouth.

'You are worried?' The question fell unbidden from her lips.

'I am worried, Eadita. William lies in a Benedictine monastery on the outskirts of Exeter. The monks are renowned for their healing skills…' she nodded, knowing of the place '…but they are confused by the King's symptoms. The monks said that you would have the knowledge, and I beg you now, my lady, please accompany me to William's side. I cannot lose him.' The echo of vulnerability and despair in Varin's voice astonished Eadita. She hesitated, digesting the full import of the job he asked of her.

'You obviously hold your King in high regard,' she replied slowly, trying to give herself time to think. She was prepared to help…but with the King?

He looked astounded. '*Of course* I hold my King in high regard. He is my friend as well as my sovereign.' Desolation flickered in his eyes as he scanned her face for signs of assent. Her continued silence irked him. 'You have no choice anyway. You can either come willingly or unwillingly. Would you rather me drag you by your hair, or be escorted in comfort?'

'You just cannot ask me nicely, can you?' she jibed at his boorish words.

'Christ in Heaven, Eadita! I've tried asking you nicely, but pretty words don't seem to work with you. Brute force often seems to reap more action!' He pushed frustrated fingers through his tousled hair, making him seem younger, more vulnerable. 'What do I have to do to persuade you to come with me willingly? Push aside your sentiments, forget who I am, forget who William is, except that he's a sick man in need of help. Help him like you helped Margaret.'

'Please?' she murmured.

'Please, Eadita.' His large hands enfolded her smaller ones. 'If there's to be any peace in this country, then the future rests on William being alive. His condition weakens by the hour.'

Eadita gathered the fur cloak around her small frame decisively.

'I will accompany you, my lord, because I cannot allow a life, anybody's life, to slip away from me without trying everything. But do not grow any ideas that I am growing fond of your Norman regime by these actions.'

'God forbid that I should ever think that.' Varin laughed joylessly.

He rushed her up to her chamber, waited outside the door while she changed her clothes, then barged in to watch her gather up muslin bags of dried plants and herbs as he rattled off the King's symptoms with grim dexterity.

'Let me come with you, my lady!' Agatha watched the couple's hurried movements in concern.

'Nay, you would slow us down!' Varin responded so fiercely that the servant cowed in dismay. Next he was bundling Eadita down the stairs to the stable block.

'Saddle the Lady Eadita's horse!' he shouted at the stable lad, who looked distinctly frightened.

'Er…!' the poor boy stuttered at the commanding tone.

'Come on!' ordered Varin. 'We must be back in Exeter before night falls.'

Eadita placed a steadying hand on his arm. 'Twas unusual to see this Norman knight so agitated. 'Varin, slow down! Listen, I have no horse. I cannot ride.'

Varin groaned, raking agitated fingers through his hair, leaving it sticking up all over the place. '*Dieu!* Well, my lady, you weigh less than nothing…you'll ride before me!' He effectively silenced her protests by throwing her up as a haphazard package on to the horse's back, Eadita clutching on to her various bags of herbs and a sack of personal belongings she had insisted on bringing.

Varin rode relentlessly, his big body bent hard around her own, his muscled torso pressing into her back, his iron-hewn arms encasing her firmly. Despite the speed of the journey with the freezing wind whipping her cheeks and her shawl wrapped tightly around her head to cover her ears, she allowed herself to relish the protection of the large frame behind her. After a couple of hours of hard galloping, her body drooping with fatigue and muscles aching, they arrived in the courtyard just before the four o'clock bell.

Eadita assessed the man lying before her with a practised eye, dimly aware of Varin in the corner keenly observing her every move. Even in the silhouetted candlelight of the monk's cell, a sheen of perspiration coated William's face. She grappled to overcome the enormous significance of the situation: the King of England totally in her power. A man who was her enemy, who she had sworn to hate. A man who she now had to save. As if reading her thoughts, Varin spoke.

'Don't even think to try it.'

'To try what?' Her purple orbs lifted innocently to his.

'Brother Geoffrey, the infirmarian, will watch all that you give him.'

She sighed. 'Do not doubt me now, Varin. I helped your men when you first came to Thunorslege. And you too. I could have poisoned you all if I'd had the inclination.'

'Don't remind me.' His bleak eyes explored her face, luminous in the flickering light. 'I take no chances with the King of England in your care.'

Eadita shrugged her shoulders. 'As you wish. I can only do my best.'

Varin folded his arms high, tilted his shoulders back against the wall. His head nearly touched the ceiling. 'Just make sure that you do,' he responded drily.

Laying a featherlight hand on William's forehead, she was astounded at the heat emanating under her fingers. 'We must bring down this fever immediately. Geraint—' she acknowledged the other warrior standing patiently by the door '—please fetch me some more tepid water.' Turning to Brother

Geoffrey, she began to rattle off a list of plants. The monk shook his head sadly.

'We've tried all those, my lady,' he announced tonelessly. He spread his hands apologetically.

Without warning, William yelled out and bent double as if seized by a terrible cramp. His broad face contorted in agony, his mouth dragging down at the corners to release a terrifying howl before he dropped back, exhausted, on to the mattress. Words started to spill from his lips, rapid and meaningless as he clawed uselessly at the air, trying to ward off some unforeseen evil.

'*Dieu!* What is the matter with him?' Varin had sprung to William's side at the first yell, and now gripped his sovereign's shoulders in an attempt to calm him.

'How long has he been like this?' Eadita demanded, searching Varin's worried face.

'He's not done this before. 'Twas the monks' inability to control his fever and breathing that made me come for you.' Eadita's heart jumped. It almost sounded as if he cared for her. She smothered the feeling as swiftly as if had arisen. Her tapered finger traced the blueness of a vein down to a fast pulse, her brow furrowed. The loose drooping sleeve of her woollen gunna dropped back with the movement to expose the tighter fitting sleeve of the underdress, emphasising the fragility of her wrists, the slenderness of her skilled hands.

'He's deteriorating rapidly.'

'For God's sake, Eadita, tell me something that I don't know!'

'I think he's been poisoned.' She held William's limp, sweating palms between her own dry hands.

Varin looked stunned. 'Nay…nay, 'tis impossible. He's too closely guarded at the Palace.'

'All his symptoms point to a plant called cowbane. His cramps, his hallucinations, his tight breathing.' She glanced at Brother Geoffrey, frowning. 'But 'tis rare hereabouts. I know of only one place where it grows near Thunorslege.' And that was hidden deep in the forest, she thought.

'I've not seen it.' The monk clasped his hands before his cassock enthusiastically. 'But, my lady, I think you might be right. The symptoms are correct…'

Varin was shaking his head. 'Nay, the King's food is always tasted. And the taster suffers not.'

'What about drink? A clear juice can be extracted if the leaves are pressed hard enough.' Varin sent her a hunted look. 'Does he have his own cup?' He nodded. 'Varin, cowbane is deadly. If I don't treat him with an antidote, he will suffer an agonising death, his lungs eventually paralysed. Let me try; I think I am right.'

'And what if you are wrong?'

'Varin, I can't promise anything, but you have to trust me on this one. Trust me.' Varin searched her deep, limpid eyes, trying to plunder the depths of her thoughts. To trust this woman, this beautiful, frustrating creature, when she trusted him not, seemed almost too great a risk. He shrugged his shoulders.

'I have no choice, Eadita. Do not fail me.'

Breathing in the scented, rain-laden air, Eadita followed the coarse, grey habit of Brother Geoffrey, his arm held high with a spluttering brand of straw and animal fat that cast an eerie glow over the medicinal herb garden. The breadth of different species would have filled Eadita with delight and curiosity on another occasion, but now her heart filled with dread at the task that she had to fulfil. Varin's words tripped over and over in her anxious mind. 'Do not fail me. Do not fail me.' His own regard for the King had astonished her; the depth of feeling mirroring the bond between herself and Thurstan. Was it possible that Varin might understand why she protected her brother, why she kept the truth hidden? But would Thurstan understand why she strove to save the King?

'Over here!' Brother Geoffrey summoned her to a corner of the garden, where he had found the bush of common rue. Eadita's heart leaped when she saw it; she hadn't thought to bring the plant in her bag as it was rarely used for healing. Grasping the succulent stems, she tugged out a large bunch of the foul-smelling plant, the rounded leaves blue-grey and glaucous.

Once back in the simple austere kitchens, watched closely by Brother Geoffrey and Geraint, she boiled the grey-green petal-shaped leaves in a vat of spring water, and pounded the plant until the juice had all but been extracted. Lifting the wreckage of the spindly matter left from her work with a well-worn wooden spoon, she made to carry the pot towards the monk's cell where William lay.

'Let me.' Geraint took the heavy pot as she staggered away from the fire with it, the cast-iron hook swinging above the flames. They heard William shouting and yelling as they approached the chamber. Eadita glanced apprehensively at Geraint, his face set as he walked alongside her.

'What if I am wrong, Geraint? What will Varin do to me?'

'Fear not, my lady. Have faith in your healer's knowledge.'

''Tis easy to fail,' she ventured, recalling Margaret's baby.

'Nay, my lady, 'tis easier not to try at all. Varin knows that.'

The foul-smelling liquid had cooled a little by the time Eadita sat on the small stool next to William. His breathing had quickened, and he was flushed and sweaty after his last hallucination. Occasionally he twitched violently, as if reacting to some terrible dream.

'I will try and spoon the liquid into him,' Eadita explained, almost to comfort herself that she did the right thing. But common rue was not a poison itself, of that she was certain. Dipping the cup-shaped pewter spoon into the pan of liquid at her feet, she carried it carefully to the King's lips. He sucked at it greedily, so she fed him another few spoonfuls.

'What now?' Varin asked impatiently. He had stopped pacing, an ineffectual practice as he covered the width of the cell in two great strides, and had come to stand by the bed, one hand braced against the wall. His linen shirt creased around the leanness of his torso, evidence of his agitation.

'Now, we wait. The effect is not immediate. I must keep feeding him this liquid.' William stirred fitfully, then sighed, drawing Eadita's concerned glance. 'You must be patient, Varin. Stay quiet now, for I need to concentrate.'

As the evening's hours stretched into full night, Eadita lost all track of time as she fought to save the sick man's life. Barely aware of Varin's brooding presence, she soothed William as the painful, feverish chills racked his broad frame, sponged the cloying sweat from his brow and spooned the life-giving elixir between his cracked lips.

It was only when she felt Varin's firm touch on her shoulder that she realised she had fallen asleep, her head pillowed in the bed furs, her hands clasped round those of the King, as if together, they both silently prayed for his life.

'He seems cooler now,' Varin immediately reassured her, pressing her down as she tried to rise. 'Why don't you rest? The hour grows late.' The brilliance of his jade eyes met Eadita's as she lifted her gaze to his.

'Aye, there is a chamber next door,' ventured Brother Geoffrey. Eadita jumped. Unaware of the monk's presence, his quiet, modulated tones came as a shock. Trying to reap some order from her sleep-fuddled mind, she laid a palm against the King's brow. He did seem cooler, less agitated. But she also knew that the devilish properties of a strong poison such as cowbane could fool even the most experienced of healers.

'I'm not sure…I'm not certain he's over it yet,' she murmured doubtfully. Exhaustion began to fog the outer reaches of her mind.

Varin grinned wryly. 'Believe me, my lady, I would bring you back again *tout de suite* if I thought anything were amiss. But now I think you need to rest.'

Eadita nodded, glad of his command. 'Then I will go…as long as you promise to watch him…and watch him closely.'

Varin tapped lightly on the door of the monk's chamber. No reply. He tapped again, more insistently this time. *Dieu!* He hadn't been aware of how much time had elapsed. Maybe she'd already fallen asleep? Maybe she'd…? Shoving his weight against the door, he burst into the room, scanning the contents with a flick of his eye. One empty pallet bed, furs and linens stacked neatly at one end. One chest topped with a bowl for washing. No Eadita.

'I'm here.' Her tone was faintly mocking.

He whipped around, his vibrant eyes seeking her petite form in the gloom. She carried a jug of water.

'How fares the King?' A flicker of worry threaded her voice.

'Aye, he's mending. Geraint is with him.'

Eadita squeezed carefully past him, conscious of the bulk of him filling the doorway. He followed the gentle sway of her hips as she walked to the chest to put down the jug, the curling end of her plait bouncing seductively on her hips.

'Did you think I'd flown the nest?' She faced him. What was he doing here if William was improving? Her fingers sought the cool edge of the chest behind her, the smoothness of the wood calming her sudden excitement at his nearness. The walls of the chamber shrank in his presence.

'It crossed my mind,' he replied lightly. Placing the flat of his sinewy hands over his face, he tried to smooth out the tension, the tiredness. Blue circles under his eyes lay evidence to his exhaustion. In one stride, he moved from the doorway to sit at the head of the bed, leaning his leonine head back against damp stone. The predatory glitter of his eyes unnerved her, as did his feral silence. A jittery tingling stirred her body.

'Do not trouble yourself,' she said drily, commenting on his lack of manners. Remember what he thinks of you, Eadita, she reminded herself sharply. A termagant with a tongue like sandpaper. I mean nothing to him, except what I can do for his King. He wants information from me; he will stop at nothing to attain it.

'I came to tell you not to worry,' he murmured, his eyes half-closing. 'William breathes easier now.'

'I'm glad to hear it.' Even to her own ears, her voice sounded clipped, defensive. She turned her back on him to pour the water from the jug into the earthenware bowl, slopping it over the edges.

'You may well have saved his life. We owe you a great debt.' Disloyalty clanged in her ears; what would Thurstan's reaction be to the news that she had held the King's life in the palm of her hands?

'I want nothing from you.' Her words hung in the air…too long. Twisting about, Eadita realised that Varin had fallen asleep where he sat. Guiltily, her eye roved over the length of him, knowing that she should shake him awake, throw him out, castigate him for his familiarity. But at the back of her mind, she knew that they were beyond the game of pretend chivalry, of lords and ladies, of easy-going, platonic friendship. A rough-edged desire flirted continually around their relationship, a smouldering fire that neither of them could totally extinguish. The awakening knowledge that behind the fierce, warrior-like exterior beat the heart of a man capable of much tenderness began to nibble away at her.

She inspected the taut lines of his shadowed face at length, a face that had taunted her, goaded her, frightened her. Had kissed her. Her heart lurched. His mouth had relaxed into a tempting curve, the fullness of his bottom lip vulnerable in sleep. Tracing the muscular column of his neck, a strong pulse beating in the dip at his throat, she marvelled at the way his broad shoulders stretched the fragile linen of his shirt. Maybe it wouldn't hurt to let him sleep for a while.

Turning, she removed the pearl-headed pins securing her headrail before soaking the linen cloth in the freezing water to wipe her face and neck. Checking that Varin still slept, she undid the end of her plait, letting the coils of silky hair loop out from their confinement. Rummaging in the embroidered bag that dangled from her waist, she drew out her ivory comb to deal with the dusty snarls in her heavy hair.

At the sounds of water splashing, Varin half-opened his gimlet eyes, momentarily forgetting where he was, what he was about. His breath caught at the glistening sight before him, a gleaming mass of chestnut tendrils spilling down to the maid's hips. Eadita's pale, delicately jointed hands contrasted strongly with the darkness of her hair as she bent to one side to tackle the mass of tangles. His groin jolted.

'Damn! Forgive me, my lady!' He rose abruptly from the bed, rubbing his eyes.

Startled, Eadita looked up, trying to wrench her comb through a particularly awkward knot.

'Oh, 'tis no matter.' She pulled at the comb, now stuck fast. 'Oh, curse this confounded hair!'

Varin smiled, coming to stand behind her. 'Here, let me.'

She jumped as he detached the comb from her impatient fingers and began to work at the jumbled strands. As the silk of her hair whispered against his fingers, he felt his own tension at his King's ill health begin to seep from him. The knots dispensed, he began to sweep the comb from the crown of her head to the base of her spine, his knuckles brushing the flare of her hips, one palm steadying her head.

Eadita gritted her teeth as the smouldering flame ignited. His warm fingertips against her skull set a tingling awareness racing once more along her veins. The inside of her mouth felt paper-dry.

'Enough!' Eadita turned violently, surprising him, breaking the sweet sensation. He stood mere inches from her, the heat of his body mingling with her own. 'I thought to let you sleep, that's all.' Her tone sounded defensive in its feeble reasoning. Her need to seek pleasure from him, his body, his lips, shimmered close to the surface.

'Why, my lady, did you want me to stay?' Varin laughed huskily, taking a step back to study her face, both refusing to acknowledge the jagged outline of desire circling his words.

The silence grew, rounding in its potency. Eadita refused to meet his eyes, knowing her expression would betray her, proclaim without a doubt the pure joy she derived from his gentle hands. Yes, yes, yes, I want you to stay, she yearned to scream at him.

'God in Heaven, why do you bewitch me so?' he murmured shakily.

'You said it wouldn't happen again,' she breathed, admitting to the spiralling, heady feeling that strung between them, knitting them together.

'You have an element of responsibility in this as well, sweetheart. It normally takes two people.'

Her violet eyes were huge, fathomless pools of purple liquid. He wanted to drown in them. Drawing a deep, shuddering breath, winding up the unravelling spool of his self-control, he stepped away from her, his green eyes shuttering.

'Nay, this cannot happen. I forget my duty.'

As I forget mine, she thought dully. My duty to Thurstan, to my kinsmen. Disappointment circled like an icy wind.

'Your beauty draws me, Eadita, but you'll always be a Saxon, protecting your own. I can't compete with that.'

'I'm not asking you to, Lord Varin. You are mistaken. I

have no intention of lying with you.' Every line of her svelte figure bristled with indignity.

'Then your speech tells me one thing, while your body and eyes tell me another. Which is the truth, Eadita?' He threw the comb down on to the chest with a clatter.

'Does it matter? There is to be nothing between us.'

'Nothing between us,' he repeated her words coldly, bitterly, as if he didn't want it to be. 'I fear 'tis almost too late for that.'

Geraint burst into the room.

'Come quickly, both of you.'

Chapter Sixteen

'Where in the name of God am I?' The strident, dominant tone cut across the chill air of the cell.

'My Lord!' Varin awoke with a start from an unsettled doze, a doze studded with odd dreams. In an instant he realised that William had recovered. Propping himself on one elbow, the healthy ruddy colour had returned to the wide planes of William's face; his riotous red hair and pale skin the only evidence of the poison's manic hold. Throwing back the furs with an impressively muscled arm, William swung his bare legs down on to the cold stone floor, the rough hessian chemise that the monks had changed him into barely covering his decency. The fine, blond-red hairs on his stocky legs fuzzed brightly in the feeble rays of sunlight filtering through the deep-set window.

'Varin! I am glad to see you.' The King smiled and rubbed his white-lashed eyes sleepily. '*Dieu!* Did we have a fine drinking night yestereve…or…?' William darted a puzzled look at his surroundings, beginning to scratch at his uncomfortable garment. 'What is this…this *thing* that I wear?' He plucked at the coarse material, the fine lines around his eyes creased in consternation, managing to ruck it up around his thighs as he tried to relieve the itchiness.

'My lord, are you injured as well?' Varin suddenly noticed a large purplish marking at the top of William's thigh as the King tried to find a comfortable sitting position on the edge of the bed.

'What? Oh, that.' William fingered the bruise-like patch on his leg. 'I'm surprised you haven't seen it before. 'Tis a mark of my birth. The mark of a bastard.' Born out of wedlock to a tanner's daughter and Robert, Duke of Normandy, William laughed roguishly. He scratched again.

'I need to take this dreadful garment off… Is this your idea of a jest, Varin?'

'No jest, my lord. You were brought here by two of your men-at-arms and your steward; you have been extremely ill.' Varin placed a restraining hand on his shoulder to keep him sitting on the bed. 'I would rest awhile; you must build up your strength.'

'You talk like a woman, Varin. I'm as strong as an ox!' William pushed his baron's hand aside and rose to his full height, half a head shorter than Varin, where he promptly swayed and sat down violently once more. Varin cocked his head, a wry smile touching his lips. William held his hands up in mock defeat.

'All right, all right, I relent.' He swung his legs back into the bed, and brought the furs over him once more. 'You better tell me what has happened…and…' his fingers sought again the abrasive material at his neck, leaving angry red weals on his fair skin '…get me something decent to wear.' Varin smiled once more. Even in sickness, the sheer dynamism of his King never ceased to amaze him. He picked up William's silk chemise, discarded on a chair, and helped him to change into it.

'You sickened three nights ago at the Palace; myself and Geraint were summoned back from Thunorslege by your squire when he realised that your life was in danger.' Varin explained.

'So…' William slapped him on the shoulder '…I am in debt to the de Montaigu family name once more, first the father, now the son.'

'You have more than honoured the debt to my father,' Varin murmured, remembering a twenty-year-old William, vowing to train up Sigurd's three motherless sons as knights in his court. Varin had been eight years old at the time.

'What illness did I have?'

'No illness, Sire. You were poisoned.'

'I should be dead then. No poisoner worth his salt would not give me less than something extremely fast-acting,' William replied bluntly.

'Your size helped; they obviously were unsure of the correct dosage for one of your magnitude, sire.' Varin grinned.

'Cheek, young man, will get you nowhere.' William cuffed the side of Varin's head playfully. His gaze drifted around the room.

'*Who* is that?' William demanded suddenly, noticing the sylph-like figure lying on a hastily constructed pallet in the corner. He sucked in his breath. 'God in Heaven! What a beauty!' He dropped his imperious tone a notch to avoid waking the woman. Varin's gaze travelled the same path as William's and a giant fist clutched at his heart, mashing it to a pulp.

Summoned back by Geraint the previous night, Eadita had not left the King's side, spooning the life-giving potion into him hour after hour. By the early morn, William had seemed calmer, but this time, she had refused to leave the King's chamber, instead seeking sleep on the pallet in the corner of the room. Now, her chestnut hair, shining in the cold morning light, lay in a silken, abandoned mass around her, cloaking her in its magnificence. The perfect oval of her pixie face lay turned towards the two men, a faint smile tracing the sensual curve of her lips. Flushed with sleep, her cheeks shimmered with a hesitant blush, almost matching the rose colour of her gunna that clung to her curves like a glove. Her hands were tucked under her cheek like a child. Varin was gripped by the sheer vulnerability of her repose, the magical enchantment of her beauty. He yanked his gaze away to focus on his King.

'That is Eadita of Thunorslege. The woman that saved your life. She has an uncanny way with healing plants.'

'Ravishing!' William finally announced in a whisper.

'Don't you believe it, my lord!' Varin warned derisively.

'Oh?' The king turned a raised eyebrow in his direction, 'Surely you are not about to tell me that you are unaffected by such a bewitching sight?'

'Nay…but the woman is an irksome nightmare. Believe me, I have been through much since I first met her. On our first meeting, she held a knife to my throat and threatened to kill me. I caught her again, dressed as a young lad, running like a young deer through the forests at Thunorslege. She climbs and wields a knife with practised skill. And she's definitely hiding something.'

'Incredible. I can scarce believe it, looking at her. Is her uncle aware of it?' William tried to settle himself against the straw-stuffed pillows. He was used to the finest goose feathers.

'Nay, when I went to fetch her, he was in the process of finding her a husband. Her cousin had caught her climbing into her chamber window, dressed as a boy. As a punishment, Gronwig tried to sell her into marriage to the highest bidder.' Varin tightened his sword belt, reluctant to recall his feelings from the previous day. 'There is not much love lost between the two of them.'

William's mouth went slack. 'What heathen practices is this country about? 'Tis like something from the Vikings' age.'

'Careful!' Varin reminded, his eyes crinkling with humour. 'Do not forget my father!'

'Forgive me, I was shocked. What else has Gronwig been up to?'

'He hints at things; I suspect his loyalty towards you is questionable. I have left soldiers at Thunorslege to watch over him.'

'I didn't trust him when I struck the deal over Exeter; with his mean little eyes, he would welcome me with one hand and stab me in the back with the other. I would rather have that one on my side. Her…unusual skills may be useful to us.' William's eyes assessed the sleeping Eadita.

'Wait until you know her, my lord. She's stubborn and pig-headed, refusing to listen to any rational argument or request. I have extracted her from more scrapes than I would care to name.' William smiled knowingly.

'I venture I have met her before someplace…her beauty is familiar.'

'Nay, my lord. 'Tis not possible. She is a Saxon; her father was slain at the Battle of Hastings and now it seems she is bent on avenging his death, mostly by giving me a difficult time.'

'Are you telling me that one so little gives you so much trouble? Why, I venture she doesn't even reach your shoulder!' William laughed.

'Her stature is not the problem, 'tis her tongue that gives me grief.'

'Aye, a tongue like sandpaper, if I remember rightly.' Eadita pushed herself up from the straw pallet, rubbing the sleep from her eyes. 'My lord, you have recovered.' Her delicate tone poured like soft honey into the chamber.

'My thanks to you, sweet lady.' William caught her hand as she approached the bed, and placed a kiss on it. His red stubble caught her sensitive skin, and Eadita drew her hand away quickly. She would not be simpering at this Frenchman's feet, even though he was the King of England. His fair skin stretched taut over his wide, chiselled face, his gaze direct and frankly admiring from the pale blue eyes. Noting the touch of grey at his temples, she thought him to be a little older than her mother, possibly approaching forty winters. Oblivious to

her dishevelled state, uncovered hair spilling in riotous abandon down to her waist, she fixed Varin with a glare.

'My job is done. I would like to go home now,' she announced.

Varin regarded her scornfully. 'What? And receive the
same treatment that I have just rescued you from?' William's
eyes narrowed keenly from the bed. 'Do not forget, *mam'selle,*
that we have unfinished business.' Eadita pinkened under
Varin's arrogant jade stare. 'Nay, you misunderstand me.' His
tone mocked her. 'We must return to the Palace immediately.
Do you think William is fit to travel?'

Annoyed that she had misinterpreted his words, Eadita
spoke grudgingly. 'I think you are mad to take him back to
the place where he was poisoned. Surely the perpetrator will
try again?'

'Exactly. And you, my lady, will help me catch that person. You know what to look out for.'

'But…but, I need to return to Thunorslege.' Thurstan
would be worried. Her mother would be worried.

'Despite the fact that you have saved my life, dear lady,
Varin tells me that you withhold information.' William's eyes
were fierce but kind. Eadita glared in disgust at Varin, who
stared back impassively. How dare he tell the King her secrets!
Momentarily distracted, she tried to keep up with William's
words. 'Help us catch the poisoner and we'll ask no more of
you. You will be free to return home if that is what you wish.'

Varin frowned, obviously reluctant to let her go so easily.
A thick burnished lock fell forward over his eyebrow; he
pushed it back impatiently as the two men awaited Eadita's
answer.

'It seems I have little choice,' she replied simply.

Emerging from the gloom of the monastery into the steely
light of day, Eadita smoothed down the graceful lines of her

rose-coloured overdress, before pulling the hood of her cloak over her head. She had managed to brush off the dried clots of mud from her skirts—the legacy of her precarious ride the day before; now it seemed she was about to embark on a similar journey.

'What is that?' Eadita stared pointedly at the grey palfrey standing calmly beside Varin's more fretful warhorse. Varin looked amused, his relief that his King lived palpable in his relaxed manner. He had obviously found time to wash, the wet strands of his hair spiking fiendishly around the arrogant set of his head.

'That, my lady, is a horse. Don't tell me you haven't seen one before.' Stepping over to the grey, he tightened the girth belt of the saddle with deft fingers. The lustrous wool of his dark green cloak draped over his wide shoulders with a sheen that indicated its expense, almost completely hiding the metallic glitter of his hauberk.

'Well, of course I have,' she snapped, eyeing the soft pink nose of the pretty animal as it snorted into the cold, damp air. 'I was just wondering why it was attached to your horse?'

'It has not escaped my notice, *mam'selle,* that despite all your skills, you have failed to learn to ride. In order to spare you yet another uncomfortable journey—' he raised his eyebrows '—I thought you might like to ride separately.'

'Attached to you.'

Varin sighed, watching the monks fuss around the King in the covered ox-cart.

'Tell me one thing, *mam'selle.* Is it your intention to be as awkward as possible on this journey because I have prevented you returning to Thunorslege?' Eadita folded her hands neatly, saying nothing. Varin groaned. 'I thought so. Eadita, the King has practically granted your freedom after you have helped us find the poisoner. Can't you wait that long?'

'Nay, I need to return to Thunorslege. My mother needs me there.'

'Your mother has Judhael to watch over her. You've noticed as much as I how he cares for her.' He frowned. 'Nay, 'tis someone else you need to see. William suspects you might be in some devilish plot with Gronwig.'

Eadita snorted disdainfully. 'Do you really believe that? After what he did to me?'

'Nay, I don't believe it. But with all your secrecy 'tis hard to deduce the truth. Now, enough chattering. We need to go.'

'But—'

Varin grabbed her by the waist, dumping her on the saddle as she ended her sentence with a squeak.

'Do not argue.'

St Oslac's Priory lay to the far south of Exeter, at a high point on the city wall above the salt marshes. Varin had summoned a strong guard from the Bishop's Palace where most of William's men were now quartered, to escort the small party from the outskirts of the city to the cathedral and palace at its centre. With customary enthusiasm, William had ordered a detour to view the proceedings on his new castle on the high volcanic mound on the north-east corner of the city, but Varin had forbidden it.

A faint, insipid drizzle had begun mid-morning, lending a misty gleam to all it touched, dulling colours and causing shivers. Knights in full armour carried large shields emblazoned with the royal crest, riding two abreast aside the cart in which the King lay, coddled in his furs.

Eadita had managed to stay on her little horse by riding astride and was fortunate that the wide hem of her gunna preserved her dignity. She hung on with a fierce grimness, convinced that at any moment she would be pitched over the animal's head and into the mire.

'You seem quiet, my lady.' Varin looked down at her from the great height of his stallion. 'Unusually so.' His horse, irritated by the painful slowness through the muddy main street, tossed his head from side to side in frustration.

''Tis not often I ride through the streets of the city under a Norman banner,' she retorted, conscious that the noisy throng of people caused her horse, and thus her, to press against Varin's flank.

'I had no thought that the market would be today,' Varin replied, annoyed at the mass of people who hindered their progress. Stalls had been set up along the thoroughfare in front of the townhouses, their walls constructed of drab red earth mixed with straw. Beggars held out their hands to the King's party asking for coin, their grimy faces stretched thinly from lack of food.

'There are stalls here every day of the week,' Eadita informed him dully. 'Trading ships and merchants come in every day.' Watching the faces move past her, bright with the excitement of haggling, she kept her head down, hoping no one would recognise her. She felt ashamed.

'Ooh, look, Martha, a Saxon lady, riding behind a Norman flag.' The wavering, accusing voice assaulted her. 'What have you done, missy with the dark locks?'

'Let me tell your fortune, my lady, otherwise be doomed,' another whispered.

'Traitorous whore.'

Eadita closed her eyes at the horrible words. Humiliation washed over her, threatening to break her stiff-backed composure.

'What's amiss?' Varin noted her shuttered countenance, pale and haunted.

'They think I'm your whore, Varin.' Her eyes laced with his. 'A traitorous whore.'

'God forbid,' he teased, trying to make her smile…or become angry. It wasn't like her to look so…so defeated.

''Tis no jesting matter, Varin. I have no wish to be here.' Her eyes pleaded with him to understand. She willed her hands to remain on the reins and not lift to brush away the bubble of tears that blurred her vision.

'We're nearly there.' Varin tilted his head towards the imposing stone arch of the Canongate, the main entrance to the Cathedral yard.

Passing under the arch, hearing the massive wooden gates thump behind her made her slump in relief. The jeering, clamouring sounds and sibilant taunts of the market crowds dissipated into the air. The massive stone cathedral loomed before her, its wide frontage decorated with painstakingly wrought carvings of fish, birds and beasts. The Bishop's Palace was built to the east of the Cathedral, the outside walls constructed of reddish Devon sandstone, darkened to a rough pink by the incessant rain.

The main group halted in front of the stable block, except for William's cart, which drew up as close to the main entrance as possible. Eadita heard the loud blustering tones of the King as the servants clustered around him, trying to help him out of the cart, but he threw them off with a loud roar.

'*Sacré bleu,* I can walk, you imbeciles! I am not dead yet, much as some of you would like me to be!' Pushing his sturdy legs out from the back of the cart, a couple of valiant servants managed to cling desperately to each of his arms. Before he turned towards the thick oak door, his keen eyes sought Eadita, still perched atop her horse.

'My lady Eadita!' he boomed, lifting a hand in acknowledgement. She smiled faintly. 'Please come and join me in a glass of celebration…I must thank you properly for your most excellent ministrations!' Eadita's heart sank. She had hoped to slink away from prying eyes to the privacy of a chamber. But she was to be allowed no escape.

The strapping figure of Varin appeared at her side, the feral gleam of his green eyes sparkling in the shadows of his steel helmet. Pulling off the restraining headgear, his hair sprang out with golden vitality, circling the proud set of his head with a radiant lustre. Her fingers itched to smooth his wayward curls and she gripped the reins even tighter to prevent the instinctive movement. Her eyes sparked in irritation.

'Why did you tell the King about me? I thought you said you would tell no one.'

'I've told you before, he's more like a brother to me. I knew he would be fair with you.'

'So it would seem,' she agreed reluctantly. 'I thought a spell in the dungeon might have been likely.'

'I was surprised he let you off so easily,' Varin grinned. 'I would have pulled out all your fingernails.' Was it her imagination or was he trying to cheer her after her humiliating ride through the city?

'Ugh!' She shook her head, smiling.

'You did save his life, Eadita,' Varin added, more seriously. 'He holds you in high esteem, despite your apparent hatred of us.'

Eadita stared at him. *I only pretend to hate you to protect myself*, she thought. Did he really want to know the truth? That since the day he had placed the dead baby in the fold of Margaret's arms, she had begun to realise her utter misjudgement of this man, a judgement coloured by her brother's prejudice and her own ignorance. Sweep away Varin's armour, the shield, the trappings of the Norman knight, and what lay beneath? A kind-hearted and considerate man, a man who had helped her when no one else would, a man who had plucked her from the insane punishment before her kinsmen, to sweep her under his protective arm. And she relished that protection, his nurturing, his desire. Eadita nibbled her lip, the horse shifting on the cobbles beneath her. She had embarked on a different journey now, one where Varin was in control. The thought thrilled her.

'Eadita? Do you need some help?' She shook her head to dispel her wayward thoughts, swinging her leg over the horse's neck, to slither crazily to the ground. As her leather soles hit the cobbles, she almost moaned aloud at her aching legs. Varin grabbed her arm, steadying her.

'A little saddle-sore, *mam'selle?*' he asked mildly, lips twitching.

'Possibly,' she admitted, smiling ruefully.

''Twill ease after a hot bath.' Tucking his helmet under one arm, he crooked his elbow. 'Shall we walk over?' He nodded over to the great hall into which the King disappeared. Eadita clutched at Varin's arm.

'Do I have to talk to him right away? At least give me leave to have that hot bath, to tidy myself up a little? I must look a sorry sight!' Bending down, Varin twitched the hem of her gunna down from where it had stuck to her woollen stockings. Rising, he straightened her veil with infuriating exactness, before cupping her heart-shaped chin in one big palm, his thumb resting along the line of her jaw.

'You look beautiful to me, Eadita.'

Chapter Seventeen

Eadita's toes brushed the heated silkiness of the water and she groaned in delight. As she climbed into the copper tub, burnished gold in the candlelight, engulfing her aching limbs in the hot liquid, her worries lifted away like insignificant bubbles bursting above her head. Her hair had been pinned up haphazardly by the helpful maidservant, but after the girl had folded Eadita's clothes into a neat pile atop the oak coffer and left a pile of large linen towels on a stool beside the tub, Eadita had dismissed her. She preferred to wallow in exquisite abandon on her own.

She had exchanged a few pleasantries with William downstairs as his servants flapped anxiously around him. Steadfastly refusing to be relegated to a lonely bedchamber, William preferred to hold court in the sumptuous surroundings of the Palace's great hall. A pallet bed, its simple frame laden with a mattress of the softest goose feather, topped with a luxurious mound of furs, provided the King with the ideal location to be surrounded in company. Varin had escorted her to the King's side and had then left abruptly, bidding Eadita to wait for him to escort her to a chamber so she could bathe. No doubt he hoped the King would hold her to the spot until he returned.

But William's intelligent eyes had quickly noted her own drooping lids and he had speedily dismissed her to spend some hours on her own, promising that they would talk later.

Eadita had almost shouted with joy at her chamber; it seemed no expense had been spared within the Palace. The earthy scent of the wide cedar boards lining the walls permeated the entire space, mingling enticingly with the fresh smell from the rushes strewn about the floor. Thick, quilted pieces of detailed crewelwork embroidery covered the walls, works of art completed with great skill, featuring lavish scenes of hunting, hawking and feasting, the Saxons' favourite pastimes. In the corner, a charcoal brazier threw out an intense, soporific heat, whilst beside the tub, a pair of huge, floorstanding candelabra had been stood from where a vast array of flickering candles threw their light upon the water.

As the lavender-scented steam rose to blur the glowing light, Eadita sighed deeply, sinking further into the water, relishing its heat climbing sensuously to the nape of her neck, hitting the sensitive skin just at the base of her hairline. Alone for the first time since leaving her home. By sending her up here with just a maid for company, the King obviously trusted her more than Varin. She smiled softly, a little shocked at the path down which her thoughts travelled. She had no wish to escape, and it wasn't just the heady temptation of this wonderful bath. It was him. Varin. Where she had once feared the gentle order of her life descending into turmoil at his intruding presence, now she embraced the unknown excitement of the future.

Her fingers traced light, rhythmic circles over the flat of her stomach, trailing water from her navel to the heavy fall of her breasts, absentmindedly kindling her newly awakened desires. Varin! He made her feel alive. Made her laugh. Made her angry. Eyes closed, her mind wrapped around her thoughts with a delicious, forbidden intensity. The Norman warrior had charged into her secretive, barren existence and turned it on its head. A craving fire sparked unsteadily in the pit of her stomach, a fire that flared to a brilliant light that she was reluctant to harness. The warmth of the water pulled her down to a place where her thoughts ran abandoned, out of control, chaotic. Desire pooled in her thighs, a striving madness invading her thought processes to send them on unknown haphazard routes, journeys from which she had no wish to return.

A whisper of cold draught caught her shoulder, which lay exposed from the reassuring warmth of the water, and dried her skin taut. Popping her eyes open to clear her mind, she lifted a dainty ankle, watching the water sluice tantalisingly over her smooth limbs, lending her skin a divine pearly lustre in the glowing dimness of the room.

'I hope you're thinking of me,' a low voice said. Varin stood by the door, transfixed by the heart-stopping scene before him.

Eadita whipped her head around, bewildered by his stealthy entrance. The washcloth fell from her fingers. Acutely aware of her nakedness, she groped hastily for a linen towel.

'Don't. Please don't cover yourself. You are beautiful.'

Her fingers stilled on the rough material, shock waves coursing through her delicate frame. Heat rose to her cheeks as his glowing eyes touched the rounded dampness of her shoulders, the tempting curve of her breast just visible above the lip of the bath. Lacing her violet eyes with his dragon-green orbs, Eadita shuddered, the strength in her limbs draining away. Something passed between them in that moment, a sealing of their fate as their souls connected in a rush of awareness.

'What do you want?' she demanded weakly, knowing the answer before he spoke. Her blood pooled and thickened under the dangerous, single-mindedness of his gaze, every fibre of her being jittering riotously as she ran her eye down the brawny length of his body.

'I want *you*, Eadita.' His voice held a thread of unsteadiness as he absorbed the dreamlike vision before him. A sparkling dew of moisture covered Eadita's pale limbs, emphasised by the flickering shadows. On returning to William and finding her gone, he had bounded up the stairs two at a time. But from the moment he had trodden on silent leather soles into her chamber, he had been stunned by the magical sight dancing before him. This delectable little nymph, the bane of his life, sucked him in with spell-like mastery, charming away the fiercely erected internal barriers, the emotional blockades that had existed since childhood, since his bitch of a mother had deserted the family. In her presence, those evil memories crumbled to dust. He stood bewitched, feet welded to the floor by some other-worldly force, mesmerised by her fascinating beauty.

'Aren't you going to order me to leave?' He lifted one eyebrow in question.

'Nay, Varin, I am not.' If she could just be with him once, forget her responsibilities and loyalties, forget she was a Saxon, then she would hold that memory of him close to her heart for ever. No one would ever know.

'Do you know what you are saying?' He moved behind her, powerful fingers dropping a featherlight touch to the back of her neck. She jumped violently, emitting a tiny sigh of release at the galvanising sensations pulsing under his touch. Her eyelids fluttered down.

'Aye, I do,' she uttered with deadly certainty.

'Eadita.' His voice shook as he knelt on the floor behind the tub. His firm lips brushed the elegant line of her exposed shoulders, creamy in the firelight. Her breath snagged. Sparks jumped from the slow-burning ember of desire lodged deep in her stomach. His fingers pulled at the hairpins made from horn that secured her hair, scattering them to the floor as the glossy skeins slid over her naked skin. Her diaphragm tensed with the sweet awareness, her inner core flowing with excitement. Varin twined his fingers through the lustrous strands, the wide pads of his thumbs gently kneading her scalp.

'So lovely,' he whispered. 'Shall I wash it?'

Her throat closed against the potent rapture of his touch; she murmured her consent incoherently. As his body curled forward around her to scoop water into a shallow earthenware bowl, his chest pressed against her back and the urge to kiss him became unbearable. She tried to turn her face to his, but he drew away, the outside curve of his thumb skimming her outer thigh. Through the fine wool of his overshirt, his chest shuddered against her spine.

'Nay, not yet, *chérie*. There is time enough. Now, tip your head back.'

She obeyed his husky order, throwing the dark tresses back to tumble like a river down the pale, slim column of her back, the curling ends floating on the surface of the water like fronds of seaweed. As the warm water sluiced over her head, his hands began to rub the soap into her scalp, his fingers moving lightly along her hairline, behind her ears, sweeping down under the heavy curtain of hair to the nape of her neck. She thought she would burst with the beguiling ferocity of his touch, her mind and body submerging in the glorious sensation.

''Tis done,' Varin announced gruffly, as he rinsed her hair for the last time. He sat back on his heels, amazed at the strength of emotion this woman engendered in him. Eadita turned her head, caught his vibrant green gaze, and smiled. Varin rocked forward, blood firing to wildness within him, grabbing her bare shoulders to seal her lips to his. His high cheekbones were flushed as his mouth claimed hers in a fierce, unyielding crush. She leaned into him, her wet hair plastered to the sleek, gleaming lines of her body, her hands reaching up to thread tentatively through his tousled hair. His skilful mouth roamed the soft sensuality of her lips, travelling like a feather across sensitive skin before touching the tip of his tongue very, very gently at the seam, demanding entry.

As she whimpered, he sunk inside the erotic confines of her mouth, his muscular arms roping under her own to gather her naked form to his chest. The copper edge of the tub pressed uncomfortably into her breasts, but she noticed not as her tongue clashed wildly with his and her insides turned to molten gold. An amassing, bunching desire lurched oddly within and she tried to push herself closer, closer to the man before her, to meld against him, to pour herself into his body. Varin groaned and the dangerous precipice that she neared loomed closer; a thrilling, quicksilver bolt shot through her veins. He lifted her from the tub, lips still riveted against her own, water splashing on to his corded thighs as he swept an arm under her knees to lay her on the furs strewn over the bed.

Startled, she tried to pull her tingling lips away from his as she realised she lay naked beneath him, her perfect limbs exposed to his hankering gaze. He lifted his head up momentarily, his leonine hair haloed in the golden light, raw desire sparking in his eyes.

'Do not fear me now, *mon coeur.*'

He moved away from the bed, returning with the linen towel to drape it over her nakedness. Eadita shivered as the nubbled fabric brushed against her aroused skin. In the flickering candlelight, she watched, fascinated by the utter concentration on Varin's face as he began to dry her, rubbing circles slowly over her shoulders, along her collarbone and down her flank. The devoted admiration in his eyes made her feel beautiful. The bold mastery of his touch thrilled her skin, his fingers entreating her to push beyond the bounds of her knowledge, to discover secrets of delight hitherto unknown. Eyes closed, she surrendered to the twisting labyrinth of emotion, dancing recklessly on the fringes of an intoxicating whirlpool; the heady waters of passion swirling seductively below, urging her to jump.

'Varin…I…' As his hands moved over the roundness of her breasts, she realised with a jolt that the towel had slipped to the floor.

'Shh,' he hushed in a low voice. ''Tis naught to be afeard of.' A lump of charcoal in the brazier fell, and a crackle of sparks broke into the dream-like haze of the chamber. Varin sat up, pulling his tunic over his head, followed by his linen chemise. His *braies* followed the upper garments to the puddle of cloth on the floor. As she marvelled at the naked form next to her, her fingers moved forward tentatively to touch the honed sinew of his arms. He shuddered.

'I have never touched a man like this before,' she exclaimed, her fingers running over the soft hairs on his chest, wondering at the breadth of his muscular frame.

'I know,' he replied gently. He let her fingers roam until he could bear it no more, then stretched out beside her, pulling her to him. His hard, naked frame against her own sent rivers of shock rippling through her body, the brand of his need burning against her thigh. Before she could recover, his lips moved over hers, touching and teasing as his hand meandered along her spine, sweeping sensuously from nape to the curve of her hip. She met the strength of his kiss with a passionate energy and vigour of her own. All sense of reason deserted her, logic running from her mind like water as she melted from an explosive maelstrom of need.

'God in Heaven, Varin, what are you doing to me?' she gasped.

'Something I should have done a long time ago, dearling.'

In the nebulous half-light, as he moved over her, his body seemed painted with gold, the shadowed angles of his face mirrored in the rugged strength of his body. She welcomed the pressure of his weight as he crushed her to the furs beneath, his large hands framing the delicate bones of her face. The vivid green of his eyes flamed with desire, with need, as he lifted the damp tendrils carefully from her brow.

'Are you sure?'

She traced the lean contours of his face, the face of a man she had hated and despised, a kind and generous man whom she had judged too harshly, blinkered by her own narrow-mindedness.

'Aye, Varin, I am sure.' She would hold this moment in her heart for eternity.

He groaned, hands snagging through her hair as the firelit tresses tumbled on the white pillow beneath her head. The headlong thumping of his chest matched her own as he tracked his lips from mouth to breast, causing her to gasp aloud before he silenced her once more with his lips. His fingers sought the core of her womanhood and she flushed in shame at the hot, flooding wetness he found there. He caught her slight inhibition and pushed his upper body up on thick arms roped with muscle, a fine sweat beading his face.

'Nay, my sweet, do not be ashamed.'

In heady shock, she tensed as the nub of his heavy manhood pushed against her tender folds, a sliding thickness stretching her innocence. She tossed her head from side to side, unknowing as to where she would go, where he was taking her. A wild, bubbling frenzy invaded her blood as a growing need built in the very core of her womanhood.

'Oh, Varin, Varin…!' she cried. With infinite control, Varin willed himself to stop his sweet entry, holding himself steady.

'Shall I stop?'

'Nay, never,' she answered in a rush, 'I just don't know…' He smiled into her passion-darkened eyes.

'Just trust me, Eadita. For once in your life, trust me.' He pushed himself into her, meeting the momentary resistance of her virginity before surging through to the hilt. Consumed by him, a mild ache was soon replaced by a surging, bursting fullness as Varin continued to move within her, slowly at first, then faster and faster. She moved with him then, matching his increasing thrust with a delighted eagerness of her own, wrapping her shaking limbs around his back as he rocked her to and fro. Her mind started to go black, hot pinpoints of light streaking through a yawning chasm, as an immense pressure started to build at the very kernel of her being, massing and growing, threatening to engulf her.

'Oh, Varin, I…I…' she panted, unsure what was happening.

'Let yourself go!' Varin ground out, his eyes closed.

'God in Heaven!' she breathed as Varin strove into her and the straining, pulsing bubble burst as her whole body contracted with blistering violence, heaving and quaking. A scream tore from her lips. Varin arched his head back as he shuddered in tandem, reaching his peak.

'Eadita! Eadita!' he howled her name. Her fingers gripped his dripping hair as he collapsed on to her and she clung to him as if her life depended on it.

Varin glared wretchedly at the uneven edges of the wooden planking on the ceiling, acutely aware of the sleek tangle of limbs wrapped around his rough-haired legs. God's bones! What had he done? He, Lord Varin de Montaigu, a Norman baron and knight to the King, had made love with a Saxon noblewoman, an innocent, for God's sake! A Saxon lady who openly disliked him; who, by degrees, frustrated and obstructed him; who fed him half-truths and still refused to tell him who she protected with those lies. What in heaven's name had he been thinking of?

He could scarce bear to look at her, devastated by the all-consuming response their love-making had engendered within him. How could he have expected anything less? How could he not have *known?* Since his mother had abandoned him, he had promised himself that he would never, ever, be hurt again, never open his heart to have it wounded once more. He prided himself on his uncomplicated relationships, closing himself down emotionally to seek women purely for physical solace, uncaring as to what sentiment or romance might surround such situations. 'Twas usually easy for him to walk away, but usually the lovemaking would be nothing that he cared for or wanted to remember.

With Eadita, the whole encounter had been shockingly different. His heart jolted crazily at the long-buried emotions that this maid, *this elf-woman*, had unearthed in him. How could he have forgotten the desolate faces of his two younger brothers, mouths slack with grief as their mother rode away? How could he have forgotten his father stretching pleading arms to the heavens as he begged Felice to stay? How could he have forgotten what love could do?

He struggled to quash the memories, to stifle them in their infancy as the glossy loops of her hair trailed through the golden hairs of his chest, as her vulnerable, heart-shaped face turned towards him, like a flower seeking the sun to smile in her sleep. She aroused a wild protectiveness within him, a cleaving need that he had not experienced for a very long time, damn her! He had made an unforgivable mistake, a huge error of judgement, trespassing wilfully beyond his own hard, self-imposed boundaries. He hated her for that. Groaning, he raked his fingers through his hair and leapt in one easy movement from the bed.

'Come, wench, 'tis time we were about!' he bellowed down at her as if she were one of his foot soldiers, picking up his discarded clothing to quickly don it. 'There's nothing like a little horseplay to give a man an appetite.' He flinched at his own vulgarity.

Horseplay? Had she heard aright? Befuddled from the short sleep, Eadita stretched, her whole body aching in unfamiliar places, her limbs reluctant to move as if set in mud. She regarded him warily, aghast at the cruel lines carved into his face.

'What have I done?' she whispered.

'Aye, maid, what have you done?' He laughed hollowly.

Had she hoped for anything more than this? If so, she was an utter fool. Varin had made no secret of the fact that he had no wish to be saddled with a woman, let alone a wife. This harsh treatment simply reinforced the fact. Biting her lip, she parcelled up the tiny kernel of sadness and tucked it away, deep in her heart.

'Was that it?' Openly hostile, she schooled her features carefully to a mask of icy disdain. He must not see how affected she had been by their lovemaking.

'I'm sorry to disappoint you, my lady.' He strapped on his sword, his lean hands deftly fastening the buckle. Hands that had loved her. 'It looked as though you enjoyed yourself.' He glanced pointedly at her sprawled, satiated limbs. It took all her will-power not to drag the furs up to her neck.

'I hated it!' she retorted, stung by the angry set of his frozen features. 'You used me!'

'We used each other, Eadita,' he snarled, his cold-blooded words falling like a stinging slap across her face. Bitter, dispiriting realisation hit her with the force of an axe. She had known what she was doing. She should have known what would happen afterwards.

'You bastard!' she breathed. He smiled, dipping his head slightly in agreement, as his lips stretched in a merciless slash across his face. The amiable, good-humoured grins that she was used to from him seemed to have disappeared.

'Correct, *mam'selle*. Now, if you would just put your clothes—'

'You….you *nithing!*' She threw the Saxon insult at him without thinking.

'Whatever that word means, my love, then I'm sure I'm it.' He waggled a raised finger at her. 'Don't pretend to be so wronged, Eadita. I gave you the chance to throw me out. I gave you the chance to say "nay" to me.'

He had. She remembered his words in the golden glow of the chamber, when the heady scents had intoxicated her spirit, and now…? Turning her face into the pillow, she tried to bury the misery in her heart.

'Go away,' she mumbled. 'I need more sleep. Be gone.'

'Nay, we have tarried too long as it is. Get up, my lady. The King awaits our presence.' He bent to pull the furs from her curled-up form to expose her naked skin to the cold air. He knew he acted like a cur, but he needed to push her away from him, create some emotional distance between them. He made to drag her from the bed and she swiftly rolled away from his grasp, twisting to the other side, pulling the coverlet to shield the front of her body.

'Don't you dare touch me, you…you swineherd,' she hissed, jumping to her feet to face him from the other side of the bed. Laughing, he caught the end of the bed fur and wrenched it from her flimsy grip, leaving her body exposed in the shadows. The luminous glimmering of the brazier behind her clearly silhouetted the flawless grace of her finely honed figure, the glowing light touching the well-rounded pink-tipped breasts and rounded hips from which he had so recently taken pleasure. Varin cursed the involuntarily jerk in his loins, his perfidious body once more responding to her loveliness as he grappled for self-restraint. Seeing her thus, he realised that he had not truly appreciated her exquisite physique as his eye travelled downwards to her soft thighs. A mottling bruise on her upper thigh caught his attention, and, as he picked out the shape of the odd purple splotches as big as his handspan, a recent memory sprang to mind.

He gasped.

'What…is…that?' he spat out, eyes creasing in consternation as he emphasised each word with deliberate slowness, punching a finger at her well-rounded thigh.

''Tis none of your business, Varin. Now get out of here.'

Eadita fixed him with an increasingly antagonistic look. He moved around the bed in two short strides to grip her upper arms, shaking her a little.

'Tell me what it is!' he demanded, in a tone that brooked no disobedience.

''Tis a mark from my birthing. Naught for concern. My mother has it too and—' She stopped her words before the name 'Thurstan' slipped from her lips.

'Diable!' he breathed, then continued to blaspheme heavily in French, as he realised the implications of the mark.

'What is the matter, Varin? You're scaring me!'

Not near as much as you're scaring me, mam'selle, he thought. 'Who is your mother?' he interrogated roughly.

She tried to shrug his hands away. Eadita frowned. 'What do you mean, Varin? She is Beatrice of Thunorslege, as you well know.'

'And before she married your father? Where did she come from?'

'What business is it of yours?' she demanded suspiciously.

'Eadita, I need to know. 'Tis of the utmost importance.'

'I don't see why I should tell you anything.'

'Don't be so childish, Eadita,' he rapped out. 'Forget what happened between us. 'Twas a mistake, I admit.' Dropping his hands loosely by his sides, he took a step back, his aggressive stance diminished. 'Now, will you tell me about your mother?'

A mistake. A simple, terrible mistake. She bit her lip to quell the rising tide of sadness. How could they possibly be well matched when her own experience was so woefully inadequate? Better to give him the information he needed, so that he might leave her to lick her wounds in private. She clutched at the slipping furs.

'My mother came over to this country from France when she was quite young. About my age, I believe.'

'From where in France?' he rapped out.

'From Falaise.'

'Sweet mother of God, ' he breathed, 'do you realise what this means?'

'Nay, Varin,' she replied firmly, 'I do not know what it means. You make little sense.'

'William carries the same mark.' Her heart thudded.

'W-what?'

'Aye, Eadita. Listen to my words. William, King of England, carries the same mark. *Exactly* the same. William was born in Falaise. You must be his kin.'

'Oh, Varin, don't trick with me,' she replied evenly, 'even I know that is impossible. I am Saxon, I carry the looks of the Saxons…nay, 'tis not possible.'

'I have seen the mark on William,' Varin repeated, his hands heavy once again on her shoulders, 'and it is identical.'

'Why should I believe you, Varin? Just leave me be.'

'We must talk to him. You will see I am not mistaken.'

'I sincerely hope you are, for 'tis a cruel jest you play upon me.'

'No jest, Eadita. I am deadly serious. You have Norman blood in you,' Varin announced to her forlorn figure. 'You have become what you despise so much, your own worst enemy.' He threw her clothes at her across the room. 'Get dressed. We must attend the King downstairs. I'm sure he'll be delighted to know that his kin resides at the Palace.'

'Stop! Stop, Varin, this is madness!' Eadita tried to dig her heels into the wooden planking as Varin dragged her along the upstairs corridor. He had waited outside the chamber while she donned her garments and tidied her hair. 'You'll make a fool of yourself with William! You must be mistaken!' Panic trembled through her voice at the utter determination of the man before her. He stopped abruptly.

'I am not wrong! I have seen the mark before, all too recently.' He scowled down at her, his features hard and menacing in the dimness.

'Then why did my mother not tell me so? Why would she keep her bloodline a secret?'

Varin shrugged his shoulders, bored by her continued resistance. 'How should I know? Maybe she wants to deny her heritage. Maybe she's *hiding* something.' His jade-washed eyes narrowed as he knocked his head with his fist. 'Aye! I knew it! I knew I had seen her somewhere before, yet she denied all knowledge of it.'

Eadita's heart washed cold with dread. 'What…? When?' she asked slowly. She already knew to what he referred. Her mother's odd behaviour when she first met Varin in the church, her uncustomary rudeness.

'I remember her at Falaise, a young woman then, chasing through the linens drying on the line. She spent much time with William and her other half-brothers.'

'But you cannot be certain.' Eadita began to feel terribly alone. Why had her mother not talked to her about this? Not trusted her? She doubted that Thurstan knew about this. Varin grasped her heart-shaped face between his hands, forcing her to meet his eyes.

'I am certain, Eadita, and the proof is sitting downstairs. 'Tis all you will need to see that I am right.'

The purpling depths of her eyes regarded him bleakly. 'You don't have to tell him. Just let me slip away, now. He doesn't need to know.' Defeat clouded her features. 'Oh, Varin, what have you done to me?'

His insides twisted. He stared at her pitilessly, her glorious hair now curbed and controlled by a neat plait swinging down her spine, the fragile bloom of her skin still rosy with the memory of their lovemaking. His large hand balled into an ominous fist. Bedding a Saxon lady and one related to the King of England. He must have been mad! He'd taken her innocence in a fit of uncontrolled passion, wanting to break this building need he held for her. It hadn't worked. He still hankered after her, wanted her as she shone like an angel in the shadowy depths, wanted her now.

''Twould seem that I have not done enough, *mam'selle.*' He bent his head.

Sensing his purpose, Eadita stepped neatly to one side, raising a flat palm against the gathering desire in his eyes. 'Nay, Varin, you will not touch me again, do you hear?'

'You gave me your body, Eadita, what difference will another kiss make?'

It will make me want you again, she thought suddenly. I will be unable to stop myself and I cannot bear your harsh treatment of me once more.

'This must stop now, Varin!' She stamped her foot defiantly. 'I will not be treated like a whore!'

He lifted his eyebrows, shocked.

'I wouldn't dream of it!'

'Then why, Varin, why do you pursue me so relentlessly?'

'Because you are so utterly desirable.'

Her limbs almost melted at the husky familiarity in his voice, but she pulled herself straight, physically and mentally distancing herself from him. 'Nay, Varin, that is not it. I make you feel something you don't want to feel and you hate me for it, yet you continually come back for more,' she challenged with unerring accuracy.

Rage rose, mad and blinding, as he acknowledged the truth of her words. *You feel something you don't want to feel.* He wanted to kill her. Shake her so her teeth rattled. Make love to her so she pleaded for mercy. Flames of hatred shot from his eyes as he hauled her towards him.

'You should be clapped in irons for that tongue of yours!'

'Hah! 'Twould surely be preferable to being chained to your side!'

'Vixen! I'll teach you to sharpen your claws on me!' he murmured, brutally trapping her lips beneath his own, grinding her body savagely against the wall. He wanted to punish her for her needling words, for the strange spell cast between them. Her hands fluttered towards his chest in a weak display of protest, but she hungered for his touch, despite their pitiless exchange. Something else had a hold on them, something otherworldly, beyond their ken. He worked over her mouth relentlessly, rapacious in his passion, urging and insistent as he claimed her for his own.

A subdued giggling at the bottom of the stairwell forced him back to reality, to wrench his passion-stained lips away from hers, to question his own sanity. Thrusting her forcibly away from him, he noted the rawness around her mouth and remembered that he hadn't shaved that morning.

'Enough!' He willed himself to curb his rapid breathing. 'Eadita, we must find out the truth! I am duty-bound to tell William!'

She had closed her eyes, quivering from the latent ferocity of his kiss, barely aware that she still clutched his forearms for support.

'Then I pray that he proves you wrong,' she murmured.

Standing before William in the Great Hall, watching his steward roll up his trouser leg at Varin's request, Eadita realised in horror that Varin had not been mistaken. As the mottled bruise appeared on the King's stocky thigh, identical in every way to her own, a huge wave of suffocating anguish threatened to engulf all that she believed in. A cruel heat gripped her throat though she wanted to scream and shout, to rail at the heavens, to stamp the hideous truth into the ground and bury it forever. Sinking to her knees before William in a pool of skirts, she buried her face in her hands, weeping as if her heart would break.

'Quick, fetch the girl some wine,' William ordered his steward. 'Varin, for God's sake, comfort the maid. What on earth is going on?' As Varin crouched beside her, his face a blank mask, she made as if to strike him, but he caught her delicate wrists and all but lifted her on to the stool. The steward pressed a tankard into her shaking hand; Varin steadied it to her lips. She accused him with eyes raging in despair.

'This is all your fault! If only you hadn't—' She stopped herself, realising William listened acutely, frowning. 'I can't believe this, I can't. There must be some other explanation!'

'Perhaps you had better tell me what is going on.' William addressed Varin.

'Lady Eadita has an identical birthmark on her leg, my Lord. Her mother is Beatrice of Thunorslege, but she was born in Falaise.'

'Beatrice…Beatrice!' William leaned forward in excitement. 'Varin, are you certain? How do you know about this birthmark?'

'I have seen it,' Varin declared with sonorous certainty.

'I see.' William's displeasure filtered through his words.

'Varin disturbed me at my bath, my lord,' Eadita explained shakily, trying to regain her shattered composure. William must not know what had taken place between herself and Varin. 'Twould surely tie them together and she desired no relationship with a man who didn't want her!

'I am sorry for that, my lady. Varin can be a little uncouth at times.' William swallowed the half-truth easily and glared at Varin, before smiling brightly. 'But an unfortunate encounter has led to a happier one, has it not? For Beatrice is my half-sister, lost to me many years ago. You, my dear, must be my niece!'

The King's niece! God in Heaven! This couldn't be happening! Since her father's death, she'd spent her whole existence fighting and thwarting the infiltration of the French and all the time she was one of them!

'Nay, nay!' She rose unsteadily, shaking her head wildly. 'You seek to trick me! Tell me the truth! Varin!' Distraught, she scanned Varin's face for signs of falsehood.

'No trick, my lady. The birthmark is all the proof we need.' Varin moved over to the table and poured himself a goblet of wine, raising it in a mocking toast. 'Congratulations, my dear. You are now one of us. *Bienvenue.*'

Welcome. His taunting words grated on her fractured senses, driving into her soul like a shard of glass, lacerating all she had known, all she was familiar with, all she had loved. Raging despair gnawed at her mind as her eyes locked with the contemptuous green glitter of her adversary. She wanted to fly at him, rake his face like a demon, but she clenched her fists in the folds of her skirts. What she lost in matching him physically, she could gain with words.

'You…bastard!' she yelled at him, staggering over to sweep the raised goblet from his fingers. Stewards and servants watched in bewilderment as the glittering arc of blood-red wine curled to one side to splash on the flagstones, spattering wildly. 'You're enjoying this, damn you! You couldn't wait to see me brought to my knees, scrabbling in the dirt!'

'Hardly,' Varin quirked one eyebrow, mildly amused by her antics. 'Your status has increased immeasurably!'

'I don't want it!' she spat.

'Eadita…!' His voice held a warning.

'Don't you dare tell me what to do! I'm sick of being bullied by you, manhandled and pushed about, day in and day out. Why did you ever come into my life? You've ruined everything!' Tears began to spill from her lashes.

'My dear…?' William reached out a hand, trying to pacify her. Varin put his hands on her shoulders, but she struck them away, with all the force she could muster. Reason had deserted her; she wanted to punish him.

'Don't ever touch me again! Don't you see? None of this would have happened if you hadn't bedded me!'

The Great Hall fell silent.

Chapter Eighteen

'What did you say?' The words rapped out from William's mouth, crisp and demanding. Eadita's hands fell away from Varin, as he shook his head silently at her, admonishing her. A dice clattered to the table behind them as open-mouthed soldiers stalled in their game, agog at the tense situation that had arisen.

'She said, "None of this would have happened if you hadn't bedded me",' Varin enunciated each word clearly, so the full meaning could not be mistaken, not by the King, or by the many knights, stewards and serving maids that busied themselves about the hall. A scalding flush flared over Eadita's translucent cheeks; she bit her lip guiltily. Every nerve ending throbbed in humiliation as she endured the interested, knowing looks around her.

'She speaks the truth?' Compressing his lips, William glanced from one to the other: Varin, like a statue, reserved and cold; Eadita, her slender form trembling a little from the aftermath of her anger, yet still facing both of them belligerently, her shoulders set in an obstinate line.

'Aye, 'tis the truth.' Varin replied, the flat monotone of his voice causing Eadita to wince in despair. The impenetrable mask of his face gave away no hint of emotion, of feeling, but she ached to reach inside him, to find out his true thoughts.

'Varin, do you realise what this means?' William rose, sweeping aside the bundle of furs to stand between the two of them. 'The code of chivalry demands it.' His steward rushed to retrieve the untidy heap of bedclothes from the floor and began to fold them studiously into a neat pile.

'Aye, my lord, I will marry her.' Varin folded his arms over his chest, glaring derisively at Eadita's white, shocked face.

'Marry me! Varin, how can this be?' Incredulity clouded her brain as she scoured his stern features for some hint of reason, of true meaning.

'We must pay for our brief moment of passion, my lady,' Varin replied sarcastically, 'with a lifetime of misery.'

'Nay, Varin, do not scare the little one. 'Tis not as bad as if first appears.' William turned to Eadita, but his booming tones did little to reassure her. 'I cannot let a lady, nay, my own niece, be condemned before God as a sinner. Varin knew what the consequences of his actions would be.' William rested his pale blue eyes upon his knight. 'Although I am surprised. 'Tis not like you to relinquish your rigid self-restraint.'

Varin shrugged his shoulders. 'Can you blame me?'

William laughed, breaking the tension. 'Nay, she has the beauty of an angel.'

'I am not some chattel at the market to be discussed as if I'm not here,' Eadita interrupted, turning to the King. 'My lord, it doesn't have to be like this! We don't even have an affection for each other! Why not send me back to Thunorslege where I can resume my quiet life? Nothing more need be said about the matter.'

William was already shaking his head. 'Nay, my dear. Circumstances have changed somewhat. You are now of royal blood; you cannot scuttle away and hide. You need to face up to your actions and your responsibilities. Varin is a good match. Many women would beg to be in your position.'

'But we don't love each other,' she protested.

'Love doesn't come into it,' Varin growled. 'You seemed willing enough to be sold in marriage to a complete stranger a few days ago.'

'That's unfair,' she retorted. 'I had little choice, being a virtual prisoner.'

Varin's wolfish glance glittered down at her. 'And you have little choice now, *mam'selle*. We are bound by my chivalric oath to the King.'

But you don't love me, she thought miserably. He obviously wanted this as little as she did. Better to be away from him and hold the sweet memory of their lovemaking close to her heart than suffer this heartless treatment, day after day. Nausea rose unsteadily in her gut. She clapped a hand over her mouth.

'Excuse me,' she gulped, pivoting unsteadily on her toes to flee in the direction of the main door, and beyond, to the inner courtyard. Grateful for the dim twilight obscuring her predicament, she pressed one shaking hand to her stomach, the other to the clammy grittiness of the wall for support as she wretched and wretched. The cobbles lurched and heaved before her eyes as a prickle of perspiration dampened the back of her neck. With nothing in her stomach to start with, her dry heaving left her with the acrid taste of bile coating the inside of her mouth. Eyes closed, she slumped back against the wall, unmindful of its abrasive exterior as an uncustomary weakness invaded her limbs.

'Better?' Her eyes shot open as Varin smoothed the damp strands of her hair away from her forehead. He held a tankard of water to her lips.

'Go away,' she muttered rudely, looping her arms defensively under his brilliant regard. 'You've already done enough.'

'It has been a great shock for you,' he murmured. In the half-light, all she could discern was the indistinct outline of his large frame, the hunting luminescence of his eyes and the sparkling hilt of the sword at his hip.

'That's an understatement,' she replied. With no strength to lever herself from the wall, the wetness of the stone began to permeate the cloth at her shoulders. 'Not only have I just discovered I'm the King's niece, but, because of it, I must be forced into wedlock with you.'

'Not quite the consequences we envisaged, *ma petite.*' His tone seemed kinder now, more gentle than it had been before the King. The coarse pads of his fingers sought her faltering hands and held them, strongly. 'But at least we agree on something. Neither of us wishes to be trapped in marriage.'

'Then what can we do about it? We're not even compatible in the bedchamber!' She sensed his frown, rather than saw it.

'Whatever gave you that idea?' Looming closer, he searched her face steadily 'I don't regret what happened between us, Eadita, not for one moment.' Her heart bloomed with happiness; he still wanted her. Varin squeezed her fingers.

'I wanted you then, Eadita, as I want you now. But marriage…' His eyes frosted over. 'My father went to hell and back in his marriage; I have no wish to share the same fate.' A side door opened in a clatter of laughter; the shaft of light illuminated the bleakness in Varin's eyes. The door closed, and it was gone.

But marriage doesn't have to be like that, Eadita thought. Her own parents had been happily married for over twenty years. Was there the faintest hope that a marriage between them might work?

'It doesn't have to be that way,' she whispered, haltingly.

'A marriage must be founded on truth and trust, little one. That doesn't even exist between us. Just look at the web of deceit that surrounds us now: your own mother has lied to you; you keep secrets from me. How can a marriage be grown on such a shaky foundation?'

Could she tell him? Could she tell him about Thurstan? Maybe now was the time. He was unable to trust her because she kept the truth from him. But if she told him, then maybe, maybe they might have a future together. It was a risk, but it was a risk she was prepared to take for the man she loved. His fingers linked warmly with hers and she savoured the glorious sensation for a moment.

'Varin, there's something…'

'Mistress, mistress Eadita!'

A thin, whining voice halted her speech. Varin whipped around, his arm curving protectively around Eadita's shoulders. A scrawny boy hopped from one grimy foot to another on the cobbles.

'Excuse me, my lady, but mistress Meryon begs a word with you…in private.' The lad drew a ragged sleeve over his snot-streaked face. Varin eyed him in disgust, before turning to Eadita.

'Mistress Meryon?' he questioned.

Eadita took a faltering step away from the wall, glad of Varin's steadying arm. 'Meryon is the cook at the Palace; she's also a good friend of mine.'

'Then maybe you should sit with her for a while.' Varin's eyes held concern. 'I think you're more shaken than you pretend to be. It would also give me a chance to talk with William—I might be able to change his decision about the marriage.'

'Oh.'

'Oh.' He smiled at her. 'Is that all you can say? I might be able to find some way out of this mess, for both of us. I thought you'd be happy.'

'I am.' She gulped down a soaring flow of misery, as Varin

tucked her arm under his and turned to follow the skipping urchin in the direction of the kitchens.

Organised chaos reigned in the kitchen, overseen by a tiny woman, who stood on a stool and shouted instructions to everyone. Under the magnificent vaulted ceiling, servants washed and chopped and stirred, intent on the process of creating a meal for the evening's guests. As the woman's arms waved back and forth, pointing and reprimanding, her bright little eyes caught sight of Eadita standing alone in the doorway. Varin had already returned to the King's side.

'Eadita!' she squeaked in pleasure. 'My lady, how lovely to see you!' The birdlike woman hopped down and sped over, her outstretched arms reaching and clasping Eadita's slender fingers.

'Meryon!' Eadita's predicament faded at the sight of her friendly face. 'Haven't you stopped working yet?'

'Nay, this lazy lot need me.' Meryon flung a scornful inspection around the kitchens. 'This whole place would fall apart if I left. Why, I only stepped out to the storehouses for a moment this morning, and young Aelward here—' she pointed at the poor unfortunate boy '—managed to burn a whole load of pies.' Her eyes narrowed as she took in Eadita's exhausted stance. 'But forgive me, my lady, I forget my manners. Come and sit awhile next to the fire.'

Warmed by a tankard of mead, surrounded by the sounds and enticing smells of the kitchen, Eadita began to feel more like herself again.

'So what brings you here?' Meryon sat down opposite her, wiping her wet hands on her apron.

'Why, you do, of course!' Eadita replied brightly. 'The boy said you wanted to see me.' Scrutinising the room to identify him, she frowned in puzzlement at his disappearance. 'That's strange...'

Meryon leaned forward conspiratorially. 'We've have some odd ones in, believe me. Extra hands helping with the King's party. When I saw you with the Norman lord in the doorway…' her voice dropped in a whisper '…I thought you'd come about the poisoning.'

'Oh…aye, the poisoning.' Eadita replied lamely. How could she have forgotten the incident that had brought her to the Palace in the first place?

'If you ask me, someone slipped it into his wine. There's no other way, you see.'

Eadita shook her head. ' Nay, Meryon, 'tis not possible, for Fitz Osbern tastes everything that passes the King's lips.'

'After he has tasted it. 'Twould be easy to do in the middle of the feasting when everyone's a little drunk.'

'My God, Meryon, you may be right. Only a few drops of cowbane are needed.'

But Meryon's attention was elsewhere. 'You there, boy, keep turning that pig. I want it cooked thoroughly all the way round, not burnt at the edges.'

Eadita leaned over. 'You're busy, Meryon, let's talk another time. I must go back into the hall, and tell Lord Varin what you have said. I will come and waste your time another day.' The two women grinned at each other as Eadita swung through the doorway.

Emerging into the cold night air, she stood still for a moment, watching her heated breath create cloudy puffs of steam in front of her lips. After the bustling energy of the kitchens, the damp mist on her skin calmed her senses. She wanted to return to Varin, to continue their conversation from before, to tell him the truth.

But before she had time to take a step, a large hand clamped over her mouth and a strong arm around her waist dragged her crazily backwards. Her heels bumped painfully along the ground as she scrabbled desperately to gain a foothold, to gain some leverage to spring away from her attacker, but the hold on her was unusually tight and restrictive. Her body was twisted around like a doll and pushed up violently against the wall of the outhouse.

'Thurstan!' She sucked her breath in sharply, immediately recognising her brother's face as it neared her own. Naturally he knew how to hold her so she wouldn't escape.

'Aye, you have it right, sister. Now, I will only remove my hand if you promise not to scream.' She nodded as the bubbling adrenaline in her veins subsided a little.

'What in God's name are you doing here?' she tumbled out.

'Maybe I should ask you the same question,' he answered drily. She ignored his sarcastic tone, smiling at him.

''Tis good to see you!' she exclaimed, wrapping him in a friendly bear hug. To her astonishment, his arms didn't reciprocate the gesture. 'Thurstan, what's ails you? Is it Mother…is that why you're here?'

'I'm here to sort out the mess you've landed us in, you… you traitor!' He spat the words out. ' How could you do this to me, Eadita…how could you do this to me…your own brother?'

'What are you talking about?'

''Twas you who saved William's life, was it not? After I took such risks gaining entry to the Palace…!'

She glared at him. 'I had little choice, Thurstan. Varin dragged me to the Priory to attend on him.'

'You could have lied about the remedy…you could have done anything rather than save him.'

'I have no intention of letting any man die, be he friend or foe. I've told you before. It goes against everything our mother taught us of healing, brother.'

'They are our enemy. They killed our father.' Thurstan would not be budged from his train of thought.

'Thurstan, I think they might be able to help us. Things are not as they seem.' How in God's name could she tell him that he was the King's nephew?

'Silence! Do not speak of such things!' He plucked at her arm. 'Listen, our time is short. I can't get close to William now, too many people are watching…'

'It was you…it was you who poisoned him!' Her breath expelled in a piercing whisper as the truth dawned. 'You know the hellish properties of cowbane, you know how difficult the symptoms are to diagnose… Thurstan why do you persist in this madness…?'

Varin's hard gaze circled the kitchen once before people began to notice him. Hands stopped, poised over stacks of plates, rolling pastry, immersed in hot water.

'Where is she?' he roared. 'Where is Lady Eadita?' Heads started to shake, people stared fixedly at the floor. Meryon, wiping her hands on a cloth, stepped forward, trembling.

'She's not here, my lord. I thought she returned to the Great Hall.'

'Why did you wish to speak with her?' he rapped out.

'B…but I didn't my Lord. I didn't send for her.'

'Dieu and damnation!' Varin swore, leaving abruptly.

Outside, in the soundless air, he willed himself to remain still. *Think!* he ordered himself. *What would she do? Where would she go?* A sound carried to his ears as he listened intently for a clue to her whereabouts. Immediately, he heard a thick mumble of voices. Walking carefully on the outside edges of his leather soles so as to minimise any noise of his approach, he slunk around the curved walls of the outhouses like a large cat about to pounce, until the voices became clearer, more distinct. His heart encased itself into unyielding iron as he recognised Eadita's melodious timbre contrasting with the gruffer, but still well-spoken tones of a man. He stopped instantly, listening keenly as he realised that the voices conversed just around the next corner.

'I can't believe you would do such a thing, Thurstan!' Eadita exclaimed, horrified. ' I truly believe you have been seized by some sort of madness.'

'But I failed, Eadita. I failed because of your interfering meddling. And now you are going to help me, help restore my trust in you, my faith in your Saxon loyalty…'

'I will not poison him!' she hissed.

'Keep your voice down!' Thurstan warned. 'You could do it, sister. With your innocent looks, sitting right next to the King, you could slip the drops into his drink as you hold his eyes with your own…no one would suspect you.' Eadita thought of Varin, and laughed.

'How wrong could you be, Thurstan. I am the very first person they would suspect. Varin watches me like a hawk…!'

'Aye, that's right, my lady!' Varin moved stealthily from the shadows, grabbing brother and sister by the shoulders in a punishing grip. In the clear moonlight, he had just time to register the identical nature of their features, the same large eyes, tip-tilted nose and generous mouth before a stunning blow to the head rendered him completely unconscious.

'No!' Eadita howled at the sight of the warrior's large frame crumpling to the ground. Instinctively, she crouched down beside him, sucking in her breath as the hot, sticky blood oozed through the straw-coloured strands of his hair.

'What have you done to him?' she railed into the darkness. Kenelm, one of Thurstan's accomplices, stepped forward, holding a jagged rock.

'Something that should have been done a long time ago,' Thurstan rasped, drawing a lethal-looking sword. 'Something that you should have done, sister,' he chided accusingly. 'And now it's time for him to meet his maker.'

'No, *no!*' Eadita reached towards the menacing glitter of

steel, grappling for the hilt against her brother's strength. Thurstan aimed the metallic point at Varin's exposed throat, and although Eadita fought strongly, she knew the tip inched ever closer to the unconscious Norman warrior.

'This cannot be!' she whispered, the words springing unbidden from her heart. A piercing awareness flooded her thoughts. Varin could not die! A physical wrench twisted an invisible rope connecting them; it mangled and buckled as the sword moved ever nearer, as if her own life lay under threat as well. Sweat popped onto her brow, her muscles screamed, sinews stretching painfully as she attempted to hold off her brother. Her own brother! She fought the one man who she had consistently honoured and loved throughout twenty-one winters; now she seriously doubted his sanity.

'Enough! We must run! The guard has been alerted!' Kenelm dropped the bloody rock to the ground with a dull thud and wrenched the sword from Thurstan's hand.

'Come! We must fly if we're not to be caught!' Kenelm started to hustle them away from Varin's inert figure. The thick cloud of rage that hung on Thurstan's brow cleared as he realised the danger they were in. Shouts rose from the walkway of the high stone wall that encircled the Palace.

'Come, Eadita.' Thurstan held out his hand. 'Come, sister,' he urged. 'I need you.' Bewildered, she looked up at her brother.

'Nay, I will not go with you. I must stay and tend his wounds.' Ripping her veil from her hair, she fashioned it into a pad to stem the bleeding from Varin's head. A trail of apprehension snaked in her gut as she willed him to open his eyes. Putting two fingers to the vein at his neck, she realised with relief that his pulse beat strongly. He groaned.

Thurstan spat on the ground, watching her ministrations in disbelief.

'You would choose a Norman over your own brother? If

you stay, Eadita, then I never want to see you again, never want to talk to you, or be with you. Do you understand?'

'I love him, Thurstan. I love him. Does it matter what banner he rides under?'

'Bah! Don't make me laugh. You've been duped by his knightly ways. 'Tis time to open your eyes, sister. Do you want to spend the rest of you life as a whore to the Norman?'

Nay, I want to spend the rest of my life with him as his wife, Eadita thought, surprising herself. To bear his children, to comfort him in sickness and in health, to laugh together. 'Twas a shame that Varin did not want the same end. By leaving with Thurstan she could release Varin from his obligation to marry her; she could simply disappear. Better to hold the exquisite memory of their lovemaking close to her heart, than to endure a lifetime of bitterness. He had made it clear that he had no interest in marrying her. Checking Varin's pulse once more with careful fingers, watching the flicker of his eyelids as he tried to open them, Eadita cast one long, lingering look down the warrior's body, committing his familiar features to memory, her eyes full of unshed tears. It was the last time she would ever see him.

Chapter Nineteen

'Don't fight me, *mon ami,* 'tis I, Geraint.' Varin struggled to prise his eyes open, aware that he thrashed blindly against his friend. He groaned. A thumping headache radiated unforgivingly from the back of his skull. Putting his fingers up to find the kernel of the pain, he encountered a thick clot of blood.

''Tis not as bad as it first appears,' Geraint reassured. 'At least someone tried to stop the bleeding. We found this against the wound.'

Varin stared at the flimsy veil soaked with his blood. The faint drift of lavender filled his nostrils. 'That bitch. That little bitch! She's gone with him, hasn't she?'

'What happened?' Geraint crouched low by the pallet bed, holding a tankard of mead to his friend's lips.

'I give you one guess.'

'Lady Eadita? Did she hit you over the head?'

'Nay, 'twas one of the men she was with. Have you seen her?' Geraint shook his head. Varin grimaced. '*Dieu!* I'll wring her scrawny neck when I find her.' The refreshing honey liquid slid down his parched throat, revitalising his senses. 'And I will find her.' He rose ominously against the pillows, his blood-splattered gambeson streaked and dirty against the pristine white linen. "Twas all a ruse, Geraint. The boy was obviously sent to lure Eadita away from me. And I was too stupid to see it!' He drained the tankard in a rush, thumping it down on an oak chest beside him. 'Why did I not insist on accompanying her to the kitchens?'

'Because you thought you could trust her?' Geraint suggested mildly.

Varin threw his friend a long hard look and sighed, slumping back. 'Aye, I thought I could. Instead I find her in close conversation with the man who attempted to murder the King.'

'What! Who is it?'

'Her own brother, Geraint, her twin brother. I suspect 'tis him she has been protecting all this time.'

'But she had no knowledge before that it was he who poisoned William,' Geraint said. 'Otherwise why would she—?'

'Save the King's life?' Varin finished for him. 'I agree, she had no knowledge. When I came upon them, brother and sister were in violent disagreement.' A hazy memory of Eadita's hands on a sparkling blade chased around his fragmented mind. Had she held her brother's sword away from him? Had she saved his life?

'Then why did she flee with them?'

Varin shrugged his broad shoulders. ''Tis a mystery. Unless…?' An unwilling thought arose.

'Unless…?' Geraint prompted.

'Unless she thinks her disappearance would break this accursed betrothal between us. 'Tis a marriage ordered by the King—neither of us desires it.'

'But you desire each other,' Geraint stated bluntly, lifting his eyebrows beneath his dark hair.

Varin laughed, holding his palms out flat in a gesture of acceptance. 'Aye, I cannot deny that. Oh, what a stupid maid!' He threw his legs over the side of the bed. 'Fetch me my hauberk, Geraint. Her brother's words return to me; they were harsh in the extreme.'

William's huge guffaw reached his ears from the great hall; a guffaw mingled with the lighter tones of a woman's laughter. Varin frowned. 'The King does not seem overly worried that Eadita has disappeared. I thought he would have sent out a search party by now. I must have been unconscious for some time.'

'We had no idea she *had* gone, Varin. Besides, the King is somewhat distracted at the moment. Lady Beatrice has arrived from Thunorslege. William sent for her at once; Judhael of Totnes provided her with an escort.'

'Ah, maybe she can give me some answers. I suspect she knows far more than she's telling.' Varin stood, swaying a little, the taut coil of his body tense and ready to spring.

'Sit down, *mon ami*. You are not well enough to go. Take some time to recover.'

'Geraint, there is no time. Why did her brother send that boy to fetch Eadita? Why is it so important that she goes with them? There is some evil plan afoot, and I have to find out what it is, even if I have to hunt them down to the ends of the earth!'

Both men turned their heads as a light knock heralded the entrance of an older woman dressed in a dark green gunna.

'Greetings, Lady Beatrice,' Varin murmured. Both men rose to bow formally to the King's half-sister. The unlined smoothness of her brow reminded Varin of Eadita and his heart squeezed in painful loss. He had to find her!

'Forgive my intrusion, my lords. I was anxious to see how the invalid fared.' Beatrice threw a radiant smile in Varin's direction as she stepped gracefully into the chamber, the soft kid of her embroidered slippers soundless on the flagstones. 'William tells me you were carried in quite senseless.'

'No thanks to your son.' With no deference to continued

formality, Varin's brutal, demanding words punched into Beatrice as if he had physically hit her. She recoiled, blanching, to collapse into the chair that Geraint had just vacated. Varin towered over her.

'How…dare you?' she whispered, her throat twisting. 'Thurstan is dead.'

'Nay, my dear lady, he is very much alive. I want no more lies.' Beatrice cowered, shrivelling visibly under his commanding stance. ''Tis time to stop protecting your children and tell me the truth. I fear Eadita is in great danger.'

Concern creased Beatrice's face. 'She's not here? William thought you would know her whereabouts.'

'Nay, she chose to go with her brother.'

'I don't understand. Thurstan was here…at the Palace?'

'So you do admit that he's alive?'

'Aye, he's alive,' Beatrice admitted. 'And I can assure you that Eadita is in no danger if she is with him.'

'Would you say the same if I told you he attempted to poison the King?' Varin crossed his arms across his chest as Beatrice flung her hand before her mouth, knuckles white.

'Nay, nay, he would never…'

'I heard the confession spill from his lips,' Varin disputed grimly. 'Are you still going to insist that your daughter is in safe hands?' Beatrice closed her eyes, clasping her arms about her torso, rocking to and fro.

'Methinks this news may be too much for her,' Geraint whispered.

'Fetch William,' Varin ordered. His friend slipped quietly from the chamber.

'Does he know?' Beatrice said suddenly, her long fingers reaching to clutch at Varin's leather-manacled forearm. 'Does William know all this?'

'Not about Thurstan, nay.' Sitting down on the fur coverlet opposite her, Varin took her fluttering hands into his. Beatrice appeared not to notice. 'I am sorry this has come as a shock, my lady, but 'tis imperative I find Eadita. Have you any idea where they might have gone?' A tense edge of frustration laced his speech.

Beatrice stared at him vacantly, not heeding his question. Her eyes hazed over in panic. 'What will William do to Thurstan? Can you promise that no harm will come to my son?' Her trembling fingers clutched at his.

'Do not ask me to promise what I cannot.' Irritation darkened his jewel-like eyes, as Beatrice refused to give him answers. ''Tis the King's decision.'

'Attempted murder is punishable by death,' Beatrice whispered. 'I know that much.' Her face crumpled as the horrible realisation flooded over her, and she burst into a jumble of noisy sobs.

'Varin! What on earth are you doing to my sister?' William acknowledged his newly found relation with pride as he strode into the chamber, Geraint in his wake. 'You seem to have an uncannily bad effect on women of late.'

Varin raked an exasperated hand through his blond locks, shrugging his shoulders. 'I am merely trying to find out some answers, my lord.'

'At great cost to my sister's happiness, it seems,' William returned drily. 'I want to make this a night of celebration, not one of tears and sadness. What ails thee, Beatrice?' His sister continued to sob, shudders coursing through her slender frame. 'Varin?' William looked at his knight for explanation.

'Eadita has disappeared, along with her brother, Thurstan. I believe 'tis he who tried to poison you.'

'I see.' William's tones remained calm, as he drew his thick, fair brows together. 'I had no idea Eadita had a sibling.'

'Everyone thought Thurstan died at the Battle of Hastings, alongside his father,' Beatrice lifted her head to speak, in between halting gulps. 'But he survived, returning to Thunorslege as an outlaw. He had no wish to live under Norman rule, and would steal money from the rich Norman merchants and tax collectors passing through to give to the Saxon poor.'

'Aided and abetted by Eadita,' Varin murmured wryly.

Beatrice nodded. 'Aye, you have it, my lord. 'Twas Thurstan who taught her to run like a deer, to climb trees and fight like a man.'

'So it all becomes clear,' Varin muttered under his breath, as he remembered the terrifying feel of her body clamped around his shoulders, her knife at his throat. 'She risks her own neck for her brother. Her loyalty is to be commended, despite it being misplaced.'

'She would die for her brother.' Beatrice suppressed a sob, her violet eyes red-rimmed from weeping.

'I intend to see that she doesn't, *madame.*' Varin promised. William caught his eye above Beatrice's ebony head, attracting Varin's attention. 'What is it, my lord?'

''Tis strange. Beatrice speaks of her son, *my nephew,* as a simple outlaw. Yet by attempting to poison me, it seems his ambitions have climbed somewhat. He appears to be intent on overthrowing the Norman reign, starting with me.'

'He is just an outlaw,' Beatrice insisted. 'Lord Varin, I'm certain you have it wrong…' Her sentence trailed to silence.

''Tis not something you could do single-handedly,' Varin surmised, hitching onto William's train of thought. 'The boy would need powerful allies.'

'And where would he find those?' William raised his eyes towards Varin as the two men looked at each other, the answer clear to both of them.

'Gronwig!'

From her vantage point at Exeter's southern gatehouse where they had paused to catch their breath, Eadita stared back at the Bishop's Palace. No shouts or hoofbeats had followed their precipitous journey through the narrow streets. Below her, the hill dropped away to the gleam of the wide River Exe glistening in the weak moonlight. Beyond, lay the dark bulk of the vast forests of Dartmoor.

Varin. She heard his name whisper in the wind, curling through the stone turrets of the gatehouse, caressing her, jeering at her. She hoped he had recovered his senses, the dark shape of him sprawled on the cobbles haunting her thoughts. If only she'd had a little more time to tend to him before she fled. If only. But this was the right decision, she told herself firmly, despite the cheerless desolation invading her spirit. He would never find her. Never want to find her. Her fledging relationship with Varin was over; he was probably celebrating his freedom at this very moment, pleased that she had released him from their betrothal.

'Come on, Eadita! Stop pining for that Norman!' Thurstan grabbed his sister's arm in a demon grip.

'I didn't come with you to be treated like this!' She pulled her arm away disconsolately, throwing him an accusing look.

'What did you come for then? Don't tell me it was to escape the Norman's clutches? You seem to be on the best of terms with those traitors!'

'Don't do this, Thurstan, I beg of you,' she replied despondently. 'Since when did you become so full of rage and anger? What is going on?' Her brother fixed her with a glance so venomous that she quailed in astonishment. What bloodthirsty madness possessed him?

'I should be asking you the same question, *sister*,' he snarled, 'although I have no wish to acknowledge our blood tie at this moment after your own deceitful behaviour.' Kenelm laid a restraining hand on Thurstan's forearm, but he shook it away, irritated by the gesture.

'Nay, I have no need of comfort, Kenelm. What's done is done. My sister has transferred her loyalties to the Norman side, has forsaken her Saxon duty.'

Under the thready moon, its light frayed by delicate wisps of cloud, Eadita's cheeks flamed at the insulting words flung by Thurstan. She hardly recognised him; the whites of his eyes glistened starkly as he stared at her bitterly; his face contorted with a bestial rage. Liquid fear ran through her like a flash of pain. If only you knew how I have protected you, she thought silently. If only you knew.

'Why do you bother with me, then? Why did you not leave me at the Palace?' she asked miserably.

'Because now is your chance to help us, Eadita. You have thwarted my chances to murder the Norman King, not once, but twice. You must pay for your interference.'

'Since when did you become a murderer, brother?' She ignored his words. 'You were once content to live the simple life of an outlaw, helping the poor and needy in the villages…'

'Since someone made me see sense; someone made me realise that all my efforts were in vain unless I aimed higher, unless I destroyed the Norman regime before it destroyed us. Don't you see?' His tone became cajoling, almost pleading. 'Now, come on, sister, we must make haste. Hopefully I can still carry out the latter part of my plan…' he muttered, almost to himself and strode off in the direction of the river.

'What is wrong with him?' Eadita blurted out to Kenelm, walking at her side. 'Why is he acting so strangely?'

'I am afeard, Eadita, and I know as little as you do.'

A finger of fear blossomed icily in Eadita's heart. 'He despises me for helping William…but I saw him as a very ill man who needed my help that night. I am a healer, first and foremost…Thurstan knows that…' she finished lamely.

'I understand and applaud your actions, Eadita. You follow your mother's teaching and philosophy on life. Thurstan has changed of late… He has become completely obsessed with bringing Thunorslege and the West Country under Saxon control again. The money we have robbed seems to have vanished.'

'What do you mean?' Eadita's voice rose partially, then dropped to a whisper. She didn't want the rigid, irritated back of her brother to turn around.

'Thurstan assures us that the money is in safe-keeping…but, well, the men are starving, our weapons are old and need replacing, and Thurstan refuses to buy food or pay for new armaments.' Eadita frowned. 'Nay, do not mistake me, my lady. The food and medicines you bring from Thunorslege are gratefully received, but even you must acknowledge that it is not enough for a band of fighting men such as us.' Her throat constricted with tension. 'Come, we must quicken our steps,' Kenelm urged.

'We must go over the bridge,' Thurstan rapped out, as the two of them drew level. His face, flushed from exertion, loomed crazily in the half-light.

'But this is not the direction for Thunorslege.' Eadita held her pace, stubbornly.

'We do not return to Thunorslege, sister.'

'But—'

'We travel on to the moor, my dear, disloyal Eadita. The Normans will find it difficult to track us down up there. I have arranged to meet someone who can help us—he is prepared to give us a lot of money to help our cause.'

'Oh, Thurstan, haven't you done enough? Varin will realise soon enough that it was you who tried to murder the King. There will be a price on your head.'

'The French will soon be overthrown, *before* that barbarian catches up with us.'

'I'm not so sure,' she replied, doubtfully.

'Why do you hang behind so, Eadita?' her brother growled out, frustrated by her lack of progress along the spongy, leaf-strewn path. He cast a derisory glance over her elegant garments; the hem of her gown, richly embroidered in red and gold, dragged through the wet dirt. Her long sleeves, the long points brushing the ground also, fared little better.

''Tis so long since I've seen you dressed as a woman, it comes as quite a shock,' he murmured. Eadita shivered. Wearing no cloak, due to the hastiness of her exit from the Palace, the chill of the night air wheedled into her bones.

'She's not dressed for this,' Kenelm announced, throwing the short fur cloak from his shoulders around her. Eadita held up her hand in protest, but Kenelm already shook his head.

'Nay, my lady, I have two thick woollen tunics underneath.' As the fur closed warmly around her slender shoulders, she thanked him.

'Now, we just need to get rid of this!' Thurstan grabbed her mud-spattered trailing hem and deftly sliced off the bottom, so that the gown swung back to fall around her calves, trails of thread drifting forlornly from the savaged fabric.

'Thurstan!' Eadita cried, outraged at his swift mutilation of her clothes.

'At least you'll be able to keep up with us now. Or do you want your Norman knight to catch up with you?' She shook her head, dispirited by her brother's harsh treatment.

'Then let's go,' Thurstan said, taking off at a fast sprint through the trees.

It seemed as if they travelled all night. The uneven, rugged terrain had made the journey demanding and relentless: Eadita's arms ached from pulling her body weight over boulders twice her size, to gain ascent on to the barren windswept moor. Her eyes smarted as they reached the crest of the escarpment, the cold wind freshening as it whistled along the top. Trees, high branches bent over like old women from years of constant battering, were starkly outlined in the moonlight. Walking along the edge of the plateau, the ground falling away to her left into messy groups of trees clinging to the side of the slopes, Eadita barely heard her brother say, 'Here it is', as she concentrated on placing one foot in front of the other.

Thurstan followed a narrow sheep track down an incline, heading for a group of pale birch trees, their ghostly spindles luminous in the darkness. The steeply pitched roof of a cottage could be made out amongst the copse, a thin dribble of smoke trickling from the apex of the oak shingles.

'We will rest here,' Thurstan announced, pushing the door. It appeared that he knew the person inside for she heard light words exchanged, then a bout of laughter. A woman squeezed past them to disappear into the night. Thurstan bid them inside. The smell of reeking straw and animal manure accompanied by various rustlings indicated that one half of the one-storey cottage operated as a byre. Eadita wrinkled her nose in disgust.

'Beggars can't be choosers, Eadita.' Her brother laughed harshly, chucking a few branches into a circle of stones from which a fire burned, the smoke rising haphazardly to the ceiling to exit through a hole in the roof. The large pot hanging over the fire smelled inviting and Eadita's stomach growled. For the first time since he had effected her escape from the Palace, Thurstan smiled at her.

'Aye, let's sup. I'm hungry too. Kenelm, after you've supped, I need you to return to the camp.' His colleague nodded. Soon the room was silent except for the sounds of eating, the three of them sitting cross-legged around the fire, greedily consuming the hearty stew, stuffed full of venison, carrots, swede and potatoes.

'We shouldn't be eating that poor woman's supper,' Eadita ventured, as she guiltily pushed her bowl away.

'No matter, she was glad of the coin.'

Patting his stomach, Kenelm rose, swirling his cloak around his shoulders. 'I'll take my leave now.' He smiled at Eadita. 'Take care, my lady.' His voice held a warning. Eadita remained silent as she watched the door swing shut behind him. Then she faced Thurstan.

'Thurstan, why are we here? Who do you plan to meet?'

'I've already told you; someone who can help us overthrow the Normans, so we can hold our heads high once more.'

'Thurstan…' She placed a gentle hand on his knee, then stopped. How could she tell him what had happened? How they bore kinship to King William? The news would surely kill him. 'Thurstan…as much as it saddens me to be away from you, I want no part of these plans. I will make my own way after this night, plot my own course through life. Like you, I cannot return to Thunorslege, but for different reasons. I will take my leave in the morning.'

Thurstan moved over to the door, securing it shut.

'You will do no such thing.'

Eadita frowned, throwing a stale bit of bread back on to the plate. 'But you said yourself, Thurstan, that I have forsaken my Saxon loyalty. I cannot hope to change your mind as it is and I cannot bear to see you suffer. Therefore I must go.'

'You, Eadita, are going nowhere. Perhaps you didn't hear me aright. I need you here.'

'Whatever for?'

'When I realised you had thwarted my plans by saving the King's life, I thought I could return to Exeter to persuade you otherwise.' He laughed harshly. 'God, how wrong could I be? But my plan has not run its course as yet. Our wealthy friend arrives in the morning with his gold. I will gladly accept it on behalf of the Saxon cause, and I will hand over his reward.'

'What is his reward?'

''Tis you, Eadita. 'Tis you.'

Chapter Twenty

'Varin, for God's sake, calm down!' Geraint urged as Varin strode back and forth in front of the fire. 'We need to discover their direction before we can follow them!'

'Aye, Varin, heed your friend!' William implored. 'Sit down, for I cannot think straight with you pacing the floor like this! I've sent Judhael to ask the soldiers on duty if they saw anything.'

Varin folded his brawny physique on to an empty bench, thrusting his long legs out in front of him. 'Forgive me.' His glance swept the company, the brilliant jade of his eyes piercing and intent. William, his wide stocky frame planted firmly opposite him; Geraint, throwing more logs on to the fire to generate the smouldering ashes; Beatrice, perched on a low stool beside William, hugging her knees, her delicate features ashen. Despite the lateness of the hour, a sole musician picked out a slow, desultory tune on his lyre.

'The guards can tell me nothing.' Judhael walked back into the hall, his face ruddy and flushed from the freezing air outside.

'I am concerned.' Varin raked an impatient hand through his blond locks, his fingers stilling as he touched the back of his head gingerly. The pain had subsided to a dull ache. 'I am at a loss to their direction.'

'Maybe my stones can help?' Beatrice suggested softly. She reached resourcefully for the pouch hanging from a silken cord at her waist. Varin regarded her with an uncomprehending stare.

'Her rune stones,' Judhael explained. 'Eadita's mother has a special gift. She can give you some idea of their direction.' Varin, about to roll his eyes sceptically, stopped himself in time.

'Surely it would be easier to track them on foot?' he asked.

'Nay, my lord. 'Twould take too long to discover their path.'

'Let's try your way.'

Beatrice shook the small, leather bag, hearing the stones click softly together. Drawing out just six stones marked with straight black lines, she placed them carefully on a low table beside her. William held up his hand for silence as Beatrice bent over the tablets of white bone, her brows drawn together in studied concentration. Her shining hair, tipped with silver at the temples, slipped forward from under her veil. Her eyes closed as she touched each stone, before beginning to intone her message, as if in a dream.

'Eadita—' she touched the first stone '—is in great danger. She lies at the mercy of three men.' Beatrice laid her fingertip on three stones in turn.

'*Dieu!*' Varin cursed, his breath twisting in his chest. Brushing the other stones with shaking fingertips, Beatrice continued.

'*Hagall* suggest disruption, things are out of control. I see her brother, who plays an odd game. I like it not. With this stone—' Beatrice touched on *Ur* '—I see wildness, someone not afraid of holding back his brute strength. I am unsure, but he is a stranger to her; the picture is hazy.' Beatrice appeared puzzled, before tapping on the next stone, that of *Rad*. 'Eadita is homeward bound, but has not reached Thunorslege yet. They rest somewhere.'

'So they are headed back to Thunorslege, and Thurstan's camp,' suggested William. He had made Beatrice tell him in detail about his nephew's activities.

'Nay, 'tis unlikely, for they are on high ground, wind-blown…a few trees.' Beatrice's voice held a mysterious sibilance, so the men around her leaned closer in order to catch the syllables.

'She speaks of Dartmoor,' Judhael guessed, his tones confident. ''Tis the only high ground between here and Thunorslege, and a godforsaken place it is too… God in Heaven, Beatrice, what ails thee?'

A trembling shiver had taken hold of Beatrice, the flush died from her face as it turned ash grey and large fat tears began to spill down her cheeks. Her eyes sprung open, her manner disturbed and overwrought. She grabbed Varin's arm, her grip merciless.

'Go, you must go now. There will be pain and she will suffer. You must help her now. She is fighting, but she weakens.' Varin sprang to his feet, his face ravaged in agony.

Judhael rose too.

'I will ride with you and Geraint.' Judhael offered. 'We must find her, Varin, and I know Dartmoor. I will guide you.' Eadita's sweet, angelic face swung through Varin's mind like a mesmerising charm; he closed his eyes tight at the memory.

'God keep her safe until I can reach her,' he breathed as they strode towards the stables.

'Ah! Here it is now.' Gronwig spied the cottage in the grove of birches, their delicate peeling trunks starkly white in the early morning light. He was familiar with the location, of middle distance between the Bishop's Palace in Exeter and Thunorslege and the scene of some excellent sport, the most recent being the virgin daughter of a palace servant. He'd paid handsomely for her.

Next to him Raoul dismounted, stretching his arms wide from the tedium of the journey from Thunorslege, due to the Earl's inability to ride at anything faster than a slow trot. He brushed vainly at the few mud spats on his leather *braies,* pursing his lips as the brown clots marked faintly. He ran a finger around his waistband: his trousers seemed to be tighter of late and itched at his side. Removing his helmet and leather gauntlets, he flung them towards his man-at-arms, scarcely looking in his direction.

'Come, Gronwig!' He bounded towards the cottage. 'I am eager to claim my prize!'

Eadita's mouth dropped open at the sight of her uncle and Raoul, standing like harbingers of doom in the cottage doorway, the morning mists swirling around their ankles. After a fitful sleep, marred by snatches of drifting nightmare, the full horror of Thurstan's plans for her swamped her small frame in a wave of desolation.

'Brother, you have betrayed me.' Her words, icy and condemning, produced a self-satisfied smirk on Thurstan's face as he bowed low to the two men. 'You're in league with Gronwig? Is that where all the money has gone?' She remembered Kenelm's words as reality dawned like a limp, wringing rag. 'Answer me, Thurstan!'

'Gronwig promised me Thunorslege if I could raise an army to overthrow the French,' Thurstan said. 'And I would have done it, if not for your interference.' Eadita was shaking her head now in disbelief. Why hadn't she realised? Because she had been blinded by loyalty, an everlasting fidelity that had been ripped apart before her eyes. Her brother had changed; his mind poisoned against her and all that was good.

'Is this how you repay my fealty?' she whispered.

'Hah! I haven't seen much of it lately,' Thurstan chided.

'Only because I don't concur with your twisted plans,' she cried. *Oh, Varin, Varin, why didn't I trust you sooner?*

Gronwig raked a disdainful eye over her dishevelled appearance. 'Greetings, niece. I'm glad to see you are still in one piece after you were so cruelly dragged away from us. But you could have dressed a little more appropriately to greet your future husband.'

'What foolishness is this?' she declared.

Raoul took a step towards her, his bloodshot eyes full of spite, his voice dripping honey. 'He speaks of our marriage, my sweet. Of the bargain I made with your uncle and thus with your brother. They have sold you to me.'

'Oh, no!' She stepped backwards, hurriedly. 'Thurstan,' she gasped, 'what is going on?'

'The second half of the plan.' His face remained blank.

'And of the first half, nephew? Did you succeed?'

'Nay, 'twas my own sister who went against me. The King is still alive.'

'You little bitch!' Gronwig announced simply. 'Methinks my proposal is too good for her.' He leaned heavily on his jewelled stick, watery eyes searching the room for a chair. Sighing faintly, he lowered his bulk to a straw bale, set hard up against the wattle-and-daub wall. Placing one podgy hand on top of the other on his stick, he cast a foreboding eye over his niece. 'You are the thorn in our side, my dear. Your foolhardy, ill-considered behaviour must be controlled, must be given strong direction and guidance, constrained at all cost.' He shook his head. 'I had begun to believe that no sane man would want to take you on, but amazingly, I have had an offer for you…an extremely good offer…the money will not fail to raise a large army.'

'And who might that poor unfortunate man be?' she asked, scornfully.

'Why, my lady Eadita, 'tis me.' Raoul grinned lasciviously. 'Remember, I have always admired you from afar.'

'Not far enough, methinks.' Eadita held her ground as he advanced towards her.

'Now, now, that is no way to address your affianced,' he murmured, a cruel light entering his pale eyes. 'You and I will have fun together.' His glance rolled along the svelte lines of her body, lip curling at her ripped hem before feasting on her trim ankles. 'I am prepared to overlook your initial reluctance to be with me…'

'You tried to force me…!' she spoke, outraged. 'I'll have none of that!' She attempted to brush his hand away from her arm, but he gripped more tightly, more painfully. 'You're hurting me! Leave me be this instant!' Raoul smiled tightly and bent down to her shell-like ear.

'You'll get used to the pain, my dear. Ofttimes, it can be quite enjoyable.'

'Thurstan—' she turned pleading eyes towards her brother '—I beg of you, help me, please.'

'Believe me, sister, you'll realise that this is the right decision in the end.' Thurstan smiled insanely at her. 'All Raoul wants is you…in return for Saxon rule. How can you deny me that?'

'Do I really mean so little to you?' She saw the answer in his eyes and wanted to weep.

'I've had enough of this,' Gronwig rapped the end of his stick against the earth floor. 'Take her outside, Raoul, make her your own. I, for one, will take pleasure in her screams.'

'Nay, nay!' Eadita yelled as Raoul dragged her from the cottage, trying to dig her heels into the dusty earthen floor. She clutched at the doorframe, but he prised her fingers off with surprising strength.

Thurstan wagged his finger at her, demonic in the intensity of his dream. 'Eadita, please, stop resisting. This is the only way we can achieve Saxon rule. Raoul will be a good husband to you. Go with grace.'

'And be bedded by this animal!' she threw back at him. 'I shall never, ever forgive you for this!' Thurstan shrugged his shoulders, uncaring.

'You have lost me, Thurstan,' she whispered.

Raoul hoisted Eadita's small-boned body sideways on to his hip, carrying her easily down through the spindly glade of birches. She hung limply, her head bumping against his knee, trying to conserve her strength for a greater push of effort later on. To return to the cottage seemed madness itself, for no one was prepared to help her. If she ran up the steep slope that Raoul descended, then she would be immediately exposed in the wide expanse of bleached moorland grass, studded with the occasional gnarled tree. Nay, her only option was to outrun Raoul in the messy thicket of deciduous scrub that clung to the slopes and valleys below her.

'Come, maid, I am eager!' grated Raoul, hauling her like a piece of meat on to his shoulder in order to increase his step away from the view of the cottage. Landing on his shoulder forcefully, her breath punched out as she put her hands out to grab a handful of his gambeson to stop herself falling. Laughing, Raoul rubbed a lecherous hand boldly over her rump, squeezing and kneading the soft flesh there.

'Not much meat on you, is there, my lady?' His hand moved down over her thighs, her skin crawling at his touch and she closed her eyes into the fusty smell of his garments. 'Never mind, you'll soon be waxing with our first babe!' He cast an eye behind him, the smoke of the cottage still visible. 'Let us find a little more privacy. I do not wish to alarm your relatives with the noise we will make.' He laughed; a raucous, high-pitched bark. His breath started to come in short pants: the exertion of carrying a maid, and not a heavy one, seemed to tax him. Hope sprang to Eadita's breast; she could certainly outrun such a lumbering oaf, if only she could detach herself from his manic hold.

'Here will do.' Raoul dumped her into a mossy clearing surrounded by whispering birches. At another time, in another life, the glade would have been delicately pretty, the slim pale trunks encasing a verdant, cushiony floor. But with Raoul snorting like a bull in heat, sneering at her with his stained brown teeth, the wood became a menacing trap that closed around her fragile figure. Still, she drew herself up, raised one eyebrow and regarded him haughtily, acutely aware of the demonic clutch on her upper arm.

'Surely there is a better way than this,' she proposed. 'This rape and pillage is not the way of a chivalrous knight. William would punish you severely.' But Raoul already shook his head.

'I have renounced my allegiance to that bastard King,' he spat with loathing. 'Nothing good will come of that. I am sworn to the Saxon cause and aim to take my Saxon bride, as is due to me. Give me no trouble and I will be kind to you.' His tone became wheedling.

'A Saxon bride that you had to pay much for. How touching,' she murmured sarcastically. 'I do hope I'll be worth it.' She watched the rage mount in his face and thought, calmly, how like her uncle he was.

'I'll wipe that arrogant pride from your face, wench. When I'm finished with you, you'll be whimpering at my feet, your spirit broken. And I will delight in watching it. Now I've had enough talking. Take your clothes off!'

'I shall not.' She refused to raise her voice, surmising that he would have to remove his hand in order to disrobe her. As he did so, she jumped away, twisting around to hare off through the trees. He roared in outrage, crashing like a wild boar through the scrub behind her, thrashing at the impenetrable brambles with his sword. Spurred on by fear, she had forgotten her hampering garments, the trailing skirts of her gunna catching on the brambles, slowing her pace. In a moment, Raoul threw his vast weight at her, pinning her to the floor. Her left arm was wrenched savagely behind her, so high up her back and with such barbarity that she heard, or rather felt, a sickening crack. Her senses swam as a hideous pain knifed along her shoulder and down her arm. Dizzying blackness threatened to overcome her.

'I'll break the other one if you ever try that again!' The stale mead on his breath stung her nostrils as he stuttered into her ear. Pressed into the damp ground, Eadita searched with her good right hand for the jewelled cross at her throat: a heavy lump of silver. She would not give up now; she would not let this monster lie with her, marry her; she would fight to her death.

As Raoul flipped her over, she held her body limp, feigning unconsciousness. Excited at the sight of her defenceless beneath him, Raoul stood, fumbling at the knotted lacings of his *braies*. Cursing at his inability to undo his own trousers, he looked down at the complication…and that was his mistake. A raging valkyrie flew at him, a large cross gripped in her right hand that pointed straight between his eyes. Thrusting it into his face, he howled as the bright red blood spurted from the top of his nose, and he immediately clutched his hands to his face to assuage the pain and the bleeding. The red fluid ran through his fingers and down his arms, dripping, but Eadita did not linger. Her attack gave her the advantage that she needed. She ran.

Her feet scampered along the muddy ground as if the devil himself were after her. Time seemed to expand, then contract. Uncertain of how much distance she had managed to put between herself and Raoul, she fancied she could hear his thumping footsteps and shouts behind her. A whirling grogginess overtook her; by deliberately ignoring the radiating pain from her arm as it uselessly bumped at her side, she now began to suffer. Quivers of stabbing agony threatened to trip her feet. She heard Raoul thrashing through the undergrowth behind her, calling her, as if through a mist. How had he recovered so quickly? Clamping her left arm to her side with her right, she determined to push on, her feet moving as if through cloying mud. The thudding footsteps drew nearer; the crackling of the brushwood swelling to immense proportions in her exhausted mind. Huge arms appeared from nowhere, pulling her back, clasping her to a wide, expanse of chest.

'Nay! Nay! Let me go, you monster!' She struggled against the bulky strength with the last vestiges of her power. She thrashed her head wildly from side to side, kicking back at Raoul's calves with sharp thrusting heels. 'You will not have me, Raoul, I will kill myself first!' A sob tore from her throat.

'Hush! Hush! *Doucement!* 'Tis I, 'tis Varin.' The mellow tones penetrated her petrified senses, slipping over her like warm brandy.

'Varin?' His name fluttered on her lips, as his big arms enfolded her shaking limbs into his own sturdy frame.

'Aye, 'tis Varin. You're safe now.' His sweet breath touched her hair as he held her, willing her to quieten. A moan whimpered from her lips as he turned her in the circle of his arms.

Chapter Twenty-One

'God in Heaven, Varin, is it really you?' Cradled protectively in the tight circle of his sturdy arms, she stared up at him in wonderment. His well-defined lips curved to a rigid smile as she lifted tentative fingers to touch his flushed, taut skin, the rough silkiness of his hair. She drank in the sight of him like an elixir, the pure vitality of him plumbing the depths of her numb, horrified body to kindle her back to life. He stood before her like a God, her rescuer, and she wanted to weep at the sweetness of his presence.

'Aye, 'tis me, Eadita. I am no dream.'

'I can't believe you're here…that you came.' Her frozen palm caressed his face as a flurry of nervous excitement swirled in her stomach. He curled his fingers around hers to hold them close to his chest and she breathed deep of the delicious scent of him, the smell of woodsmoke and leather.

'Did you really think that I would not?' His eyes, brilliant points of hard, green light, narrowed on her.

'After what happened?' She pulled from his loose grip to reach up to the back of his head. He winced slightly as she touched the spot where he had been hit. 'After what *I* did?'

He didn't speak for a moment, running a frustrated glance

over her dishevelled appearance. Brambles and dead leaves snarled in her beautiful hair; her face was streaked with old tears. Her wrecked gown hung in tatters. Gaping rents peppered her stockings, the pearly skin of her calves gleaming through. Mud caked the supple leather of her thin shoes. He'd never been more relieved to see anyone in his whole life.

'Would that you had stayed by my side,' he muttered, shaking his head as if chastising his own stupidity. The constant warmth of his fingers soaked into her freezing hand. How could she tell him? How could she tell him that by fleeing, she had hoped to spare him the humiliation of being forced to marry a Saxon?

'I thought by fleeing it would help us both.'

He shook his head uncomprehendingly, his lips compressed as he probed cautiously along the arm that was dangling limply by her side. Blond-tipped lashes fanned across his impenetrable gaze as he focused on the task.

'Whatever gave you that idea?' he murmured.

You did, she thought, *you did. You made it perfectly clear that you hated the very thought of marrying me.* A whimper of pain broke loose from her numbed vocal chords as he encountered the damaged part of her limb.

'Forgive me. 'Tis broken.'

'Are you sure?' she croaked out, startled by the intensity of the pain. He grimaced wryly at the doubt in her voice.

'We don't just kill people on the battlefield,' he announced acidly. 'I know about broken bones…and tended to many.' Shamefaced, she met his eyes squarely.

'Varin, I'm sorry. That was rude of me. I've no right to insult you after what you've done for me today.'

'No insult taken, my lady.' He quirked an eyebrow. 'Now, do you think you can ride before me? Otherwise, we'll have to wait in the cottage for a wagon to take you back to the Palace.'

'Aye, I will ride,' she shuddered. 'I have no wish to return to that…that…hovel.'

'Good girl.' From beneath his padded gambeson, he drew out his thick leather belt from the woollen loops topping his *braies,* proceeding to wrap it around her twice to strap her broken limb tightly to her side. He left her good arm to swing free. Although his fingers remained brisk and efficient, his touch sent a leap of desire arching through her dainty structure. 'This will make the going easier for you until it can be set in splints.' The unsteadiness in his voice as his hands left her body belied his cool demeanour.

Varin's horse stood cropping the velvet mounds of grass under a copse of whispering birch. The conker-like sheen of the animal's back stood in stark contrast to the pale trunks, as Varin helped her towards the destrier. A twig snapped and she started nervously at the brittle noise, her limbs turning to water.

'Where's Raoul?' Anxiety imbued her voice.

'Dead. I ran the bastard through.' Varin bit the syllables out.

'But—'

'I saw you on the ground before him. I thought he had killed you.' A scrappy desperation spiked his tone.

'But he is—'

'I thought he had killed you.'

'You killed him because you thought he had killed me?'

'Aye.' Varin stopped. The glittering green of his dragon eyes searched for her gaze and snared it. She sucked in a fluttering breath.

'Aye, Eadita. I thank the Lord that you are alive.'

He pushed unsteady fingers through his golden hair and suddenly wrapped her in a huge bear hug, enfolding her. Leaning into him, she let her eyes drift closed, lapping up the strength pouring into her own body, nourishing her frazzled mind and wiping away the dreadful images of the past few hours. The steady bumping of his heart reverberated through the many layers of cloak, gambeson and tunic and she rubbed her cheek absentmindedly against the downy fur of his cloak. The need to sleep safely, to sink down into a dreamless oblivion, loomed before her and a long sigh of relief escaped her lips.

'I thought I had lost you,' he murmured into her hair. 'Why did you run from me?' Her belly knocked crazily at the gamut of sensations his body aroused within her as her reply forced its way out from muffled confines.

'My brother, Thurstan. 'Twas him I was protecting all along. I owed him my loyalty.' Her speech sounded wooden and hollow, hurt by the utter betrayal.

'And how has he repaid that loyalty?'

Unshed tears gleamed dangerously at the bottom of her eyelids as she focused on his firm mouth. The intense desolation she experienced at her brother's treachery was indescribable.

''Tis hard to accept, when your own blood betrays you.'

'What would you know?' she responded caustically, dashing the tears angrily away with her good hand.

'Oh, I know only too well.' He pulled her stiff little body that bristled with hurt into his own once more. 'Come, we must get you back to the Palace and into the warmth.' Sensing her silent wretchedness, he placed his hands about her narrow waist to lift her carefully on to his horse, mounting up effortlessly behind her.

'Where is he?' she asked reluctantly as they started off at a slow walk through the trees. 'Where is Thurstan?' His shoulders moved in a shrug against her slim back.

'The cottage stood empty when we reached it. Geraint, Judhael and their soldiers have gone in pursuit.'

'Thurstan has betrayed me, Varin. I must try and find a place in my heart to forgive him.' Her voice rose a notch.

'Hush, Eadita. Do not distress yourself.' The flat of his hand spread protectively over her stomach.

'He tried to kill you, you know.' She struggled to keep the sob from her throat.

'I know. And you stopped him.' His memory had long since confirmed that Eadita had held the blade away from his throat.

'He has changed so much since we lost our father,' she intoned sadly. 'He called me a Norman whore.' Her voice quavered as she remembered Varin's naked body bearing down on her own. 'Which I suppose is what I am.'

'Nay. Never that.' His grip tightened around her, trying to reassure her frozen conscience. Words of love threatened to tumble out, but he held them back. Now was not the time. He flicked the reins as they reached the top of the valley slope to push through the bracken and on to the moorland beyond. Eadita's slight weight fell back against him as the head of the horse rose and he savoured the feel of her.

''Tis not so much the losing of a loved one that turns the mind, but often the battle itself. War affects men in different ways,' Varin explained gently. 'Some harden their hearts or they suffer the agony of memory. They cannot pull apart from the scenes they have witnessed…or the lives that have been lost. It eats away at them like a maggot in an apple, wrecking havoc on a man's mind.'

'Thurstan has become so,' Eadita acknowledged. 'Will he ever be the same again?'

'We can never go back, Eadita. Life and its experiences will always change us…as people do. I am only just starting to understand this myself.' There was a note in his voice that she strove to comprehend. It was if he were talking of something else, not Thurstan at all.

'I feel he is lost to me. Gronwig has warped his mind.'

'Gronwig! We suspected he might be involved. Now you confirm it.'

'You didn't come to Thunorslege as his bodyguard, did you?' she demanded, suspiciously. 'You came as William's spy.'

'I did, Eadita,' he confirmed. 'Ever since William struck

the deal in Exeter with Gronwig and Bishop Leofric, he maintained grave reservations about your uncle. I came to keep an eye on him.'

Eadita nodded. 'That man is a monster. He has made my life a misery.'

'If only you had placed your trust in me sooner, Eadita. I could have helped you, you know.' His ridged thighs bunched behind her softer hips.

'If only the Normans hadn't come to Thunorslege,' she stated, miserably. 'Then none of this would have happened.'

'I doubt that,' he countered. 'Gronwig would still have carried out some evil plan.' He paused, his golden hair stirred by the breeze. 'Besides, I would never have met you.'

The horse stepped high over the prickly gorse. Weak sunlight touched Eadita's face as the haunting cry of a curlew rendered the still air.

'Do you wish that you had not?'

'Nay, Eadita, never that.' He laughed suddenly, a deep rumble in his chest. 'You have certainly made my life more… interesting.'

Her mind hazed over, then cleared again to cruel, reasoned logic. So he had confirmed it. She had been nothing more to him than a passing fancy. An *interesting* passing fancy. He had made no secret of the fact that he wanted her body…but nothing more. No commitment, no future. How could they possibly go through with this marriage imposed by the King?

'Then you're obviously better off without me!' she returned, rawly. 'Varin, we must break this betrothal between us!'

He jerked on the bridle so abruptly that she almost fell off. The animal bucked slightly, unused to the rough handling. 'Is that what you want?' he rasped in her ear.

Nay, 'tis the last thing I desire, she thought. *But it's obviously what you want. I have no intention of tying you to my skirts with a gaggle of children, watching you chafing at the bit, resenting the domestic restraints on your freedom.*

'Aye,' she lied, anguish plucking at her heart.

'Then Fortune has smiled on you, my lady,' he returned, mockingly. 'Before you decided to disappear, I spoke to William. He agreed he had overreacted. He decided to break the betrothal…if we both wished it. And it seems that we both do.' His voice dripped ice. Eadita clamped her eyes shut at the pain of losing him once more.

'But why did you never tell me, Mother?' Eadita murmured several hours later, snuggling into the warm furs as she lay beside her mother on the wide bed. 'I would have understood.' Despite the gloominess of the afternoon, cloth had been fastened to the inside of the window embrasures to allow both women to sleep.

'I hadn't spoken of my past for so long, that when the time came to tell you, when you and Thurstan were old enough, the lie had become a truth,' Beatrice tried to explain, lines of exhaustion creasing her brilliant eyes. 'Can you forgive me?' She turned her head on the linen pillow to her daughter resting beside her, frowning at the heavy strapping on Eadita's arm.

Eadita bit her lip. So many lies and half-truths. So much heartache. If she had been honest with Varin from the outset, would any of this have made any difference? The uncompromising lines of his face tormented her memory as he had carried her up to the bedchamber to sleep after her experience. Why had he seemed so ill humoured when he had just been released from the enforced confinement of marriage?

Beatrice reached over to touch Eadita's fingers. 'When Varin recognised me at Thunorslege, I was going to tell you then. But I was afraid of losing you. Both of you had been brought up as Saxons…and after your father was killed, you hated everything about the Normans.'

Not any more, thought Eadita sadly. Not any more. 'Varin remembered you from when he was a young squire at Falaise?' she enquired brightly, trying to cover her misery.

'Aye, he was but eight years old. Felice, his mother, had just left them. It was a terrible time for him and his brothers. And Sigurd too.' Eadita's heart twisted. Varin's words returned to her. 'Never trust a woman.' As she had been unable to trust him. To be honest with him.

A soft rapping at the door intruded into her thoughts.

'Enter,' Beatrice called, half-lifting herself from the bed as she drew her shawl loosely about her. William's steward appeared, his expression agitated.

'Forgive me, my ladies.' He coloured slightly at the intimate sight of the two women under the covers. 'I think you'd better come at once. The soldiers have found your son. They have found Thurstan.'

Beatrice had to help Eadita down the stairs; the poppy juice she had administered to her daughter for her arm seemed to be wearing off and now Eadita's face was white with the effort of controlling the pain.

'Why not stay in the chamber, daughter?' Beatrice whispered, as the expanse of the Great Hall came into view. 'You are not well enough for this.'

'I want to see Thurstan.' Eadita gritted her teeth. The two women suddenly halted their slow descent, wide-eyed with shock as Geraint burst in, valiantly clutching the thrashing, spitting figure of Thurstan. His face, twisted almost beyond recognition, hair standing out in matted tendrils, reminded Eadita of a caged animal.

'You…will…not…hold…me!' Thurstan gasped out in anger, trying to smash his knuckles into Geraint's face. 'I am a free man!' Varin, slouching indolently beside William, pushed himself away from the wall. At his command, two knights ran forward to help Geraint, eventually securing one arm each to hold the protesting, bucking man between them. Geraint approached Varin.

'We cornered him in an old quarry…he's given us a devil of a run. Gronwig was dead at his side. I think he died of an apoplexy…or attack of the heart.'

Noticing the two women hesitating on the stairs, William beckoned to Eadita and her mother to come and sit by the fire. Thurstan's eyes widened in astonishment as he followed the King's gesture.

'Nay, nay, this cannot be.' Thurstan rolled his eyes wildly. 'She's supposed to be with Raoul…what's she doing here?' Varin moved swiftly before him, impassively confident before Thurstan's writhing, uncoordinated movements.

''Tis over, Thurstan.'

'Never!' Thurstan howled, thrashing his head from side to side.

'Throw him in the dungeon,' William commanded, moving to stand beside Varin. 'We will talk to him when he has calmed down.'

'I fear that may never be,' whispered Beatrice, worriedly. At his mother's words, Thurstan stilled his movements, before fixing his sister with a steady unwavering eye.

'I don't want to hurt you, Eadita. I thought I was doing the best for you and you betrayed me…with him!' He tried to jab his finger at Varin, but the restraining hands of the soldiers were too powerful. ' All I want is to have the country back under Saxon rule again…to live in peace. Raoul would have been a good husband to you.' Varin swore under his breath, attracting Thurstan's intense stare.

'Aye, Norman,' Thurstan continued. 'I hope her loyalty continues towards you. I held it once, but now it seems she has found another man to tryst with. She saved your life, grabbed my sword hand when you were inches away from death.'

'I remember,' Varin confirmed his words coldly. 'But she still loves you.'

'Our father's blood is on your hands, Varin, yet she still runs to you. What further proof do I need that I no longer hold her love?' A strangled gasp issued forth from Eadita.

'Lock my nephew up!' William ordered, pointing a commanding finger at the two guards either side of Thurstan. 'I've heard enough of this foolish prattle.' A puzzled frown crossed Thurstan's face. William moved to stand before him. 'That's right, Thurstan. It may amaze you to know that your own mother is my younger half-sister and you, surprisingly, are my nephew.'

'I do not believe it.' Thurstan's voice was barely audible.

'Then believe it now, Thurstan—' Beatrice stepped forward, her face etched with distress '—for he speaks the truth.'

'Nay!' Thurstan cried out, pulling roughly at the strong arms holding him. 'You're trying to trick me.'

''Tis God's honest truth, Thurstan. William and I have not seen each other for over twenty-two years.' She smiled shyly at her half-brother. Thurstan, watching their linking glance, slumped in defeat.

'Before you clap me in irons, I have something to show Eadita. I beg of you, bid your guards to release my arms. I will not run.' William regarded him for a long moment before nodding his assent to the guards. Varin stepped closer to Eadita and placed his hand on the hilt of his sword as Thurstan fumbled in a leather pouch that dangled by a silken cord from his belt. Thrusting his fingers inside, he drew out a handful of shiny black seeds that winked ominously in firelight.

'You may have need of these in the future…' he held out the bright, sparkling pips in the palm of his hand '…but I for one will take mine now.' Before anyone thought to act, he stuffed the handful of the seeds into his mouth. Eadita forced her feet to move towards him, her muddled brain finally working out what he had held. Belladonna seeds! As horrified comprehension dawned across her face, he smiled at her.

'All is lost, Eadita. I can't live with this any more.' He sank to his knees as the belladonna started to take effect. Eadita's damaged arm wrenched painfully as she sprang across the room towards him, Varin moving like a shadow at her side. He plucked the pouch from Thurstan's belt and ripped the gathered top apart to view the contents.

'What is it?' he demanded, as Thurstan's eyes closed and he swayed, as if in deep prayer.

''Tis belladonna. Deadly nightshade.' Eadita dropped to her knees beside her brother. 'Pure poison. He has chosen to take his own life.' Her explanation left an acrid bitterness in her mouth.

'Is there naught we can do?' Varin questioned, as he caught Thurstan's sagging form to lay him flat.

'Nay, there is nothing we can do. The poison affects the heart almost instantaneously—see, his face turns blue; he sinks into a sleep from which he will never wake.' Her detached gaze touched on the staggered faces around her—her weeping mother, Judhael, a stern-faced William. Varin touched her shoulder, wanting to shield her from the sight.

''Tis too much,' she whispered and collapsed into his arms.

The rain spattered furiously against the cloth covering the window. Sighing, Eadita pulled it aside to view the wet, drizzling evening. Down in the courtyard, she watched her mother whisper with Judhael in the shadow of a covered archway, their pale hands linked intimately. She caught the threads of Judhael's low murmur, Beatrice's tinkling laughter in response. She sighed again, letting the window-covering slap back into place. Even her mother's obvious happiness failed to lift her despair.

She hadn't seen Varin for days. Since her brother's funeral, William had begged Beatrice and Eadita to keep him company at the Palace before he left on campaign to Cornwall. Judhael had also elected to stay with his entourage. Her mother had bound her arm tightly with splints and the restriction of not having the use of her limb had become a constant source of irritation. 'Twas the only emotion she felt apart from an aching, listless grief that dogged her days and nights. She had soon realised in a wave of guilt that it wasn't Thurstan for whom she mourned, but Varin.

Sitting alone in the Palace bedchamber, she realised it was time to be honest with him. At least she could absolve her conscience in that respect. Nobody in this horrible mess had been truthful with her; she had constantly been lied to, by her uncle, by her brother, even by her own mother. But not Varin. He had never pretended to be anything other than himself. And she loved him for it. Trying to summon up the energy to change for supper, she began to unlace the ties at the neck of her gunna, wondering vaguely how she would dress with her arm immobile.

'Let me help you.'

She froze, her violet eyes seeking the source of the rich, melodious tone.

'Varin?' she breathed unevenly, speaking a name she hadn't voiced aloud for days for fear of making herself more miserable. He stood in the doorway. Her eyes travelled the crushing, irresistible length of him. His vibrant tunic of dark-green wool clung to his broad frame, caught into his strong wrists by thick leather cuffs. His leather *braies* served only to emphasise the interminable extent of his legs. Wet strands of hair spiked around the bold set of his head, giving him a fiendish look. Her heart raced, unstoppable as she absorbed the essence of the man she loved, detail by heart-stopping detail.

''Tis I.' He scanned her face to drink in the smooth, velvet softness of complexion, the dusky pink of her lips. He frowned at the dark circles under her eyes. Was it too soon?

She flushed under his green cat-like scrutiny, her legs weak despite being seated.

'I…er…I was thinking of coming down for supper tonight.' She spoke the obvious without thinking, shy under his unnerving gaze, his devastating presence.

'I can see that.' He moved into the chamber with animal grace, smiling gently. ''Twould be good to see you in company again.'

'I…my brother…' she forced out the limp excuse, haltingly.

'I understand, Eadita. But it has been over a sennight now. William is becoming concerned. And so am I.'

'Why you?' she squeaked. 'Why are you concerned?'

'Why do you think, Eadita?' He stood so close now, the worn leather of his *braies* almost touching her knee. The virulent masculinity of his nearness threatened to overwhelm her.

'Because you want us to return to Thunorslege?' Her eyes, deepening to indigo, sought his.

'Nay, because I want you by my side.' His voice held an unspoken promise.

'There's no need to be with me any more. You know the whole truth.'

'Do I?' He lifted a lean, tanned finger to stroke her cheek. The simple contact pulsed shafts of arousal through her slender limbs. Rising awkwardly, she moved from his magnetic presence towards the red, glowing coals of the brazier. Tell him now, she urged herself. You have lost him already. You have nothing more to lose.

'Nay, Varin, you don't know the whole truth.' She traced her fingers nervously along the carved edge of an oak coffer as she took a deep breath, preparing to speak. 'You do not know…that I love you.' Her feet rooted to the spot, unwilling to turn round to face his mocking laughter. At his continued silence, she quivered, tears gathering at the corners of her eyes in bleak anticipation of his rejection.

'As I love you, Eadita.' The words brushed around her like heated liquid. Bewilderment clamoured in her mind.

'W-what? What did you say?' Had she imagined it?

He pulled her into his muscular frame, arms lapping around her waist carefully. She stared in amazement at his fingers meshed over the blue wool of her gunna.

'You heard me, Eadita. I love you.' His lips grazed her ear, a butterfly touch. 'From the moment I first met you, you have taunted me, bossed me around, goaded me beyond belief and driven me half-mad trying to protect you. You've made me feel, Eadita, something I thought I would never experience again. I sleep you, dream you, smell your perfume wherever I go, feel your soft skin under my hands. It has been this way since we first met, but I stubbornly refused to accept it.' He laughed. 'I was arrogant enough to believe that no woman would ever master me…' he clasped her more tightly into his embrace '…but it seems I was mistaken.'

'But the betrothal?'

'I was angry at being forced by William into a situation I resented. But when you announced you didn't want to go through with it, *mon Dieu,* Eadita, for the first time in my life, I wanted to weep.'

'I thought you didn't want it,' she mumbled in her defence. 'You'd already made your thoughts on marriage abundantly clear.'

'But I do want it, *chérie.* I do. With all my heart.' His lips touched the back of her neck, just below her hairline.

'You must be mad.' A jumble of excitement began to stir in her belly.

'Nay, Eadita, I am completely sane. I have been a fool for allowing my father's experience to colour my thinking, my whole life. I want you beside me for the rest of my lifetime, to bear my children, to protect you, to love you. That is my wish.'

Head reeling, Eadita extracted herself from his embrace to

move over to the window. She raised the covering and lifted her face to the cold, fresh air that blew through. Out in the courtyard, she could see the guards gathered around their fires, holding their hands out to warm them. Of her mother and Judhael there was no sign. She knew the exact moment Varin came to stand behind her, sensing the heated steadiness of his large frame.

''Tis my wish too, Varin. I wish it with all my heart.'

Turning her into his full embrace, he bent his tawny head into a kiss to make her his own.

MILLS & BOON®

Live the emotion

Look out for next month's
Super Historical Romance

BRIDE OF LOCHBARR
by Margaret Moore

Lady Marianne dreamed of returning to her
Normandy home away from the cold, wild highlands
of Scotland. Away from the doddering old man to
whom she was betrothed.

Neighbouring chieftain's son, Adair Mac Taran,
hated all things Norman – until he met the beautiful
Marianne. He swore to free her from a loveless match,
little realising what old hatreds would be stirred
and what new dangers begun...

**"Margaret Moore's characters step off the
pages into your heart."**
—*Romantic Times*

On sale Friday 2nd December 2005

*Available at most branches of WHSmith, Tesco, ASDA,
Borders, Eason, Sainsbury's and most bookshops*

www.millsandboon.co.uk

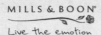

Make your Christmas wish list – and check it twice! ★

Watch out for these very special holiday stories – all featuring the incomparable charm and romance of the Christmas season.

By Jasmine Cresswell, Tara Taylor Quinn and Kate Hoffmann
On sale 21st October 2005

By Lynnette Kent and Sherry Lewis
On sale 21st October 2005

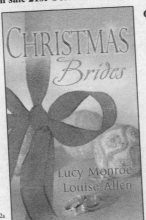

By Lucy Monroe and Louise Allen
On sale 4th November 2005

*By Heather Graham,
Lindsay McKenna, Marilyn
Pappano and Annette Broadrick*
On sale 18th November 2005

*By Marion Lennox, Josie Metcalfe
and Kate Hardy*
On sale 2nd December 2005

*By Margaret Moore, Terri Brisbin
and Gail Ranstrom*
On sale 2nd December 2005

*By Lisa Jackson, Barbara Boswell
and Linda Turner*
On sale 18th November 2005

1105/XMAS/LIST 2a

1105/059/MB146

Experience the magic of Christmas, past and present...

Christmas Brides

Don't miss this special holiday volume – two captivating love stories set in very different times.

THE GREEK'S CHRISTMAS BRIDE
by Lucy Monroe
Modern Romance

Aristide Kouros has no memory of life with his beautiful wife Eden. Though she's heartbroken he does not remember their passion for each other, Eden still loves her husband. But what secret is she hiding that might bind Aristide to her forever – whether he remembers her or not?

MOONLIGHT AND MISTLETOE
by Louise Allen
Historical Romance – Regency

From her first night in her new home in a charming English village, Hester is plagued by intrusive "hauntings." With the help of her handsome neighbour, the Earl of Buckland, she sets out to discover the mystery behind the frightful encounters – while fighting her own fear of falling in love with the earl.

On sale 4th November 2005